The
OPENERS OF THE GATE
Stories of the Occult

The
OPENERS OF THE GATE
Stories of the Occult

by

L. ADAMS BECK
(E. Barrington)

DEVORSS & COMPANY
P.O. BOX 550, MARINA DEL REY, CA 90294-0550

I dedicate this book
to my Jock—
an Opener of the Gate

Preface

These stories are founded on the deepest and highest range of Asiatic thought though the scenes of some are in the West. That thought is as vital for the West as for the East. The background is fictional but the stories are all true. In this connection I draw attention especially to the two entitled respectively ''Hell'' and ''The Man Who Saw.''

L. Adams Beck.
(E. Barrington)

Contents

The
OPENERS OF THE GATE
Stories of the Occult

The Openers of the Gate

IF I MEASURE THE EVENTS OF THIS STORY BY THE effect they have had on my own life and beliefs they seem to me stupendous in their simplicity, but what they will mean to others I cannot guess. Only I know that, when I gave the stark truth of these flashes of insight (for so I will call them) to a man well qualified to estimate their value from the material and psychic angles, he considered a moment and said: "I can well understand that it might be distasteful to you to give the public the facts, and yet when one remembers how the world at present is trembling on the verge of realization of the undiscovered continent of the superconscious faculty in man I believe that every atom of reliable evidence should be added to the common stock. And I think it the more in your case because of the very unusual way in which what we call the lower consciousness of animals was involved. Therefore, though you have not asked my opinion on this point, I say, 'Write it down. It is a true record.'"

That decided me. It may mean as much to some others as it did to me.

I will be brief with the preliminaries but some are necessary. Two people were concerned, my distant cousin, Helen Keith, and myself. She married as a very young girl, and her husband had died after ten years of a very unhappy marriage. She had no children. I am unmarried, a doctor by profession, my name James Livingstone. I scarcely need name myself, however, for, though the great results are mine also, the story is hers.

She had a charming little house near Tetford, the lawn sloping down to the Thames, and there, after release from her miserable bondage, she settled down to shape her life as best she might into some semblance of future hope and happiness. My practice was in one of the western suburbs of London lower down the river and my chief pleasure when I got a spare hour was to motor over and sit under the great trees on her lawn, watching the river glide by in the eternal serenity, and there talk the sun down the sky in the harmony of perfect understanding. I know there were people who said it would be a very suitable arrangement if we married some day—she was only thirty when her husband died, I thirty-eight. But I also know that such a thought never occurred or would have occurred to her nor at that time to me. We possessed the treasure of an equal friendship—rare enough, God knows, between a man and a woman—helped by the touch of kindred blood, and she with her wretched memories of marriage would have shrunk with horror from the notion; the bird set free has no yearning for the cage— while for myself my profession engrossed me body and soul.

I had made some mark with work on the endocrine glands, had written a monograph which attracted notice, and it was Helen's opinion as well as mine that I might yet climb out of the ruck and do some useful stuff. Marriage had no more interest for me than psychology, and if I could put it more strongly I would. But Helen and her life interested me enormously. She was so bruised, so wounded in the battle, that I wondered sometimes if she would ever regain heart and hope and march onward as man or woman should.

She had fallen by the wayside, and the world went by her. From the medical point of view too it was interesting; one of those obscure cases of jangled nerves which are most difficult of all to deal with because there are hardly any pronounced symptoms. The only really definite one was insomnia—you could see that in the feverish brightness of her eyes and a twitch sometimes of the eyelids. Beautiful eyes, brave, honest, and kind, in a white intellectual face with sensitive mouth and chin, but they had a tortured look still, if one caught her off guard. Otherwise she lived her life like other people, had her friends and saw enough of them to escape the reproach of eccentricity and, I hoped, was gradually beginning to take peace of mind for granted.

Yet I doubted. She could interest herself in nothing; she—with exceptional intellectual gifts, with money enough to set her free from material fetters, with health behind it all, as I was assured, if only one could touch the hidden spring and set the nerves working smoothly again. But, there seemed to be no point at which she could take hold of things.

I came over one Sunday afternoon of many to Tetford and found her sitting under the great sweeping beech, staring at the river where the boats went up and down with happy young people gay as flowers, whose dresses and blazers made bright reflections in still water. The lily-leaves swayed gently in the little bights, and bulrushes stood on guard along the banks. The meadows on the other side glittered like cloth of gold sheening into cloth of silver with buttercups and daisies. A blackbird sang divinely from among flaming rhododendrons. It was a perfect setting for perfect content and yet—her book had fallen on the grass, and with chin propped on her hand she saw no beauty, no peace, only the nightmare of the past.

She stared and looked up smiling as I brushed over the lawn, but the smile did not deceive me.

"Helen," I said, flinging myself on the grass beside her with my hands under my head so that I could look up into the towering green above me, "I've been thinking of you. Not in my honorary capacity of cousin, but as an eminent medical gent, and I say you can't go on as you're going. Did you sleep two or four hours last night? Be honest!"

She evaded details.

"Not brilliantly, but enough. It's surprising how much less sleep one can do with than most people think. And it isn't half bad in a way. The night goes so quickly—there's such a lot of interesting things to think of. If only one weren't rather tired in the morning, there's no other drawback."

"Exactly. But that being so we can't go on living on capital. Now I've come down with a definite proposal."

"I hope it's not a proposal of marriage," she said gaily. "Only yesterday old Mrs. Lowther told me that was the clear intention of Providence as regarded us both. Will people ever learn the noble and simple art of minding their own business?"

"Well—why should they? It amuses them and doesn't hurt us. Old Lowther lives in a perpetual drama of other people's imaginary adventures. She'd die of her own company if she didn't. But what I wanted to say is this. We've often agreed that 'The Way of All Flesh' is probably the cleverest novel written in English, haven't we?"

"Yes—and what's the proposal? A sequel in collaboration? You'd much better stick to the endocrine glands."

"Gowk! Do you remember that the hero goes through a beastly experience which simply leaves him

drained and flattened out? His doctor gives some very
remarkable advice: 'He's not strong enough to travel. I
should take him to the Zoo. The animals have the most
remarkable curative effects. I don't recommend the
influence of the felines. They are apt to be too stimu-
lating, but the larger mammals, such as the elephants
and greater bovines, are immensely soothing.' I haven't
got it right—I'm mixing my own notions up with
Butler's—but the point was—"

"The point appears to be that I'm to ride up and
down the Zoo on elephants. Well, Jim, I won't. So
now you know."

I liked Helen's laugh. It pleased me even more than
the blackbird's song. The worst was that one heard it
so much less often.

"You idiot!" she added. "Every word of that stuff
is pure irony and excellent irony at that. I've often
enjoyed it."

"I'm not so sure. I think Butler's right and that the
society of animals is the most soothing in all the world.
Look at the shepherd in poetry. Look at the milkmaid
with diamond eyes and cheeks of rose! Look at the
hunting horn and the gay tally-ho!"

"Yes, and so nice for the hare and the deer!" she
said sarcastically.

> " 'We'll all go a-hunting today
> All nature looks smiling and gay—'

so let's go out and kill something. Why not a little
blood in the picture!"

I raised myself on my elbow and protested.

"I aspired neither to elephants nor hunting for you.
What I was leading up to was simply that I should
like you to have a dog. I believe in dogs. They're
gentlemen."

"When they're not ladies. Well, I respect animals. I'd die to save them from cruelty, but I neither know nor understand them. I've never lived with them. And I don't like soulless things about me. It's bad enough to have no soul myself. I don't want to see my mortality repeated on a lower scale. It's tragic to me."

This was an old story. Helen had no instinct of immortality, no blind belief in a spring after the winter of death. Nor for that matter had I. We both had had our upbringing in families priding themselves on a scientific view of life and no nonsensical theories. My father had liked to call himself a Positivist, though I never troubled my head as to what that might imply beyond the agreeable fact that we never went to church. If Helen had not been in much the same case to start with I can imagine that her life with Moray Keith would have pretty well killed any spiritual romance in her. But I could not agree that it bore on dogs one way or another.

"My dear Helen, you're talking crass nonsense. What have souls got to do with it! A dog's the best company in the world, bar none, and that quiet non-intrusive kind of companionship is just what you want."

She would only ridicule me.

"If I can't have an elephant—but I really almost could on this lawn, and he would just love wallowing in the river!—why not fall back on a dog, you think! No, thank you. I'd almost as soon adopt a baby. I believe you get fond of dogs and then they die in about a year. I prefer to have all my troubles under my own hat."

So we argued and she was obstinate and the talk drifted to other things. But each time I came down her eyes were brighter and more wearied, and she could interest herself in nothing. Each time she dragged herself more tragically through days that must be endured, facing life as if all were well, but crippled—crippled!

"If only you had a touch of genius or anything like that!" I said one day with more anxiety than flattery. "Then you'd put things at their right values. You'd see Keith isn't worth a curse, much less a memory. But you're so confoundedly commonplace."

I wanted even to make her angry if I could. But she took that smiling too. Then more seriously.

"Jim, I have a genius for one thing and yet in that I've always been a mute inglorious Milton and I expect to die unhonored and unsung. But I really have a genius for loving, as sure as you sit there. I could *be* someone else and make them me. But that'll never come off."

If it couldn't there was no use discussing it. I waved that aside. I was not fool enough to suggest the usual tonic and a little gentle distraction of the mind. So it lapsed and I grew yet more anxious about her ultimate recovery of the instinct of happy living. And then a remarkable thing happened.

But before I go on to that I pause to hope I have made it clear that we were neither of us people with an ounce of what are called psychic instincts or promptings. If I have not, I must put it clearly on record that there was nothing of the kind. Helen had rather a cold critical intellectuality. I was just what I have described. And now for the beginning.

Once in a way she would coax me to a theater in London, and then I would motor her home and return to my own diggings. On this particular night the play was excellent, and we had enjoyed ourselves to the full. I remember we came out laughing and I suggested supper at Prince's and she agreed; and I left her stand-

ing on the edge of the pavement while I hunted for
a taxi in the throng. Suddenly there was confusion and
a general hold-up of traffic; I heard shouts and a
woman screamed near me, and I made my way back
hot-foot to where I had left Helen, and she was gone.

I could not even dimly imagine what had happened
nor where to look for her. She might have forgotten
something in the stalls and have gone back. In my
bewilderment and with the crowd hurrying past it
seemed safer to stand where I had left her until she
appeared. And then to my consternation the crowd
parted, and Helen emerged from the street, her white
dress torn and stained, her wrap gone, clasping something in her arms.

"Good God, what on earth is it? Where have you
been?"

"It's a dog!" she gasped. "A puppy. It was right
under a taxi and I swung it out and fell down. Do
let's get away! Look at the crowd."

"But are you hurt? My dear old girl!"

For she was white as death, and the bystanders were
very much inclined to cheer her for a regular sport.
The London mob loves pluck and it likes a dog. A
crowd was certainly gathering and a swift getaway in
a taxi strongly indicated. We achieved it.

"Little brute! You might have killed yourself. Will
you swear you're not hurt?" I said indignantly when
we were bowling along.

"Honest Injun! And he isn't hurt either. Look here!"
she said.

She showed me the smallest black Scotch terrier I
had ever seen. How such an infant contrived to be
wandering in the Strand at half past eleven will never
be known. At least we never found out. Helen declared
when she knew him better that it was his audacious

pluck and curiosity which had sent him out into the world to seek adventures when the rest of his family were nestling (figuratively) under their mother's wing in a padded basket. That seemed probable enough. He had the look of it now, though trembling all over with nerves and amazement.

He was evidently a gentleman of the bluest Scotch blood, perfect, with sharply pricked velvet ears, bright wise eyes, large head, and quaint little sturdy legs, the promise of a square well-set body—every point as it should be; and I speak with authority for I know a bit about that breed. I liked the look of him, the feel of him, the minute I saw the creature.

"Well, you have never ceased bothering me to get a dog. Now I've got him. The gods have spoken. And the first result is that we can't go out to supper. I look as if I'd been in a drunken scrap. And, good heavens! where's my wrap? I never thought of it till now. See what it is to have a dog!"

She would not be serious, but as a matter of fact it was rather a splendid thing to have dashed into that whirl of cars for the small scrap ot life in her arms. I doubt if I should have done it myself. I stated that fact judicially.

"Oh yes, you would! He's so ridiculously small, you see. You never would have let him go under just because he wanted to explore. The courage of the thing! What shall we call him?"

"Then you mean to keep him! But he's a valuable little chap. I don't know whether we shouldn't advertise. . . ."

"I do," she said decisively. "If he was valuable to them they shouldn't have let him be parading the Strand at night. I'm—well, I'm *damned* if I advertise. He's mine."

I noticed she was holding him up so that he lay with
his head on her bare breast. It seemed the soft contact
pleased her. I withdrew the motion about advertising
and suggested "Sandy."

"Yes—that will do. Sandy." She repeated it in a
voice with a new note in it. I suppose if one has saved
a life—even a dog's—at the risk of one's own it may
mean more than a little to one. Anyhow it was clear that
the gods knew best. I took them home and still she held
him to her breast.

I pass on to the next time I went over to Tetford.
Sandy had made good. She said he had reconnoitered
the house and garden and decided they would do. There
was indeed everything to recommend them. The lawn
was a velvet couch for dreaming in the sunshine, and
the trees here and there were full of promise for in-
vestigation and scuffling rushes. There was a rabbity
paddock at one side of the garden from which nothing
but a bowl of milk would coax him, so did it fascinate
the hunter in his queer little scrap of a body. Then also
he was a born swimmer and even in those first gropings
of exploration had tried to dash into the river to what
Helen believed would be a watery grave, and had spoiled
a second dress as she hauled him out. Delicious secrets
were evidently hidden for him in the clumps of rhododendrons, and when at last, exhausted with adventure, he collapsed upon the grass with a pink tongue
extended disclosing teeth as white as new ivory, it
needed no words to assure her that his cup was full. He
asked no more of life. She told me the story of these
first days with a kind of amazed interest—amazed that
such a trifle should have got hold of her. But it had
with a vengeance!

She had a tendency at first to call him the elephant
and to assure me that she found the presence of such

a huge mammal inexpressibly soothing. It had been
exactly the right prescription! Well, she might laugh
but it was true. From the minute that dog entered the
house she was a changed woman, and I had only to
stand aside and watch the miracle of love. I own it
interested me enormously, for I had never seen her
under that especial sway before—there had been only
decorous family affections and then a marriage of terror
and repulsion. Now—well, even from the medical point
of view it was interesting. I was not a little proud of
my intuition and began to think there was something to
be said for her theory that she had a genius for love.
I must have sensed that truth unconsciously. Her old
nurse, Mrs. Bramham, who adored her, proposed at
first that Sandy should sleep in the kitchen in the character of a watch-dog. His size made him ridiculous
from that point of view in any case, but I saw Helen's
eye harden with resolve.

"No, Brammy dear. He means to sleep on the foot
of my bed. I saw that the minute he walked into the
bedroom. I should have put my foot down then, but I
forgot to. We'll have to put up with it."

"But, heavens above, Miss Helen—you that can't
sleep as it is! You'll never get so much as a wink! A
nasty dog picked up in the street!"

She sat down on the floor and he scrambled into her
lap, and the two looked up at Mrs. Bramham—who saw
it was a lost cause and shook her head groaning audibly.
I also had misgivings on that head I own. A lively
puppy is scarcely the bedfellow for an insomniac.

Yet when I next came over—and I came oftener,
from curiosity, and to see my treatment through—
Helen assured me that she had slept like a top after the
first night. That had been a terror.

"He had so much to see to that he was scuttling up

and down the bed and burrowing under the pillows all
the time, getting to know his way about, you see. He
had to do that before he could settle down. And once
he fell off the bed with a fearful plop and I thought he
was done for. Then I tried to make him take his milk
and we spilled it and broke the basin. It was a perfect
Walpurgis Nacht of horrors, and Brammy nearly
preached me to death next morning, for I was a wreck.
But after that—mark you! the *very next night*—he
curled up at the foot of the bed and never stirred till
six nor did I. And it's been the same ever since. Look
at me!"

I looked. Her eyes were beaming—no tension in the
light of them. The strained pucker between the eye-
brows was gone. There was the indescribable radiation
of happiness that indicates health alike of body and
mind, and her lips and cheeks bloomed like the flowers
in the garden. The little miracle-worker sat looking
gravely up into her face, and she snatched him up,
struggling for freedom in her arms, while she asked
triumphantly:

"Was it worth dashing into the taxis to save such a
worthless little bit of goods? *Was* it?"

And I answered yes, with fullest conviction.

Now here I must indicate the extraordinary love that
bound those two together because it bore on what followed. Night or day they were never separated. Wherever Helen went, Sandy went. Even on shopping days
in London he followed, but on his leash for safety.
Whether she read or wrote he was at her feet. When
she punted or paddled on the river he had his cushion
in the stern. Even in his garden and meadow adventures she must follow or he was soon at her feet again.
Their walks were heavens of romance to both, for a
Scotch terrier is a born scout and he made her one too.

In a word, he cured her. I saw the Helen of eighteen again, expectant and glad. And under the influence of this constant human companionship (for as regards other dogs he was a little stand-off and high-brow), intellect in Sandy developed together with his adoration until I solemnly declare I have seen that dog do things that no hypothesis but reason could account for, and highly complicated reason at that. I have seen him think, consider, and act on his thought, and I have known that speech itself could not make clearer either his love or the wishes and resolutions he shaped in that queer, intelligent brain-box of his and proceeded to carry into effect. Sometimes I have wondered whether his very speechlessness did not presage that higher form of communication when we shall desert the clumsy medium of words for something better.

Certainly Helen thought so, and their mutual understanding and contentment was in its way a most beautiful thing to see. I told her frankly one day that there had been a time when I began to think her mainspring was broken and the joy of life past resurrection.

"And look at you now, and you owe it all to Sandy!" I said: "Wasn't I right? Wasn't it a resurrection?"

"A thousand times right. But—" She paused on a long sigh. "Isn't it strange and fearful to think that for all that love there's no resurrection? My little Sandy will die and it will all be poured out and wasted like spilled water. All that love!"

"No worse than for us!" I answered shortly, "I never yet heard an argument about the mortality of animals that didn't cut at ourselves too. We have nothing to plume ourselves on. Your love will be as much wasted as Sandy's, if you come to that. And yet you would give your life for him. You very nearly did, even before you knew him."

He lay with his head between his paws and bright eyes fixed on his mistress, as though he drank in every word she uttered. That was a favorite attitude of his. I could almost believe he understood and followed our talk.

"Oh yes, I claim no exemption for ourselves!" she said sadly.

> "Strange law of every mortal lot!
> Which man, proud man finds hard to bear,
>   And builds himself I know not what
> Of second life, I know not where.

No, I'm not so weak as that. Sandy goes out like a blown-out spark and I too. Well—let us live and love, for tomorrow we die. Only—I wish I might go first!"

"And what for Sandy then?"

"I did think of your taking him. But I knew even that wouldn't console him. I'm a poor thing, but his own. So I've put it in my letter of instructions that you're to give him the mercy of sleep and then we're to be burned together. Tell me, Jim, did you *ever* see the roses so lovely as they are this year?"

I knew she shied at the subject from sheer inability to face her own position if the order of the exit should be reversed. And indeed I myself—and here the medical man comes in again—was very apprehensive of what might happen in a nature so highly strung as hers, keyed by fate to such suffering, if such a thing were to be.

There are so many possible tragedies, you see, in those strange little mysterious lives lived so close beside us. I used to watch Sandy (and indeed I myself loved the wise little creature) frolicking about the lawn in the winning clumsy way those Scotch terriers have, and think how quickly the scene might change. He had his adventures too—the day when a bull-terrier attacked him, and the little Scotchman stood up to him game as a rat and took his punishment like a man, until Helen, badly bitten herself, dragged the bulldog off and carried home her little warrior dripping blood along the road. But—it might have ended otherwise, and then what? I did not like to think. They were all in all to each other. Could one say more of God or man? Love is a queer thing. I have learned a lot more about it since then.

Reflecting, I brought her a present I knew she would dislike at first though from me she would not refuse it—a beautiful big Alsatian puppy, a harmony in cream and brown deepening into black on the back, with noble mask and keen ears and eyes, taut and alert in every nerve-cell. There is no dog more beautiful and faithful nor a better guard to his own people, and after the bull-terrier episode I thought Fritzel's care might not be amiss. She accepted him graciously and he was adopted straight into the family. After a while she said:

"Jim, I love Fritzel with all my heart. But Sandy and I are *one*. Do you see the distinction? I decipher Fritzel's mind from the outside, but I live in Sandy's brain. You would not believe it—no, not even you!—if I told you how I can be in touch with him and he with me. Something far more intimate than words. Look now. I'll call him."

He was rollicking round the paddock far away—a gentleman at his hunting and naturally engrossed. The grass ran down to the river bank and there were alluring water-rats among other attractions too many to be told. That paddock was his happiest hunting ground of all, and his business interests there growing daily.

She put her hand over her eyes and sat very still for a second, the other hand lifted for silence. In a moment came a nearing rush and he was at her feet, panting, staring up into her eyes for instructions. A strange thing to see. In a moment more his round black paws were on her lap, his tail wagging furiously. Then he was off again, her eyes following him.

"I called him with my mind," she said. "I discovered that quite accidentally one day when I wanted him. And he can call me. If he were in difficulties now I should know; isn't it strange? Do you believe in telepathy, Jim?"

"Certainly. There are all sorts of queer mental by-ways unexplored as yet, but I'm not sure I've heard of an animal case. I should like to see you do that again : it may have been chance."

"Oh no, it wasn't. I do it often. But Sandy has taken me in hand. You haven't been here for so long that you don't know the new development," she said. "You know there's a *crêche* in the village for the kiddies whose mothers work in the factory at Felton. Well, I couldn't help thinking how they'd like the lawn and Sandy and Fritzel, and so a woman, brings up the three- and four-year-olds twice a week and we all have a great time. I've got to know some of the mothers too. Fritzel is perfect with children—and as for Sandy!" Words could not express that perfection.

We discussed it at great length, and again it interested me profoundly. She was opening out in so many ways—I could see the heart of universal compassion growing in her—that heart which brings understanding of all the world, and is to my mind the highest form of human development. I could give singular and beautiful instances of the effects I noticed of this, as more and more the dogs brought her in touch with the humanity about her. But I must come to the stranger parts of my story. I have given indication enough to show what they sprang from.

Four years had passed since Sandy's arrival. Fritzel had grown into magnificence. A dog may have beauty as noble as that of a lion or an eagle and he had it all. He was a very present help in the troubles that the little Scotchman's indomitable courage often invited, and the three walked abroad secure. My mind was at ease about them as it had never been yet. But be Fritzel what he would—and Helen loved the ground he walked on—their brains and hearts were not interwoven as were hers and Sandy's. He would lie on her knees sometimes, looking up at her in a mute communion and interchange beyond any speech. They understood each other in the most intimate and beautiful fashion I have ever seen. Love had worked its miracle, and that atom of life had rebuilt Helen as doctors and philosophers could not. A singular thing to watch.

Then came the end. An agonized telephone from Helen:

"Sandy is dying—poisoned. I have the vet here, but for God's sake come."

I raced down, but I could do nothing. I will not describe the scene. I have no wish to play upon emotion and there are things that pierce me still when I recall them. The last convulsion came and she sat with her head dropped upon the little stiffening body. I shall never forget her face when she looked up then. Her words startled me:

"I saw an idiot child at the *crèche* yesterday. If God can do that—and *this*—who can forgive him? Is there any law anywhere at all in all this hell?"

I pass this time over. Again I have no wish to write emotionally and it was too pitiful for any words. I stayed that night, for it seemed to me that she might relapse into her old listlessness, and that Fritzel and I were her only safeguards.

It was then with senses sharpened by anxiety that I began to notice singular things about Fritzel. He had been devoted to Sandy—no closer dog-friendship ever existed, and they had formed certain habits which had all the authority of routine. Every morning after breakfast they trotted off side by side into the paddock to call upon the water-rats and other interesting families, and they allowed half an hour for this invariably.

Now on the morning after Sandy's death he stood in the dining-room by Helen as we finished breakfast, bewildered, looking about him, looking up at her, like one lost in a world unknown. It touched me more than I like to say, coupled with her hopeless look of pain.

Suddenly I saw him turn to the French window open on the lawn. He froze into attention as if someone were coming up the drive. Do you know that amazingly beautiful attitude of suspense in a dog, when with head erect and one paw held up he thrills from nose-tip to tail-tip with hope and expectation? We watched him in amazement—there was no one he welcomed like that.

A breath of roses blew in at the window and ruffled the curtains. Fritzel's paw dropped. He laughed all over his face, his tail wagged delightedly. He leaped to the window and was gone.

"So soon to be happy—to forget!" Helen said brokenly. "Sandy wouldn't have—" But she could not finish the sentence. I went out and watched. Fritzel was hunting round the paddock in his usual way, alive with interest. He came back in about half an hour, found his mistress under the beech tree and lay down beside her. But again I noticed a curious thing—it is a part of my trade to watch seeming trifles. He had had a way of lying that made a hollow for Sandy's repose, and there they would doze in a heap of warmth and tranquil comfort, all tangled up together. He stretched out in the same attitude now, with of course the difference that it exposed the thinly haired under-part of his body to the air—a thing a dog always avoids if possible unless in very warm weather. Helen noticed it too. She pointed at him.

"Poor Fritzel—dear Fritzel! I was wrong. He doesn't forget. But that'll soon pass over. It will be cold in winter without the little one and the fire will take his place. Well—we must do the best we can for each other, old boy."

Before I left that day I had seen Fritzel do another thing which I thought the most extraordinary of all.

Their dinners had always been brought out and put a little apart in two basins on the veranda. Each took his own in perfect confidence that there would be no interference, and when that delightful moment ended they went down a certain path that led to the river, and then sat together under the beech tree waiting for Helen.

Now when the solitary dinner was brought out Fritzel looked about him with the bewildered air of the morning. He walked up and down the veranda, hesitated, ate a little, nosed a bone out of the way, walked about again evidently much perturbed, then returning ate a large share of his dinner, leaving a portion untouched, and went slowly down the path to the river.

"He doesn't care for his food today. Take it away, Mary," Helen said slowly. She had eaten nothing herself.

"No, leave it," I said quickly. From the window we could see Fritzel sitting under the beech where so much of Helen's life was passed. Twenty minutes and more went by. Then suddenly he came leaping back with great arrowy bounds, his feet scarcely touching the ground, and so into the veranda. He finished his dinner hun-

grily, took possession of the bone and went off with it
to the tree. I think Helen was disappointed in him. I,
on the contrary, was constructing a possible drama in
my mind. Which of us was right?

After that I did two things. I came over to Tetford
whenever I could spare the time and I got certain of
the proceedings of the Society for Psychical Research
and began to consider them, and when at Tetford I
divided my watch between anxiety for Helen and interest in Fritzel.

Of Fritzel I cannot enter into all the details which
carried conviction to my mind that he was leading
exactly the life he had lived with Sandy and that he
saw and interpreted things on a different plane of being
from our own. But I saw it in his every movement. All
Helen's habits were riven by the change and loss. None
of Fritzel's. She stooped under a growing weariness
though she continued the little pleasures for the children and so on because she felt she owed them to her
memory of Sandy. All else which merely appeared to
concern herself she dropped. Fritzel on the contrary had
dropped nothing. He was content. It may seem a kind
of folly thus to analyze a woman's mind side by side
with a dog's, but knowledge comes by many paths, some
of them little more than tracks. Knowledge was my aim
now and then, and I was trailing Fritzel.

I was all this time profoundly interested in the literature of the Fourth Dimension—that singular world
which is our own but which cannot be seen or realized
through the blinding, distorting medium of the five
senses. It has always been a vague traditional belief
among the peasantry of many nations that animals have
the faculty of seeing spiritual apparitions, and even in
the Bible occurs the celebrated instance of Balaam's ass
who was so much less asinine than his master. Have

certain animals anything of the Fourth Dimensional outlook which is denied to reason but open to the subconscious? I seriously asked myself whether, looking to our utter ignorance of the working of a dog's consciousness, I should prove myself a lunatic if I entertained the hypothesis that Fritzel was still conscious of some impress, if I can so put it, of Sandy's presence.

I would not say anything about it to Helen, for her wound still bled, and she was sleeping badly again, relapsing slowly into the state from which Sandy had rescued her. On that head I had a right to real anxiety, but I understood her, and Fritzel I could not. The one appeared to me blind, the other awake and aware. There were perpetually times when he would get up and smile (you know the delicious smile in a dog's eyes) and stand with uplifted paw, and after giving the welcome, settle down into peace at Helen's feet, when we could see nothing and yet I would swear he hailed a friend. The weirdest thing to watch, and yet breathing joy and security. I would have given more than I was worth to get behind his brilliant eyes and see with him. I began to know it would have meant a voyage of discovery to wider realms than man has sized up as yet. I asked myself perpetually, did she notice all this? Could it escape her? Amazing that it should!

At last came a letter from Helen:

"My dear Jim, I am writing on a subject that may bore you, but I know your endless compassion—and who has tested it more than I. So here goes! I am beginning to think I did Fritzel an injustice. I thought he cared so little when Sandy went—I have sort of undervalued him ever since. To see Sandy forgotten was more than I could bear. But once or twice lately —I had better tell you what happened last night. You know Fritzel has slept in the upper veranda into which my bedroom opens. He *never* moves at night. You could not tell he was there. But last night—I could not sleep and I am ashamed to say I was crying and very lonely, when suddenly he pushed the door open and came in. He walked straight to my bed, put his paws on the side and so stood, looking not at me, but at the place where Sandy always slept, wagging his tail and smiling. Then he lifted one paw and laid it on the very place (you remember how he would touch Sandy like that in the garden?) and so stood for a second talking—you know the way they used to talk to each other?—and then dropped on the floor and went off to the veranda satisfied. Now this sounds a trifle to you. You will laugh! But something in the way it all happened made me ask myself whether it could be possible that life once lived in a house leaves some kind of emphasis behind it—not, of course, survival in any spiritual sense—which a dog can realize? I seem to have read some such theory somewhere. Tell me if you have ever heard of that kind of thing. I can easily see it might be only memory. Or even perhaps a sense of smell—or some quite natural explanation. Do tell me what you think."

I told her I had noticed the thing from the very beginning and had watched with the utmost interest because I felt certain something was going on beyond our comprehension and well worth following up, but that her explanation did not, I thought, meet the case nor the intermittent character of Fritzel's manifestations. I said I should prefer to defer giving my own until I had studied the subject more deeply, and ended by begging her to watch and make notes.

This she did, and I have those notes lying before me now. They are far more acute than mine, for a woman of Helen's type brings intuition to aid observation, and her knowledge of the dogs and their ways was far closer.

She came to the definite conclusion that Fritzel thought he was not alone. He still, at close intervals but not continuously, enjoyed the companionship. But the odd thing was that she drew no deduction from this of life-persistence. Sometimes she would call it "idealized memory" or "a kind of reflex action of the brain cells" and so forth. I, reading and thinking steadily forward into the new worlds of psychology opening on the dazed eyes of materialistic science, felt all this to be a little—shall we say?—unenterprising, more especially as I passed her notes on to a man working high and far along the line of indications of the higher psychology, and his flashing interest in Fritzel's problems enlightened my own. I have already mentioned this friend of mine.

It was about six months after Sandy's death that Helen was taken very ill with influenza. In reality it was grief plus a germ. She had never been herself since her loss. The moment the news reached me I went over and saw Dr. Marsham, who had the case in charge, and gained his permission to look in when I would and consider with him the turn it took. I knew we were in for a battle.

Mrs. Bramham knew it too.

"I wish Miss Helen had never seen that dog!" she wept to me. "You couldn't help loving the thing—it had such a way of its own, and she was never one to do things by halves. She'll kill herself over it yet. Why, even that Fritzel has more sense! He don't fret nor worry about it. If Miss Helen knew half what was going on in that dog's head she'd have more sense than she has."

This was a dark oracle and I asked for more, but

Mrs. Bramham was very shy over what would be called "the superstitions of the lower classes."

"Animals knows things we don't. Just like we knows things they don't." Which was so incontrovertible that it ended the discussion.

Influenza took Helen in its manifestation of high fever at first and utter exhaustion later, and I thought she would slip through our hands. Dr. Marsham and the very excellent night and day nurses thought the same. The day came when I may say I was sure of it.

Fritzel had been permitted to go in and out of the room all the time, partly because his perfect training made it possible, partly because it was evident that Helen suffered in his absence. Briefly, we regarded him as one of her slipping holds on life.

On that afternoon I was in the room with the nurse, Fritzel lying beside the fire, the room in full daylight reflected upwards on the ceiling from a great fall of snow outside—a desolate landscape with the river running black through it. Helen lay in a white exhaustion. Nurse had taken pulse and temperature and silently showed me the result. I will not dwell on what I felt —reason told me it was a question of hours. We stood by the wide window and waited. There was nothing more we could do.

Suddenly and silently Fritzel rose to his feet and went towards the door. It was closed but not shut—I mean it was not ajar. There he stood gazing at it steadily, one paw in air, ears stiff as iron with intensity of listening, quivering from head to foot in the dead silence. I had the impression that he might break out into a great cry, and held my will against his that he should not, for I feared to move lest it should excite him more.

Nothing of the kind happened. The door seemed to move a very little ajar as doors sometimes do of them-

selves, and instantly Fritzel relaxed into joy. Not a
sound, not a movement, but joy unmistakable, at gaze,
watching, glad. At the same instant Helen raised herself in bed, white as death, radiant.

"Sandy, Sandy!" she said, and fell back on her pillows again.

I thought it was death and the perception that sometimes comes with it, and was at her side in a moment—
nurse at the foot of the bed. The light flashing up before extinction—that was in my mind. But she opened
her eyes on me.

"Lift him. He's trying but it was always too high for
him. Lift him, Jim."

I went as if in a dream to the other side of the bed.
Fritzel's eyes led me to where Sandy would have been
standing, supposing—! I passed nurse to do it and shall
never forget her expression.

There, because Helen's eyes were on me, I stooped
and made the motion of lifting something that stood
with paws on the bed struggling to get up. And, as I
did it, she opened her arms and made a place for him
and laid her cheek over where his head would have been,
and so convincing was the drama that for an instant
I believed I saw him myself. That Fritzel did I cannot
doubt. He went back satisfied and silent and lay down
by the fire.

Now what I am going to say is as true as truth and
yet I can scarcely find words for it. I felt no weight as
I lifted, but I felt something in my hands which I can
only describe as life. Something vital. A man of my
profession may recognize the faint vibration of life
under the very mask of death, but it was not with
knowledge or reason that I knew this thing. It was by
that new quality beginning to bud in me which I called
the extension of consciousness. For the instant it struck

me dumb. I had lifted life and laid it by Helen. I knew it but understood nothing. The thing *was*—that was all you could say.

Then instantly reason reasserted itself in us both, and we busied ourselves with her. Nurse gave her a restorative. Her pulse was stronger. Her attitude was one of rest not of collapse.

An hour went by and still she lay content. She had not moved and we dared not shift her. But there was a glimmer of hope.

After Dr. Marsham's visit, nurse, an educated young woman, whispered to me in the firelight:

"That was the most wonderful thing I ever saw, doctor. Can you explain it?"

I could answer nothing. I had not adjusted my mind. But I assert this: when she left the room for a moment and I stood at the foot of the bed looking down on Helen, now asleep, I declare as solemnly as man can speak that I saw Sandy's bright eyes looking out at me from under the shelter of her cheek.

It has been said by a great Indian thinker that when one meets a true ghost one is never frightened—fear denotes that the appearance is only imagination. I believe the reason of this would be that being ourselves a part of the psychic we cannot fear it, whereas phantoms created by the imagination may be monstrous and alien as the skeleton shadows of tree branches flung on snow, not having any relation of truth to us at all.

Before I leave this part of my story I wish to state that I acquired the power of focusing so that I could see the dog when I would. Call me insane if you will, but remember that when we chatter of consciousness it is in the first place a word more misused than any other, and in the second that what we ordinarily call consciousness is nothing but a film thin as tissue paper between the depths of the subconscious and the heights of the superconscious. It is little surprising then that human beings should now and again tear a way through it by which they pass to one or the other of the vastnesses above and below.

I knew now that Helen would recover and awaited her revelation with indescribable interest. She had never uttered a word about Sandy from the moment of her cry of "Lift him." She was for a long time weak as water and what was passing in her mind I could not tell. But the double life of the dogs went on about her, and focusing, as I have said above, I could see (whether with my eyes or no I cannot tell) that they were together and went and came as naturally as in life. With one exception. Sandy would disappear on his own occasions for hours together, but where, I never could tell. There was always Fritzel's delighted welcome when he returned. I have the impression and give it for what it is worth that Fritzel did not understand these absences, had no part in them and disliked them. But this is guesswork. I saw Sandy constantly lying on Helen's bed, and Fritzel conscious that he was there and satisfied. Of this there is no doubt.

It was not until spring had come and Helen was able to be in the veranda that I had any real talk with her, and by that time I had much advanced in knowledge of the difficult subject I was studying. Nurse was still with her but she strengthened every day, and it interested me when I could go over—which was not very often—to see how her eyes dwelt on Fritzel, and his passion of devotion in response. That increased steadily. He was taking up Sandy's lead and developing immensely in reason and heedfulness. I began to have hope that he might yet be her life-belt as Sandy had been.

On this particular May day the sun was shining and

it was warm as June. She lay on a sofa in the veranda propped high on pillows with something soft and white flung over her. Sandy lay at her feet, his head on his paws, his eyes fixed on her face, Fritzel on the ground within reach of her hand. I thought she had acquired a most touching and spiritual beauty—but I will not dwell on that, nor on the first part of our talk. I pass straight on to what I waited for.

"Jim, do you know why I recovered?" she asked at last. "I was slipping straight down into death—and by the way never let anyone be afraid to die!—I—I liked it."

"They never are when they reach that point. It's the lookers-on who get up the wind," I said.

"Well—I hope so. Anyway I was all but there, when —can you guess?"

I said nothing. I was not going to color her story with any reflection of my own. She went on.

"I saw you and nurse like figures in a dissolving dream. You were ghosts to me. The door opened and Sandy came in. He stood up and put his paws on the side of the bed next the door—he never could get up alone because it was too high for him. So I don't know what happened, but in a minute he was in my arms. I felt his heart beat. He was much more real than you and nurse. He lay there thinking love to me exactly as he used to do. A dream—but it cured me. So don't laugh it to scorn."

A dream! And as she said his name Sandy raised his head from his paws and was "thinking love" to her under her very eyes! I could almost see the vibrations passing from him to her. It was very strange. I sat in the presence of a truth she could not see and that concerned her most intimately. And I saw it and she could not. She went on.

"When I woke up he was gone, but I knew I should live. A line of Shakespeare's haunted me—'For in that sleep of death what dreams may come.'—I wish you could know how real that dream was. You have been so kind and patient with me about Sandy."

I considered a moment. "Do you happen to remember if Fritzel was in the room?"

"Yes—yes—" she said, hesitating as if fishing for a memory. "I think he was near the door. Yes, I am sure. And in the dream he knew Sandy was there."

"As you say in your notes he had often seemed to do before?"

"Yes, I had forgotten the notes. But, yes. Was he there really?"

"He was lying by the fire and got up and went towards the door," I said.

A long pause. Then very slowly:

"Jim, did I speak in my dream? Is there anything you can tell me? All, except Sandy, was like moving in a thick white mist. He seemed real."

Again the dog looked up. He moved slightly, and curled up with his head against her foot in an exquisite attitude of trust. I saw that. God knows what thoughts flashed through me of the wonders about me to which I myself was blind—the clues everywhere about us for the picking up; we moving through them confident and arrogant in our blindness!

I told her exactly what had happened. It was taking an emotional risk, but I saw her mind was questing weariedly and restlessly. I chose the lesser evil and spoke. I did so with no emotion or exaggeration of any kind; flatly, if I may use the term. She stared at me with her soul in her eyes.

"Jim! You say you felt him. Have you gone mad? And you saw him later? What is one to believe? For if that were true—there is no such thing as death. Do you know what you're saying?"

"Certainly I know. There *is* no such thing as death. The body comes and goes; the soul never comes or goes; it includes all the universe in itself. It is the universe."

"But a little dog—a little dog!" she repeated wonderingly. "Oh, Jim, how you have changed!"

"Yes, I've changed. You think in terms of time and space, Helen, and I think in very different terms now. I have at all events a shaft of light shining into my darkness—and I owe it to the dogs."

I changed the subject then. She had had enough for mind and body and I knew she must do her own thinking. No one else can do it for one. She made me promise to come again when I could, and I left the three with an extraordinary longing to come back and get into closer touch, if I could, with the Mysteries. Not the least of them to me was that she on whom such love was lavished had felt only the back-wash of the wave and still took it as a dream. I put that to the man who had read her notes on Fritzel. He answered:

"She loves intellectually not absolutely. She can't forget herself and that is not the right approach. The dogs love her with utter faith and absorption. They never think of themselves, and are *her* in the deepest sense. They couldn't lose touch with her if they tried. That's one of the reasons, though there are others, why the bond between man and dog is forged of steel. Dogs understand—no, *feel*—no, *are*—the very essence of love in a way to which very few men and women attain. Does that wound your pride? It needn't. Very strange forces and mystic states are involved in the relation of man to animals, as they know in Asia. But in that of man and dog most of all."

He said more, which I will not record here though

it impressed me profoundly with its truth and beauty. He ended with what he called a hit at a prophecy.

"I believe that when Fritzel goes your cousin will not survive him long. The two will draw her. Sandy has been doing it steadily, as love will, and he nearly won. The two together will succeed. I don't mean in the least that she would die of grief. You understand better than that now. They will want her to go on with them. She will go. What we call death not infrequently happens in that way. They will go on educating her."

Again he said more that I shall not repeat because of the simplicity of its high truth. That obscuring simplicity stands in the way of much revelation, for men will have the long words and complicated processes if they are to give the tribute of even a passing belief.

Helen remained in ignorance. The outlines of the "dream" blurred a little into vagueness for her, though it remained always the most beautiful memory of her life. My vision she attributed to "the nervous tension of the moment." "One understands so well," she said sadly, "how anything can be imagined at the moment of eternal loss. I know that when my Sandy went— unless I had held my mind very steady I could have believed any wildest possibility. But I am where I was, though I wish I could dream again!"

I said no more—what use? I never told her that when I went to Tetford I always saw Sandy at her feet, watching her with the worship of a perfect devotion. Once, unseen by her, I tried to touch the velvet of his ears as his head lay against her dress, but as I did it he blurred and was gone like a reflection in water when a stone is flung, returning at once when it settles into calm. I loved him, but his concentration was not for me. I could not touch him.

So she went on grieving when she might have lived

in sunlight. For one thing, she never recovered her health after the influenza. And it was a shock she could ill stand when one day quite suddenly Fritzel died in his sleep beside her. Sandy had won his friend back, and Fritzel had pulled with him. They wanted to be together without the stupid limitations of this dull three-dimensional world of ours. I could understand that well enough now. I grew a little tired of them myself.

But I remembered my friend's prophecy and knew what to expect. They were always about her after that, happy, eager, like dogs who stand sentry at the door for a walk, hearing the beloved footstep coming down the steps, knowing that perfect delight awaits them. It was astonishingly beautiful to see their eagerness and expectation. They were tense with hope. I could hardly forbear telling her, assuring her, every time I came, but her sad fixed unbelief held me back. Helen needed so much education, but that I could not give her. I knew it was in store for her now, and soon.

The day before she died I was with her. She lay with Sandy at her feet and Fritzel standing in the veranda outside and looking in as if to entreat her to come out and romp in the paddock or swim in the river.

"Why do you lie there all the stupid day, beloved," he said with his eager eyes, "when all the world is before us? Come out—out, and have done with it all! Have you forgotten how lovely it is in the wide open? We want you. Come! It's heavenly out here."

The dog glittered with energy and invitation. You have seen it yourself on a happy day when the dog you love drags you out and will take no denial. But this was intensified tenfold. It ran through me like bright spring sunshine. Little Sandy, more patient, lay awaiting his moment tense and confident, his eyes fixed on her.

"Jim," she said faintly, "I'm *dead* tired of being ill and a nuisance. I crave to be out in the open and blow in the wind over a great moor like a bit of thistledown. Can I? Shall I? Is it a dream? You've got so much further than I. Tell me."

"That and better," I answered. "And with the dogs."

"The dogs!" she said with a note of weary wonder. "I believe you believe they're here. I wish I could. I wish I could!"

I did then what I could not have done before. The moment had come and I cannot tell how I knew it but I knew. I did a thing and with a result that I never could have imagined. I put my hand on hers and clasped it. I sent my will through her eyes, saying, "See!"—in the inmost of my being. And I saw perception run through her just as when the sap runs up a bough like wine and the leaves thrill with life. She raised herself and looked at the window.

"Fritzel!" she said. "Fritzel! Yes—soon—soon! And Sandy!" As he sprang into her arms, she looked at me like one stunned with revelation. "You knew and you didn't tell me. Oh, thank God--thank God!" I won't dwell on it. It was a passion of recognition. Let that suffice.

She died next day. Died: what a word for the supreme reality! But so, I suppose, it must be stated until we acquire the new language with the new wisdom. For myself, life goes on to its inevitable developments. I am a busy man in my profession and I find this inward knowledge adds much to my usefulness. We are only beginning on the psychic side of medicine but its promise is vast. I could tell so much more, but here I must call a halt. Of all subjects this is one where one must be guarded.

I shall not marry, for the woman I loved is not dead

as far as I am concerned. Only two evenings ago I
pulled down past her house by the river. Other folk
live there now and the garden is tended and happy. But
as I neared it I allowed the boat to drift past as I
always do that I might watch Helen running and laughing in the meadow opposite like a girl, with Sandy
leaping about her and Fritzel circling them both with
his great arrowy bounds—the perfection of grace and
strength. She ran to the edge of the bank and waved her
hand to me smiling, and the dogs stood at gaze beside
her with welcome in their eyes. I drifted on and the
sunset, less radiant than they, absorbed them into radiance.

I envied them.

"But we like sentries are compelled to stand
   In starless nights and wait the appointed hour."

And I have seen and known. I have the Key of the
Fields and the time will not seem too long though I
could wish it shorter.

Lord Killary

IN THE MOST REMARKABLE STORIES OF PSYCHIC DE-
velopment it is often difficult to obtain verification and
when this occurs I, for my part, let the matter drop
so far as the public is concerned, hopeless of conveying
the atmosphere, the intangible nothings which convinced
me. That this is often a severe loss to those who study
these subjects I know, yet the rule is a wise one. Sometimes, however, I present, as an imaginative story,
something that I myself know to be true, and those who
read may then accept or refuse it according to their several capacities. Perhaps the truest things are best conveyed thus. In the story I tell now, I know the man. I
had seen with pleasure the perfection of the relation between himself and his son (his wife was dead). I had
realized a psychic development of the noblest type, but
I little guessed the poignant story conveyed in a manuscript which he caused to reach me after his death.

It permitted me under certain restrictions and pre-
cautions to tell facts which I myself would have found
it difficult to believe had I not known the man whom
I have called Simon Roper. As a last preliminary I have
only to say I have kept the faith. No one will trace the
personages from the words I write.

Roper's mother was left a widow when he was four
years old. They were very poor and the boy attended
the village school and did extremely well there. The
mother was remarkable—a deeply religious woman and
an omnivorous reader. The father had been a doctor.

This village was within two hours by train of the great manufacturing and shipping town of Lilchurch. Centuries ago it must have been beautiful and it still holds the treasure of a noble old Carthusian church dedicated to the Holy Cross. Roaring streets cover the site of what was once a vast priory, the center of all the arts and education of the shire, and all that memory retains of its sacredness is the name Holywell Street, a trough for horses and dogs and a jet released by a spring where thirsty passers-by may drink, little guessing that the Middle Ages believed this water to be a drink divine, curing all hurts of soul and body, and that it drew pilgrims from every corner of England. None come now and the world would say the power has departed with the belief. The world, however, has not the last word to say on such matters.

Mrs..Roper had good right to be hopeful about her son's career. He passed on to the age-old grammar school at Rifden near Lilchurch, where he won scholarships and otherwise distinguished himself. He left school and—no work was to be had. No one wanted an unusual young man with a taste for literature which he did his best to hide as a known disadvantage in the labor market. At last he got a temporary job as a commercial traveler, and when that was coming to an end their thoughts turned to Canada (they had friends in Saskatchewan) as the only hope. And then the unexpected dropped like a shooting star from the blue.

Business took Simon Roper one day to the stately office of the biggest firm in Lilchurch. It had world-ramifications; its own line of ships, and what not. To be in Parker Walter's was to be safe and secured from all the slings and arrows of struggling commercial life. Lord Killary was the chief, though all the directors were great men, and when Lord Killary was spoken of

people thought of the man who had given and created
the Great Central Park which was the glory of Lilchurch, the man to whom all charities looked for sympathy, whose club for all the young men employed was
the finest thing in Europe, who knew them all personally and made friends with them when it was at all
possible. Yes, of all institutions in Lilchurch, Parker
Walter's was far and away the greatest and Lord Killary was its brain and heart.

Simon Roper was leaving after ten minutes' audience
with a man who scarcely pretended to listen. Fate, on
the watch as he came down the marble steps into the
great hall, brought Lord Killary at the same moment
and landed him with a sprained ankle in young Roper's
arms. It would have been a broken leg otherwise. He
sent for him next day to Laytonhurst—his great place
eight miles from Lilchurch—that he might thank him
personally. And the two liked each other. A billet in
Parker Walter's followed. Simon's life-tangle was
smoothed out.

I wish I could dwell here on the loving care with
which Killary was drawn in Roper's manuscript. He
was of good Scotch blood from above Inverness, a
man of forty-eight, slight, dark, distinguished, hair
brushed with silver—a man who had known trouble,
for early in his married life a riding accident had made
his wife a cripple and there would never be heirs to his
honors. A lonely man too, said Roper, for his tastes
led him to things very far apart from the usual business
drive. It was his habit to allow and encourage his clerks
to come out on Saturdays and Sundays to borrow books
from the great library at Laytonhurst, and it may be
suspected that he glanced over the old librarian's lists
now and again; for, catching Simon one Saturday
afternoon buried in the Greek Anthology with an open

Plotinus beside him, he spoke to him not like chief to
clerk but like one human being to another, and after
that Simon felt he could not avoid thinking of the great
Lord Killary as a friend. Here I must insist that Roper
was as remarkable in his own way. Something quick,
unusual, sympathetic, met me on every page of his
manuscript. I can see very well what Killary surprised
in him. I can see the two leaning over the table in the
library and Killary's delicate finger pointing to a verse
in the Greek—Plato's famous epitaph on the boy Aster
—the Star, as his name betokens, who fell from the
firmament so young.

"Shelley translated that!" says Killary. "Would you
have the courage, Roper? His isn't literal, you know."

He repeated lingeringly Shelley's lovely lines.

> "Thou wert the morning star among the living,
>   Ere thy fair light had fled;—
> Now, having died, thou art as Hesperus, giving
>   New splendour to the dead."

"Difficult to beat!" he said and smiled. "The Star
of Night—Hesperus—eh?"

Young Roper looked up eagerly: "I've done it, my
lord."

"Say it."

Very shyly Simon repeated:

> "Thou, living, wert the Star of breaking dawn,
>   My Star, and now thy loveliness withdrawn
> Has risen in other skies and there thy light
>   Is Hesperus in that eternal night."

"Not half bad. Literal too. Shelley would have liked
it. Well, Roper, come often—and you know there's

always tea at the Dairy for the boys and girls from our show."

That was Killary. His own share of his great place could not have been very radiantly happy, for the ordinary amusements of bridge, drinking, hunting, did not appeal to him, and Lady Killary was too suffering to allow of the usual house-party gaieties. Killary rode a great deal—alone. Read a great deal—alone. Traveled —chiefly to visit the big business interests abroad— again alone. His life appeared to be thrown much inward—if outwardly his concerns were world-wide. Simon's thoughts centered much about him. They had met more than once in the library at Laytonhurst and always his manner was that of a man who lays little stress on social circumstances but much on inward sympathies. No one would guess this at the office. There, business was business with a vengeance. Perhaps it is not too much to say that Killary became a hero to young Simon Roper, and he had a strong and romantic affection for the man. It was about this time that Roper's mother died and that he made a new friend at the office, Lord Killary's secretary, Katharine Picard.

He had seen her at a distance of course, but one day they came down in the lift together and she spoke.

"How are you, Mr. Roper? I'm so glad you've joined up. I hear you go out to the library at Laytonhurst. Are you living at the club?"

"No, there isn't a vacancy now. I'm on the waiting list. But I have very decent rooms in Storm Street. They were on the firm's list."

"It's rather wonderful the way they think things out," she said. "That's Lord Killary. He will have it. Don't you like him?"

"Who wouldn't?" Simon answered joyously. They were standing in the hall now, and it was clear she was

going out to lunch. She listened with pleasure. He could
see that. He added:

"One can't even remember to be astonished he has
time to think of us all. He makes everything seem so
natural."

Killary passed them, talking with Mr. Parker, not so
engrossed in business but what he could nod to the two
as he went. Her eyes followed him.

Roper had the impression that like himself she had
known the seamy side of life. She had a pale intellectual face with wistful gray eyes, tranquil and reflective
under broad brows. Her gray dress with white turned-
back collar and cuffs was nunlike in its severity and
suited the little round clipped head with one long lock
which draped the forehead. He felt he would like to
know her better. They might have something in common. Simon liked everything in the manner of a fine
silver-point, gray, illusive, delicately imaginative. Katharine Picard was all that.

They stood perhaps a moment and then as she turned
to go he ventured:

"Miss Picard, I often lunch at the Thatched House.
Could we lunch together today? Do!"

She gave a rosy smile of pleasure and blushed up
like a child.

"Why, yes! Oh, I would like it! Thank you so much.
Let us go."

They went down the great steps. He thought how
pretty her little feet were in gray suède shoes and silk
stockings to match. Yet as a whole her face was not
really pretty—except indeed the eyes—it was attractive.
He decided that was better. It would wear—the other
might not. It had another advantage also. The many
young men employed at Parker Walter's preferred a
much more striking style of good looks. They liked

highly colored lips, full and fruity, darting eyes with sleek mischievous glances. They liked the cravings of the sexual nature in a man to be understood, answered, even prompted, and they certainly had not far to seek. There was plenty of all that in the young women who graced the Parker Walter offices. These boys did not mind occasional tantrums and a little vulgar violence in their charmers, and they not only condoned but invited a perfectly brainless frivolity which sailing along the surface of things asked no more.

Every Jack had his Jill on every floor. Only Katharine Picard went her way in a kind of moonlight quiet. She had a tiny office opening close to Lord Killary's, and her business was with him and no other. That being so she had an assured position of her own and received a kind of deference from everyone, which made Roper feel it to be something of a distinction that she should lunch with him. They grew to be friends and it became a habit. He was glad when one day on meeting Lord Killary in the street the great man stopped him and said:

"Miss Picard tells me you lunch together, Roper. That pleases me. She's such a good girl, but too grave for her age. You and she strike me as having many things in common. Brighten her up if you can. Why don't you bring her out to tea at the Dairy? I don't think she has seen it."

He smiled and went on. Extraordinarily kind for a man in his position to give a thought to his secretary and clerk. But that was Killary's way. No wonder people loved him. The thought struck Simon: could he have any budding romance in his mind about the two of them?

But no—he was out there! They never would attract each other in that way. He loved her company better than any other. She cared for the kind of things he did—could brood for hours over "The Earthly Paradise" or the myths and legends of lovely dead days. They had come to Christian names; they could sit in Laytonhurst woods in the silence of intimacy and perfect contentment. She took him to her home and introduced him to her rather incapable mother, the widow of a clergyman. He sculled her on the river on long summer evenings; and the Jacks and Jills of the office said it was "a case" and they wondered how his Lordship would stick being robbed of the perfect secretary —the secret, the reserved, the unapproachable Miss Picard. But it never was "a case." The two concerned knew each other and went their way. Roper used to think that if he had had a sister it would have been like that—a perfect kinship.

Yet after a time Simon too felt the soft cloud of Katharine's reserve. He was not altogether happy about her. One evening on the river he spoke his mind in the dusky starred veil of coming night, as they drifted down to Lilchurch with the current.

"Katharine, what's the matter with you? You're not happy; your mind's troubled. Everything's changed."

She flushed up rosily. He saw the pulse from the heart flood her pale cheek and was half sorry he had ventured. Yet, friends must be bold, and he could not see her paling and saddening daily and take it for granted. He held to his point.

"Tell me, Katharine. I'll stand in with you whatever it is. Tell me—is your mother hard up?"

Her salary was fine, but still—the little house in the Axmere suburb took some keeping up, and Mrs. Picard's rheumatism had added on a maid to the establishment within the last six months.

She shook her head.

"For if it were that—Katharine, you'd let me know, wouldn't you? We've shared things together that— Well, it isn't like the every-day boy and girl."

She leaned forward and laid a cold hand on his, but her eyes were not cold. They brimmed with gratitude— and yet behind it all was that impenetrable reserve which made her the best secretary in Lilchurch. He was shut out. He was not to know.

"I can't thank you, Simon. We're friends. I knew that from the first day I met you but—No. I've no trouble. I want a change, p'raps—or a tonic."

"Then ask Killary. He's such a decent sort that he'd give you anything—or any of us for that matter."

She agreed. His secretary would be the last to dispute Lord Killary's generosity. Simon knew he was reserved with her as with everyone, but there was always the Absolutely Trustworthy behind it. The whole office knew that. This went on for a month, and still Simon could make no headway against his doubts and fears. Katharine's sister had died of consumption four years ago. Could that be the hidden terror? He began to be seriously afraid it was.

One day an amazing thing befell him. A brief letter from Lord Killary.

Dear Roper,
I wish to speak to you on a matter of importance. It is private. I need say no more for I know you can be trusted. Come down to Laytonhurst on Saturday afternoon and meet me at the gate by the Home Farm at four o'clock.

Very Truly yours
KILLARY

Laytonhurst was open to the public on Saturday and Sunday afternoons—that was a part of the man's exceeding generosity. But the Home Farm was private and it abutted on the Wichworth pine-wood where no one might go except by invitation. Here, you might suppose you were in a Canadian forest, so great were the red tree-boles, so majestic the whispering silence. Simon went, divided between pride and astonishment. He knew that he had been singled out in more ways than one and felt certain that he was to be used in some new development of the business, possibly in one of the coveted posts in the great Asiatic seaports. He would like that immensely though he knew it would be a pinch to leave Katharine—that was a companionship he could hardly hope to repeat.

His heart throbbed as he saw Lord Killary's tall slight figure by the gate, with Jock, the little black Aberdeen, at his heels. Jock came every day to the office and had his own place and position as definitely marked as Katharine Picard's—an indispensable part of the personal retinue and much considered and courted. They said Killary thought the world of him.

Killary was in country kit and it suited him far better than his office wear. He looked younger than the forty-eight years given in the Peerage, though a little worn and sad-eyed. Looking at him Simon recalled the lines:

"I felt at once as if there ran
A shoot of love from my heart to the man."

Yes, one could feel that for this master of millions. It was give as well as take with him and his own heart threw out answering signals.

He welcomed Simon briefly and kindly and led the way into Wichworth Forest, down the wood-ways carpeted with silence from the heaped pine-needles. The slight figure in gray took Simon on—on—into a part

he had never seen before. Still as a temple, pillared
with woodland columns propping the hidden blue. There
was a small seat, and he motioned Simon to it, leaning himself against a mighty bole, the black Aberdeen
sitting and looking up into his face stedfastly.

"I can't, my lord, while you stand," Simon said.

Lord Killary made a gesture. "I wish you to."

Simon sat down and felt a something weighing upon
him unlike anything he had ever confronted in his life.
That he should sit—a young man, a mere clerk—and
the great Lord Killary stand! Could this be the preface
to a business offer? The solemn silence of the trees
formed a background very hard to reconcile with the
office atmosphere to be expected. The first speech was
startling.

"I can't beat about the bush. The matter is too urgent.
I must come straight to the point. Do you feel I have
been of any use to you, Roper?"

In his profound amazement, centered on the belief
that some further promotion awaited him, Simon found
words inadequate.

"I should say so, my lord. You've simply made my
life. And much more than that, too. I've felt I wasn't
only a number at the office. You spoke to me as if I
was human. I can't thank you, but I know it."

He had leaped to his feet, and Lord Killary smiled
at that a little sadly but protested no further.

"If you feel this, would you be inclined to help me
in a very difficult delicate matter? I feel the shame of
asking any return for what I did freely and as a matter
of justice. But would you?"

He needed no answer. Simon made a step forward
and the joy in his face was radiant.

"But could I, sir—I mean, my lord. If I could—by
George, I'd be glad!"

Killary's lips contracted with a little spasm that was not a smile.

"I expected that answer. You're a good fellow, Roper. I've always known it, but this is a matter most painful and difficult to break. I wish to God you could guess it without words—but that can't be."

Simon's mind ranged wildly over possibilities. Money. No—ridiculous. Lady Killary? No—he was a devoted husband. All the world knew that. He was silent from utter bewilderment, staring at the chief open-mouthed. At last Killary said slowly:

"Is there any other person in the world you would step very far out of the way to help?"

"My mother—is dead, but then—" He hesitated an instant for courage and added: "Miss Picard, my lord. I like her more than any other girl I ever knew. Since you ask me—yes, I'd do a lot for her."

Killary looked at the ground. His voice was like marble as he said:

"Does that mean that you—you love her? Her value to me will perhaps excuse my asking. I mean no intrusion."

Not in the least knowing what to do with this amazing interview Simon clung to the unvarnished truth as his sole guidance. The case was beyond all diplomacy. One just had to tell the truth and let her rip. But that was difficult enough. It was like having one's bowels probed with the surgeon's knife, revealing things wholly unexpected to oneself. Could Killary have noticed anything? Could there be more in Katharine's feeling for himself than he had ever imagined? Simon was not a vain man but really this seemed the only glimmer of revelation. He said hurriedly:

"I don't love her as perhaps you mean, my lord, but we're great friends. We trust each other—and I don't think there's anyone like her, but we don't want to marry each other if you mean that. Not a bit."

Did Killary sigh? He was still looking at the ground. His hidden eyes could tell no story. But the little Aberdeen drew nearer and looked up stedfastly into the beloved face. He knew.

"I gather you would sacrifice something for her happiness," the monotonous voice went on. "It would trouble you to know she was distressed."

For a moment Roper was sure he had guessed. But Killary was wrong. She felt nothing like that for him —clean strong friendship no more.

"I'd do anything to save her unhappiness. Anything."

"Anything? You mean it?"

"Anything. But what does she want, my lord? Why didn't she ask me? She knows I'd do it."

"She doesn't want you to do this. Yet—I see I must tell you the whole. Roper, I know I shall never regret giving you my confidence. She has spoken of you— But—it tears me."

"Certainly you shan't regret it, my lord," Roper said quietly. There was a moment's silence, then Lord Killary straightened himself and looked him full in the face.

"I am going to say something that will shake your whole opinion of me. Something dastardly. On that head I make no plea."

The fixed face opposing him! Even then Killary wondered if any sense of what was coming penetrated Roper's amazement.

"I have put Miss Picard into a terrible position. She is to have a child, and though I would do all in the world, I can do nothing. I cannot break my wife's heart to marry the woman I—to whom I owe all. My wife would never divorce me. It would kill her. Miss Picard would never accept the sacrifice from her. And her own sensitiveness would never stand the publicity. I can—"

He stopped so suddenly that it was as if some last strength in him had cracked and left him helpless. Stunned, Simon could only stand in stiff silence with his heart in a whirl of dizzying emotions. Katharine! Her suffering, her suffering! What other girl would agonize as she would over her ruin—for it would be no less. Her work broken. She and Killary could never meet again. Her mother—that little home gone. She could not stay there and face it out. A hundred points of misery for Katharine met and splintered in him as he slowly adjusted his confused thoughts to this new conception of Katharine and Killary. But what could he say—what do? Why was *he* told? It seemed that everything he said must be wrong, clumsy, impossible. Yet, Killary was waiting—waiting. At last Roper stuttered out something about regarding her as a sister. "If anything could be done." Killary turned upon him with a dying fire of hope in haggard eyes.

"Something could be done. Otherwise I think she'll go mad and kill herself. Her mother—no, the whole thing is impossible. Of myself I must not speak. I've lost all and deserve it. She must marry—"

A rush of enlightenment. So that was why he was told. He was to be the paid tool to make a hiding place for Killary's shame. The foul insult. He flung out his hand. "Stop! How dare you? How dare you?"

Even as he spoke he envisaged the whole plot. Oh yes, it was very clear now why Killary had been so good to him! How long had she been his mistress? He was to be Killary's convenience. He could not suspect Katharine—no, not even in that furious moment—but he saw they were both to be put respectably away out of the rich man's life when she became troublesome,

with a poultice of bank notes to heal her bleeding
wound. Even if she knew—who could blame a woman
fighting to save her child and herself from ruin at the
hands of a scoundrel? Yet he was sure she did not
know.

But Killary—the arrogant, insulting brute, paying his
way with money and hiding behind his invalid wife—
the rich man who could buy other men's honor as he
could their labor! He loathed the very thought.

Roper turned in silence to go. He had once loved the
man. He would control his fury while he could. It was
a voice he would never have recognized that called to
him in stark anguish.

"Roper—for God's sake! Not for me. If you like I'll
swear to shoot myself tonight if you'll do that for her
—for *her*. You know her—pure and good and true. If
I go out tonight, will you? I make no offers. I ask
your life, for she loves me and no other man would
ever be anything to her. Are you the man to save a
drowning woman and child?"

Yes—and to act as a screen that Killary might use
for future meetings with a woman whose name was
safeguarded by marriage. He scarcely heard the agonized voice.

"My money is dross. I know no man but you to
whom I would trust her for a day. I could buy a hundred men but I can't buy you—"

It was the wrong word. It drove Roper mad. He
thought of all the stories the world knows of men who
get their fat billets by their complaisance and climb by
shameful concessions. So that was what Killary thought
of him? He was purchasable because he was poor and
dependent. Had there been a tone, a gleam, of arrogance
in Killary's manner he would have dashed his fist in
his face and walked off. But it was only a try-on, and'

he could safely leave him to use his wealth on someone
else more supple, more keen-eyed on the main chance.
Loathing for money and its arrogance filled him. He
stiffened and straightened himself for his last words.

"My lord, we'd better end this talk. I needn't say it's
to me as if it had never been spoken, but you misjudged
me from start to finish. I'm not that kind of man. And
I'd like to say here and now I had better leave the business. It would be disagreeable to you to see me and—
well, I shouldn't like it. I ask one question. Does Miss
Picard know you spoke to me?"

Stiff against the tree like a man nailed on the cross
Killary said:

"No. She would never forgive me. Nor will she
either take money from me. My money is my curse.
My one hope was that you might win her confidence,
for she trusts you. And what she will do I can't tell.
She loves me—but money—no. You may be right. I
thought for a minute there might be a larger outlook
but no doubt such things are impossible."

He was silent for a moment, then added:

"You are right too about leaving Lilchurch. Allow
me to mention to Parker you are going and leave him
to use his discretion. I swear to suggest nothing. One
last word—believe it or not, if you had been my chief
instead of my clerk I would have made this appeal to
you. For I think only of her. If I could see her safe—"

His voice broke horribly on that. A kind of sob.

Roper shook his head. It might mean anything and
he did not himself know what it meant. He only wanted
to get away and think what he could do for Katharine
now that this man had used her and cast her off. He
went quickly along the silent path with contempt and
fury battling in his heart. At the corner he turned.
Killary had dropped into the seat. He was stooped to-

gether in a heap of misery. His face was hidden with
one hand; the dog on his hind legs was pawing at the
other, for love's sake, but unnoticed. Roper went furiously on. So men should suffer who ran up the debt and
called others to foot the bill.

He got to his rooms and looked at the telephone.
Should he call up Katharine? He must see her, and
though he would not add to her burden she must know
he was leaving, but never why. On second thoughts—
he would sleep on it. That interview would be one calling for the utmost tact and sympathy, and tonight he
could not count on his outraged self. The morning
would bring calm. And he had his own affairs to think
of—and anxious ones the moment he could find time for
them.

But as to sleep—that shy bird perched out of reach,
woo her as he would. The roar of the city slackened,
the lights dimmed. The measured tread of the policeman on his beat became audible as he marched along,
and still Roper could not sleep. Katharine—Katharine.
Her face, pure as a disembodied soul, floated on the
stormy background of his cruel thoughts of Killary
with closed eyes, not hoping, not pleading any more,
enduring. And in that vision he fell asleep at last as the
first dawn showed a thin gray edge over the serrated
house roofs, and a dream detaching itself from a heavenly crowd entered its home—his heart.

Strange. They were walking together down Holywell
Street—the roar of thundering motor-busses and trams,
motor horns, the unbridled rush of traffic, filled their
ears, and the gaudy glitter of wealthy shops dazzled
their eyes. Why were they there? Katharine loathed
those big streets. Always they went round the little by-
ways, evading and avoiding, so that they could talk
happily of their books and plans for meeting on the

river. Now she looked up and tried to make him hear and could not. That angered her. She threw her hand out with a gesture of disgust and lo—the amazing was upon them! The curtain rolled up on a new scene.

Holywell Street was gone. The air was full of healing silence. There were May-trees about them, snowed with blossom, the white almond-like scent filling the air with heavenly sweetness. In long meadow-grass two golden-haired children were gathering buttercups and stringing them with daisy-chains. They had wreathed one looped garland about the horns of a white cow, and her great eyes with their purple bloom gazed in mild bewilderment at the flowers dangling about her.

"Isn't it heavenly—the peace?" Katherine said, clinging to his arm, her breath coming quick with delight. Sadness had dropped from her like a veil.

The very soul of things ancient and lovely swam in blue air about them dreaming awake. The children were immortal youth, bright-eyed as seraphs. Surely that grass, those flowers, never grew on earth—but on the lawns of Paradise. Beyond great trees was a high-pitched roof as of a church—that also built the unearthly quiet. And before them, at the end of the meadow among the flowered grass, was a little village well, with a trodden track leading to it. There was a turning handle and a rope and a little wooden bucket dangling, and above it a stark cross with the dying Figure with outspread arms to which the whole world bows as the epitome of its sorrows.

"It's the Holy Well," Katharine's voice said beside him, "and it has power to heal all griefs. From every part of England men and women come and drink and go away glad. Let us drink."

He could hear his own voice edged with bitter irony —surely some memory of the day's struggle.

"If that were true it would be so crowded that the fields would be trampled bare. We couldn't get near it, and rich men would buy the land and form a Holy Water Company, Ltd., and sell it at a guinea a drop and the virtue would go out of it. No—don't let's drink! A monks' fraud, and we have real trouble to fight."

But still she led him on with soft insistence through the scattered gold and silver of the buttercups and daisies.

"Very few people understand. You must bring your own vessel to carry that water away. You must give as well as take. There are no miracles— But, come, let us drink. It may do nothing. It may do—this!"

She waved a hand at the dreaming beauty about them. One of the children ran to the well and turning the light handle brought up the little bucket, dripping and sparkling with living water. He cupped his hand and drank, waving to them after, glad as the Angel of the Resurrection.

"Come—come, and drink! Everybody drinks here."

They went forward hand in hand. Katharine filled her hands and drank eagerly. It seemed to Simon that he saw pure color flush into her cheeks and lips, heavenly azure into her gray eyes, as the living water ran divinely through her. She shook the drops from her hands and where they fell white flowers sprang, unnameable and starry. Roper cupped his own hands to drink—and as he did so became aware that a man lay prone beside the well. It seemed that neither Katharine nor the radiant children saw him and yet he must have struggled to reach it and there had fallen with thirst unquenched. He lay on his back, arms outflung, head thrown back, blood on the brows, on the mouth, on the hands.

Forgetting his own thirst Roper hollowed his hands
and kneeling by the man drained the water between his
clenched teeth. It fell upon the tortured brows. Again
he filled his hands and Katharine stood, pallid with
watching. The dead lips quivered, the closed lids trembled to the opening, and suddenly she fell upon her
knees and covered her face with her hands. The children knelt also. There was the sound of a far-off bell.
Roper looked up. The Cross was empty. The Figure
that had hung upon it lay at his feet. The bleeding
brows, the hands—he knew them.

There are things upon which one should not dwell—
even in dreams. What man could bear that knowledge
and live? A roar like the thunder of crashing worlds
broke upon him. They were walking in Holywell Street
again and the roar of traffic drowned all else. As she
drew him up into Charterhouse Street leading to the
Monks' Close, Katharine's voice said beside him as if
the rest had been a dream or nothing:

"There was once a holy well here. Kings and queens
came on their knees, they say. Now only the dogs and
horses and poor people drink there. Strange!"

He woke that morning in an extraordinary quiet,
the spring sunshine flooding his room. He knew very
well that revelation had come to him and life would
henceforward march to another drum-beat. Others
would not hear it, but he supposed even they would
be conscious of a new rhythm. The first step lay clear
before him. How could he hesitate? How small and
shameful appeared his denials and self-respect and
wounded vanity in face of the human agony that had
met him in Killary's hopeless appeal for help. How
could he face his own contemptuous refusal, the brutal
selfish cruelty springing in hatred from his lips? And

why refuse? Is a life so great a gift to offer before
the overwhelming Love that rules the world? It seemed
as nothing, remembering how he had thrust Killary's
gold against him as a bar to all human pity, and left
him beggared—Killary who had trusted him, whom he
had loved. Scarlet with shame he stood remembering
the bowed figure and his own pitilesss contempt. Now—
he envied the dog who had clung to him in love un-
changeable.

For in this flooding light he recognized the utter
loneliness of Killary's life, wifeless, childless, and the
generous outflow of sympathy to himself and others.
Roper understood the story now in every fiber of his
being. Was it wonderful that he should have turned
to Katharine—whom he himself loved as the friend of
friends? But he would atone. His hands trembled so
that they hindered his mad haste to be writing the
letter to Killary that should be the beginning of hope.

Life gives and resumes its opportunities. On the
breakfast table lay the paper branded with huge black
capitals. The letter would not be written.

SUPPOSED SUICIDE OF LORD KILLARY

When at last Roper could brace himself to read the
necessary words they were few and simple. They had
found him in the Wichworth woods. He had apparently shot the dog first and then himself. They lay
together in the deepening twilight. A letter was beside
Roper's plate.

Dear Roper:
    I am doing what is best for all concerned. She
will accept now what she would not while I lived.

I ask your forgiveness if I wounded you and I believe the time may come when you will accord it and understand I turned to you not as the rich man who can buy but as the beggar who has lost all. I recognize it was too much to ask, but you must believe that a very high estimate of you was implied in my request. You refused it and were justified in so doing. I venture another request—my last. Stay in the business. You are wanted there and Parker knows your worth. On the other matter I have nothing to say. I conclude with my best wishes. and they are sincere.

Very truly yours,
KILLARY

Roper did three things. He pressed the letter to his lips. He tore it into shreds and let the morning breeze take them. Then like Peter who also cast away an unreturning opportunity, he went up, locked his door and wept bitterly. Through that crisis of the soul no human understanding could accompany him. He mentioned it in his manuscript and passed on.

At the inquest he was the principal witness—apparently the last person who had seen Killary alive. Had they met by appointment? Roper, calm and self-possessed, answered, "Certainly not." He had Lord Killary's permission to walk in Wichworth Forest, and was going for a Saturday afternoon tramp. They walked a little way together—as far as the grove where the bodies were found. Then Lord Killary stopped and told him, if he came back that way, to have tea at the Dairy.

Was there any sign of perturbation, trouble, anything unusual? Nothing, Simon answered. Exactly his usual self, kind and calm. The many questions elicited no more. It was a case of absolutely motiveless suicide, so far as the world could tell. There might have been another meeting after Simon left him, but his life lay bare and blameless before the world and not the greediest paper could snatch at any solution of the mystery. Killary had gone free.

Let us take the story up on the day when Katharine Picard at last desired to see Roper.

They met at his rooms, for it was a part of her anguish that her mother could know nothing of the facts. All Lilchurch must grieve for Killary, and his confidential secretary might be allowed a little extra license in her lamentations, for in addition to the shock such a position is extremely personal and really cannot be reconstructed. Mr. Parker had his own Miss Wareham, whom it would be impossible to dispossess. The money loss was therefore appalling. Mrs. Picard felt that breakfast in bed was certainly indicated and would be appropriate also on the day of the funeral. Did not Katharine think that a wreath with "In Grateful Remembrance" would be expected? Very pretty ones could be had at Gardner's for ten and sixpence.

There was much more, and when she came into the room on Sunday with her stricken face Roper with his new-born understanding could distinguish all the different strands of pain that wove her garment of agony. He had no thought now of the strangeness of the position or of any delicacies or indelicacies—he burned with love for Killary and Katharine, and as for himself, except as a channel of help he had forgotten he existed. His chief preoccupation was that Killary should know. Yes, he was there watching—watching. Roper could see him, bowed and despairing no longer—eager and hopeful, with Jock beside him eager also. And Killary should be glad—by God, he should be

glad! Roper swore it to himself as he pulled the chair
for Katharine and sat down resolutely before her. Her
face—it wrung him. All color had fallen from her
cheeks and lips. Gray shadows deepened the hollows
about her eyes. Pain, the pitiless sculptor, had modeled
the features pitilessly—the lips a mere cipher of suffering. Her dress hung loose about her. Even the young
shoulders stooped under the accepted burden.

"I wanted to see you, Simon, before I go away."

"Away?"

"Yes. You can see I couldn't bear it. Don't make me
say it."

He interposed hurriedly: "Yes. I know—I know.
You could never stand it."

"Could *you?*" she asked, with eyes that sought some
fellowship in suffering.

"Yes. I shall stay," he said slowly. "I love Killary.
I shall stay because he would have wished it."

"That's a good reason. You loved him?"

"I love him."

"Who wouldn't!" she said and broke into low and
bitter weeping. He sat very still. She must lead the way
now. Presently, drying her eyes, she said:

"Simon, wherever I go I don't want our friendship
to drop."

"Nor I. But it never could."

"I know. But there's more. The night he died I had
the most amazing dream with you in it. So beautiful—
so marvelous, that I've written it down to keep forever
and ever. I want you to read it and tell me if there
mustn't be something wonderful between us to have
made me dream that. I wouldn't show it to one man
in a hundred but you are the hundredth."

He unfolded the paper and read swiftly. His own
dream; his very own. Except—a strange exception—

that the dying man to whom he had given the water of life kneeling was—Killary.

"He was dying," she said. "He had shot himself. The blood was on his forehead, but you knelt beside him and gave him the water. You, Simon. I shall love you forever. I'll tell you now. I loved him."

Disguises had dropped between them, though there was one secret which would be his forever—for Killary's sake. He knelt on one knee before her and took her hands. She stared at him in wonder as he spoke.

"Katharine, I dreamed that dream too. We walked together in true things that night and he was with us. We saw the truth. All that you knew I knew. How can we ever be apart again? If you loved Killary keep that love. Who am I that I should butt in? But don't go away. Don't, for God's sake, leave me. Marry me. Be Killary's, but be my friend. I want no wife. I want you, and because the world will have it we must marry."

She looked at him in white amazement, trembling from head to foot—in a long silence. Presently, she strained herself to answer with perfect simplicity.

"You must hear the truth. You may think me wicked —how can I tell? But Killary—we loved each other. It was only lately. He was very lonely—he had no wife. Now I am to have a child, and I'm not sorry, I'm so glad that I'm afraid I may die of joy before it's born. Oh, they say women have hard times in this; but think! If I had died first he would have had nothing, and I— have heaven."

There was a long silence. He knew Katharine and this did not startle him. She would not—could not think like other girls. Already the pale Madonna clasped the child in the arms of her spirit, confronting death, shame, ruin, with the altar flame in her sunken eyes. But at her next words he trembled.

"Simon, there's one thing I must ask you. You saw him last. Was there anything about this that drove him to death? With me he was always happy. If I thought *I* had brought him to it—"

No need to finish that sentence. With what an effort he met her eyes and held them Simon never knew. It seemed to his imagination that Killary stood behind her with uplifted hand. "Be silent—be silent!" He would keep the faith.

"Put that straight out of your head forever," he answered. "From something he let drop I believe he may have thought of Italy—somewhere happy and far away. I couldn't understand it then. No—you gave him happiness. Nothing else, my dear. Nothing else."

Their talk was broken by many silences, and the look in her face rewarded him. Presently he touched her hand again to recall her thoughts.

"Katharine, love is love. I have nothing to do with you and Killary. But the child. Will you injure it in any avoidable way? Won't you give it the best you can —a name, a home, a man to stand by it?"

She opened her lips to speak, but was silent, looking at him with eyes so searching that they pierced his very soul. He answered their question.

"Yes, I care for you but not in that way, and I believe I'm a man to whom friendship is more than the other. Frankly I tell you that Killary means more to me than any man living or dead—and I can't tell you why—or any woman. I loved him—I love him."

She laid her hands on his and said eagerly:

"Oh, because he was so wonderful, so single-hearted, so dear. You *knew* what he was."

"Perhaps. Anyhow, he meant more to me than you do and always will, though I love you in my way. Will you take it at that? I'd have done my best for your child. I'll do better than my best for his."

The battle was won. She said eagerly:

"You understand. You knew what he was. Yes—I could live with you. But, oh, consider, Simon. Think. Another man's wife—another man's child. And if you meet the right woman—"

"I've met her! When will you marry me?" he answered unwavering, and took her hand and kissed it. In that action he dedicated his life to Killary. Perhaps the moment of purest happiness he had ever known was when she drew his head to her shoulder as he knelt before her and kissed him on the forehead. She could not measure the magnitude of his sacrifice, and he could rejoice in that, for in himself thankfulness overpowered all sense of human loss. But Katharine would never know.

It was when she went and he sat alone, looking out into the sordid street that he realized and accepted in full the austere beauty of life. It is only possible for a man to participate in the heaven about him by the heaven within him, and Roper tasted heaven that day in its purest essence.

They were married immediately and certainly no surprise was created anywhere. Had he any moment of distaste when Killary's will announced the bequest of ten thousand pounds to his secretary? None. It was a natural thing in relation to his immense riches and her good services, as far as the world's opinion went. From Roper all illusions of personality had fallen away, and he and Killary walked as brothers in their joint trust for the girl and the child. I must suppose from what he told me that he had long before developed to the point of high perception, but it is certain that all Killary's power of thought and love and realization, new-won or enhanced by death, projected itself to Simon now and not to Katharine. That was a part of his reward.

"I shall see him until his next rebirth, and then we shall be together!" he said. "We are leaves of the same tree. I know now that was what I always felt about him. It was no chance that brought us together. There were deep things between him and me. He knew it then. I know it—not too late."

On the birth of the boy new happiness dawned for Roper. From the beginning they were one in everything—in games, thoughts, hopes, all that makes a child's life. Roper realized as few parents do that—

"The thirst that from the soul doth rise,
  Doth ask a drink divine—"

and the child had it—shall I say—clean from the flowing spring in the Meadow of Flowers. He told me he often saw Killary watching the boy in silent delight, with Jock at his feet—both happy and sharing in the starry vibrations radiating from the child's happiness.

"But not the real Killary," he would add, "or the real Jock. Both are up and away about their business. These are his thoughts of us and I love them. My God, the wonder and gladness of my life!"

Under these influences and with her own latent psychic powers Katharine developed a relation of great beauty with Roper. I think no woman of perception could have avoided it, but it became a much closer thing than any sexual relationship could have been. They dreamed the same dreams often and one of these so extraordinary that it has given me a story I must tell later. Holding Roper's hand, not otherwise, Katharine could see Killary at moments and rejoice in that beloved thought made manifest. Shall I say I believe that at last she scarcely could tell one influence from the other, nor cared to tell? That she made no distinction between their love of her and of the boy? That appears to me to be the crowning achievement of the selfless beauty of Roper's devotion. For it is the truth. It is love that *is*, and the person through whom it is manifested matters as little as the pipe through which the living water runs.

She died twelve years after the marriage from an accident. As she lay dying in his arms he asked her whether her life had been happier than it would have been without him. She answered that she thanked the eternal Love in every memory of him and that her last entreaty was that the boy should never know that the father of his soul was not the father of his body also.

He never will. This story can be written because he walks the world proud in the memory of a father who never failed him or any other, whom all men trusted and honored. He will never recognize the mystery I have revealed.

So Killary's instinct was true and what he wished befell. There are much stranger psychic interweavings in this story than appear on the surface, and thoughts which I do not dare to suggest save to those who walk the Way of Power. For them they lie open and beautiful and need no more words of mine.

How Felicity Came Home

IN THE STORIES I TELL OF THE GREAT REAL WORLD
that interpenetrates the little one in which most of us
live I know their truth will need no protestation to
minds which have reached a certain point of evolution.
Others will take them as fairy tales; but this has been
the fate of much wisdom hailed at first as the madness
of sick-brained enthusiasts. Wisdom, however, is but
another name for strength. It serves its sentence of
contempt and later ascends the throne serenely. Therefore when I tell this story of how Felicity returned I
covet no converts. I state what I know. Their belief is
to them. The telling is to me.

It is the story of what befell Paul Rivaz and his
wife Magdalen—he a delicate dark-eyed man of deeply
introspective habit touched with melancholy and dis-
appointment even in his happiest days, she a beautiful
young woman, life and health running in every vein
like clear water, meant by nature to be a living song of
joy wherever life had cast her lot, dark, vivid, passionate, eager. And when I knew them, both had been
struck down by a blow so dreadful that it seemed that
even Magdalen, the stronger and younger of the two,
would never again think anything on earth worth a
desire. Their faith in life was shattered. They crouched
under its cruelty as a slave may crouch under the whip
he can never avert.

Briefly his career had been in the civil service in
India. Their only child died there. His health failed

64

under repeated attacks of bronchial asthma, which weakened the heart, and he was ordered to give up his profession and return to Europe. It might have been worse. They had enough money to put more than comfort within their reach. They could buy climate, which was necessary for Paul, and beauty of surroundings—as necessary. But they could buy nothing more and had no treasure that they knew of within themselves which could in any way help them. The earth was iron under them. The skies were brass.

It was not Paul's asthma. They could both have borne that and its sad limitations. They did not lack for that kind of courage. And they loved one another so that Magdalen could give and Paul take the tenderness of care he needed. It was the loss of Felicity.

Felicity with her eight glad years, her dear impish face lit by elfish green eyes in curling black lashes—the little cropped black head with heavy locks tossed about her eyes like a pony's forelock. Paul always declared that Magdalen put a bowl over the child's head and clipped the thick hair round its edges—so round and black the little head, so quick and lithe the little active body—so beloved, so inexpressibly dear to them both. Their very being met, centered, and expressed itself in Felicity. It was easy to see who would rule that household, people said, when she grew a little older. Paul and Magdalen knew who ruled it already—the gay adorable elf who was so miraculously theirs and life of their life.

They all knew the time in India could not be long, because Paul's health would not stand it. Therefore India could never be even as much a home to them as it is to the ordinary exiles who, compelled to live there, never make the Mighty Mother their own, but turn their backs upon her as she glides by them in the dark with a mysterious whisper and the muted sound of bare feet. And Felicity, knowing this, dwelt in a dream-home which would come true some wonderful day in a country that she, born in Rajputana, had never seen. It would be southern France because the English climate could not be trusted. France was only a name to her, but the beautiful, gallant sound touched some chord of romance in her heart. They all often talked of that home to be.

"I see it in the night," Felicity said very seriously and often. "A great hill like Murree. Lovely green trees—oh, lovely!—with birds that sing! And doves; white doves and gray. A lovely, lovely garden all cool and shady, and a river. Not poor flowers kept alive by watering but strong ones wet with dew, and grass paths and roses—roses. My room has hills far away to look at and one day we shall climb them. And there is a most beautiful dog called Bru who loves us, and a cat gray like a cloud. When shall we go home? I want to go home."

It was always the same story, though sometimes the house had a tower, which could scarcely be true. They tried a little to discourage her fine fantasy, but that was hopeless.

"Then it shall be two towers," Felicity said, "and my room is in one of them. I want to go home. I want Bru. Dogs are too sad in India."

The house became a reality to them, and Bru a personage though they never knew how she had found the name. He was to be an Alsatian, cream and black, the perfection of beauty and—

But there was to be no home for Felicity. A swift Indian fever seized her. Even on that terrible Sunday morning when flaming sunshine parched the garden she smiled and spoke of the home in France—dear France

—cool, the rain falling like silver—Bru at her feet, roses—roses. Even when delirium took her she spoke of home and smiled. How could Paul and Magdalen realize it when a few hours later the doctor who had seen her born told them that all was over?

Death exacts his rites swiftly in India. Next morning she lay under the Indian trees. All was over indeed.

It is useless to dwell on their agony and the incidents of their flight from a country which had become dreadful. Dreadful to leave, for Felicity must stay there. Impossible to endure, for Paul was dying of it and of the cruelty which had broken and ruined all hope.

They landed at Marseilles half-dazed, stupid with grief, yet with the imperious necessity upon them of finding some home where he could endure life and where Magdalen hoped against hope that he would cultivate his frail little gift of writing about the people, faiths and superstitions of the Indian villages—a weak barrier between them and despair. Felicity—Felicity! Oh, the home-coming they had hoped! Oh, the desolation of reality!

They moved from one small southern town to another, trusting that chance would send them what they needed. It did, and swiftly. There is a little village which I shall call Clermont-Tourville standing far back from the great road which runs on to Avignon and finally to Marseilles. They were motoring through it one day and stopped to lunch at the little *auberge*— so plain and simple, where nevertheless such good southern cookery could be had, and wine—the warm blood of country grapes—was red in the thick glasses. They would stay a few days, he decided, and madame, pleased with her foreigners whose name was so easy to pronounce (and indeed Paul's ancestors were of a good old Huguenot stock) and who spoke such charm-

ing French, became a happy gossiping friend and devoted much time to sounding the praises of the country
round.

"A house wanted? But, *mon Dieu,* why then did not
monsieur et madame go and view Les Tourelles on the
hill? The most beautiful of gardens! Partly furnished,
only, it is true, but then how easy to order all one would
from Sallières! Let *monsieur et madame* view this
sweet place which was so fortunately for sale!"

They went next morning in the sunshine of a perfect day of early spring. Let me describe that house,
for much turns upon it.

It stood far above the poplar-edged road which runs
straight and true to the south, and Magdalen Rivaz
thought it must suffer in its flight from a place so
lovely. For the village stood in the richly wooded hollow of a great hill, which shut off the north and east
and fronted to the south and west. Snow had never
been known to lie in that happy garden. Daffodils were
earlier there than elsewhere, and the banks of violets
were mines of amethyst jewels nearly all the year
round. And the roses! The late owner from whom
Rivaz bought the property had prided himself on having seventy-six different varieties growing in flawless
perfection. They bowered the house and pergolas,
clothed the bushes with lamps of fragrant color, or
stood in stately standard ranks like court ladies parading in beauty for presentation. The place was snowed
over with jasmine when first I saw it. The waves of
perfume in still air recalled to me the most beautiful
of Zola's stories—"La Faute de l'Abbé Mouret"—
where the girl swoons under excess of perfumed deadly
breath from the heaped flowers in her room. But these
were pure as a child's heart. And through the paradise,
tumbling down from great heights above, ran a small
river.

The house, though comparatively small, was built in the fashion of a French château. It had a beautifully gabled front and two small *tourelles,* one at either end. Having been the dower-house of a noble family it owned grace and distinction which of their kind cannot be found outside France—something ethereal and austere, as of some great lady who has shone at courts in scenes of gallantry and gaiety but now, relinquishing the world, retires into sweet solitude, to be alone with memories and assemble them in a faintly beautiful *pot-pourri,* to perfume a life passing away gently as the drifting shadows on a summer day gather into gray twilight.

They wandered about the garden almost in silence and suddenly Paul turned upon his wife.

"Have you seen, Magdalen? My God! Wonderful. This is the house—" His voice broke.

"I know!" she said, her voice choking in her throat. "The garden—roses, roses! The river. The two little towers. Oh, Paul—Paul!" For it was as though Felicity spoke in their ears.

For a moment neither could speak, but each knew that cost what it would, it must be theirs. Trees—trees, a little wood at one side with delicate wild flowers at home in it. Great hills hovering like clouds in blue distance. From a window that might have been Felicity's own they faded into beauty that brought a moisture to Paul's sensitive eyes. Had the child's inner vision opened upon them? Felicity's home. But without her! What bitter mingled in how sweet a cup!

But there are no doves. Look at the old pinnacled dove-cote—empty. The place is silent, dead, deserted, except that the garden has been kept up. "Can we face it?" he asked.

Magdalen's hands were gripped in one another till they hurt.

"Could we live away from it and disappoint her? If she can give us any thought it would be here she would see us. Even if she is gone out forever and ever, still she thought of this. We can fill the dove-cote. We can bring life to it." She could say no more. The tears were spilling down her face.

On the very next day, Monsieur Laplace, the notary who was responsible for the house, was sought. Within a fortnight Les Tourelles was their own and in a week more they had moved into it with a worthy French couple as servants in addition to Magdalen's own faithful maid. To build it into the perfect similitude of Felicity's imagination seemed to be the first, the only thing which had stirred any remnant of eagerness in either since the day they had laid her beneath the blazing fire-flame tree in India.

They wandered through the garden hand in hand, curving its grassy paths, leaning over the violet banks to catch their sweet breath, standing by the rocks where the little river sang its crystal song on its way to serve humanity below. There was no house above theirs. They were nearest to the sweet Provençal sky, gentian blue-eyed, looking through the crowding trees, friendly and near at hand.

"Can we be happy here?" Magdalen said in a low voice, clinging to her husband's arm almost in awe at the over-brimmed cup of beauty held to her lips. The beauty Felicity had dreamed on the torrid plains of Jalabad.

"If we could be happy anywhere. But when I think that Felicity had to live and die in a sun-baked Indian town and this was waiting all the time—this green flowered paradise—it's bitter. Think of her flitting among the roses, climbing the hill under the trees—"

His voice failed. Neither were of the type who could

comfort themselves with dreamed beauties of a rose
garlanded, gemmed, and golden paradise, pieced together from Jewish or Mohammedan desires, painted
in excelsis above the clouds. India had destroyed those
fairy tales for them but had not peopled the void with
her own wisdom. They had lived too much on the surface of things to reach that mighty heart beating below
in its own silence and mysterious light and darkness.

"But we have to live," Magdalen said trembling,
"and here—"

"Yes—we have to live," he assented. "Perhaps when
I get stronger it'll be easier for us both. And there'll
be my writing."

They had not surrendered all hope of rescue in that
rather beautiful miniature talent for writing small
sketches of Indian life. Village tragedies, comedies,
which were beginning to be accepted as delicate
aquarelles, perhaps more convincing than the heavily
loaded oil-paintings in which Asia is presented to the
West by the gifted tourist who scampers there to collect pen-material which will impress the untraveled.

She threw her arm about his shoulders.

"Yes—your writing. Now that I can type—we'll
work together. It will be a new life for us both. You'll
see it will be happy."

Suddenly her voice turned to a cry. She clung to
him shuddering.

"Paul, there must be somewhere, something in the
world that would bring us to her again if only we
weren't blind. I feel it—but, oh, I don't know the way!
It's like the hopeless quest in a fairy tale—the impossible riddle."

"But the prince always solves it in the long run,"
he said, gathering her tenderly to him.

"Yes—by supernatural helps that don't exist. I'm a

fool. It's the human lot. Why shouldn't we have to bear it as well as others? But why were we ever born? Why was she?"

He put the thing aside. It was too heart-breaking. They passed the empty dove-cote, very beautifully pinnacled against the trees.

"Empty! Let's fill it, Magdalen. Let's surround ourselves with young life. Marceline must have a cat—no, it shall be ours, a smoky-gray beauty like a drift of vapor with great green eyes. Felicity's. And all the air shall be full of wings—I'll put up little bird-houses in the trees—"

"Stop!" she said. "I have a wonderful thought. Let's deliberately make it *all* Felicity wanted. The things she used to dream of. 'When we go home,' she'd say. Do you remember she said once, 'If I want to I shall sleep by the river. You'll find me there.' We never shall. But as she dreamed of it—let it be for her—not for us."

In that way came the beginning of a kind of story which was to mean so much to them that they hid it with painful care from others. This was to be a home where, if from some dim mysterious land, vague itself as a dream, she could ever send a thought to them, it might find a home to rest in before it must swim the bare starry space again to its mysterious source.

They used that little room with windows looking out to the far hills lost in blue air. It opened from their own and nothing quainter could be found. One side of it was rounded, for it was in the tower on the right aspect of the house. There was a small carven bed in the room with four delicate poles, long curtainless, and beside it a cabriole-legged table, and an *armoire* of the same period, where once the dresses had lain of the young demoiselle of blood so noble that presentation at

the court of the most Christian king was hers by right
of birth. But all pride had long since left the room.
The swallows built over its eaves, and roses and honeysuckle thrust in at the windows, and the bare polished
floor had responded to no high-heeled little feet for
many a long day. A vestal spirit of quiet brooded there
over the passing years in much peace, and since it
opened from their own bedroom like that of a girl
carefully guarded by her parents, all that was necessary was to have the polished floor kept glimmeringly
clean like stilled water, to set the windows wide and
a great jar of fresh flowers on the table every morning.
That jar was the only new thing in the room. The rest
had always been there.

That done, and Felicity's Room a part of daily life,
they filled the dove-cotes with snow-white inhabitants.
The air was thrilled with wings. The garden was less
their own than that of the birds who built in the trees,
sang, loved, nested, and lived in a sanctuary which,
alas! is rare in France. The peasant people laughed in
the village below and said that madame was *"folle"* for
birds; yet after all a lady *si gentille* had a right to her
own fancies, and thus the children had orders to safeguard bird life in the woods which clipped Les Tourelles
in their embrace. It was but just. *Cette petite dame
Anglaise* had a heart—yes, she had a heart of gold for
sufferers either in purse or body.

The cat was also realized—a magnificent vaporously
furred creature with eyes beryl-green or hazel as the
light took them. Her name was Lilith, from some story
Felicity had picked up of the lovely lady who lived in
Eden before Eve beheld it. A child's Lilith, beautiful
and kind. But the crown of the animal family of the
budding paradise was Bru, the great Alsatian, beloved
by all from the moment he came—a puppy adopted

instantly by Lilith and the winged friends of the garden, who used his back as a resting place from the
beginning.

He was Felicity's realized dream of her own Alsatian—"when I come home."

Does it seem absurd that Paul and Magdalen Rivaz
realized and built up this home of dream which they
were so sure Felicity would never inhabit? It was not
really absurd even from their point of view. They man-
aged through this carefully cultivated imagination to
strengthen their memory of the child and in that way
often spoke of her together, though in truth Paul could
never make up his mind whether that memory was not
too poignant for endurance and whether a prayer for
forgetfulness were not wiser. It is hard for human
beings to live on waking deams. But they did their best.
When Bru—now in the brilliance of his black and
cream beauty—stirred in his sleep and lifted a listening
noble head, Magdalen would say:

"That's because she is coming round the corner of
the house. See, she's in her white dress with the blue
ribbons. She has left her hat upstairs and all the thick
black locks are tumbling over her eyes. Now—Paul,
she's running into the wood, and Bru gets up and follows her. We needn't take him for a walk this morning.
He's going with Felicity."

And Paul would answer, but with an effort:

"Yes, and look at Lilith on the pedestal of the sun-
dial. Now she stalks them—close along the grass. I see
the muscles ripple along her body. And the doves fly
that way in a white cloud—low—just above the ground.
They will brush her hair with their wings. If we could
follow too—" And then the sigh—the bitter unsatisfied
sigh. It is well to tell oneself fairy tales, but how if
one does not believe them? He could only seize his pen,

and Magdalen would click at her typewriter like rattling thunder-drops but sometimes a drop, not of rain, would fall on the keys when Lilith and Bru and the white cloud of wings disappeared in the green growth. They envied them their pleasures, the close wholesome contact with all earth scents and sounds—the spirit of the woods slipping in through eyes undarkened by grief, alert senses, the supple bodies clothed with the loveliness of fur and feather. And most of all they envied them their care-free joys.

"I sometimes think we should be happier if we could take to the woods like Lilith and Bru," Magdalen said wearily enough one day. "They have a million pleasures we know nothing of. Listen!"

They were sitting under the western rose pergola and from the wood came the sound of quick rushes, smothered hunting cries, fluttering wings—a hundred delightful excitements and soft explosions of pleasure like little rosy and blue fireworks let off in the green fire of the secret woods with all their happy incantations.

"But we're growing happier, I think," Paul said anxiously. "We don't dwell on the misery of loneliness as we did. I have taken up my work again, though it doesn't go as well as it used. And you're able to type now. Only a little while ago we could neither of us sit down to anything. Yes—I think it's healing. Not that one could ever forget but—"

Even as he spoke his lips twitched. He pushed the papers aside and went to stare down into the river singing at its work among the little rocks and pebbles.

There was a small nook there, a mossed curve in the rock overgrown with strongly rooted ferns where a child could crouch or sit—if a child knew its delicious secrecy. He always stood there, Magdalen also, because Felicity had said long ago that she might sleep by the

river "when I go home." But taking it at the best their
bird was nesting now by some vague river of which they
could know nothing, hidden away somewhere in space
behind the locks of adamantine secrecy to which they
had no key. Who could believe that? Joy must be our
right, he thought, or else we could never so bitterly
resent its loss. Who—what cruel Power is it that plun-
ders us with violent hands and leaves us broken and
bleeding to endure the bitter hail of misery in the cold
No-man's Land of immitigable loss? A tyrant, a rob-
ber, an ironical devil, he thought, staring with lost eyes
into the singing crystal of the radiant water.

Bru dashed down the rocks tense with delight in
sunshine and the wine of the high sweet air. His eyes
danced, his brilliant pink tongue hung over the picked
pearls of his teeth. He looked up at Paul almost
shouting:

"Be happy, master. Be happy. Joy is here now ior
the taking."

He made a great leap into the deep pool beside the
rock and swam and floundered, wild with delight.
Lilith sprang silent-footed to the low gray rock above
the stream and watched him with eyes slumbrous with
content in the sun. Sometimes she extended a deft,
unsheathed velvet paw and brushed the surface of the
playing water like lightning, as if to touch the shadowy
shoals of minnows fleeing below. The doves wheeling
above cooed and curved in circles and ellipses of
delight.

"I want their secret. I want to be happy with them,"
Paul said fiercely to Magdalen. "Who has the right to
torture us like this? This is the home she wanted—
longed for, and it's too late. And as for us—" He made
a hopeless gesture.

Bru scrambled out of the river for a long refreshing

shake, which sent diamonds dazzling over the ferns.
He came and laid his head against Paul's hand, searching his face with eager eyes. Young he might be, but
he knew the smell and sound of grief—the close un-
wholesome atmosphere of that earthy contact. Lilith
knew it too. She looked from her rock with elegant
disdain of Paul's bowed shoulders and the swelled and
reddened lids of Magdalen's eyes and glided away on
small gray velvet-shod feet. Bru remained, but anxious,
alarmed. Why could they not see? Why would they
not know?

They went back to their work like two galley-slaves
chained to the oar—partners in misery as chilling as
age; and all day, forgetting them, the gay life of the
garden went on in glittering sunshine; and plants and
birds and animals—those whom Nature loves and understands so much more nearly and tenderly than she
does man, her rebel—rejoiced with her gladness, and
when the twilight shadows deepened over their happy
weariness curled themselves to sleep in the warm and
fragrant bosom of their mother.

All but Bru. Dogs have reached that higher plane
where they share the sorrow and joy of those they love.
Very closely and consciously Bru had grown up in the
shadow of grief from a gleeful babyhood which prophe-
sied a careless heaven. Now he knew it would not be
that. These twin gods who reigned in Eden were so
sad that nothing comforted them. They smiled in the
necessary modulation to assure each other that they
were not broken-hearted at the moment. They worked
with sighing pauses. When work was done they walked
about the garden, absorbing its beauty and that of the
blue hills and stooping sky with detached admiration
which carried none of the passion of the marriage joy
given by nature with ardent lips and arms to her devo-

tees, gathering them to her fruitful breasts where all
the world may come to rest.

To himself they were kind—none could be kinder—
but they did not understand. They were blind, deaf, and
dumb to all the things which Bru's deep subconscious
union with nature, so far higher than his normal perception, told him were true and of immense weight in
setting one's life to the key that nature demands for
comprehension.

To these he was tuned by the perfect undisturbed
harmony of his nature. They had fallen out of tune
altogether. Their relation to his heaven, the garden and
the woods, was only that of people who have paid in
gold for some dim beauty which they cannot appre-
hend. He could not know this but he could know its
effect, and it set a cold shadow at the gate of his own
happy world.

That night, much disturbed by the aspect of those he
loved, he decided that the glory of the day had not been
enough. The moon was nearing her full, and he must
stay out with the pale lights and dewy shadows all
night. He did not put it in that way. He only knew
there was a despotic hunger upon him and he could not
sleep in Felicity's room as was his wont. There were
things to be done outside the house and he must do
them.

Therefore when he was let out at ten o'clock according to custom and he looked back at the two lonely figures standing on the shallow steps he did not come back
at the usual whistle. Hidden in the wood, shoulder-deep
in long grass and fern scattering scented dew upon his
creamy fur, he looked at them stealthily as a wolf, gone
wild and happy for the moment. For twenty minutes or
more they called—his god and goddess—but still he
stood rigid as a dog cast in pale metal, and only a little

night wind with moonlight in its eyes sighed on the
wet grasses. Then he heard her say to his god:

"Bru must have gone hunting. Well, it doesn't matter. Come to bed. He's big enough to take care of
himself now."

The two went in. The pool of light made by the open
door vanished. A lock turned. He was alone in the
moon-drenched garden, and moon-drenched woods
holding the mystery called him. Oh, the garden, and
the moon's mighty beauty swimming pale through the
ocean of night, a naked divinity brimmed with charms
and spells! Bliss unutterable filled his soul and a calling
voice from far away to which his quick pricked ears
and glittering eyes responded.

The leaves were bathed in moonlight like water falling from lunar heights. The pale splendor overflowed
and dripped in pools to the earth. The garden had forgotten the man and woman, and every flower was no
longer posing for them but intent on its own business.
Bru knew that well as he went quietly past the house
on his way to the river and the woods. Looking up he
saw Lilith crouched on the sill of Felicity's window,
watching him intently with great eyes brimmed with
moonlight. She knew, she understood. The doves knew
also though they pretended to sleep in the pinnacled
dove-cote, the foolish birds! Bru came to the nook by
the river where the glittering stream broke itself into
splendor among the rocks. He was right. He stooped
his head and smelled the little recess among the crushed
ferns. Yes—the wild thing, the free thing he sensed,
had been there. Now, black nostrils to fragrant earth,
he followed the trail up the grassy path past the rockery
by the rose-crowded pergola into the wood. Not even
their massed perfume crimson on the air could drown
it. The lights were out in the house. The divinities

inside had laid wearied heads on pillows. Probably they were weeping mysterious tears for that mysterious loss which embittered all their days.

Under a tree in moonlight half in shadow stood a naked girl, a dark-haired, green-eyed imp whom Bru had never seen there before though he had seen many strange things in that wood, unsuspected by its owners. She might be eight years old though he did not count in that way. He only knew that to sit and stare at her all night or to play hide and seek among the ghostly trees would be more of a heaven than to stay in the posed garden with the people he loved. For instantly he loved her more. She was free of his world and knew the language of the scents, the frail noises, the thin delicious flavors in the air, which made his drama. Her eyes and nostrils and ears were alive like his own.

She dropped on her knees in the grass and stretched her arms and he walked straight into them. She locked them about his neck. Her face smooth as flower-petals lay against his beautiful cream-colored mask and glittering eyes. They talked long and intimately in that language of the senses unknown to or forgotten by humans. She told him how she had come over great seas walking on the moon-path by night or springing from glitter to glitter on each leaping wave by day.

"As the sea-gulls do, because I was obliged to come home and they had left me far away. They thought I lay under a tree blazing like fire with flowers, but I never did—that was the shell of me. And they said, 'Dead'—but I was trying to find my way home. You know, Bru, *you* know that they must call before one comes. And now I have come. This is my garden—my nest by the river. I knew you were coming and I ran in here to meet you out of *There*. Did you see me today when he stood by the river?"

And Bru's unfathomable eyes answered: "I saw."
"And Lilith—look, she's coming! See, in the shadow!
She's climbed down the trellis."

She came winding smoothly through the ferns, lifting filmy paws from the dew-drops and with arched
back and curling tail pressed her vaporous softness
against Felicity's stooping body. The doves knew; they
flew softly in a snowy cloud and settled on the trees
about to see, or was it a dream of them—white dove-
thoughts hovering in moonlight? Not that it could be
a wonder to them or to Bru and Lilith. Their innocence
is wide-eyed to things which the knowledge of man-
kind misses. But it was joy; a new playfellow in the
garden; an influence sweeter than all fragrances of all
flowers, and their own. It had waked them from their
little soft dreams, or the dreams themselves may have
flown out into the woods. Who can tell?

The house was dead as a grave, locked in silence and
darkness when she came out into the garden where the
stars were dancing in the river. Her hand was on Bru's
head. Lilith caressed her feet, the doves flew in a white
cloud above them. Yet if the blind souls within had
looked from curtained windows they would have seen
nothing but Bru and Lilith and have called them impatiently back into the dark.

Felicity curled herself into the nook and stretched
one foot to break the ripple of the river. Lilith leaped
into her lap with sheathed paws. The doves settled
softly about them.

No pen can write the long communings of that night
because no words exist for it. It came and went in wafts
like the little breezes whispering to them. But they
knew. After moon-set, before the darkness waned,
Felicity, lighter than Lilith's lightness, climbed up the
trellis and like a lost moonbeam into the empty room.

A great bowl of syringa filled it with honeyed sweetness from cups of ivory.

Bru standing below and Lilith climbing after her felt her thought:

"I have come home,"

and answered in this hidden language:

"Felicity has come home."

Next morning—it was Sunday—Magdalen waked with an extraordinary sense of happiness. Paul was still asleep in his own bed by hers—a look of pain fixed on his thin lips and about the hollow of his eyes. His asthma had gripped him half the night.

She rose and opened the door softly and went into Felicity's room. The pale morning sun washed the floor with gold. The scent of the honeysuckle fresh as dawn was like the language of all sweetness in the world. Yes, the gold and silver flowers were crowding in at the window also, pushing the white and crimson roses aside as if to storm the house. Lilith was lying on the bed. She must have been curled up on the pillow at first for a little dent was there. For a moment one could imagine—but no, one must not imagine. That might break a heart so frail, of such thin vibrating crystal, that one must play no tricks with it. The dent was warm —she laid her hand on it and Lilith purred softly, blinking with enormous eyes of beryl-green that hid all the secrets of the night under ocean-deep slumbrous content.

Magdalen remembered Bru. She put a gray kimono about her and went quietly down into the garden to look for him, her feet thrust into little Japanese slippers.

The house still slept and the garden had not had time to compose the face it must present to its masters. It was wild and sweet—sweet beyond all but in-

stinct. Presences walked in it as their own, every blos-
somed bough dripped dew. The rose-cups held attar of
roses, the grass flung diamonds back to the rising sun.

Bru stood outside the long window she unlatched and
an ocean of azure air crested with fragrance flowed into
the dead house like the cry of the Angel of the Resurrection. He sprang to meet her. What was in his eyes?
What knowledge struggled to express itself in his leap
into her arms, his dumb yet most vocal insistence that
she should follow—follow? She obeyed.

He led the way, wild with joy, to the river. To the
little nook, moss-cushioned, where they always stood
when they grieved most for Felicity. Felicity. There
was a dent in the velvet of the moss. So that was
where Bru had spent the night! And who could wonder—with the radiant river for his companion. No—
he had not been hunting. Perhaps he had even been
dreaming as she had dreamed. That dream came slowly
back to her as she sat on the moss already sun-warmed
in its sheltered niche.

She had dreamed of Felicity as she had never done
since the day when they had composed her little elfin
face into the dignity of the last sleep. Even then it was
impossible to think her dead. A faint smile not heavenly but innocently elfish lingered about the edges of
her lips. It seemed to say with sly sweetness—a child's
trick:

"Yes—I am cheating you. Very soon I shall open
my eyes and laugh because you believed it and were
sorry."

The little black head with heavy short-clipped locks
had no relation with death at all. It had lain like that
a thousand times playing at sleep with a glimmer of
mirth under thick curled lashes. But yet that very same
day the child who in the morning had breathed and

laughed was carried out to be committed to the keeping
of alien earth beneath a tree that flamed a wild splendor
to a tropic sun.

That was how her mother had always dreamed of
her. Elfin, impish, but utterly withdrawn, the immeasurable gulf of a grave between them.

Last night, however, in her dream Felicity had come
naked, ivory flushed with health and life, running along
the grassy paths and into the pergola where she sat.
She flashed through the roses like a white bird and into
her mother's arms.

"I was only pretending, I told you so. Now I have
come home. You made it for me and I have come. Bru
knows."

Was it the sweet broken ripple of the river which
had brought this memory to her? Or Bru's deep eyes
fixed with unutterable knowledge, if she could take it?
And see—Lilith had come too and was circling about
her feet, looking up with tiny weird cries. Passionately she wished to pass into their vibration—to understand. Oh, proud humanity which thinks it knows all
and has lost the Key that unlocks the doors of Night
and Dream! It appeared to her now that she knew why
she had awaked so happy though she could give no
reason for it at all.

She slipped her kimono off and stepped into Bru's
pool. He followed her while Lilith, the princess, performed her morning toilet on the rock. The heavenly
coolness of the water clung about her like the cold
soft hands of friendly elves. Softly they laved her
limbs and washed the stain of sorrow away to flow
through happy corn-fields to the Rhone, to the pure
purgation of unsounded seas. She rose from it as from
a rite of initiation. What was that whiteness flitting
away through the pergola? A sunbeam? But Bru

bounded after it shaking rainbows from his coat, and
Lilith suspended a dainty gray paw in mid-air on its
way to the satin-soft ears, and followed swiftly.

She would say nothing to Paul—what was there to
say?—until she had consciously worked out a problem
which she had never suspected to be a problem until
that morning.

When they began to build the nest for a dead bird
it had seemed a bit of tender hopeless imagining which
people ignorant of anguish might very well smile at,
saying: "They were afraid of forgetting so they concentrated on this fanciful little plan to keep the thing
alive in their hearts against the inexorable law of forgetfulness which grows the mosses over the deepest-cut
inscriptions in any graveyard. They will tire of it one
day."

But it seemed to Magdalen in the flash of revelation
in her dream that in concentrating—yes, that was the
word—on the thought of the child and making the
home her heart desired they might be employing some
power—ignorant of its rules—that would build better
than they knew, evolving cell by cell as it were some
living influence unimaginable to them when they set out
upon their building. A verse of old Vaughan's recurred
to her in its delicate simplicity:

"He that hath found some fledged bird's nest
        may know
    At first sight if the bird be flown;
But what fair dell or grove he sings in now,
    That is to him unknown."

Could that heavenly bird be tempted by wisdom to a
lower sphere to give and take comfort with its song?
Love dies at the gate of Death so far as communion
goes; can wisdom do more?

It will be observed that Magdalen, though no Christian, felt instinctively along Christian lines when she tried to shape her thought. Yes—the darling was in some far-away sweetness impossible to be understood. It never occurred to her that Blake and the other mighty mystics are right and that this earth is heaven and all the universe, or nothing. One has but to open one's eyes and paradise is here, and here and about us walk what we ignorantly please to call the spirits of those who have slipped the fetters of length, breadth, and height that cripple all our movements—until we know there are no fetters but only drifts of mist blown across our eyes.

Magdalen sat down that morning in the niche by the river while Paul collected his papers, and tried to remember what she had ever heard of prayer—a curious unreasonable effort which sometimes came off and sometimes didn't. If it came off it was a coincidence; if not, exactly what might be expected. Under her eyes a little golden beetle was trying for some unknown reason to roll the seed-pod of a violet to some hole where it appeared to him to be wanted. It was nearly as large as himself and his exertions were piteous. He fell and struggled, went to the little hole near the sundial to prospect, returned assured that he could do it, and failed and fell again and again. Evidently he was convinced that it was possible and a mighty urge of strength rushed along the feebleness of his legs, but not enough. She watched fascinated. It became a symbol to her of all her own hopeless struggles to regain Felicity—but more pitiable for she had never believed in her powers and the beetle was convinced of his. She took her watch and noted after she had already watched long; and for half an hour the small golden creature pushed and thrust and fell and at the end had moved its burden not at all. Kinship stirred in her. She knew the faithful hope in the golden body; with a tube of grass she pushed aside the uphill morsel of earth obstructing the advance and the beetle took triumphant charge and along the level thrust the treasure home.

Magdalen sat rigid—a new lesson learned. Can it be that when in perfect hope and energy we assert our power the whole universe must harness its strength to ours? Could it be that she herself by some cosmic force outside her own will was compelled to respond to the pull of confidence in another life however lowly and help to reinforce its powers? And, if so, might it not be that every star and wind and tide and their power was hers and her, and bound to fight shoulder to shoulder with her that her will might be done on earth "as it is in heaven"—heaven meaning the true reality about us, obscured by the world of our senses, where nevertheless also the Universal Will must work to its perfect ends? Well, then, if that were true she would harness the power of the universe, the whole mighty rush of strength at its work in star and insect, to her feeble powers, and they should be her slaves to realize her will on earth. Not in any way that should hamper or cripple the child's spiritual evolution, but that she might ensnare some memory of her love and thought for her mother and father and enable all three to realize that in deepest inmost meaning this home being theirs must be Felicity's also. Joy was her due. She would command it. She rose radiant. It could be done—as the beetle had triumphed, though on another plane. Every wandering thought, every dream awake or asleep, every power of insight, instinct, intuition, must be concentrated into one burning focus of desire every day to realize the life in the child and make it one with her own, so that they could never again be apart in life or death. It was not Felicity's fault, it was her own, that there had been division, but that was ended.

There were energy and direction in Magdalen's character. They were to help her now. Each day she went for an hour into the wood and sitting under a great tree, utterly unconscious that she was following the greatest system of psychological training in the world, she composed herself to immobility of mind and body, breathing within herself a formula for quiet and insight. If it rained Felicity's room was her sanctuary.

At first it was difficult.

Thought wandered. The birds twittering in the boughs, a butterfly's winged voyage in blue oceans of air deflected her, and she was obliged to close her eyes and that induced a dull drowsiness which overcame her so far that more than once she found herself asleep against the great smooth-skinned tree-trunk, uplifting its fountain of dewy green spray to the sky. But that passed. Lilith would sit beside her with fathomless eyes fixed on the glades of green, and Bru draw to her feet but not for sleep—wakeful, watchful, hopeful, on guard. They were in her sphere of consciousness, but how she could not tell.

One day a very singular thing happened. Rain had fallen in the night and a large curled leaf retained some drops. She happened to be looking at it steadily as she willed the reunion. A sunbeam slid through the branches and touched it to brilliance, and as the glitter caught her eyes some imprisoning shell of outside consciousness shifted and left an open door. There was a roar in her ears, stunning, deafening. It ceased and absolute void followed. Emptiness. She could summon no single thought or word to aid her and yet was conscious of an appalling solitude.

When she told me of the Dark Night of the Soul, paling even in the remembrance, I remembered certain words of my own written in the knowledge of a like experience:

Then a quick thunder and I thought the world
Like some great globe uplifted from its base,
Roared from me down some dizzy orbit hurled
And left me lost in space.

Time had ceased for her and she could not tell how long it was before in an immense distance she saw Felicity rushing to her across time or space or both—she could not tell. Like a white bird skimming the depths and heights she came, not borne on wings but by some terrific speed that sent her across the Void and stayed her before her mother. Felicity's voice or thought—she heard it clear as a lark's note at dawn: —"Home. Call me and I come. I run over the bridge and Bru knows and Lilith. Call me, call me!"

She cried, "Felicity," and the flight ended gently as the shock of a falling rose-petal in her bosom. The little black cropped head lay there; the little brown arms entwined her neck.

No—I must be silent here. All but silence is profanation. No words can tell that rapture of reunion.

After a while, whether long or short Magdalen could not tell, she floated up to the surface of daily thought and to a transfigured world. Bru and Lilith sat like guardians with wise eyes fixed upon her. The radiant garden burned in a flame of color through the tree-trunks. Paul's voice was calling her, but she sat dazed with knowledge. She had learned another lesson. She studied it with stern analysis.

The point clearly was to lull the objective mind to

sleep. By a mere accident she had hypnotized herself with the glitter of the water. That would certainly be only a beginner's crutch, for she had already gone far enough to realize that there are powers in the subconscious self which can effect the same release but bitted and bridled by the will. Concentration, meditation on psychic power, the will fastened stedfastly on the aim of transcending what are called mortal limits, and realizing that in all the universe are neither time nor distance unless the illusion of the human will creates them. If Felicity had ever lived she lived still. If she had ever been near she was as near now. But as the music of the spheres may wander weeping in space for want of aerials to receive it, so Felicity's thoughts concentrating into shape must wander homeless unless home awaited her in her mother's breast.

"It is we who are at fault, not they," Magdalen said to herself with solemn certitude. "And we talked of the division of death and there is none, and it is we who are blind and deaf to the beauty that walks about us and holds out its arms beseeching for recognition. Felicity, my darling, forgive me."

But she said nothing to Paul. Some deep instinct warned her that he had not yet reached the point of penetration. Fear, disbelief, doubt—she could not tell which to expect, but she knew none of them could help him and any would cloud her own newly risen dawn. She turned instinctively to Bru, to Lilith, and the birds. Those children still sheltered in Nature's vast bosom had not deserted her powers for those of reason. They knew. The compensations of life, understanding of the marvelous adjustment of its mosaic, delighted Magdalen with a sense of fulfilment as she saw these creatures, our despised servitors from the point of view of reason and logic, yet so rich in wealth which appeared to her to matter more for the hope of humanity than all the degrees of all the universities and all the inventions bridging sea and sky. But there again, if man's is the harder way home it is the more triumphant. Compensation everywhere.

It was her delight now, when the typing was finished and Paul took the rest he needed, to go out into the hollow of the heart of the green wood and there sitting leaning against a tree-bole to give herself up to concentrated meditation. Bru lay beside her intent upon his own thoughts, not asleep but with head couched upon his paws regardant, waiting. Lilith lay a vaporous cloud of gray with fathomless eyes of ocean-green fixed on a certain glade. It appeared to Magdalen that the force throbbing along her own nerve-threads and the channels of its course was no longer bounded by her body. There was a day when she knew this certainly, for it became visible. Filaments of light rayed from her like the strands of a cobweb and enveloped Bru and Lilith, and at the same moment that she perceived this she was conscious that from the body of each of them light also emanated—neither vibrant nor rayed as her own but throbbing like that of a glowworm and continuous and clear. She had the impression that this was a constant and natural condition with them for seeing eyes but that she herself was obliged to use tense spiritual force to maintain her own. Was this light connected, she wondered, with the electric crackles and sparks which she had noticed in the fur of Bru and Lilith when the air was charged with thunder—or rather was electricity a different manifestation, a side-current as it were of some vast primal force including all in itself?

• But even as she perceived the light, Felicity blown like a leaf or a breeze fled down the long glade to her arms, and Bru leaped about her wild with joy, and

Lilith's vaporous softness caressed her naked feet. There were things to notice of extraordinary interest. Felicity loved the wild flowers—even better than the garden ones. She would kneel over them in a trance of adoration springing from some deep inward unity, but she never gathered one. She had some means of absorbing them that exorcised covetousness. Magdalen entered later into that experience herself. Unison; that was what Felicity had achieved. She climbed a tree one day and looked into a nest—a late brood. The mother-bird perched on a spray watched her with delight as she stooped to kiss the little ones, then sitting on the child's shoulder sent her joy-notes thrilling through the wood. Another day a strange thing happened. There had been an outbreak of rabies in the village, which with Magdalen's Indian experiences seemed a thunder-cloud of dread. A child had been bitten and had died.

As they sat in the wood, lost in their lovely learning, down Felicity's glade there rushed a great dog, snapping with jaws pouring with foam. Magdalen knew. She had seen it when the madness caught from the jackals breaks loose and living things flee before it.

Felicity put herself in his way with outstretched arms not to repel or guard but to welcome as she welcomed all living things, while Bru and Lilith stood on watch. For a moment Magdalen sickened with terror. She had forgotten that pure life is guarded with shields of diamond and spears of fire.

The dog fell exhausted at Felicity's feet. She sat beside him stroking his head with monotonous passes. Into the little bubbling spring she dipped her hands and poured the icy-cold water on the head bursting with pain and fever. His cries ceased. She opened his locked teeth and poured it down his throat. Then put her arms about him and lulled him to sleep. Sleep. The air was full of sleep. It breathed in the light tremble of the leaves, in the gentle unhurried bubble of the spring, in the soft come-and-go of sunshine and shadow.

Did Magdalen herself sleep? Certainly she lost herself in a dream of conditions where pain and sickness and terror are meaningless names, and it might have been eons afterwards when Paul's voice called her with a note of terror and she started awake to see him standing pointing with a shaking hand at a great dog who lay dead a few feet from her, his jaws still trickling with bloody foam.

"Did he touch you?" he gasped. "That's the one—"

"No, he never touched me," Magdalen answered. "The poor, poor creature! No, not poor now. Let us bury him here."

But considering this event it brought Felicity at once nearer to her and set her higher. So the child's touch could give the peace of death. So she was a part of the mighty force of nature now—her little light resumed into the fierce flash of lightning, the ripening glow of summer sunshine. Yet, how near. How dear. She would lie in her mother's arms, the dear round black head on her bosom, the eyes clear like pure water in a fern-fringed pool fixed on her mother's. Was there speech between them? That question Magdalen could never answer. Sometimes she thought, Yes,—sometimes, No. It was at all events the very essence of speech, though to herself in considering it afterwards it had to pass through the medium of the words which cloud and limit the human understanding.

"Are you so happy, Felicity?" it seemed she asked. And the reply from the little shining face was:

"Not happy. Happiness. Come and see."

"But I do see. Joy flows with you like a river."

The answer was, "Joy," in a dove's note. So it seemed.

"Shall we be together, Felicity?"

"We are together. How could we be apart?"

"Is it so different from this? Dear—tell me. Tell me. My heart breaks to know."

"It is this, but—"

Now it seemed in this strange communion that Felicity laid her child's hands across her eyes. And she saw farther than mortal sight can see—a world at rest. Joy on shining seas and lands, blown in the clarion winds, vibrating in showering stars and happy planets. No— hush! It could not be told. It could not be seen in full. A corner of the darkness was lifted—one beam of the Eternal Sunshine struck a blinding shaft.

She said, sobbing with terror as when the human thing beholds the heavenly:

"But where do you go, my darling."—*"My!"* The heavenly thing was still her child.

"I never go," it answered, "soon you will know that." Then after a long pause of vision. "But people come. Bru is coming."

"No, no. I can't spare him. He saw you first."

"Bru's coming."

"Will it be good for him?"

Felicity smiled.

Bru looked up with his beautiful soul in his eyes and smiled also as dogs smile for love. It is not possible to say how lost and lonely Magdalen was in that moment. Her ignorance was agony. They knew. They could come but not she. The door swung in her face.

That night Bru refused to sleep in Felicity's room as he had done once before. They found him next morning lying on the mossy roots beneath the tree where Felicity sat, where Felicity climbed for her birds. It was a bitter blow to Paul.

"Everything I love is taken from me. All things grow sadder one by one."

But to Magdalen it was a very different matter. Bru was always with Felicity now and with them came the dog buried in the woods, a little timid at first, then rejoicing with the others—free of the real world instead of the prison of poverty and pain in which he had lived, and died. Lilith knew, but Magdalen saw with dread that their happiness drew the little cat-soul also as a magnet. She too beat against her bars.

But it was the unexpected which happened. The days were shortening, the moon visible earlier, when one evening in the wood which was Magdalen's true home now, Felicity lay in her arms, entwined with her mother so closely that all youth and sweetness and joy seemed to lie on her breast in a treasured burdenless burden. Communion was between them more close and intimate than any speech, as star to star strikes fire, and if it must be put in words its beauty dies. Yet, what other way?

Bru lay at their feet, and the other dog, whom Felicity called Joy as though it were a love-name, lay beside him. Lilith in Felicity's lap. The child stirred and pointed through the trees at Paul bowed over his table.

"He is coming."

"No—no!" cried Magdalen's soul as the silver arrow pierced her heart. She noticed for the first time that the child had never called her mother, that she only spoke of her father as "he." Yet with no unhappiness in that. She understood that it meant dearer nearness than any earthly parentage. They were one—what do names mean? But the announcement left her bleached and drained with fear. How little she had learned—and how far from the meaning of her achievement!

Felicity's grave child's eyes regarded her with surprise.

"Do you wish him to be ill? I hear his heart crying

for me so loud that it drowns my voice. His tears blind him."

It was like an elder sister counseling a younger. For the first time the immense wisdom of the process we call death struck Magdalen with blinding force. A child —the little cropped black head—the little hands—but yet—

> "She has seen the mystery hid
> Under Egypt's pyramid:
> By those eyelids pale and close
> Now she knows what Rhamses knows."

She trembled in looking.

"If it is best—" she tried to say.

Felicity smiled.

It came next day as they sat together—Magdalen in Felicity's room. He had been ill in the night and the doctor came early next day and said the heart was very feeble and he must not go downstairs.

"It will be only a day or two, madame, you see well! It is a heart—not diseased—oh no, but feeble. It tires itself. It needs rest."

Therefore his writing was put on the old, old table in Felicity's room where the noble young demoiselle had perhaps written her faded love letters. A great blue bowl of late roses was beside him, and Magdalen sat by the window breathing in the sweetness of the broad blue air outside. Bru and Joy lay on the grass and Felicity beside them. Lilith sunned herself on the window sill watching the three. Suddenly Felicity uttered a cry of joy. It rang through the garden like a lark's wild exultation at sunrise. She sprang to her feet, looked up and began climbing the strong trellis to the window. Magdalen watched fascinated as she laughed and climbed. A sigh recalled her—a long sigh. Paul was sinking sideways in his chair as if overcome by sleep. His head fell slowly back on the cushion, his eyes were closing. Felicity standing behind him put her hands above them as Magdalen sprang to the stairs and shrieked to the servants for the doctor, then rushed back to the room.

He half opened his eyes as from a happy dream. She saw the faint line of darkness under the lashes.

"Felicity," he said, and then a pause, "Magdalen."

No more. It was as though the undertow of some great tide resuming itself into the ocean carried him with it. Slowly, softly, floating in pure moonlight. For one wild moment Magdalen did what she could to drag him back, but Felicity smiled above him and the outward-drawing current was mighty. The vast arms of the deep received their child.

Not even in that moment could the true soul in Magdalen weep for any loss. She had trodden too far along the way of wisdom, she could gaze with undeceived eyes upon the truth.

When the kind old doctor came, weary from his long round, he saw a dead man lying upon Felicity's bed, composed by tender hands to the eternal sleep. But Magdalen standing by the window with Lilith in her arms, stilling her weird tiny cries, saw a living man walking in the garden she had never truly known, carrying Felicity in his arms, her dear black head upon his heart. Her little arms laced close about his neck. They went and stood by the river, and Bru and Joy went with them, and all stood looking into its living light of joy as it flashed singing through the rocks to the village below and onward to join the Rhone and so, growing in strength and power, to lose itself in the ocean.

There is not much left to say. Of all the women I

have known I think Magdalen was happiest. Why not? She had learned to see with the double vision and such words as death and parting had no meaning for her any more. She lived companioned in that garden of paradise though her only "living companion" was little Lilith, tender, loving and faithful, who, seeing what she saw, scarcely knew how to translate her knowledge into the food of daily life. She was with her friends, but knew a bar between them not yet possible to understand, and often her alarmed little soul vented itself in tiny cries for more intelligible vision. But when Magdalen took her in her arms there was peace. Mysteriously she saw through that higher wisdom and was at rest.

"I understand it all now," Magdalen wrote. "What I see is their thoughts of me and mine of them, blent in a heavenly life that is more real than anything we know. It has much power—and even divine power to console and uplift. But beyond and above this and far away in the unknown their divine spirits are pursuing the trackless way for which we have no words—the way that leads to the eternal. But I know when, weary of your wanderings, you come to this happy house, whether I have gone on or stayed, you will see and enter into the loveliness of understanding which fills the place and the shining feet which tread its paths and fill it with content."

Magdalen has joined them now in that trackless way, carrying Lilith with her, and I shall never again see the dreaming house and roseate gardens. Happy are those that dwell there in the happy airs that blow from pure heights, lulled by the eternal singing of the little river on its way to the ocean.

But it is only the wise who can distinguish symbol from absolute truth and live by both.

Waste Manor

THIS STORY WAS TOLD ME BY THE MAN WHO HAD LIVED through its strange experiences. Part of it may be read, I think, by the light of modern western psychology, but the greater part stretches out into that vast ocean of wisdom of which India and her daughter-nations hold the chart—they and no others. For myself, I have long since formed my own opinion. I leave it to others to form theirs.

The man was a descendant of one of the old English families of Cumberland; by every instinct and tradition a gentleman. I met him on one of my many voyages from Marseilles to the East on a Japanese Nippon Yusen Kaisha liner which I shall call the Hana Maru.

To my secretary and me seats were allotted at a little table for three in the corner of the dining saloon. We looked at the third seat with the traveler's hope that something pleasant would come of its owner. That is always likely on board the Japanese boats, for the company is full of interest to those who love their Asia. Men of the great Japanese families, diplomats, soldiers, sailors, professors, students, artists, and many more are always coming and going on the long blue highway which begins in London and ends at Yokohama. I have made lasting friendships between port and port and have opened many a shut Asiatic door.

But it was an Englishman who walked quickly up to the table as the busy little waiters were serving the soup. He was of middle height, dark-haired with deep-set

dark eyes under brows straight as bars across a notice-
able forehead. The face was intellectual and oversensi-
tive. I felt certain of two things—that he had been ill
recently and that he had hoped for Japanese company
where ignorance of his language would leave him in
untroubled quiet.

He bowed coldly, said his name was Wendover, and
relapsed into silence.

But on such a voyage continued silence becomes impossible, and little interests sprang up along the Medi-
terranean as he realized gradually that we were harmless
and had plenty of interests of our own to keep us going.
The door of separation moved on its hinges. It appeared that he was in the Indian Civil Service, that he
shared my love of Asiatic art, that he had of late taken
up the study of Indian thought, and was a really deep
student of history. These were bridges upon which real
communion might pass to and fro, and I grew to like
him, to understand that the realities which lie below the
level of daily life were more to his taste than the surface which is enameled so smoothly and coldly that not
a living root may ever grow in it nor flower blossom.

Sometimes he would sit with me on deck when stars
were lucent in the black polished marble of the sea,
silent more often than not in a world of his own, and
I knew instinctively that he had thoughts worth hearing
if ever they should float up to the surface like bodies
long drowned and lost to the world of the living. Indeed there was something poignant and melancholy
about the man which marked him out from others.

We had long passed the narrow gut of the Suez
Canal and were far down the Red Sea, plowing past
the wildly peaked and pinnacled islands which lie lonely
as death with sundering seas washing on desolate
shores. Weirdly colored and beautiful they rise, flat

against the sky as painted scenery from the harsh blue of the sea and pale sands.

It was sunset and they stood stark against the burning gold of the west. Oceans of gold billowed upon them from the sinking sun like a triumph of victorious gods. They took on splendor as though a flame in their hearts responded to the awful glory.

Wendover came along the deck and leaned his arms on the rail, absorbed, unconscious of any life about him.

Such a crisis of Nature's passion cannot last long, and very swiftly the wild pomp faded and night was gliding over the western sea to imprison the world in her net of stars. Then he turned and came slowly to me, his face still vibrant with a kind of pale triumph.

"That was orchestral. A mighty music!" he said.

The evening star emerged like a bird's clear song after thunder. He listened to its unstruck music for a moment, then spoke again abruptly:

"I've had a strange experience in England. That appealed to it."

"And you are coming back to India for the clue?" I asked. "She holds all the clues of the soul."

"That's true. True."

It is indeed. How many have I known coming consciously or unconsciously that India may unravel their destiny and free them from the complexities of the West! There they may sit, holding the hand of the Mighty Mother, looking from beneath her brooding brows into the all-revealing mirror where each man may, to his peace or terror, see himself as he is in naked truth.

That night he began the story which I am permitted to tell here. I give it in my own words because it came by fits and starts as if some inward spring welled and subsided. There were hints, implications, and these he

looked to me to understand. Sometimes a word helped
him to understand himself and he would look at me
gratefully and say: "Yes—that's it. That explains."

So, though I add nothing whatever, I give here and
there a little comprehension. But I am a voice, no more.
The story is not mine. I shall give his name as Stephen
Wendover. Obviously it cannot be the real one. His age
was thirty-eight. The family house and lands had been
sold in his boyhood. He had but one relation—a sister
living in Australia whom he had not seen for twenty
years. These are the preliminaries.

Rather more than a year before our meeting he was
in England on a year's leave after a sharp attack of
malaria, and needing rest of all things he went down
to Tanswyke, a small village under the Sussex Downs
for a couple of month's fishing. That was the excuse.
Drowsing and dreaming in the great woods which
clothe the valleys beneath the downs were the real aim.

It was that rare delight in England, a perfect summer, calm and laden with country scents, the flowers in
cottage gardens floating like birds upon still air. In that
of the old inn, old as the Plantagenets, where he lived
they were almost unbearably sweet.

He had a little guide-book of the district for his
strolls and noted in it the names of the stately parks
and manors carved out of what appeared to have once
been the mighty inheritance of one family—the Thorolds of Bydon.

"The Thorolds of Bydon," said the little book, "seem
for the last three hundred years to have chosen the los-
ing side in war and politics. They had already incurred
the wrath of Henry VIII and Elizabeth, and in her
reign the great Tudor mansion was dismantled and
from the remains were built great walls enclosing a
much reduced park and a comparatively small but beau-

tiful house suited to their fallen fortunes. In their later misfortunes this house also fell into ruin, the estate dwindled into four acres of garden, and this patch of ground has lately been bought by Lord Wickington, first baron and owner of Wickington Park once a part of the great Thorold estates. But a very curious fact is that the family has always attributed its ill luck to the marriage of a Thorold in the reign of Henry III with an heiress of the Tracy family whose father had led three knights to the murder of the saint and archbishop Thomas à Becket in Canterbury Cathedral in the year 1170. It is well known that a curse was pronounced on the de Tracy family that neither they nor any of their descendants should ever know prosperity thereafter, and it is certain that the Thorolds never throve after the de Tracy blood ran in their veins. Waste Manor is now a fern-clad heap of ruins. *Sic transit gloria mundi.*" With this Latin tag the guidebook story ended as guide-books will.

But it left a kind of dim pity on Wendover's mind as he thought of the stately houses in their waving woods and acred gardens flaming with blossom, flaring with hothouses, where the new-made knights and peers whose glories were founded on bacon and oil and alcohol, shone resplendent and the last four acres of the Thorolds were swallowed up by Lord Wickington, formerly Jimmy Jicks, proprietor of Jicks's Vitamin Cattle-Food.

"Lord save us!" said Wendover to himself. "I wonder if the Thorold ghosts come and gibber at night in at Jimmy's windows. I would if it were me."

He sat in the little coffee-room of the Crosslets under the pewter plates in glimmering rows on the rough oak dresser, as Mrs. Eves, the landlady came in with a question about his day's fishing.

"Too much sunshine, and water as clear as a looking-glass. Nothing doing," he said. But he hadn't wanted to do•anything except lie under the hazels and blink at the shining little river. He had hidden his basket and rod and forgotten them and drowsed away the day except when he ate his luncheon and flung his crumbs to the Jicks pheasants, tame.as the fowls at the Jicks model farm. Something in him thrilled responsive to something in the green solitude, and he camped there and drowsed until dusk hung in the trees like smoke.

"It looks as if the whole countryside had been forest," he said to Mrs. Eves. "Did it all belong to the Thorolds?"

The taproom was full of babbling rustics but she had a spare minute. "Lord, yes, sir! They owned from here to Corrington in the old ancient days, but they never had no luck after one of them married a Tracy. It's said the Tracys killed some bishop down to Canterbury and they got a curse on them heavy enough to sink a man-of-war. Anyhow it sank the Thorolds all right. They was great court cards once. Lord Wickington bought the last four acres from Mr. Thorold before 'he died."

"And whereabouts was Waste Manor?" Wendover was glad to hear Thorold was dead. That would be less bitter than life for a man who honored the past.

"That's hard to make out unless you know the lie of the land. It's to the west through the park, all overgrown with trees, and you come on it all of a sudden. But there's nothing to see, without it's great heaps of old bricks all overgrown with bushes and stuff."

Wendover sat alone, smoking and thinking until the moon came lamping over the woods, drowning the stars in pale glory.

"Queen and Huntress, chaste and fair"—he could

picture her glimmering through the long glades and
wished he could follow her flying feet. At last he turned
in, with a window wide to the moonlight and fruit-
smelling honeysuckle and roses, and slept in a maze of
dreams changing as softly as the shadows of breathing
boughs on the walls.

Next day it seemed necessary to retrieve the basket
and rod, and a notion possessed him that he would like
to see that pathetic little four acres now swept into the
rich man's pocket with all the rest. He thought of the
curse as he went up the narrow winding lane between
deep clematis-wreathed hedges and so into the woods.
Remember he had lived in India where the curse of a
holy man may be a thing more real than the food you
eat. In the girdling of the Himalayas it would not seem
strange that it should blot out the light from the eyes
of the murderer's descendants. Why not? In the reckon-
ing of the gods is neither past nor future. For them the
spilt blood still lay in pools on the pavement, the consequences of the deed still rippled outward like the rings
in rudely disturbed water. Crime is the root and misery
the blossoming of that deadly nightshade. It is impossible to live in India with open eyes and miss these
implications. Even if you do not believe them they color
all the air.

So thinking, he went to the nook of meadowsweet
where he had left his basket. It was gone. Some mischievous boy must have made his own of it. No matter.
Wendover got out his book—the "Chronicle of Walter
of Lincoln," an old monkish history—and half read,
half dreamed the hours away in a spot where the ancient
chronicler himself might have fished for the abbot's
Friday dinner. Rest sank into his blood as he followed
the story of the red Plantagenet, Henry II. "A king
very passionate, round-headed, showing a lionous vis-

age, strong, light, hardy, and amorous with women," the lover of Fair Rosamond and many more. He turned to the scene where the fierce anger of Henry blazed out against the unyielding archbishop, Thomas à Becket, and grinding his teeth until the foam-flakes fell from his lips he summoned de Tracy and his three knights, de Morville, le Breton, and Fitzurse, crying, "Who will rid me of this proud priest?"

Without let or halt they mounted and galloped to Canterbury, and there in his own cathedral, before the very face of the Crucified God upon the altar, they closed round him as he stood haughty on the steps above them, and they broke his skull and pierced his heart and left him lying in his blood before the unchanging gaze of God.

A great story, greatly told in the sonorous monkish Latin. It possessed Wendover.

He laid the book on the grass and dreamed awake of the noble arcades of the vast cathedral echoing to the onset, for Thomas had defended himself with his crosier like a man of the Lord of Hosts Who is the God of Battles. He could see the four, maddened by their own blood-lust, devil-driven, hacking with Norman swords at the dying man, wild with hurry lest the awful Figure on the Cross should strike them into worse than death and drive them shrieking from the holy precincts.

Now it was done, and the unchanging Face followed them as with slowly invading terror rising about them like chill water, the tumult of their yells died in the dead quiet of the church, and they rode back for their reward. They received instead wrath and curses from the king turned craven at the thought of the wide world's horror. Outcast they would live, outcast die. Did any Nemesis haunt them in careless England later or did all the hate and fear drift into nothingness?

He sat and thought of these things and ate his food
and drowsed again in the heavenly cool of leaves, and
the shadows lengthened, and at last some shadow of
pain or fear startled him awake to see day dead, the
dusk in the trees, and a woman in white coming down
the long glade. She carried his basket. Still weak from
illness he got on his feet and went to meet her.

It seemed that they met in the deeps of a green ocean.
The topmost leaves swaying in twilight were the ripple
of the surface. The shadows below were its profundi-
ties. He thought she seemed to float in dim green light
as she came on. Perhaps he was still a little confused
with sleep.

(I remember Wendover paused here as the moonlight
swept the flying waves with silver and a lost island
drifted by us like a ghost. I asked if she were beautiful
—a woman's question. He could not say. It was certain
he had never seen anyone who conveyed the same impression, and that impression he was quite unable to
define. She was pale and her eyes extinguished all the
rest but the black background of her hair. They conveyed absolute and watchful stillness like those of a
wild creature on guard—unwavering and fixed but intensely alert. That was all he could tell me, except that
his feeling was one of extreme constraint amounting
almost to a slight repulsion.)

"We found your basket in the copse last night and
kept it for you. One of us saw you hide it and knew
it was yours." She tendered it gravely. Her words gave
him a strange sensation. He had thought himself absolutely alone all day and had taken his ease as a man
does in solitude. No one likes to think that curious eyes
have been upon him in those conditions.

"I'm extremely grateful," he said with reserve, "especially since you've been good enough to bring it to
me. I hope it wasn't much trouble. Do you live near?"

"Near," she answered. Then, looking at him with a steadiness that caught his eyes and held them: "You should not sleep here. It is dangerous."

He noticed then that she spoke with a curious deliberation which seemed foreign, avoiding all the little contractions of daily speech. It was as though she repeated a lesson and with some effort. But the matter of her words took his attention from the manner.

"Dangerous? But how could that be?" he asked in astonishment.

"Perhaps you would not understand. One of us watched you all the time."

One of "us"? Of what strange family? She added: "There are heavy dews here. Your clothes are wet, and as you have been ill—"

He stared at her in ever-growing amazement. Certainly there was a drenching dew, but why should she care and—

"How do you know I've been ill?" he asked suspiciously. The interview grew stranger every moment.

"You are ill now. You should not sleep here. It is dangerous. You should come and sleep in our house."

She spoke with a kind of authority, her face and figure growing dimmer in the dusk. His astonishment was so great that it took the form of deep anxiety, as if he must safeguard himself from some danger. And yet there was nothing alarming in her words. They were unusual. That was all.

"I'm really very much obliged, but as it's getting dark I must be moving on. It's four miles to the village and—"

"It is much more than four miles. You would be unlikely to reach the village before tomorrow morning. Perhaps not then. You do not know the place."

"I beg your pardon. I come here often. I know the

way as well as I know—" His voice failed suddenly. Was he so sure he knew? Something was closing in upon him. Perhaps the coming dark gave the trees the effect of marching, of drawing nearer and nearer. That something in him was himself yet not himself and it began to be afraid.

She replied: "We know you come here. We have seen you. But you would not know the way back. You had better come with me."

"But I beg your pardon. I go down here and turn to the left and—" She drew back as if to let him pass.

"Try."

Wendover made a few steps forward. Did he recognize that huge clump of pyramidal hollies, stiff as if shears had trimmed them? Did he know that alley of yews clipped into fantastic shapes? A thin light stole through the trees from a rising moon. Could that be a lawn—and a sun-dial? No, surely. Impossible. Only vague shadows. But he halted and turned, confused.

"You're right. Sorry. Somehow I don't know. But unless I walked in my sleep—" He hesitated.

"We know you did not do that. The forest changes at night. It is better for strangers not to stay out in it. . . ."

She was standing some paces from him. Her voice sounded cold and strange as the sound of a distant bell. The sense of a far greater distance than appeared crept from the inmost of the outer self and gripped him,— something alien such as a man might feel on landing in an utterly unknown country among people inhumanly different. But her attitude had nothing menacing. It seemed to be watchfully passive. She waited.

"But the thing's ridiculous!" he said loudly, to hearten himself. "Of course I know the way. You go down that glade, and turn to the left—no, to the right.

No—not that glade. That one. At least—" He turned
about helplessly. His brain swam, and it was growing
dark. What was he fighting against? Resisting, and
uselessly?

"Couldn't one of you show me the way?" It became
of immense importance to him that he should get back,
yet he could not tell why.

"We never go to the village. The roads are not safe.
You are in danger at this moment."

They stood looking at one another. Were they test-
ing each other's strength? He could not even be sure
she looked at him at all. It was too dark. He spoke at
last with difficulty, conquered.

"It's really very good of you and I suppose I must
accept your hospitality. I mean I'm most grateful, but
a stranger doesn't like to give so much trouble, and if
you had a gardener or anybody who could come as far
as the—"

"The gardeners all went a long time ago. You are
not a stranger. We saw the name on your basket.
Wendover. One of our people married a Wendover—
a great many years ago. Do you remember?"

(He stopped here to tell me he had never been a man
who cared for pedigrees and such things. There was a
pedigree at his lawyer's office in London, but he had
never looked at it.)

He shook his head helplessly at her question. "Sorry.
I don't know a thing about it. Who was it? Perhaps
I've heard."

She moved slowly towards the clipped yews, if yews
they were, and he could do nothing but follow. She
spoke over her shoulder. Was he walking in sleep?
The air was heavy with dream.

"It was in 1624. Your ancestress Sophia Wendover.
She married one of us—Sir Aylmer Tracy. Her

daughter Cicely Tracy married her cousin, a Wendover. No, you are not a stranger."

He could neither contradict nor assent, but it seemed to matter to him more than anything in his life—more even than the terrible strangeness of his loneliness with this unknown guide in the night and the phantasmal unreality of the tall hollies and clipped bushes shining in vague moonlight through which they passed. A lawn with the rabbits loping over it—could it be? Never— that was the glade down which he passed daily to the village. But the village seemed as distant now as the cold moon lost in arid space.

"Is this the garden?" he asked at last.

"It is what you see." She went steadily onward.

"And the house? We seem to be going deep into the wood."

"It is beyond those black hollies. You would never find it. People never come here. I am often in the wood at night but no one comes."

"But you said the wood was dangerous."

"Not for us," she said and added strangely, and with what he took for glee, "But the people at the big house find it dangerous. Lord Wickington is rotting with cancer. The heir is demented and the daughter is worse. I tell you the place is dangerous."

She turned and looked at him, and so strange a light gleamed from her eyes that he shrank. She grew bolder now that they were in unknown ways. But he was too bewildered to think of flight.

Was it a garden or a long grassy glade? To use Wendover's strange phrase, it appeared to pulsate between the one and the other and he could not tell from one moment to the next. There were great walls of ancient brick mossed and plumed with fern. Were they broken here or there or lost in gulfs of darkness? He

thought, but was not sure, that there were gaps filled
with hazels and tangled rose-bushes, wild and tall. Half
circling the walls ran a little river—the one in which he
had fished so often, but it looked strange in the moonlight.

There were dim relics of splendor, a noble iron gate
where gilding glittered still on the bars. It was two-
winged and pillared, and on either pillar a stealthy grif-
fin drenched his recumbent stone coils in shadow. Trees,
trees, everywhere drowning out the light. The place had
gathered ill about it, an opiate breath unlike the pure
air breathing in the woods outside.

She led the way over a bridge that crossed the river
and they stood in the inner garden. Inexpressible re-
pugnance loaded Wendover's feet, but he went on. If
he had stepped over the confines of the world into blank
space he could not have been more utterly lost and
bewildered. Under the moon, now bright, the house appeared a huddle of shapes, rooms, roofs, blocked out
with ruin. Impossible to say how much was lived in,
how much given over to desolation. There was a broken
balustrade from one corner, and from the gutters of the
roof leaned gargoyle heads grinning down. What had
they seen? What could their stony out-thrust tongues
tell if in the darkness they came awake and yelled horror
through the trembling woods? Below them was a slug-
gish lake choked with great lily leaves.

Wendover made one last struggle to be normal, to
convince himself that all was well. "It's a large garden,"
he said as loudly as he dared.

"Four acres," she answered, leading on to the gate.

She was right. Instantly he knew he was no stranger.
They entered, and as it swung creaking behind him, he
remembered. He had seen those windows lit, raying out
light into the black woods. People had come riding, in

coaches, haughty cold people who lived their lives in disdain of those who only existed to serve them. He saw the house no longer ruined but with a stately air befitting that of a great family, and the moon was glittering like a silver fish in the lily pool before the great front. She spoke again:

"This is the house. It is here you must sleep. Those woods are full of—"

"Of what?" He stopped and looked into her glittering eyes with chilling fear.

"You know. At night they wake and lie in wait."

"And you?"

"I wake all night." She turned and went on.

(It may seem a strange thing, but when Wendover repeated those words to me, though couples were pacing the deck and the gramophone on the other side brazened out the last Charleston, I forgot them all. My nerves tingled. The sinister secret words lent voice to the awful loneliness of ocean and hid beneath its vast veils of darkness.)

She walked up a wide flight of steps to where the hall door stood blackly opened, and as she set foot on them suddenly the dead house sprang into lights as for a festival. Lights broke forth at every window and poured like revelation into the black garden, showing crowded dreadful faces, slinking things, half-shaped forms that fled the light. A woman towered above them on the uppermost step as if for welcome. Her look was hideous and inhuman.

Wendover halted on the lowest. Strength returned to him. He cried aloud: "I'll go no farther. Not a step. I know now I often felt you in the woods. And there are more of you. Your name is legion— Devils! In God's name, who are you?"

There was a muttering of distant thunder. It grew

and grew, swelling into such a roar as when lions answer each other in reverberating deserts. It shattered in
his brain.

The woman descended the steps to him, menacing,
burning with evil passions. Her eyes shot out the flames
of hell. Her hand stretched out to claim her own blood
in him. It passed human endurance. The world rushed
from him on thundering wings that sounded in and
outside his tortured brain and through the universe.
His senses broke and he knew nothing more.

(Here it will be said: Could such a wild dream be
seriously taken without assuming lunacy in the man who
said he saw? Yes. I have heard darker stories than this
where ancestral memory broke through the bars and
invaded the present. Psychologists know them well and
are helpless before them. But this experience has a
stranger ending than any for which the West has any
explanation.)

Morning.—Wendover waked as if from tortured
sleep in a strange place, a whitewashed room with jars
and bottles ranged on shelves. A little country surgery.
He lay on a long couch, his head propped on pillows,
and beside him was a girl holding a bottle of some
restorative. The air was still pungent with it. A man
stood behind her, obviously a doctor, bending forward
to see. He straightened up as Wendover opened his eyes.

"That's all right. He'll do now, Miss Thorold. Lucky
you found him, though! It thundered and rained last
night, and it doesn't do to lie out in the woods if a
man's not too strong to start with."

"It was good that you had the ambulance ready when
I telephoned from the lodge," she answered in a clear
low voice. One knows those clear-cut voices and trusts
them.

Silence. They both stood looking at him. He could feel it through closed eyelids. He tried to pull himself together, weakened by a great shock, unaware of its cause, quivering in every nerve. At last he dragged himself up on his elbow.

"I'm most awfully ashamed, and I don't know what happened. I've been ill and I suppose I fainted. After that I knew nothing. Where was I?"

"This young lady found you on her morning walk in Wickington Park. You were lying under the trees near the East Gate close by here and we brought you to my house in the ambulance. She is Miss Thorold. I am Dr. Bowstead."

I pass over the thanks and protestations. The girl had slipped away before they were ended, and Wendover was alone with the doctor.

"I'll take you back to the Crosslets presently, Mr. Wendover. You're all right but I may as well say you're not a well man yet and must be careful."

"But I never fainted in my life before. I can't imagine how it happened."

"You never must again if it's going to involve lying out all night in Wickington Park. Why didn't you knock at the lodge door if you were feeling seedy?"

"I never thought of that. Indeed I didn't see it," Wendover said in a low voice.

He remembered no details of the shock, but knew that consciousness left him in the wood at least six miles from the East Gate. How had he come there? What had transported him. Was it his own feet fleeing from unbearable terror? or something mysterious and terrible which had possessed his soul? But he was silent, and the good doctor motored him to the Crosslets and left, recommending at least two days' rest.

He felt the want of it himself and besides it would

give him time to think and remember. To that task he set himself.

Two days later he asked Mrs. Eves, the landlady for some particulars of his rescuer. Did she live in the village? Now that he had recovered he must surely go to offer his gratitude. Mrs. Eves comfortably flashing her knitting-needles over a cup of tea in the bar parlor was perfectly ready to dispense information.

"Why, as to that, sir, Miss Cicely Thorold and her ma live very retired in the Cottage beyond the church and a very nice-brought-up young lady as you'd wish to see. They belong to the old ancient Thorolds that owned Waste Manor when there was a house there long ago, but the money's gone and her brother in India—"

For a moment Wendover heard no word she said though there were many. Waste Manor. The desolate name, lightly spoken though it was, unlocked the floodgates of memory, and the torrent rolled again through the dry channels of his brain, bringing strange jetsam with it. Again he saw the white figure moving down the glade to meet him, he heard the ambiguous, sinister replies, he saw the trap laid into which his bewildered brain had driven him. How nearly its jaws had snapped he knew with terror. What had saved him from the madness of herding for a loathsome night with the powers of evil he could not tell, but believed it was some strong gesture of the invincible human will, which is in its foundation divine and free. That did not as yet matter—he was saved. But had the experience left any mark? What had *they* done with him while he lay unconscious and at their mercy? Who were they— what?

With these and many other questions rushing through his brain he never asked himself if the whole thing had been a hallucination rising like miasma from his attack of malaria, for he was as sure as of life and death that his eyes had seen, his ears heard, though in some deeper sense than the ordinary vision and hearing. Still, being human, he would seek for corroboration. He would find it also, he was certain. Slowly his mind returned to cognition of Mrs. Eves's discourse.

"And her father had an appointment in India, sir, and come home and died, and her mother's an invalid, and if ever a girl's home was as dull as ditch water it's hers. So she has a kind of solitary way with her and keeps herself to herself as the saying is. You won't see her if you go sudden. She'll like a note first."

Before they parted he asked Mrs. Eves a question which had its importance to him.

"I hear Lord Wickington is in bad health. Is that true? And his only son out of his mind?"

"Lord Wickington? Why, sir, a healthier stronger man doesn't walk on ten toes! I won't say he's got a nice temper. He don't seem a happy man for all his money. But as well as well! You could light a fire at his face it's that rosy. The son—ah that's a bad business. His horse bolted four years ago at something that frightened it in the woods, and he was dragged and his head smashed something awful and he's never had his senses since. He lives with a doctor up in a village on Shackleton Down. There's no heir. And the daughter—" She shook her head.

This was corroboration with a vengeance in its circumstance and otherwise. He noted it and in spite of Mrs. Eves's opinion would have refused an insurance on Lord Wickington's life.

Alone again, he sat down and wrote a letter to his solicitor in London:

Dear Thicknesse:

I remember that before his death my father deposited in your care our family pedigree and some

miniatures and other little relics for safe-keeping.
I do not wish to remove them from your care, for
I am returning to India before long, but I wish to
ask two questions.

Can you have the pedigree looked through and
inform me if you can find my ancestress in the
reign of Charles the First, born Sophia Wendover,
and tell me who her husband was? I also wish to
know who her daughter Cicely married. If there
were more than one it would probably be the elder
daughter. My second question is—are there
among the miniatures any likenesses of this ancestress and her husband? Because if so I wish to
examine them and if you send them down I will
return them immediately.

(This letter and the reply were shown me on board
the Hana Maru by Mr. Wendover.)

Having written to Miss Thorold and received permission he went next day to the Church and through
the little rose-garlanded churchyard, lost in its dream
of heaven, to the cottage which lay a quarter of a mile
beyond down a green byway.

It stood in a great copse of beech and elm trees which
half hid it, and not only was the seclusion cloistral but
the church appeared to rear its medieval barrier between
it and all the life of the tiny village. The garden was
walled with old brick mossed and plumed with fern.
Tiny toad-flax grew along the upper ledge and fruit
trees showed above it. Wendover noted also that a
brook, crystal-clear, ran over bright pebbles before the
garden and a little rustic bridge led to the gate. This
strengthened the impression of a dwelling set apart by
choice and circumstance.

He crossed the bridge with some diffidence and as

he did so saw Miss Thorold coming down the little path between the rose-standards to meet him. She wore a white dress and was bare-headed, and a kind of shuddering memory ran through him of another woman also in white and bare-headed who had come down a long glade to meet him. It was strange that this dwelling reproduced in a little the features of the den of darkness once known as Waste Manor. Trees stood about this also, clouding it with shadow. Water cut it off from the commonplace world. The cottage was hundreds of years old, beamed and tiled and modernized with difficulty. A woman in white had drawn him to either.

Yet the width of the spiritual world lay between the two. The eyes raised to Wendover's were so frank and lucent in their serenity that had he known nothing else of her they would have won his eternal confidence. Here, too, he was not a stranger—but with how great a difference! Difference and coincidence repeated themselves all through that strange but happy interview. After he had left he asked himself if she had beauty in addition to her mystic charm and could not answer the question. When there is instant assimilation and union how can a man stand off to criticize and appraise? And that was his case. Neither then nor after could he inventory her face and presence. He tried to—that I might understand—but I could only gain the impression of selfless quiet, of something refined almost to tenuity, of utterly elusive beauty, if beauty there were. Brown-eyed, brown-haired, a little wistful, but with a kindling smile. I must leave it where Wendover left it—an impression. No more.

But in his mind, he said, the name "Cicely Thorold" was like music, and it recalled strange evanescent pictures, painted by Rossetti and his school, of maidens lily-pure and solitary, mysteriously secluded amid holy emblems in lost churches and castles, like still white flames burning in the dark.

After greetings and inquiries and thanks she led him up the little garden to the low cottage.

"I wish I could introduce you to my mother but I can't. She's a great invalid and as she never sleeps at night it must be in the day—when she can. She is asleep now."

They passed two yews bowed blackly into an arbor and within Wendover saw dimly a couch and the outline of a woman's figure lying upon it like one at rest or dead. Their footsteps made no sound on the grass as they went by. It emphasized the great quiet of the place.

The drawing room was larger than could have been expected. Two rooms had evidently been thrown into one; the ceiling was strengthened by rough but magnificently carpentered beams, and two stout pillars of cedar supported the plain arch which united the rooms. The furniture was scanty but extremely beautiful and ancient, the whole room possessing an atmosphere of distinction which impressed Wendover very powerfully.

It was not until near the end of his visit that anything interesting transpired, but when it did it was startling.

Cicely Thorold said gently:

"There is a curious thing, Mr. Wendover, about which I will ask you a question if I may. Your name isn't a common one and in our pedigree there is a marriage which connects us with it. May I tell you? We have the pedigree here."

It may be imagined how the rush of blood quickened Wendover's heartbeat. He laid his cup down with a shaking hand and looked at her.

"An ancestress of mine was Cicely Tracy, daughter of a marriage between Sophia Wendover and Sir

Aylmer Tracy. Cicely married her cousin Stephen Wendover of Casson Hall, Cumberland. Does that mean anything to you?"

He answered with an attempt at composure: "It means a lot. I am Stephen Wendover of Casson, though the house is gone. I believe Cicely Wendover was an ancestress."

They sat looking at each other with great eyes as those who wake from a dream.

"Wonderful!" she said in a low voice, and he echoed the word. Presently she added:

"Then we are far, far off cousins and you are a Tracy too. Her daughter married a Thorold. I never thought you were a stranger—"

"Something spoke," he said slowly. "It spoke in me too."

There fell a silence between them. The old clock which had measured out the lives of the Thorolds and Wendovers ticked loudly beside them in its recess, allotting and resuming their minutes of life.

"May I come again?" he asked in a low voice as if it were a secret between them. "I'm a very lonely man. Not a soul belonging to me but a sister in Australia. Don't shut me out."

If his pleading was a shade too urgent she forgave it. She granted his wish. He might come in four days. Perhaps her mother would see him, knowing the kinship. As he stood on the little bridge watching her go up the garden another thought struck him. He had spent that afternoon in the fairy land of the ancient Morte d'Arthur. He had emerged "from the Forest Perilous guided by the Strange Damsel and had entered the House of Adventure set in a right fair woodland and surrounded by running waters and girdled of high walls."

(At this part of the story came reserves. I think Wendover did not wish me to know how closely his heart had clung to this sweet woman of his own blood —a plant of the same root, whose white blossom lit his loneliness like a star. Yet I read the story rightly, I am sure, when in my mind I divorced it from all sexual hope and experience. It was love untainted by any covetousness of earthly expression.)

He paid two visits before Mrs. Thorold saw him— surely the frailest thing that could breathe and live, a body holding the spirit as insecurely as a cobweb holds a dew-drop.

Her black hair was oxydized with silver, her sad gray eyes as blackly lashed as her daughter's, but the look of wan suffering was her own. She met Wendover kindly but with a touch of pity.

"So you share the unhappy Tracy blood with us, Mr. Wendover? Tell me if you can, has it used you better than it has us?"

Difficult question to answer! He hurriedly reviewed his own life. Loneliness, the loss of house and lands, exile, health none too strong, a solitary future. And yet—

"Is life ever entirely happy for anyone?" he asked. "Have the Tracys more to complain of than others? Would you say so? I think the root of our trouble lies deeper still."

He saw Cicely's eyes quicken and shine. Mrs. Thorold shook her head sadly. "No, our forefather committed a wicked and most sacrilegious murder. We all pay for his devil's temperament."

"It seems a little unjust!" he said thoughtfully. "And I know many worse off than the Tracys."

A little more passed and then she was wearied and closed exhausted eyes. Cicely took him to the quiet drawing-room with its air of breathless ancientry and pale distinction.

"My mother might be well if she could escape from that belief," she said sadly. "But she never will. It has doomed her. Is that part of the Tracy curse? I think not."

What could Wendover say? His experiences in the Perilous Wood colored all his thoughts with fatalism. He had told her of his letter to the lawyer; now he held out the answer. It confirmed his own vision and Cicely's facts completely. There the marriages of Sophia Wendover with Sir Aylmer Tracy and of Cicely Tracy with Stephen Wendover stared him in the face with legal precision.

"As to the miniature," wrote Mr. Thicknesse, "we hold a miniature of Lady Tracy and one of Mrs. Wendover. The latter is extremely attractive; the former I own is not to my taste. I shall send both down by a confidential clerk for your inspection on receiving your authority."

Silently Cicely rose and opened a cabinet of ancient English oak barred with iron hinges. She took two miniatures from it and laid them on the table.

"Copies," she said. "We didn't even know the originals existed."

Copies, but fine ones.

The face of Cicely Wendover reminded her descendant of Cicely Thorold's. The same delicate and pensive grace, brown-eyed, faintly smiling. But the other! The corpulence, the retracted nostrils and flat sensuous mouth were the woman of his horrible vision branded in upon his brain by revelation. She was magnificent in brocade and pearls with a high fan-shaped lace ornament upon her heart—the Lust of the Flesh, the Pride of Life, the Desire of the Eyes, made visible in a gross body. And she had married a Tracy—two meeting streams of evil.

Cicely looked at it shuddering. "The vile woman. I've asked mother to let me burn it and she won't. It's like an evil influence in the house."

"Yours will hold it at bay," Wendover said. He pushed it from him with loathing, and it slid on the polished table and crashed on the floor. It was painted on thick glass after an old Dutch fashion and it flew into flinders. The thing was gone.

The joy in Cicely's face balanced his consternation.

"Thank heaven! If I had had the courage— No, I don't want yours, thank you? The original that that woman sat for and saw with her own eyes would be worse than the copy. Mother need never know."

That day too he left with a bewildered sense of the ways of fate that nothing could explain. What are the blendings of heredity? What the doom they impose? The riddle was beyond him.

The time was drawing near when he must leave Tanswyke and prepare for his return to India, and each day Cicely grew dearer to him. He loved her not as men commonly love, but dearly. We are ill served by words where this passion is concerned. The same term must widen to wings that overarch the heavens and shrink to the fan-flutter of a base little flirtation.

He met her sometimes moving quietly along the sun-flecked forest paths on the near side of the park. Though he had said nothing, some delicate instinct in her divined that the other must not be spoken of. It held some instinctive horror for both—some racial nerve that quivered with the same wound.

Then she would stop and smile and they would fall into step for a while and then sit under the listening trees. It must have been a relief to her. Her life was so

lonely; her mother's stark conclusions so unlike the
fine intuitions that built her own strength. Once or
twice he ventured to hint at the desolation of her life.
Must it always be like this—always?

"One gets used to it," was all she answered.

"But here? In this prison of a place? Surely the wide
world—"

"Wherever we went it would be the same. After all,
we are Tracys. We can't evade our doom. It has taken
us all in turn. My father—my brother—my mother.
Have you ever heard a verse of the song about us?"

He shook his head. She laid her small hands quietly
in her lap and repeated without any inflection:

"Woe to the unborn sons of the Tracys
(Say what redemption is left through all time?)
O, could they win to the land where God's grace is,
Baffled and faint with the storm-wind's embraces,
(The wind that wails for their forefather's crime)
With ever the wind and the rain in their faces—
Never again, till the end of time."

Silence. They were sitting under a great beech by a pool
starred with white cups and buds of lilies. Not a leaf
stirred, and the quiet was cloistral. He looked at her
and again the thought of the story of the Grail floated
from the deeps of his mind.

"So Sir Percival looked on the maiden and had great
pity of her, for so well shapen was she of limb and
body as that nature might not better have fashioned
her, and all the beauty that may be in woman's body
was in her and all the sweetness and simpleness."

It protested against her hard fate with a voice sadder
than tears. He tried to remonstrate against his own conviction.

"But surely you can't believe that a long-ago crime

of one of your ancestors could crush you like this? Life has hardships and contradictions, but such a cruel injustice would be impossible in any world not ruled bv devils."

"There are many strange things we don't understand. The consequences—the way things are bound together—" she said.

"The very belief in it, the very life here, are enough to bring about the certainty of doom and insure its fulfilment. You ought not to be here: you and your mother— It's horribly bad for you. Couldn't you get away? Forgive me for venturing to say this, but we are friends."

"I know. I'm grateful. But there's nothing to be done. We have no money. You could never think how little it costs to live here. And if we can save anything it must go to my brother. He has married unhappily. He—"

It dawned dimly on him then that he had heard of a Thorold—Tracy Thorold—who had been in one of the native regiments, who had mysteriously left it and vanished. Men said he had gone Indian. They say that sometimes when they can account for strange things in no other way. Wendover resolved he would hear more when he got back. Now he slid past the subject.

"But you?"

She saw he cared and looked up at him with the hidden soul in her eyes. He had never seen any so strangely beautiful. Clear as deep gray water set in the midnight of blackest lashes they had a magnetic power that sent a faint tingling along his veins.

"Don't be sorry for me. I have compensations," she said and paused, then added: "You have been so kind to us. Shall I tell you? One may be a Tracy and yet find wings."

He caught at that. It is impossible to say how much the place and the two women interested him. No—that is too cold a word. They pulled on something in his heart. He understood. They were in the same plane though he could not define what and where it might be. Wings? And a Tracy?

"You will believe it," she said, and seemed to search for words to express an experience too great for her. "I was born in India, and mother and I came back when I was eighteen months old. She was too ill to stay there. You will see I could remember nothing of the country. A strange thing happened six months before we left. The wife of a Brahmin near us, who had no children of her own, was very fond of me. When my ayah took me to the grove near the temple of Vishnu the Preserver she was nearly always there. My mother says she was a beautiful young woman, very silent and gentle. She interested her husband in me. He was always at the temple and he would come out and stand looking down upon me, lost in thought. One day my mother asked him to say what was in his mind, for many people knew he could see hidden things. You will think it strange, but he said a wonderful thing."

"Why should I think it strange?" Wendover said. "Don't I know India? Sometimes I think the only clear sight in all the world is there."

"Then you'll understand. He said: 'Looking at this child I see strange joys and griefs. I see a vast building of the gods, as it were a mountain of stone carved in noble shapes. Dark inside—dark, set with small lights and I see a great Rishi [a holy sage] proud and terrible of aspect mounting some steps to the altar. And four men armed wait for him in the dimness.'"

She paused and looked at Wendover with a question. He answered:

"But yet—might not the story of your family connection with the Great Murder have got about? I know from my own knowledge that there is some secret wireless in India we've never fathomed."

She made no comment, but went on:

"And he said: 'I hear them cry aloud to him and he fearing nothing—as how should he?—answers: "Here am I. No evil-doer but a Priest of Him that Is." And the wicked Four try to drag him from that holiest place, but he will not and resists like a warrior, and since the gods wait their time the evil-doers have their will and slaughter him. And so, to meet their doom.'"

Again she paused and said:

"Have you thought it strange he should see Canterbury Cathedral in darkness?"

"Does it invalidate the time?"

"No, it confirms it most strangely. Thomas à Becket was murdered at five o'clock in the afternoon of December 29th. It would be black dark in the great cathedral then, but in India it would be light. That is the true sight. Then he said: 'For this child because she has been swept into the karma of the great murderer there can be none of the transitory joys that men follow to their destruction. Alone she shall live, alone she shall die. Yet that Eternal within her shall take wings and escape, and the night repay the sorrows of the day.'"

"They should never have told you!" Wendover interrupted with indignation. "It was to doom you. They must have been mad."

She looked at him strangely.

"They never did. You shall hear. Then he did a thing almost impossible for a Brahmin. He took a little stem of the sacred tulsi plant and dipping it in water traced the symbol of Vishnu the Preserver on my fore-

head saying: 'Come home, poor child, one day from the
cruel West. Your peace lies here.' My mother was
furious. She rubbed the mark dry, glaring at him, but
he turned away smiling like a man who makes allow-
ances. 'What is done, is done'—that was all. But I
was never taken there again."

(It is hard to describe the interest with which I
heard this part of Wendover's story. No more incredible thing could ever have been told of a Brahmin and
a priest. But it elucidated much that followed for I saw
plainly that he had followed the girl's rebirths and recognized her as a daughter of India swept by a faulty
karma or some need of her soul into the vortex of the
Tracy curse. This should be borne in mind.)

"But what happened? What did it mean?" asked
Wendover, bewildered. He had felt in her an almost
visible dedication but to what? to whom? He begged
her to tell him more.

"I began an inner life when I was very young, I can
never remember a time when the nights were blank.
Directly I fell asleep the doors opened. I was much in
India—I saw, I knew. I walked along the roads and
few saw me. Here and there one who had the sight
smiled and blessed me. That was my real life. I saw
no reason in it; no child does, but it was life. The day
was a dull dream. I awoke in the night. When I was
six I saw the Brahmin and knew what he had said and
told my mother. She was terrified, but would say nothing. Much later she owned it. She hated my dreams as
she called them. But *I* know I only dream in the day.
I wake all night."

She smiled as one who has a secret to keep. Her face
had taken a strange expression—her eyes like the
luminous depths in some sea-cave obscurely dark. They
seemed to ally her to strange secrets of nature, to wake

a nameless fear in the man who heard her. Was it a
dawning likeness to his strange guide in the Wood
Perilous? Did the tangling fibers of kindred blood go
as deeply and terribly as that? Were there dark possibilities as well as noble? There was power in her as
well as delicacy, and power is a two-edged knife.

"Gradually I saw connection in my pictures. Certain
currents played upon me—not others. I saw what the
opening of the door meant. I know now that all the
thoughts, ideas, of the world are real and eternal. They
never pass away, but are a great store of knowledge
which anyone may use who can, according to his own
self-knowledge. Well, I have the key of a room in that
palace of power and I know enough to be certain there
are rooms upstairs to which I can't climb yet—but they
are there. Every day it grows clearer as my inner and
outer life blend."

He repeated the famous prayer of Socrates aloud to
see if she would recognize the thought.

" 'Beloved Pan and all ye other gods who haunt this
place, give me beauty in the inward soul, and may the
outward and inward man be at one.' "

"I know—I know! The woods are full of lovely
Presences, but they never come inside this garden except when I open the gate to them at night. We are
too sad. Then the inward and outward are at one without contradiction. That's just what I wanted to say."
She stopped and added: "Did you know there is a saying of a great prophet, 'When the outside becomes the
inside then the Kingdom of Heaven is come'?"

He had never heard it, but it reached his heart. The
wisdom of the subconscious uniting with reason and
the intellectual forces. Yes, that would be the Kingdom
of Heaven indeed.

There was a long silence. What right had he to intrude into the secret places of her soul? And yet there were things he burned to ask. He had been a student of these things in India. He knew some of the teachings of the ancient and modern schools of thought. It can be imagined with what interest he heard her young lips uttering the mysteries which bewilder the wise. He ventured a step farther.

"I can quite believe it is possible that pictures of the past are mysteriously preserved, amazing as it is. But the future? The past *may*—I don't say it is—be traceable to latent or hereditary knowledge of your own. But the future? That's the test!"

"Not as you think. In the world where I live time is not marked off as we have it here. The present and future are pictures in exactly the same way."

"Can you give me any proof of that? What have you seen?"

"Proof?" she said. "There's no proof about it. That belongs to earth. Things there *are*."

Something in her manner impressed Wendover more than her words. She was careless whether an outsider believed or no. She knew.

"I have seen pictures of you." she added. "I saw you in a tent on the mountains somewhere with a dark man behind you in a green turban, and another man, light-haired and very tall, came up to you, and the dark man brought a table and chairs out of the tent and you both spread out a map and marked it. There were acres of forget-me-nots all round you as if the sky had fallen and made blue pools of peace. The mountain had two peaks like the Breasts of Sheba in 'King Solomon's Mines,' and a huge overhanging ice-cave pushing forward into the valley, and a river running from it. Do you remember?"

Remember? Wendover was pale with memory. Kolahoi, the great snout of the glacier, the cold river. And Edmond Hall had run over from Aru, and they had planned to trek from there to the Sind by Khem Sar and Zaiwan and he remembered in a flash that this Hall had said to him idly: "I never see Kolahoi that I don't think of the Breasts of Sheba in Haggard's book."

Wendover pulled himself together. "Can you tell whether you saw this in the past or future?"

"Not in the least. I tell you time has no meaning to me there. But it will certainly happen if it hasn't come already, for it *is*."

"Have you seen more of me?"

"Yes, much more. That's why I know we are tied together by something more than blood. All the people I see have touched or will touch me. I saw you here— walking in the garden. The house weighed on you like lead. It would on me if I had to live in it. But I escape."

"You must know your own future from your past and present," he said earnestly. "Tell me—shall you escape for good? Will your life be cast in brighter surroundings?"

"They are bright as stars!" she answered with her inscrutable smile. "But I shall never have what people call a good time. It will be better than that. Much better. Remember this life is a very short act of the play. Sometimes I can't tell whether what I see belongs to this act or the one before or to come. How can I? You outside people all look on this as something to be made use of, to be planned into this life as if one had a telephone fitted or any other convenience. I can't make you see how little account it takes of the kind of life we live in the day. That's only like the little bit of an island peak that shows above the sea with the rest of the continent drowned in deep water. *We* know which matters."

The thought struck Wendover then that he had lit by chance on the most wonderful medium—invaluable in the desperate quest of the Dark Continent which lies beyond our ocean of thought. He told her a little of what the wise men of the day are seeking, hoping to interest her. She shook it off her as a wind-wafted rose shakes rain.

"I have nothing to do with all that," she said. "It sounds horrible to me. My world is quite different. I don't care whether they succeed or no. These things come to the people who need them. They make us make beautiful thought-forms—but I can't explain, and it doesn't matter. What does matter is that one sees all life is law and you build your nest straw by straw like a bird and if the wind blows it away it's because you built badly. Build again! I've built this wonderful House of life for myself and I am content with it. The next will be higher up on the mountain above the clouds."

He entreated her to tell him more, though he saw very well he was not to hear the things which most concerned her. Indeed she said one thing which he held for true in all relations of life.

"You can never truly hear anything unless you know it already yourself. What's the good of telling? Perhaps I should not have said as much as this."

They walked back slowly through a grave sunset in wind-washed trees, and he little thought this would be the last chapter in a very wonderful experience. He counted upon some parting confidence before he left in two days, which might clear the outlook for both. But it was not to be. At the bridge she stopped and held out her hand.

"You have been so kind—and the only one of my own blood—that I will tell you that when my mother dies I believe I shall go to Burma and wait and see what happens. I have money enough for that. Do you laugh? Ah, I want only work and thought. The vision draws me that way."

He would have interrupted with some eager protest about money but she smiled and went quickly up the garden.

Next day came a note to say her mother was so ill that there could not be a minute for meeting.

"But I wish you all good. May I call you Stephen, for I think of you in that way, and we shall never meet again. Our lives have touched very strangely. We are bound by the fetter of a great wrong, but it can be slipped. I have seen your fate—peace like mine and perfect release from things which do not matter and vex the quiet of our souls. I send my love and hope to you. The wind and rain may blow in the faces of our people, but they will not vex you and me. We have known the secret and have found our way to the back of the North Wind."

Here Wendover's story ended, for a few weeks after he embarked upon the liner where I met him. Gliding over the surface of the Indian ocean we often sat at night watching the moon and stars drift by in solemn procession; and I did my best to learn from him what conclusion he had come to about the vision, if so it can be counted, of what he called the Wood Perilous. He believed it was a true sight, that it had in truth happened, that for an hour he had been swept into the world of spirits and had there been a spectator of the strange drama eternally surrounding us and rarely visible. This he thought received confirmation from the fact that we met one day at the board for wireless news and there read together the information that Lord Wickington had died under an operation for cancer of the throat.

"And who will they strike at next?" he asked as he turned away.

"They?" I could get no definite opinion from him on that point though it was obvious that he leaned to the spirit hypothesis. To me it appeared rather a mystery play of evil passions still sending their vibrations through a place which had been their playground for many centuries. The kindred blood in Wendover and something sensitively responsive in him to these aerial messages had dramatized a dead and living evil into human-seeming forms. In this connection I noted keenly that the out-of-the-world seclusion of Cicely Thorold's home and many other incidents, including her strange saying, "I wake all night," repeated, as it were, on a noble plane his meeting with the embodied evil of the Perilous Wood. I believe this foretold the transmutation of the curse centered in Waste Manor, that one day larks will sing about it and doves dream on the tiles of the ancient roof and happy children will play in the pleached alleys of yew and the dead evil blossom as the rose in fragrance and innocent beauty. There is much still to be considered in this matter, much that seems inexplicable, but I steadily believe the first incident to be a black shadow cast by the light of the other and to be dissolved by it one day into radiance.

As to his difficulty about the injustice of the descendants of de Tracy suffering for their forefather's crime, to me with my Buddhist training that presented no difficulty at all. Those souls were naturally drawn by affinity into the sweep of the de Tracy karma who had something to learn, to suffer, or to perfect, by sharing that experience. It was not because he was their ancestor. He became their ancestor because their experience needed some training or experience from his. They were swept into his vortex because things in it made it their own necessity, and each turned it to account according to the stage of evolution which he or she had reached.

Wendover and I had many interchanges of thought before I left the ship, on Buddhism, the ancient Vedantic philosophy of life and death, and we each learned something from the other. He said on parting that he would let me know later what turn his life had taken.

This promise I thought he must have forgotten, for no letter broke the silence. "Ships that pass in the night," I thought, but did not forget him.

Two years later I received an invitation to attend the ordination of a bhikku or Buddhist monk—one who has renounced the world of transient appearances for the way of peace and renunciation.

It took place at a temple near a lake, where on a platform above the water a little hut decorated and screened had been erected, for the ordination must take place above pure water. I stood with the gathered people and watched the little procession of children carrying brightly decorated wands and leading the way. The yellow-robed brethren followed and with them the priest to be ordained.

Passing, he never lifted his eyes from the ground, but I saw the face of Stephen Wendover. I cannot say it was either a surprise or a shock. At the moment it seemed the right, the logical conclusion to all pain and trouble of mind. More I cannot say though I know much more. The monks crossed the bridge to the hut, none others following them, and there the ceremony was performed. It was a long time before they emerged, the new brother walking gravely, the white European shoulder emerging strangely from the flaming yellow of his robe. They proceeded to the white tent where he would receive congratulations.

The faithful bowed before him and kissed the ground at his feet. I myself made salutation with joined hands, remembering very strangely how often we had sat side by side talking as friends of matters which I alone of those present knew had influenced him to this high decision. Our eyes did not meet. A whole world of experience divided us now, and yet never perhaps had we been so near in thought and purpose.

He repeated the necessary prayer. The tom-toms beat their guttural music and it was ended.

A week later he wrote me a few words which included these:

"Your kind interest in my singular fate bids me inform you that I have made a fuller study of the Buddhist faith in the past two years and have found in it an answer to all my questions. You will recognize the words of the Perfect One with which I end and you will ask no better.

" 'Tranquil is the thought, tranquil the word and deed of him who is delivered and brought to quiet through the perfection of wisdom.'

"I have found the Peace. May you also find it! I thank you for your presence on the happiest day of my life."

For the last time this was signed with the initials of the name he had discarded on passing into the quiet life. It is because he has done so, and the noise of this world is less to him now than the little sounds in the inside silence of a grave, that this story can be written. If he read it, it would be with the indifference with which a man reads the history of an alien whom he will never know.

Of Cicely Thorold I know nothing, but I believe I shall know one day.

The Mystery of Iniquity

THERE IS A VILLAGE IN SWITZERLAND HIGH UPLIFTED among the mountains beside a little lake of gentian blue. Nothing could be lonelier, nothing more detached from the lower world, nothing lovelier. It is still approached by the old-fashioned diligence, toiling up mountain ways whose scanty population would not reward any higher enterprise in approach. The tourist does not know its name and from me never shall. Therefore I shall call it Geierstein after Sir Walter Scott's famous novel, and there leave it.

But I was free of the place. And when I took my yearly holiday I took it always at Geierstein partly because I loved the place for its beauty and quiet, partly because I had valued friends there—Pastor Biedermann and his wife. He was a Cambridge man like myself though a Swiss, and our friendship grew in value to us both with the years.

It followed that when I arrived at Geierstein regularly every fourth of August I boarded with them and fell immediately into their life and that of the village as to the manner born.

Their house alone would have won the day—a chalet, long and low, with balconies up and down stairs where you could smoke and read or work or stare at the Jungfrau and her giant companions swimming in blue air or the splendors of sunset and dawn. It was a generously gabled house with running bands of decoration which somehow expressed the simple and pious

hope of the pastor's ancestors who had built it in the
year 1740. Across the front in fine old German letter-
ing ran the verse designed to express the spirit of the
house and hope of the builders:

> *Wer Gott vertraut,*
> *Hat wohl gebaut.*

(Who trusts in God has built well.)

They had built well. Years of sunshine, rain, snow
and storm had beaten in vain at the high pointed windows, the generously sheltering eaves, the dove-cote
chimneys. Warmth and strength were still the guardians of the house when the cold wrath of the mountains broke in fury down the valley and over the lake.

Peace was the atmosphere of the house; sunny
golden peace in summer, warm fire-lit peace in winter.
It began with the garden, Biedermann's own special
charge, crammed with bushes of lovely old-fashioned
roses brimming with perfume. I felt that the very dew
on their petals must be attar of roses, their true spiritual essence. There was a rainbow of crowded asters.
Round them crowded tawny wallflowers, lavender
bushes, campanulas—God knows what. The perfume
rose divinely to my balcony where I often slept in the
open and woke to the dew-drenched glory of the garden with earliest dawn's call to my plunge and swim in
the lake.

Biedermann was an unusual fellow, deeply religious
in stanch Lutheran fashion, but with affections and
consciousness wide enough to float his bark to heavens
never conceived in the Lutheran limits. His wife was a
household sweetness. Her low voice singing old ballads
or hymns as she went about her work will always be
a background in my thoughts to the strange events we
were to share.

It began as simply as any household happening. It was the day after my arrival and we were sitting at supper. We had reached the stage of wild strawberries and whipped cream, when Biedermann said carelessly:

"Since you were last here, doctor, I have let the old Parson-House again."

He preferred living in his own house, and it was an understanding that he should keep up the Parson-House and make a little profit by letting it to eke out a tiny income.

"And who now?" I asked.

"An English lady and her daughter and I'm really glad to have you near to discuss them. They're getting on my conscience."

That meant on his compassion—a raft capable of supporting all the shipwrecked of the universe. Mrs. Biedermann sighed.

"The mother's a beautiful person but hard—hard as your toast this evening. Toni! were you dreaming when you made it?" she said laughing to the little flaxen-haired maid.

"The daughter is beautiful too," said Biedermann, "but in a most peculiar way that I can't describe. I should very much like your opinion."

"But why are they here?"

"I don't know. She's very reserved. Only said her daughter had been ill and was ordered quiet and mountain air. She took the house for a year and came in April."

"Then they mean to be here in the winter?"

That was unusual. I had never seen it except for a week but I knew what the terror and beauty of the falling snow, the raving winds would be. After October Geierstein was as cut off as a planet on the outermost orbit of the system. Everyone drew into their own concerns and family life—and what on earth would an English lady and her daughter do then? People who know the great hotels and winter sports have little notion of such a place as Geierstein when the Snow Queen sits enthroned in the valleys of the Bernese Oberland.

"And what's their name?"

"Saumarez. The daughter's name is Joyselle. They come from London and—"

"What?" I said. "Why, I knew a Dr. Saumarez, a most extraordinary—"

"Her husband was a doctor. He died some time ago."

Now it became interesting. Saumarez was a hard-bitten fellow with keen watchful eyes and set lips through which no secret would ever slip that he meant to hide. We had been medical students together and even then he was like that—ready to join in anything going but always outside it, a looker-on in spite of himself, a man no one honestly cared for. I had heard he became a clever aurist and had a house near me in London but at the other end of the street—a world away as London goes. Dead? I did not know that either, but these strangers became faintly interesting to me because of their association with Saumarez.

Biedermann said slowly:

"I should like you to meet them. I have an idea— Should you not say, Hilde, that there's some hidden trouble?"

She answered:

"Certainly. Frau Saumarez speaks from the lips outward. What is in her heart she never tells. More strawberries, Herr Doktor?"

As she spoke a girl passed along the road, going slowly towards the old Parson-House. She had no hat and was the slim short-skirted slip of a thing one sees in every street. What was her own was the distinction with which she carried a clipped satin-smooth head set on a long throat. It was too far for me to see her features, but the figure defined against a sunset sky had the confident beauty of a young birch tree alone in a clearing of the woods. A Dryad—a tree spirit, blown for a moment across human vision.

"That's the girl!" said Biedermann.

Next day, on our way to see a case in which he wanted my advice he introduced me to Mrs. Saumarez as she stood by her garden gate with the village milk-woman milking a cow into a pail at her feet. She bowed with the usual smile when I was presented but, directly I suggested a possible acquaintance, froze. Her face stiffened and she was on guard instantly. The very tone in which she met and dismissed the subject disclosed some wound which I knew she would have held back with tooth and claw if possible.

"My husband died two years ago. Have you noticed how beautiful the Caroline Testout roses are this year, Herr Biedermann?"

That was all. We talked a few minutes and said good-by and began our tramp up the steep little mountain road. Suddenly she called after him and I went slowly on, piecing her together.

A locked face. Cold only (to use a contradiction) because there were volcanic elements at work under it which must be kept in check as granite hides boiling lava. Her few words were the puff of steam revealing the fire-heart within. She was handsome and had a kind of chilly dignity—a woman of whom I should have guessed that the Saumarez I knew would be the very last man she would admit to her intimacies. Well—marriage need not mean intimacy beyond what a man may have with the chance choice of a night!

Presently Biedermann came up behind me.

"She wanted to say a curious thing," he said meditatively. "Now what could she mean? It was—'Please ask Dr. Livingston if he sees my daughter not to mention her father to her.' I'm afraid we were right. There's something painful behind it."

That was plain. We said no more on that hand but climbed on and up to the little woodland cottage set in stark and stedfast pines and staring out through low-browed windows at the giant crests of the Oberland, surging like a wave petrified in eternal defeat in some wild war on the heavens.

I saw the case he wished me to see there—a girl of about nineteen, named Lili Schneiderling, suffering from obscure nervous trouble. I diagnosed and advised and was leading the way out of the room when she called me back, speaking hurriedly and low in German-Swiss. Biedermann turned in astonishment to hear:

"I want to tell you—I want to say—how can I get well if—" She gasped and paused, putting up a hand to hide her eyes.

"If what?" I asked encouragingly, bending over her.

"If the English fräulein comes at night. Tell her not to,—promise me. It should not be allowed. It should be stopped."

She panted as if the effort of getting the thing off her mind were greater than she could endure. I looked at the mother, a comely blonde Swiss with troubled eyes, who stood on the other side of the bed.

"What does she mean?"

"Indeed, sir, I can't tell. She has said it more than once. The young English fräulein passes the window on her way up to the waterfall in the woods but she never comes in."

"A lie!" said the girl harshly. "She came in the day after they went to the old Parson-House."

The mother smiled patiently. "Why, yes, Lili! But that was only to ask her way. She never came again."

"She never needed to. She had spied out what she wanted to know. Well, all I say is—if you want me to get well tell her not to come here. *I* don't want her, the dear God knows!" She turned and caught my hand in a hot painful grip: "Will you tell her? You're English too?"

I promised—and Biedermann and I went off together.

"Is there any madness in the family?" I asked when we had set our faces upward once more.

"None. The parents are as ordinary as can be, and she's an only child now. For what it's worth, my opinion is that Lili is jealous of the other girl's health and strength. She goes out in all weathers night and day. A week ago in a storm—I give you my word I thought she would be blown over the edge of the cliff road before my eyes. I saw the wind lift her. Actually, for a second! Right off the ground. She flung out her arms and laughed.

"A great storm goes to the head like drink sometimes, but I think she must have given a hop, skip, and jump to help it! I expect Lili has had a jealous dream. Half the antipathies of the world center there, and the dreamers forget the cause when they wake."

We went off on dreams then, I telling him all the newest notions and guesses on that most mysterious subject, and gradually as we talked we climbed up to a ragged track on the way to the waterfall. I must describe the place for my experience turns on it.

We were now four miles from Geierstein. The frightfully steep narrow little road had come with us as far as the shoulder of a crag and there deserted us, turning abruptly to the left on its winding way upward to another village two miles farther in the mountains

and known as Donnerstein; a few chalets collected in
the cup of a mountain valley, hugely uplifted as was
Geierstein in the arms of a mountain only lesser than
the Jungfrau and her mighty companions. Here we
turned up the steep track. Half a mile of it led us to a
great wood of pines, somber and sighing even in the
hot sunshine of the late afternoon. The far distant
murmur of water came on a waft of wind as we entered where a thick carpet of golden pine-needles
dumbed the sound of our feet.

Otherwise, what a silence! Not a bird sang, not a
cricket trilled. We were in a great cathedral of Nature's making, too high, too vast, for human worship.
One could imagine the cold spirits of the mountains—
no, that kind of thing has been said often enough. It
means nothing except to those who have seen. Biedermann spoke low. The place enforced quiet.

"Now for a surprise. We're lucky, for the wind is
the right way. You see that crag in front? You hear
the silence? Now prepare to be deafened. It's fuller
than ever this year."

A crag plumed with firs blocked the way perhaps
two hundred yards in front with a steep fall downward.
We climbed round it cautiously, for it was a place for
a slip and a nasty accident and the difficulty absorbed
me. In the next moment my ears were filled with the
thundering roar of a terrible dance of water over mad-
dening rocks, plunging for life, for safety, for escape
from hell, as it were, down an awful precipice to the
unseen lake, in a world too far below to be its own.
Never before had I seen it like this.

Vain to speak. Thunder and spray and foam filled
the world, deafened, half blinded me. This was the
Geierstein Fall. I stood staring at it in silence, and
suddenly I saw a sight entirely new to me.

About a hundred feet below at the left side jutted

out into the water a jut of the forest darkened with pines. The extraordinary thing was that I could not remember having seen this promontory before. It was as strange to me as the rest was familiar and I stared in astonishment. At first I thought it was an optical illusion caused by the shimmer and slide and spray of the water. It appeared to change and flicker. I rubbed my eyes. I would have called Biedermann's attention to it with words, but the noise was thunderous. I pointed and he laughed and nodded. Finally he put his mouth to my ear and shouted:

"There's a little hut about a quarter of an hour on where I go and read a psalm or two with an old cowherd. Will you wait or come?"

I shouted, "Wait," and he went off, climbing with hands as well as feet round the bluff. I was glad to be alone in the wild and terrible place and stood looking at the water, meditating on the unfamiliarity of the promontory.

I could imagine how a weak brain might feel the fascination of the long pale green slide of water glittering in sunlight, and dream of plunging with it down through airy space in quest of life—more life—to be sought through that marvelous smooth motion. The names of more than one of my patients flashed through my mind whom I would not willingly have trusted for a moment to stand by the ever and never changing phenomenon.

I looked downward to where the strange promontory with its trees shimmered and danced through spray. It was like a mirage I had once seen in Egypt, quivering at first then settling down into what seemed to be reality. Suddenly something slipped through the gloom of trees. What in the name of God!—a woman—a girl, mother-naked. It—she appeared to lay a hand on the rough bark of one of the pine trees, and she stood staring at the plunge. I saw her clear as ivory on ebony. The trees still shimmered through driving spray. Presently she left them and advanced out on the jut as if to meet the full rush of water, going confidently. My first thought was the medical one—Was I going to see a case of suicide before my eyes and do nothing?

I put my hands to my mouth and shouted, yelled—I don't know what—that she might know she was watched, guarded. My puny voice shattered in the enormous vibrations about me and was tossed to bits. She stood bending forward unconscious of my presence. Suddenly she looked up, laughing and waving her hand. I turned, more by instinct than reason, and began to make my way back round the great bluff of cliff that we had circled to reach the waterfall. In the hurry I slipped, fell, picked myself up again and scrambled on with the blind conviction that I should find some way to the rescue in the wood beyond.

Presently I regained the breathless quiet of the trees where we had first entered and began casting about for a trail to the lower level. My brain was clearer now that the all-stunning noise had ceased, and I hunted with purpose and direction. It must be a madwoman, but life is life in the maddest brain, and life attempts its salvation. I found what I thought was a foot-track going directly downward and began the descent, using my alpenstock for the pine-needles made it slippery as glass. Cursing my delays I slipped and fell and struggled down and down to a point where the trees ceased and bare rock began.

A shout above. A great cry. Biedermann's voice.

"Come back. BACK! Have you gone mad? No way there—Come *back*. Back this minute!"

It broke some tension in my brain. I drove the alpenstock deep into the earth and yelled. "A woman down there. Must get on. Wait!"

He was not far above me as distance goes and I saw some shock strike him right in the center. He shot out an arm, waving frantically. I remember the thought struck me that the quiet self-contained Biedermann had gone right off his head.

"Come back, I tell you. Danger! Come!"

It caught me. He knew some better way. I dragged at the alpenstock and scrambled up, reaching the boles of the pines ascending like a stairway, gained his level and leaned against one of them, gasping with the effort. I could not speak for a moment.

"In the name of God"—his voice had the solemnity of an invocation—"where were you going? What did you see?"

"A naked woman—down there!" I got out in a series of gasps. "I saw her from above. I thought—suicide. I was going down."

He said low as if to himself: "Thank God I came in time!"

Then after a moment:

"Rest—get steadied, and we'll make for home. There's nothing you can do. Nothing!"

I yielded in deep perplexity—I had had a shock far deeper than anything my scramble up and down could account for. Something that struck me deep in the heart of my consciousness, and that by no means the consciousness of the average man, for mine had been trained beyond the common by experience and discipline. I noted how if my eye turned for a moment to the downward way Biedermann's grip tightened on his stick. I had the feeling that he would have attacked me sooner than see me attempt it. Once or twice he looked up apprehensively as the shadows darkened. It was not sunset, but the sun had dropped below a tremendous peak and the chill of nearing night was perceptible.

Presently I got up. "Ready now. Let's go. Queer experience!"

He led the way along the track I have already mentioned and said not a word until we had reached the road running upward to Donnerstein and downward to Geierstein, then halted a second, and we both looked back to the wood—black in advancing shadows.

"I want you to make me a promise," he said.

I laughed uneasily. "No blank checks for me! Give me the reason and I'll give you the promise—if they click."

He said, "That's reasonable," and was silent again, leading the way.

At that moment I heard a light step on the road above us as if of some woman coming down from Donnerstein. I turned instinctively to look. Nothing there. Let me say that during the whole time of our descent that step went with us until a point which I shall mark. I did not like it. I did not know at the time whether Biedermann was conscious of it or no, and hesitated unaccountably in asking.

"You heard something?" he asked.

"Nothing of consequence. What were you going to tell me?"

"First tell me what woman you saw? And where?"

I described the lower pinewood. The trees falling back from the mighty rush of the waterfall. He turned his head over his shoulder and looked at me fixedly. Then the naked girl:

"And the queer thing is I never noticed that promontory before. I made a scramble for it. I was as sure as I walk here that she was going to fling herself straight in. I'd been thinking it was the very spot for a crack-brained man or woman. However, if she's done it she's in the lake by this time and has got through the Great Experience. Now for your story, Biedermann."

He looked unlike himself—a queer constrained look —and what gave the lie to my assumption of ease was that those footsteps kept us steady company a few yards behind on my left. I could not rid myself of the notion that someone who wanted to hear was keeping up with us and might draw nearer.

"I hate the subject but I see I must speak. First, there's no such jut into the fall as you speak of. Cragsmen who have climbed down beyond where you attempted to go describe a huge and terrible crevice—a crack or fault in the mountain that goes down to— heaven knows what. Just beyond where you were is a smooth face of rock; a slip—and you'd have glissaded down and nothing could have saved you."

There was that in his face which made it impossible to doubt he was in earnest. I said what naturally occurred to me:

"Then how did she get down—why did I see it? There's another way?"

"I tell you there's no such place. That phantom you saw doesn't exist."

I halted for an incredulous second. The footsteps halted too.

"But I tell you I *saw* it. I would have said it only for the infernal row of the water. There was a dazzle of spray on the jut but I saw it. Let's go back and—"

He dragged me by the arm. "Come on. I never dreamed you'd see it."

"Hasn't anyone else?"

"Yes, two men and—"

"And you say it isn't there. It's some change in the

rocks." But for the echoing footsteps I could have laughed aloud. If either of the two of us was going dotty it was not I.

"If you *will* have it!" he said, and halted. Then went on quickly: "A young fellow, Lili Schneiderling's brother, Arnold Schneiderling, saw it. His companion didn't. Then he lost it. The wooded plane was gone. He saw it no more than his friend. There's a sheer plunge there, straight as the side of a funicular. Two days after, Arnold and another man were going along the track you and I took. Suddenly he left the other and clambered like mad down the way you went, shouting. A yell and Untermeyer going down after him as far as he dared saw a frightful crevice and saved himself just in time. Arnold was never heard of again."

I reflected. "I should like to cross-examine Untermeyer."

"I've done it," Biedermann said. I noticed that his step and therefore mine had fallen into the rhythm of the footsteps behind. Was it conscious or unconscious?

"Helfman saw it next. The carpenter's son. There were three young men there at the time. The others saw nothing. He saw the wooded promontory and the naked girl. He said she looked up and laughed and waved. They had to rope him to prevent him going down. They thought he was mad and so got him home. Two days after, he was seen going up into the wood, running. He was never seen from that day to this."

I reflected. I could have done it more clearly but for the echoing footsteps. Then I said:

"The thing is perfectly clear. It's a mirage from the spray and whirl of the water. I can hardly believe the promontory isn't there, but, granting that, the woman is not difficult to account for. The dazzle and flash and smooth plunge of the water act as an intoxicant. It would affect some brains and not others. But I'm surprised it should affect me. I'm as hard as nails."

"That's a legitimate explanation," said Biedermann, "but it scarcely covers all the facts. That girl you saw on the way up—Lili Schneiderling—has never been to the waterfall, but nevertheless she gets curious attacks of—shall I call it trance?—what I described to you— in which she speaks of the woman."

"How could you expect otherwise when all the village is chattering?" I asked. "When did these things happen?"

"Within the last four months."

We walked some way in silence.

"Is there an old story about the place?"

"Yes. Four hundred years ago—you remember the little old castle on the lake?—the Baron von Falkenwald fell in love with a girl of foreign blood. Nothing is known of her but that she jilted him cruelly and he leaped into the waterfall, the first, as far as we know, of a long series of suicides there. A woman is said to have been seen with him, pointing with glee to the water."

Again I reflected. "Is that story known in the village?"

"No. I discovered it by accident when I was searching the archives at Einsiedeln in connection with a property claim. As pastor I judged it right to keep it to myself. The place has a bad enough reputation. After the happenings this year the more superstitious folk talk of a water-spirit; the wiser, of mirage, as you did."

"And you yourself?"

"I have had some reason to think there is more than meets the eye in life. I suspend judgment."

We walked a little way in silence. Suddenly I said: "Can you hear light footsteps following us?"

We stopped to listen. The footsteps also stopped instantly, and he shook his head. We went on. They did the same. I had a horrid notion that something unseen and evil was overshadowing all our talk. I should rather say I knew this, and with anger that it or they should attempt to frighten me like a beginner.

"I hear nothing," said Biedermann, striding on.

The rest of our walk was nearly silent. But as we reached Geierstein and were passing the garden gate of the old Parson-House the footsteps suddenly stopped. Immediately, Biedermann spoke:

"I have given you reasons. Now for the promise. Will you promise me never to go up alone into the Falkenwald?"

"Don't ask it. Can't you see that all this has made me doubly eager to get to the bottom of the thing? Remember my profession. If there's danger, surely it's my duty to investigate it. In your calling and mine can we show the white flag in any risks, bodily or psychic?" He agreed seriously. We went on and nothing was said in my hearing to Frau Biedermann of what had happened.

Next morning a note was brought to me from Mrs. Saumarez. It had the same effect upon me as her appearance. That of dull, secret persistence. I am sensitive to atmospheres and even those given off by letters and personal objects.

Dear Dr. Livingstone:

I should be glad to consult you on a private matter of importance. It is desirable that no one should know a consultation has taken place and I shall be in my garden at 5 P.M. today and if

you could pass as it were accidentally the meeting
need not seem to be arranged. I shall be obliged
if you will not mention the matter. Your friendship with my husband will excuse this unusual
request. No answer is needed.

Sincerely yours
ANNETTE SAUMAREZ

Friendship! I thought that assumption cool after
my slight admission and her grudging reply. I knew
she must have been put to it before she would use that
plea. My impulse was to send a polite refusal, but a
doctor cannot estimate needs nor decline a duty. I
sent no answer and at five o'clock was walking up the
mountain road feeling strange premonitions. Sorceries
were closing about me and I could not tell whence. I
neared her garden.

A profusion of roses—a hard-faced woman among
them in a wide-brimmed hat. The milkwoman of the
village stopped to see. She would be able to report that
Mrs. Saumarez looked up quite casually, went quite
casually to the garden gate and made a polite remark
to which I replied politely. That I then strolled in and
she pointed out one or two garden triumphs. Now in a
position to satisfy the unslaked hunger of Geierstein
for events, the milkwoman went slowly on, and instantly (we were invisible from the house windows)
Mrs. Saumarez turned to me and the mask dropped.

I saw straight black brows drawn across a forehead
where the sharp downward line dividing them spoke
to experience of angry temper. Hard glittering eyes in
a handsome tight-lipped face. Such gentleness as one
might expect from a steel trap waiting to snap on
an unwary animal wandering nearer and nearer. She
spoke abruptly:

"I want to consult you about my daughter. I have heard in London that you make a specialty of nervous troubles, and I believe she is in a serious state. Will you keep the matter utterly private?"

I thought the tone offensive and replied coolly:

"Your husband was a doctor. You should know the medical rule of secrecy. But if you prefer to take her elsewhere—"

"I don't prefer. You must excuse me if anxiety makes me abrupt. If—oh, if I could make you understand!"

"Is the patient ready for a visit?"

"The patient? My God! She's not to know I have seen you. She's away up the mountain. That was my chance."

"Then may I beg particulars?"

She did the most unexpected thing—laid her hand for a pleading second on my coat-sleeve. The action revised my whole conception of her and rebuked me as I have been rebuked a hundred times before for the cruelty of rash judgment. Now I saw that what I had thought temper was the iron strain of self-control imposed on wincing nature too weak for it. The hardness was the despairing clutch on strength out of reach. The face was a mask of endurance that must ask no sympathy in its griefs. A most miserable woman stood before me. I said instantly and with acute shame:

"I beg your pardon. I misunderstood. Shall we sit down?"

"Thank you. Not here!" she said hurriedly. "You see she would come in this way. We'll sit at the back in the arbor."

A tiny green bower with a rustic table. She looked nervously round for listeners and plunged straight into an extraordinary revelation.

"Dr. Livingstone, did you ever think my husband mad?"

No question could have caught me more unprepared. I stared in astonishment, and answered with some constraint:

"I knew him so little, that really—"

She flashed in before I finished.

"Not in the ordinary way. Listen! He was crazy over psychological experiments. He dissected the mind as coldly as doctors dissect bodies. He believed people could be used as slaves if you find the right strings to pull. He was a bad man. Did you know that?"

Now I began to remember dimly that I had heard some doctor speak of him as a man who was making daring experiments in what my students persist in calling "psykes" when any mental and nervous states are under discussion. He laughed about it, called him an empiric, a charlatan and so forth. I imagined he had not achieved the success of renown or wealth, but really the whole thing interested me so little that in the press of my own work it went clean out of my head and never recurred.

"Hypnotism and so forth?" I asked.

"Partly, but much more. He believed people could be taught to project their thought-forms visibly as they do now by chance through death-bed apparitions and in other ways. He thought telepathy could be brought under scientific law and could always be accompanied with visible presence."

"Possibly it can," I said, beginning to be deeply interested.

"Yes—but for what ends? He thought the way in was by the influence of certain drugs. He called it 'The Drug Revelation' and terrible people came to the house and terrible experiments were made. A

woman and a man went mad under them and there
was more than I ever knew. He used the brain until
it broke. There's one drug that makes all the powers
flare up for a long time and then drop, as it seems,
forever into idiocy. I know its name but even to you
I won't breathe it. A fearful thing. I have come into
the room again and again and found him stupefied,
and when he woke he would pour out horrors that
turned my soul to fear incarnate. Can such things be
true?"

I would not discuss it with her though I held a
strong opinion of my own. But here the case was clear.
A bad man drawing into his own evil vortex all the
evil influences to which he had thrown wide the door
—I knew the way he had trodden, the point marked
"Danger," where disregarding every instinct and warn-
ing he had plunged to ruin and not alone—a blind
guide of the blind. I said briefly:

"Pray go on. I shall be better able to judge when
the whole story is before me."

She sighed patiently.

"This went on for two years and then came a
change. He called me into his room one night and
before I had time to speak or see caught me
and pressed a sponge over my mouth and nostrils
and held me down. I saw nothing, felt nothing but
green meadows and immeasurable rest—green pastures,
a Shepherd leading his sheep. I wished never to wake
again to the unspeakable weariness of life. But I woke
lying on my bed exhausted and he cursed me and told
me I was no good—no good. He must find a better."

"You had safeguards," I said with profound pity,
"spiritual safeguards he could not break down. You
need have no fear."

"Fear? I had nothing else. After that, he never

drugged me again, but going about the house I would see strange faces, figures horrible and despairing. Thought-forms, he said, but horribly lifelike. They could speak and move but they were spectral—not human. Light did not frighten them. They went and came as they would or he bid them. Did I see them or did I not?"

She was an image of entreaty with shaking hands held out. No words can tell my pity. A good woman in the den of the only devils that exist—if the word exist may be used to express the inexpressible. But I concentrated in listening. This related itself to certain studies of my own with a very different aim and object. She sighed again when I made no answer and went on.

"My mother was dying and I was called to her. I left my daughter Joyselle in charge of an excellent old French governess, Mademoiselle Payot and an old servant, Margaret. Joyselle was then thirteen, unusually young for her age—her chief interest in life a lovely little West Highland terrier whom she loved almost as tenderly as she did me. A beautiful generous child. It was a sharp pull to leave her, but my mother was dying of cancer and it was no house for a girl. I had been away for two months receiving nothing but good news when a letter came from Mademoiselle Payot."

She drew it from her bag and laid it before me. It was in French.

Dear Madam:
    Circumstances which I very deeply regret oblige me to leave my position without delay. I will not refer to them further than by saying that Dr. Saumarez's manner leaves me no alternative. I

should not go in this way but that I know your confidence in Margaret and my own experience confirms it. But I think you should return as soon as possible.

There was more, relating to arrangements which I need not quote. She put it away and went on, the nerves in her face and eyelids twitching nervously. She was a patient too, if she had known it!

"I was in Carlisle and my mother clung to me. What could I do? Joyselle's letters were those of a child. Margaret wrote seldom and without detail. 'Missy was well. The house was all right,' and so forth. I wrote repeatedly to my husband. He always answered that Joyselle was in the best of health, all was well, and Mademoiselle Payot had left because her temper became unbearable. She had frightened Joyselle terribly more than once and she herself had grown alarmed at her own want of control. Several times he wrote like this. Four times he came up for a week-end and quite reassured me."

There was a pause. In far distance were the crystal peaks of the Wetterhorn and Schreckhorn, awful in beauty. All round us, roses, roses in the sweet old-fashioned garden, bees making a low drowsy bourdon in the air. Peace everywhere—but on a cracking surface disclosing rifts of horror beneath.

"My mother died and I came back. I had been away three months. At once I saw the change in Joyselle. She had been fresh and sweet as a bunch of pinks, innocent and trustful as a baby. *Now* her eyes held the knowledge of evil. They were quick, glancing— proud, concealing. She met me with a kind of hardy assurance. I should have hated it in any girl. It terrified me in my own. She might have been a woman of equal age, polite enough but holding me off with her reserves. Her dog Darroch was dead, she said carelessly, making nothing of a thing which would have rent her heart when I left. I had a feeling that love also was dead between us. She looked the picture of health, her lips crimson, her eyes sparkling as if with some inward satisfaction I could not fathom. She was then just fourteen."

"Did you make any effort to fathom it?" I asked.

"Every effort. No use. I questioned Margaret. She answered doggedly. 'Missy is well. Anyone can see that,' and so forth. Then I began to watch—to spy. A mother must! She cared for no associates—no society. She was happiest in her own room—a large one on the third floor, and there she had the most extraordinary collection of books on the brain and mind. Horrible for a girl of her age, but her father would not let me interfere—All spiritual things were dead in her, but her brain-power was wonderful. It was as if"—she hesitated for a while—"as if it were breaking loose like fire. She said she was writing a story. I couldn't keep up with her intellect. It was beyond me and she despised me."

Her voice trembled. We were drawing near the heart of horror.

"One night my husband and I had been to the play— Macbeth. It was near twelve when we got back, and the street was empty with a full moon glaring down it. I looked up at the house and saw something white fluttering down from Joyselle's balcony. You will think me mad when I say I thought for one wild minute that it was she herself coming down hand under hand on a rope. I caught my husband's arm and pointed up, shaking from head to foot. He stood, his eyes fixed and I heard him muttering to himself 'Clever girl!—

well done!' and madnesses like that. I got out my
latch-key and flew upstairs. Her door was locked. I
rattled and banged and at last she seemed to wake
and came to me. I shall never forget her face. The
stiff smile, the sly anger in her eyes. Doctor, she
looked a criminal! Yet what could it mean? She was
there in her room—had been asleep. I saw the dent
in her pillow."

"You mean," I said, "that her father had taught her
his tricks? She could project herself."

"Yes—yes!" she said eagerly. "I watched. He had
taught her to drug herself. He used to watch while
she disengaged herself as he called it. I have seen it
happen—she would fall into a drugged sleep and then
leave the drugged body like a butterfly off a flower
and flit about the house or out and away. I never saw
where. She did awful things."

She stopped, shuddering with memory. To be honest
I was by no means certain at the moment that her
brain was not touched and a great part of her story
hallucination. For though I knew the thing could be,
on a very different plane, its perversion and openness
were out of all my experience. If it were true the girl
must be watched and rescued somehow or frightful
dangers lay ahead. But how? I kept my most guarded
professional manner and it steadied her a little.

"It's almost impossible to suppose a father would
subject his daughter to the risks of drug-taking. Had
he been attached to her?"

"Never. He hated her for not being a boy. But don't
you *see*? He never thought all this wicked. He thought
it power, riches, everything the world has to give. The
magnificence of brain-power. There were rich women
and men who simply poured out gold in return for
what they called his magic. And remember I had failed

as a subject and he wanted one to show off his power on. He said she was wonderful— People were beginning to talk of her when he died—"

She gasped and moistened her dry lips with her tongue as if to enable herself to speak.

"This went on for some years. I lost all hold of her and was afraid to complain to anyone. She was too strong for me. There was nothing she could not do. He died two years ago when she was sixteen."

"Had she access to the drug after that?"

"I don't know. But it grew worse. She began to talk quite openly about her experiences, and they were like his—ghastly and terrible beyond words. The vilest."

I said thoughtfully: "The brain had probably become diseased under the drug-taking."

"I don't think that!" she said eagerly. "She had a strong brain always and even her father did not dominate her. She hated him. But he opened a door and let her in to all the horrors of the ages. A kind of form of him haunts her and she would drive it away but cannot. I have seen it in the room staring at her as if he had slipped behind and she was the teacher now. But I tell you—and it's true, believe me if you will, that the *will* in her, the desires in her, can slip out of her body in her own shape and do what she chooses while she lies drugged on her bed. She is off and away all night and often in the day."

I said slowly: "The saints and divinities have had that gift and we call it miracle."

She said: "Ah yes—yes!" with a smile sadder than any tears. "If her power could be turned into the spiritual channel! But that could never be; with her the brain is everything. And what terrifies me is that I see her body being drawn into it too. The flesh longs to share in the mental creations. And that means— open ruin. She's shaved it more than once."

There was a long silence. Then she half rose.

"Will you come up and see her?"

"But you said she was up in the mountains!"

"So she is. Do you think I don't know the stories of the waterfall? I'm coming to that. But her body is asleep upstairs. Come up."

Can I express the feelings with which I followed her upstairs into the quaint low-browed room looking out upon the guarding Alps? The scent of the garden made it sweet as a bower of roses. The curtains were white, the bed draped with white—a girl lay on the square white pillows as in the chalice of a lily. I stood beside her, lost in thoughts for which I can find no name.

She was a slim maid of eighteen, white as pearl, no tinge of color in her cheeks, lips ardently crimson as hibiscus blossom. She had that look of decadent divinity which appears to be the last word in fashionable and intellectual beauty. One might picture her as the evil goddess Ashtoreth of the Zidonians, stiff in a golden shrine glittering with encrusted jewels, the winged doors half open that her rigidly outspread hands might rain abominations on her worshipers. The shut eyelids and black lashes sealed on the marble cheek gave her the air of stiff hieratic mystery seated above all human law, unmatchable in evil.

"You could touch her and she would not wake," whispered the trembling woman beside me. "It's a trance. Not sleep."

I stooped again and close to the delicate nostrils where the faint breath fluttered. Yes—there was the smell of a drug which I dare not name. And very soon she would need no outer help of that sort but could set herself free, unaided, to roam the world, a danger more dreadful than a wandering tiger to every human being who crossed her path. The case was plain to me now. I followed her mother down into the garden.

There in haste as the sun neared the mountains she repeated to me the stories of the young men which I had heard from Biedermann.

"There's no kind of magic of all the ages she doesn't know!" she ended. "Look!" she picked up a book and showed it to me.

That too I knew. It has been the source of deadly dreams to the world for millenniums—"The Book of the Lady of the Great Land." It opened at the Invocation of the Maskim—the seven evil spirits before whom Assyrian men and women trembled in the guardian shadow of their winged bulls known as the Kirubu—later to become our cherubim and be hymned in Christian churches that little guessed their origin. Into what deadly perfumed evil, long hidden, mummied in nard and cassia, bandaged and bound and hidden in temple vaults and bricked tombs, and now awaking insolently in the sunshine of a later day, had I stumbled?

The invocation stood out in black capitals before my eyes:

THE MASKIM, THE EVIL ONES, THEY ARE SEVEN. THEY ARE SEVEN. SEVEN THEY ARE! TO OUR WILL WE MAY BIND AND HOLD THEM, FOR IN THE CLAY OF MAN IS KNEADED THE BLOOD OF GOD!

The beauty of the last phrase caught me. The perverted truth that might yet save the miserable girl. Seven Evil Ones—and I remembered how in the Christian Scripture seven devils were cast out of the Magdalen leaving her snow-white and virgin-pure.

We went slowly through the garden and stood for a moment each thinking our own very different thoughts. Then Mrs. Saumarez said hurriedly—the old look of panic upon her face:

"You must go. She'll be waking. But come again when I send for you and tell me what to do."

I went off, carrying the book with me unconsciously, and a little way up the steep mountain road, looking out over the blue lake as from the ramparts of a great castle. I could not go straight back to the Biedermanns' quiet circle after that experience. I must have time to assemble my thoughts and fit them to a line of action opening before me.

The hell that Mrs. Saumarez must have lived through! And I could predict with certainty that the time would come when she would either be drawn herself into the orbit of the evil or go raving mad. Those who meddle with the perversions of the mental processes little know the ghastliness that lies in wait for them at a certain turn of the road. They will learn when they near it how frightfully the surface of power and pleasure cracks, disclosing beneath it illimitable woe. For if within us is the Kingdom of Heaven (and that is God's truth) within us also is the Kingdom of Hell. Not indeed that which frightened our parents in grim sermons and mechanically repeated prayers but that which set our ancestors half mad with tales of witchcraft and dreadful rites where the polarities of good and evil meet—the deathly clay of man mingled with the blood of outraged divinity—to use the parable in the book in my hand. I opened it again.

"My Father," it cried a page farther on, "the disease of the thought has issued from the abyss! How shall the man find healing?"

How? For man too is a creator, and if in his thoughts he creates forms of terror and wickedness they will surround him living and clear, walking in sun or moonlight, visible to those who have eyes to see—his own self-chosen companions dooming him to the Pit in this life and a terrible future in others.

I reached a height where the road turned and stood meditating these things in their innermost. My work had been directed in part by a great psychologist from whom I had heard true tales which exceeded in deeps and heights of mental process the heavens and hells of our early imaginings. He had his own methods of healing for some such cases, but all differed, all needed different handling. Could I dare to thrust my hands into the delicate machinery of a brain working on lines I knew, strong with its own evilly trained power?

As I stood considering this problem I heard steps approaching the corner behind me—a woman coming down from Donnerstein; I thought no more of it than that.

But they rounded the corner. They were close on me, invisibly—and then I knew. They stopped beside me. Unseen eyes surveyed me sharpened by evil to wicked, almost spiritual power of perception. I felt the cold vibration play over me like a wind of frost. It held me for a moment—perhaps longer—and then the steps went slowly down the road. It was as though a spirit had lifted up the curtain of the dark, held me with glittering eyes for a moment, dropped it and gone on its way.

I stood to watch the dying glory of the afterglow flush the sky, dye world and heaven into a divine rose, then slowly furl its petals and abandon the world to night and the creatures who walk in dark places. I went stiffly down the hill to the Biedermanns' home, looking up as I entered to the old legend carved along the front:

> *Wer Gott vertraut,*
> *Hat wohl gebaut.*

Yes, that is true. Man holds the talisman of safety in his own divinity—the blood of God is kneaded into the clay of man. He need not drop it unless he will. That house will stand.

The question in my mind was—should I consult Biedermann? I did not forget the doctor's obligation of secrecy, but none the less the woman had demanded help, and if I could reinforce my own powers the obligation lay on me to do it. But I would approach the subject cautiously and so make my decision. I have indicated already that he was a man of much spiritual power; of deep piety; and, though my own inspirations do not lie along the Lutheran path, power is power, meet it where you will, and all the streams have their source in the skies.

Frau Biedermann went up early to bed, with a headache. We lit our pipes and sat in the great shadowed balcony beneath the eaves where the mountains stood bathed in moonlight, gemmed with stars, their own glory of eternal strength submerged in a greater. I led the talk with care to the point I chose, so that my question was natural when I asked it:

"Biedermann, do you believe in what is called possession?"

He turned mild blue eyes of astonishment upon me. "Naturally. Is it not in the Bible?"

"It certainly is, and yet modern science might have other explanations to offer. Would you accept the theory that a man could be so saturated with evil that his will could obey none but the evil presences formed by his own thoughts and that objective devils of his own creation dwelt in him and used his body and brain as their vehicle?"

He reflected a moment. "I think I could admit that explanation. Mind you, I believe in a real Power of Evil—call it the Devil for short—who has his own realm of power and acts in it."

"That I cannot admit," I answered. "The universe

is one, with no duality, and man and nature are alike divine, but I know that man has the power to create frightful thought forms which dominate himself and may dominate other natures weak or wicked. It is a horrible stage of evolution but the seed of good—of power is in that also. The man who can create horror will turn his creative power to good and glory one of these days when he stops at another station on the long railroad of life. Am I a heretic?"

I quoted from the Gospel: "If Satan cast out Satan he is divided against himself; how shall then his kingdom stand?"

"That is true and interesting," he said eagerly. "You mean if a man can be stimulated to—as it were—rend his own flesh apart, endure the agony and fight the fight, he is sure of deliverance and the evil things may be cast out forever? I think that may be called Gospel teaching."

"If Gospel means 'good news' I think so too. I name these things differently——but I think we can shout across the road to each other. Have you seen such cases?"

He laid down his pipe and told me a dreadful story and another. Men of his profession, like my own, see the dark places that the hurrying world skirts or forgets. The second one bore most singularly on the secret my own mind was guarding and related to the young man Arnold Schneiderling of whom he had told me on the way from the waterfall. In the speech of the world the lad would be called a degenerate. Deep had called to deep with a vengeance when the English girl came his way. This threw a more focused light upon my problem.

It was late when we parted and Biedermann made a curious remark as we went upstairs.

"One should never allow oneself to be deceived by facts. They are the veil of reality."

Did I not say all the faiths coalesce at a point? I had heard that doctrine elsewhere than in a Lutheran Parson-House and had known its truth.

Facts gave way rather rudely that night—or was it the other way over? I went to sleep with the book on the table beside me and the moon looking in at the windows making two white pools of light on the black floor—a haven of peace.

As if a blow had struck me awake I sat up in my bed to face a horror. Groveling on the floor, crawling along it, passing in and out from gloom to gloom I saw the naked body of a woman. More snake than woman she propelled herself, lying flat with oaring hands and elbows. Humanity was obliterated in the attitude. It survived only in the head, horribly lifted, with the short hair running in a sparkling crest over the ridge of the skull. Her eyes fixed on mine without any intellect were patches of darkness in a white face above stretched lips. She wallowed in and out of light and gloom. I knew my own repulsive thought-form of the girl in the old Parson-House and with a swift spiritual gesture destroyed it. The room was empty in a second, flooded with pure moonlight. To see her thus was no way to help her. As I sat thinking I heard swift steps outside and sprang to the window to see the figure of a girl in white running fleetly up the mountain road, looking behind her now and then as she ran. She vanished round a corner.

A moment and after her came a young man running desperately as if for his life. I could hear his gasping breath as he passed the balcony. It told of a pumping heart and bursting veins, but still he ran as if the devil were after him instead of before him.

They were out of sight—a parable of many things; when I turned again there was nothing but silence, and the peace of sacred centuries filled the little house.

Next day Biedermann brought in the news that young Franz Rieder, son of the postmaster, had disappeared. He was known to have been heavily in debt and to have been led into dissipations at the market town of Hegenburg twenty miles distant and was only at home to demand money from his father. The supposition was that he might have done a bolt towards the frontier, but the village was alive with fear and conjecture, for this was the third disappearance in four months.

I thought it right to mention to Biedermann that I had seen a young man running up the mountain road, and ten minutes later a search party which I joined was formed, and we started for the Falkenwald, the men looking doubtfully at one another in fear and dreadful expectation. As we made the first turn we met the English girl coming down, walking lightly and gaily. She carried a long-stemmed white rose with dewy leaves in her hand and held it against her red lips to inhale the perfume. Biedermann lifted his hat and she smiled to him as she passed. I noticed two of the men whispering together and looking at her. They did not smile.

For the first time I had seen her eyes—they swept me in passing. Dark, extremely long and narrow. One could almost have said in the old Indian phrase that they touched her hair, and this gave her an oblique glance extraordinarily unusual and attractive. But I was conscious of a tingling along my hands and arms as she passed, and the Shakespearean line crossed my memory:

> By the pricking of my thumbs,
> Something wicked this way comes.

I turned to look after her in a minute and saw her standing looking fixedly after me. She went on at once.

Reaching the Falkenwald we divided and searched. I had the curiosity to climb round to the place of my last visit to the waterfall—where it made its mighty plunge from the heights. I stood there looking down for the promontory where I had seen the naked girl. Biedermann was right. It did not exist. Nothing interrupted or diverted the smooth and awful shoot of pale green water shot with flying foam, leaping to destruction leagues below. It had been mirage painted on my eyes as I saw her there. But how?

I rejoined the men. Roped, two had clambered down beyond the point I had reached on that eventful day. On the edge of the crevasse they found a shoe, a bloody handkerchief, and recognized them. What more? Columns of print could not have better told the end. But why? That question remained unanswered.

Biedermann, lost in thought, made but one remark as we reached Geierstein and separated—he to go to the boy's mother, I, to the balcony.

"The mystery of evil is at work here. We must not rest until we confront it with the Cross."

My own thought, but in other words. After sitting awhile on the balcony and strengthening my resolution, I got my hat, put her book under my arm and set off to the old Parson-House. It was noon and hard sunlight dwarfed my shadow on the white road. I opened the garden gate and went in.

Between two linden trees an orange-colored hammock was slung and in it lay the girl reading. She turned, hearing steps, and threw her legs over the side and sat facing me.

"My mother is out!" she said, without a pretense of ordinary civility. Her manner was insolent and

haughty as if something about me angered her. I was
equally unconventional. Beauty blazed at me from the
long narrow eyes and red lips, but I knew her and
she knew it.

"I must have a few words with you," I said and
pulled a garden chair under the tree to face her.

"I refuse!" She sprang to her feet. I shook my
head smiling.

"You accept, for, if not, a few days will see the village break loose upon you, and if they tore you to
tatters or dragged you to the asylum—and it's a
toss-up which—I for one would not blame them."

Silence and the light breeze fluttering the leaves. Her
fierce pride did not falter. She sat down again and
stared at me.

"Are you mad? What have I to do with the village?
I live my life—I go nowhere but to—"

I interrupted. "The mountain road. The Falkenwald!
Did you guess where we were going this morning
when you met us? Did you see me when I looked
down from the shoot of the waterfall the other day?
You looked up. You waved."

She laughed a little. "You're as mad as a hatter! It
takes roped men, they tell me, to get down the side of
the fall."

"It would take more than roped men to get where
you stood, for in the world about us that place has
no existence. Drop fencing! Come to reality. I tell you
you are in danger."

She looked at me sidelong and warily, measuring
her own weapons against mine. I read her thoughts
as she set her mouth so that the lips trembled pite-
ously, like those of a child who entreats for forgiveness in all innocence. But no obedient tears obeyed the
summons to her eyes. It is an old superstition that

witches cannot shed tears; which is as it may be. The pose of the young and terrified girl did not deceive me for one moment. She was folding and sheathing flamboyant power— "As though a rose should shut and be a bud again."

"How am I to help it if men go wild for me?" she asked meekly. "It happens to other girls and nobody blames them. You're a man. You should understand. Is it likely I'd have anything to do with these village louts? Not I. I despise them. We simply came here to have a little peace. When young Lethington shot himself—"

She halted in a breath at the look on my face. She had made a slip and knew it. I remembered the shouting newspaper headings, the evil room where drugged men lay and dreamed their hashish dreams. Much more also, not uncommon in the great cities. No wonder they were in hiding. She saw it all in my face and flung out into her true self again, defiant, hard as steel. I considered her a moment in silence; we were face to face now, preliminaries past.

"You never had a chance," I said. "Your father opened the wrong door for you when he might have opened the right one."

"He told me there was no other. But this *is* power. I've had a good time if I've had no more. I live on the desire of men. They go mad for me when I look at them. Hardly one— Where's the harm? I'm not bad-looking, am I?"

More than beautiful, my brain answered. A charm perilous and deadly. A bitter wine to drink. A honeyed sweetness, poison in the throat. The secrets of wicked forgotten worships were in those long agate eyes fringed with midnight. She represented what men will always find worth pursuit when the worst they can do

has been done and unslaked longing seeks for more—
yet more. But though my brain acknowledged her my
heart was silent, my flesh revolted against her.

"It's no use with you," she said savagely. "Well,
then—what do you want me to do? Hands up for me
this time! I never spared anyone. I can't expect you to
spare me. Give me back my book!"

She snatched at it from under my arm.

"What's *your* amulet?" she added. "You can't de-
stroy my witchcraft with crosses and black cats. You
know better."

"I want to ask you a question," I said slowly. "Is
there never a moment when you remember yourself
before your father took you in hand and wish yourself
—well—what you were then—or like other girls whom
men love?"

"That's a queer question!" she said with a smile in
her long eyes. "No, never! I suppose I used to sometimes, for it's rather frightening at first when you see
what you want to see and do glide out of you and
take shape and force others to see it. I used to faint
and cry, but he kept me up to it. I was a triumph of
'psykes' he said. No, I never want to go back. But I
have to lie low when the papers get hold of me and
sometimes I get most awfully tired and drowsy. Then
I have to draw strength from other people. Not the
good old blood-sucking vampire! You get into their
vibration. You know."

A thought struck me. "That's what you're doing to
Lili Schneiderling."

She nodded laughing. "But I must have more. I
have to be asleep nearly all day. See, I've no color.
Wait till you see me with a faint, faint color like the
last of the Alpenglow. I'm six times as good-looking
then. I'm seedy now."

I ignored that and returned to my question. "If you could be set free would you prefer to remain what you are?"

"Infinitely. Don't let's talk nonsense. Can't you go away? I want to sleep and there's nothing to be done."

"There's a good deal to be done. Your mother consulted me—"

Her eyes narrowed. Her lips drew apart dangerously. "I'll make her pay for that!" she said under her breath.

I shook my head and answered coolly: "I think not. Mr. Biedermann and I will remove your mother today and leave you alone in the house."

"But *I* think not!" Her teeth showed like a cat's with retracted lips tightened above them. "She knows and you know that I can come through walls and windows while I'm asleep in my bed. There's no part of the world where you could hide her from me, because she'd call me herself. I've mastered her. She'd have to build me if I couldn't build myself."

She sat up facing me proudly.

"Death?" I suggested.

"There's no such thing! Don't try to frighten me with fairy tales. My father lives in this house as much as we do. Look up. You'll see him at the window."

I looked up involuntarily.

The detestable face of Saumarez was looking down upon his daughter and me. As I looked it was gone but I had seen it. What a thought to have moving all but incarnate about one!

"Did you think I don't know that?" I asked coolly. "But did your father tell you of hell after death?"

"Fire and brimstone?" She laughed aloud. "No, he knew better."

"Did he tell you that men make their own hells and

need no other devils and that it goes on and on? That what you most hate will be your surrounding—bodily, mental——for what will seem to you forever and ever, though it will be only a moment of eternity?"

She looked up sharply. "That's queer! I dream that sometimes."

"You will dream it for a considerable time," I said, "There's no evading that law. That marigold could sooner come up an oak than you not reap what you sow. Now, what will you do?"

"Sorry you don't like me as I am!" She laughed ironically. "You should have known me as a nice little girl in pigtails adoring my dog—" She paused and added in a different tone, "I'd like him back," and then sank into silence for a moment. Presently she lifted her head fiercely.

"What else am I to do? Even if I didn't like it— and I do—there's no turning back. You know enough to know that. When you can do as you like and herd men like sheep and dip your hands in their pockets you don't go back to the maundering jealousies and help-lessness of the average woman."

"There's no turning back. True. You have learned one secret of power. You can't unlearn it, but you can go past it and on. You must decide now. This place is finding you out; and if they lynched you who could be surprised? Such things have happened and will again. You're nearing it."

Her eyes dilated on me with terror. This kind fears death very exceedingly, knowing enough to know cer-tain things. But this kind also does not own it. She shot a look of hatred at me.

"I'm always being hunted from pillar to post. I might do better in Asia. They understand better there. But go on. You've got me—in a way."

"Naturally. You don't want your brain—your instrument of power—broken and scattered. But it's coming. One way or another it comes to women like you. You're the curse of great cities—you and your like. You drench your victims with the false occult—the intellectual, and of the spiritual you know nothing. You trade on vices and fears. You waken the devils in your victims' hearts with your obscene magic that you may wring gold and power from them and trample them into the mud. And then one day—these women and men like you—they make some fatal slip, and the law gets them and holds them up in public for the devils they are, and the prison doors shut on them."

I could only appeal to her fears, but every word I said was God's truth. The world knows too well the trader on hidden evil cults and influences. That would be her escape when the pulse of beauty flagged in her and life ran low.

She looked up and said violently: "What could I do?"

"You could throw away your drug. You could come to London and be my patient."

"Oh—I see. Money!" she said impudently. "Well, I could be a profitable patient! I have lots of money. Good for you, but I don't see what you have to bribe *me* with. You don't know these things.. And I shall get more power as I get experience. I made you see my father now. I got your brain, though I couldn't get more. But I may later."

She laughed dangerously. I also, but to another tune. The scene had its humor—the rival magicians before Pharaoh, let us say! I told her in a few words that I was ahead of her there. That where she could make thought-forms to play upon the vilest strings of human nature I could command spiritual resources that were powerful to create and restore. Her instrument was the brain swayed by the primitive consciousness of forbidden things; mine was the spiritual and evolutionary consciousness of the universe mighty to unfold and develop the divine in man.

"Match yourself against me and try!" I said. "Try, though I acknowledge myself a beginner in a school that takes ages to perfect its pupils."

"It all sounds mighty dull!" she said and yawned. "Haven't we gassed long enough?"

I was silent a moment, considering, for an inspiration had shot through me—an answering flash, as I thought, to the indent I had made for a sword in the struggle. But could I speak to a debased creature like this of the most sacred experience of my life, founded on a lower consciousness and rising to infinity from the story of two dogs to the heaven-height of the woman I loved?

What is one's own but to be shared with the needy?

I told her the story in simple terms. At first she sat, marble hard, presently the sullen obstinacy of her face stirred, became more human, finally she listened intently. I ended.

"I like that," she said. "I can swear that's true. I love animals, but I can't get it in on them, have no pull on them. I can't even ride— Horses go mad if I try to touch them. They don't register me a bit, and I wish they did. Look now at that beast"— She pointed to a fox-terrier belonging to the next house down the road — "I've given him bones, biscuits. He'll not touch them. It's queer, for I want to make friends."

"Try," I said. I wanted to see, but I could have told her what would happen. Animals, especially dogs, have a very highly developed instinct against spiritual evil. That has been a common experience in all countries and times. It is not for nothing they lead a dog at the head of a Parsee funeral procession. I gave her a biscuit. I had always a supply for dog friends. He growled low and deep, disclosing shining teeth. The hackles along his back rose stealthily as he edged towards me for shelter. She flung it at him, and he leaped at her furiously. I dragged him back by the collar and he looked up in amazement that I should avert righteous judgment, then, sheltered beneath my knees, watched her steadily.

I said: "They know. They see."

She said scornfully: "Devils?"

"What else was or is meant by them? But to return: I believe you can be cured. Will you put yourself in my hands? Will you try it for a year? I know you're no coward, so I tell you frankly you'll go through hell while you're learning my way and discarding your own. But if you're game I'll stand by you shoulder to shoulder."

"There's nothing I care for except what I am and there are things one can never drag out of one. You're talking putrid nonsense. There's nothing I want but what I have—I am power."

"Power!" I said ironically. "And afraid of being driven out of a Swiss village! Afraid of death! Afraid of life! Power! Come and get your eyes opened and you may talk of power then!"

"Never. You drive me mad; you frighten me. Go!"

"Wait," I said. "I give you a few minutes to decide. You're on an awful road. You think you're safe because you keep your body out of it as far as you can. Fool! What strength has the body against the brain? And yours will weaken daily. You'll be dragged in. My consulting rooms are full of people like you, damned on earth whatever they may be hereafter. In a year or less you'll be open to man's justice, and when he gets you he does not spare you. You'll rot in a prison or asylum for the snake of the great cities that you are!"

"Never. Never. Go away," she said, and made as if to thrust me from her.

As the words left her lips two things happened. A man looked over the fence near us, glaring at her and muttering to himself. He shook his fist at her with a curse and went on, turning and cursing as he went. It was the father of Franz Rieder. And her mother broke from behind the roses and sobbing wildly fell upon her knees before her, clasping her about the body with arms of desperate love.

"For God's sake—for God's sake!" she cried, and could say no more. The girl was pale and shuddering with a fixed face above her. I cannot word that scene nor say how long it lasted. That is beyond me. I will only say that at the end she rose and stood looking at me, mocking, insolent, defiant, yet with a look like a shadowy rainbow in black skies.

"Well—perhaps it'll be a wow. There may be some fun. I'll give you six months and if you fail—"

Her mother had crept into the house weeping terribly. The dog sat and looked at us both bewildered.

"You promise?"

"I promise."

"Then go into the house and pack. We'll start for London tomorrow."

She went without a look behind her. There was stuff in the devil that might yet make her a flame of pure fire. After deep consideration I told the story to Biedermann, asked his prayers for the fight and received his promise. Why? Because every prayer of true faith and belief, let it come whence it will, is a draft on the power of the universe which will be honored.

I took them to London, settled the mother in rooms at Henford, the northern suburb, and put the girl Joyselle in the house of a doctor friend, a remarkable psychologist, who took in only one mental case at a time and had a house and garden perfectly adapted to his work. I gave him the fullest details, and she had not spared me on the way over, so that I knew of what I spoke. The arrangement was that I should visit her three times a week and oftener if necessary.

I shall never forget the flash of fury in her eyes when she found that another beside myself was to be concerned in her cure. She defied us both openly. If Eliot had not been seasoned and armed she would have got him under her influence before my eyes. As it was he watched her with coolest professional interest. The nurse was a stolid, unimaginative woman from whom she could have no hopes and who frankly regarded her as a lunatic. Her fury was terrible when she saw herself what she called trapped—but I rejoiced to see that its very violence exhausted the powers of evil concentration on which she worked. She was draining her own reserves with every shriek and struggle. If Eliot and I had ever disbelieved the stories of demoniacal possession (with a difference) we should have been converts now. There were times when a devil and no woman struggled, swore, yelled obscenities and blasphemies, on the ground before us. I have seen Eliot wipe his forehead, pale as ash, and say:

"Done in! The asylum is the only place for her."

And yet the brain was perfectly sound all the time.

But there was another side. When I told her she must either be searched for the drug or put upon her honor that she had none, she gave her word—and cheated. We knew it next day. After I had ordered the nurse to search her I turned on her and said the one word, "Coward!"

In a moment her face and neck were flooded with the crimson of deadly shame, as if the vessel of her heart were shattered by the insult—the only one that could touch the savagery in her, nurtured on the brutal lusts and greeds of modern life. A slur on her personal hardihood—her only ethic! She could not stand that. She made a dart for the window and would have flung herself out, but I was there before her. I had got the key to her cipher and used it.

She stared at me as I left, a dumb fury with loathing eyes.

I concentrated on her that night with all the power of all my knowledge and training, knowing that Biedermann would be at the same work in his own way where the stars stand sentinel on the high mountains. We had a fixed time together. Later I telephoned to Eliot. She was asleep, exhausted by her devilries.

It is impossible that I should give all the details of that long struggle with misdirected power and the degrading influences of modern brutality. Men of my profession *know;* others must take it on trust. Satan was casting out Satan with a vengeance and rending himself in the process. It was ten to one whether she could live through it.

Eliot dealt with her on material lines and the influence of a fine personality. I, on the psychic. I brought to bear upon her the oldest system of psychology known and focused its withering light on her aberration, and at first with no result whatever. She grew more hardened. She defied us, tried to bribe the servants, made cunning efforts at escape. I began to think we must give her the status of a certified lunatic, for the position was fast becoming untenable, and yet Eliot and I agreed that with her brain-power cool as ice it might be difficult to carry that matter through.

"She's so poisoned in every fiber that I see uncommonly little hope," Eliot said one day. "There are moments when I wish she could be reduced to imbecility and built up from the beginning if it were possible. Is there any hell hot enough for the devil who brought her to this!"

I agreed, but added:

"Look at the force in her! She's a perfect wellspring of misdirected psychic power. A cataract that destroys but may yet make light and warmth for the world. Don't despair. It's the fight of our lives, old man. Don't crab it."

He was stanch as steel. Besides he had moments of real pity and liking for her misspent courage. So one may sympathize with a rat showing its teeth in a corner in the last despairing struggle against death.

She would talk with me when I came—and that was a useful influence. I harped upon the note of courage and that always whipped her failing strength. She would not be beaten if she loathed the victory. But I began to realize the possibility of her death in the trenches. She looked a dying woman.

One day a very unexpected aid reached us. There was a high wall round the garden, unclimbable (for Eliot occasionally had certified lunatics), and a well-guarded lodge at the only entrance; therefore I cannot tell how this thing happened. As she and the nurse walked along the shady south walk at the end of the garden they saw a dog lying dead, as they thought, on the grass border. The head had been brutally clubbed, so far as we could judge. A West Highland terrier. The nurse said she fell on her knees beside it in a paroxysm not of pity but rage, threatening the brutes in language that made the woman's blood run cold. Finally she looked up.

"You damned fool, go and get stuff to wash him. No, I'll carry him in. Tell Eliot to come."

"Can't leave you!" the nurse retorted, with not unreasonable anger.

"I'm coming. Get on."

She lifted the dog in her arms with his blood dropping over her dress and carried him into the surgery. No animal had ever come near her since she went down to hell, nor would this have done so had he been conscious. She held him with fierce tenderness while Eliot removed a fragment of bone pressing on the brain and dressed and bandaged the little head. He was quick to see the points of the situation and, while he washed his hands afterwards, said artfully:

"Nurse is too busy to look after him. We'll send him to the Vet to take his chance."

I had better not record her words. She would nurse him herself. After a show of resistance it was granted. We had gained a powerful ally.

Again I must condense. I believe that but for that living interest she would never have fought through the agony of disusing the drug. Eliot and I appreciated this and left neither that nor any other way of help untried, but it was agony under which I say deliberately I think she would have died but that she was fighting for the dog's life. I gave that up more than, once; she never.

He was lying in a box one day when I came in and she had just dripped some milk and brandy through his teeth. Kneeling beside him she looked up quickly, and the picture impressed itself on my mind.

The dog breathed. That was about all, and you could not say much more for her. She was deadly ill. Her eyes burned with a waning fire in the long hollow eye-caverns into which they had sunk. All beauty was

gone. The face was more like a death's head than a
living one, every bone jutting through sickly skin
drawn taut over it. Her body was shrunk to such
emaciation and weakness that she lay on her bed all
day. What wonder? She was fighting on, but against
what odds! Nightly she walked through the hells of
insomnia, daily through the hells of tortured nerves.
Food and drink were like ashes in her mouth. I will
not swear that she always kept her promise to with-
hold her evil powers of concentration, but on the whole
she held them down. A strange and terrible sight.

Only one energy survived beside the fighting instinct—her passionate care for the dog. She called
him Darroch after the dog she had had as a child and
once gave a hint that she believed he had come back
to her. A piteous thing to see, and yet her one hope.
She would crawl to tend him. No one else must touch
him, and though she cried out for the drug while Eliot
allowed the graduated doses, the moment he told her
that stage was past she never asked for it again. I
have seen the blood run down her chin from the teeth-
marks on her lip, but she endured savagely. I could
respect the strength in her, if no more. There was
always that background to the horrors and degrada-
tions through which she dragged herself and us, and
of those I dare not speak out of my own profession.

Now as she crouched by the dog he stirred and
moaned. He laid a paw unconsciously on her hand as
she stroked his little breast. She bent over him and I
could not see her face. I said:

"He'll live. You've saved his life."

She said, so low that I could scarcely hear: "Must
he have died? Did I save him?"

"Certainly. You saved him."

Silence. I saw a dreadful trembling begin in the

poor bony hands and arms. It flowed like water up
her body, up into the rope-like throat muscles. It
reached the quivering nerves of her face, and shook
her fiercely like a storm from head to foot. She collapsed into a heap on the floor, sobbing wildly. Dry
rending sobs at first. Then merciful tears to relieve
the frightful tension. They poured down her face;
she was too weak to raise a hand to dry them, but it
was to my thought as if the granite of her heart had
softened and was pouring away in rivers of living
water. We laid her on the sofa, her heart's action so
feeble that if it had given up the struggle I could not
have wondered.

"Perhaps so best!" Eliot said, looking down upon
her as she lay, tears still pouring like thunder-rain down
the jutting bones of her face. Yet even then, when
the dog stirred and uttered a cry to his only friend,
in a moment she was dragging herself across the floor
to the rescue, half sitting, half crawling with her
hands. It reminded me of my horrible vision of her
crawling along the pools of moonlight in my room at
Geierstein. Like; but the width of heaven and hell
was between the two. We did not stop her. She reached
him, tended him, and then fainted. We thought she
was gone.

I draw near the end. A strong soul greatly sinning
is easier to redeem than a weak one when a certain
stage is past. We passed it that day. Darroch recovered first and was power and strength, for he loved
her—her first revelation of selfless Love, the Great
Seducer whose flute all must follow when they hear
its heart-piercing music. He would not leave her, so
it became worth the up-hill climb to strength that she
might hope one day to take him into the garden. But
it needed all our pull—including the dog's—to get her

through, and I would not have had her die then. She was not fit to face that problem before she had mastered this.

Then came the moment when by two minutes at a time I began to reverse her father's evil lessons and teach her the true approach to power. I dared not neglect it. She knew too much to be left with any weapons lying about which she had not been trained to handle. No dangerous vacuum must be there. Power she would have; then she must have the best.

I have never seen so apt a pupil. That was natural. I had only to reverse her learning, and the Way began to open. It interested her profoundly; in her clear, merciless mind the majesty of unalterable law presented itself as awe-striking and utterly desirable. She had the mathematical instinct and I put the right books into her hands, which connect it, for those who can see, with the ancient science now building up all her waste places. She leaped at that learning. The marshaled beauty of order presented itself to her. But, no— it would need a book to record the stages of evolution which she passed through, pressing steadily onward to her goal. She was fighting on my side now. Satan had cast out Satan, and how could his power stand?

I came one day to find her sitting in the garden with Darroch, now as healthy a little fellow as you would wish to see, at her feet. Her extraordinary education along psychic lines made communion between them possible in a way I have never seen before, but into that I have no space to enter. She lifted him and he lay in her lap while we talked.

"Tell me this," she said slowly. "Should I remember the things I did? For I can't. They're all blurring— they'll go. What about remorse? Is it another angle of my callousness?"

"Not it. It's a sign that the strength in you looks to the future. Why look back? You have tremendous reserves of power. You'll do great things yet. I back you against the world."

She smiled faintly, then:

"Do you remember the Maskim—the seven Assyrian devils? I'm like the Magdalen that had seven devils cast out of her. Mine are getting as unreal to me as dreams. Did hers, I wonder? I'd like to ask her. What happened to mine?"

"You know best. You cast them out yourself."

"No, not I. Love," she answered quickly. "Love's the conqueror whether you get it in a Christ or a little dog. I never knew such a thing existed, and now—I see nothing else. Who can stand against it? It sweeps you away like that great green glide of the waterfall at Geierstein. Nothing has a chance against it. It broke me."

At the beginning of the talk I should have dreaded that memory. Now we were swept on together. There was nothing to fear. She stroked the dog's coat gently while she spoke, and the movement of her hand was not more tranquil than her face and voice.

"I remember it all so well. No animal would ever look at me. It's strange, but I always wanted them to like me. I think now that was the only instinct that kept me human, though I could have tortured them one and all because they hated me. Not that I did. I was not devil enough for that. There are other things I shan't remember until I can laugh at their folly, and then perhaps they'll have gone right out of my head."

Her strength and curative power were astounding. I had seen what the world might call a miracle wrought under my eyes. To what shall we put a limit?

"And don't I know what I owe you? That's one of

the things I'll work for—to be *your* victory. But I owe more to this than even to you. You are Wisdom. *This* is Love."

She lifted the little dog, looking into his eyes and he into hers, and added slowly:

"For in the clay of man is kneaded the blood of God."

Is it worth while to give any outer details of her triumph? Scarcely. The world knows her name but only a tithe of her greatness. The story can be told thus far, but like all true stories the best is hidden and there are no words for it.

Many Waters
Cannot Quench Love

THE STORY I TELL IS SO STRANGE THAT THERE ARE times when I could hardly credit it myself but that Tyliol is still alive to assure me it is true. Not that I ask him—God forbid—but while he exists I know that at any moment I can go up the hill to where he lives in the lonely bungalow with the swaying palms about it—the fronds creaking monotonously in the dry wind. I can stand by the veranda in the starlight and call "Tyliol" as she used to do and hear the matting curtain before the door creak also as he pushes it back and stands there. We would stare at each other and never a word said of the name in both our hearts before he went back in bitter silence to his solitude. But I would know—he also. For Lilavati's chair is empty.

He was a planter in Ceylon—tea and rubber—at the Gaunt-Willock Estate in the Upper Country; and I had come out to learn my business, a creeper—as they call them there—paying something solid for the pleasure of hearing Tyliol damning my ignorance ten times a day. Of course I hadn't been there twenty-four hours before I knew he drank like a fish, was a hard-mouthed bully and a man that should no more have had men and women in his power than one of the two big elephants that pulled and hauled on the land. Far less for the strange humanity of the big, gentle beasts struck some deep-down notion of com-

mon understanding in me. I've seen Dilshankar, the
biggest bull elephant, lurch silently down the track
where the carts, each drawn by a pair of tiny brown
bulls, went up and down almost night and day, and
curl his trunk about a coolie sodden with arrack and
lay him carefully out of danger in the ferny hollow.
There would certainly be leeches. There might be a
cobra or two, but to Dilshankar that was all in the
day's work and he knew that at all events there would
be no Tyliol, more pitiless to drunken coolies than
either, especially when he was half seas over himself.

You must understand there are estates and estates
in Ceylon. There's the gentlemanly kind with a handsome house and *pukka* drawing-room and big veranda
with handsome chairs and a highroad outside where
the cars roll up from Colombo or Kandy and the *appu*
serves a jolly good dinner, and pretty girls out from
England and Australia chipper on the veranda with
long drinks and cigarettes and admire the green glittering diamonds of the fireflies eddying over the cannas
in the garden when the sun drops.

A man can easily ask one of them to stay with him
there for good and help to run the show, and if she's
a fool she takes the risk and there's a white-satin
wedding at Colombo and "the Voice that breathed o'er
Eden," and the place is Eden all right, only something
has gone badly wrong with the Voice. Women should
think twice before they marry men who have to live
in the tropics and run the Dravidian brother, for sometimes he gets on their nerves badly, especially to the
accompaniment of pegs and endless cigarettes, and
when a man's nerves go dotty so near the Equator he
isn't always nice to live with, and if the overture was
angelic flutes and harps the opera isn't.

And mind you those estates are the pick of the

basket. Ours wasn't. It was forty miles from anywhere, which perhaps would have mattered less if there had been a road, but the nearest road was four miles away, down hill by the track I have spoken of, and that wouldn't have mattered either but for the sweeping tropical rains that kept it either waist-deep in mud or baked by the grilling sunshine into brick ridges. Both gave me a twinge when I saw the patient little bulls pulling gamely up the hell of a place until they dropped often enough, and the coolies would rub chillies in their eyes or light a fire under them to make them stagger up and on. I put a stop to that and to the further activities of one of the men, but Tyliol never interfered—in that way.

In others he did. I was told later that if I had had the advantage of a talk with young Morrison, my predecessor at the Gaunt-Willock, I never would have signed on. But I believe nothing would have stopped me. Morrison was at the Galle Face Hotel the night I slept there after landing. He sat, almost touching my elbow, at the next table by one of the windows that look on the rolling surf at the bottom of the garden. We sized each other up; and I simply saw a fellow with a twitching white face and dry lips and thought, "Too many cocktails and girls," and never guessed that a talk with him would have sent me back on the boat he was going home on next day. Hadn't so much as a hunch who he was. If I'd known, it would have put the lid on an experience that made the Gaunt-Willock, Tyliol, the hell of it all, worth while. In the fright of hearing Morrison's bleatings I'd have chucked my chance and I wouldn't sell that chance now for all the gold that ever was coined in India. So it was to be and would have been even if Morrison had let himself go as he did to others.

The day I went up to the Gaunt-Willock Estate and it dawned on me what Tyliol was and that I was to share the bungalow with him I own I didn't recognize my blessings—they were so uncommonly well disguised. It was a damned uncomfortable house, low and dark and snaky, and the furniture the cheapest Colombo brew, creaking and sticky with new varnish.

The *podian*—which is to say the boy—cringed and slunk with a wary black eye over the shoulder suggestive of a frequent well-aimed boot. There was no sign of the softening influence of a woman's presence anywhere—but that I didn't expect. Not so much as a vase of flowers, though outside they hung the world with tropical beauty. The dinner was the wateriest soup and the toughest curried hen that ever teeth stuck in, and as I don't take kindly to spirits and there was nothing else, lime-juice and lukewarm water completed the banquet. After dinner Tyliol lit his pipe and hunched down the veranda steps into the dark, and it took some pluck to sit down there under the glare of a swinging kerosene lamp darkened by clouds of mosquitoes, to square my elbows and write to my mother in London that Tyliol was a reserved sort of fellow (he had spoken scarcely two words at dinner) who would no doubt be a topping sort when one got to know him better. I garnished my tale also with the usual palms and flowers and spectacular hills and so forth, and felt all the time like a convict with the prison door slammed on him, and the more so because I had been a bit of an artist in London, a lover of all such beauty as came my way, and I had expected better things from Ceylon.

I wrote until pretty late, and was wondering whether it was Tyliol's habit to doss down in the jungle with the cobras and jackals, when I heard steps coming up the garden path. Light quick steps that didn't sound like Tyliol and interested me so far that I leaned forward and stared into the dark.

Not a thing could I see. The violent light of the lamp made a dazzling patch of the veranda and a wall of blackness beyond, lit only by the glittering pin-points of fireflies flitting low. But in the dark came heavier steps from another direction this time and a halt and Tyliol's voice snarling like a dog at an invisible someone.

"So you've come back, have you? And stayed a day longer than you said you would. I can tell you the next time you go to see your aunt you'll stay there for keeps and see how you like life in the coolie lines. Temple's here and we had a damn bad dinner and—"

A clear ringing voice—a woman's—cut across his like a whip-lash.

"I'll go when I must and come back when I like and if you turn me adrift plenty will be glad to pick me up. And any damn dinner is good enough for a sot like you and the man that's fool enough to come here. Let me pass!"

I heard a step now, and light as a leaf on a wind a girl in white ran up the veranda steps and halted before me.

Beautiful. She blazed on me in the coarse light of the kerosene lamp swinging above us. I couldn't analyze her or itemize her looks in that flashing moment. She was beauty—no more, no less. She had the end of a white scarf flung over her head and her eyes flamed under it. It seemed a long minute that we stood and I saw that though I am a tall man she topped my shoulder. Then Tyliol hunched up the steps and lurched and nearly fell, recovered himself heavily and stood behind her.

"Good little boys should be off to roost before twelve," he said thickly. "But since you're here—this is Lilavati."

It would have been ridiculous to call her Miss Anybody or attempt any ghost of the proprieties. She was Lilavati, and the whole story was told in the look of dominant proprietorship she flung at him and the sullen mastery of his "touch-if-you-dare" stare at me. "Stand off at your peril," it said as plain as print.

Of course it was to be expected. A man doesn't live alone in a God-forsaken bungalow in a God-forsaken jungle with only the dark men and their women and children herded in the lines where they have their homes and not try to make some sort of companionship for himself with some sort of woman. But—Lilavati! It was not her beauty that knocked me off the deep end with astonishment, though that was enough to do it in all conscience. It was her being English in spite of the Indian name. In a perfect fog I tried to think why an English girl—a raging, tearing beauty like that!— should have taken up with Tyliol and the Gaunt-Willock Estate—a girl that might have blazed on London or New York like a comet and been a gold-digger of the best either in the marriage market or the other. A best seller anywhere, anyhow! What in the devil's name had brought her down to this?

She walked up to me and held out her hand frankly and unashamed. "Glad to see you. Sorry we butted in with a row first time you saw me. I'm not always such a hell-cat as I seem. As a matter of fact I've got to hold my own you see, so maybe it's as well you should know it sooner as later. Sorry the dinner was a washout. Have some bread and cheese?"

I shook my head feebly and she turned on her master.

"You get to by-by. You've had more than you can carry!"

His eyes were glazing with sleep and drink. He glowered at her owlishly and slipped without a word into the long chair beside us. In a moment more he was as sound off as a church.

I looked from him to her. "Shouldn't we get him to bed somehow? Don't they say the night air—"

"He often sleeps in the veranda. The podian wouldn't touch him for gold and I can't. So he takes his chance. Stop a sec! The podian's gone off to bed and I'm dry with thirst. I must get some water from the filter."

She pulled the scarf off her head and went into the house. I was alone with Tyliol who was already beginning to snore like a pig. Now I could recollect and describe her beauty to myself.

It was worth it.

Her hair was dark brown with a red glow in it. Her great eyes green as the fire-fly diamonds and as bright, starry in dark clouds of lashes. You never see such lashes west of Suez, nor, I think, such richly curved lips, crimson as pomegranate buds. Her nose was haughty and well-bred as a princess's should be if she had her rights, and her figure in the clinging white dress swayed like a mermaid's to the arch of a green wave. Daylight might bring disillusionment but now—words, thoughts, failed me. Except that I felt her to be as hard and bright as the snap of a steel spring in spite of all the flaming beauty, which would have leaned to the sensuous side if the lips had been fuller.

I stood waiting and Tyliol snored. She came back presently with a little tray and two glasses of water on it and set it on the little table and looked at me dangerously.

"I don't offer men drink. I know too much. It makes them brutes one way or the other and I'm not sure which I like least. Yes—I am! The water's clean. It won't give you enteric."

She drank thirstily, and her lips shone like wet coral, then set the glass down, and pulled a sit-up chair for herself and motioned me to a long one. But I preferred to sit on the end of it. There was no ease in her company or hard clear voice. I felt something like a new disease had up for analysis.

"We're alone. He won't wake till six in the morning. I'd better introduce myself and let you know the worst."

"But is it safe for him to stay here all night? Leeches—snakes?"

The look she cast at him was not unkindly but utterly superior; she let it fall like a ray of frosty sunlight.

"He'll do. He often does it. Let sleeping dogs lie. Won't you light up?"

I lit a cigarette and offered her one. She took it.

"Now for a nice little Sunday-school story! I've got to explain myself," she said. There was a pause and the fireflies dipped and flickered in the dense branches of the tree outside. The coolies were all asleep down at the lines. A dog howled, Tyliol snored, and except for such music the world was hers and mine.

"Didn't I see what was in your head? You couldn't hide it—and you didn't think it very nice. I can relieve you so far. I'm not English—I'm a mongrel, a half-breed, and indeed I should bless my stars because Mr. Tyliol has condescended to—to look after me. Now you know!"

Her tone forbade any reply and I felt she wanted the stage to herself anyhow. She went on:

"Lilavati, indeed! I've got a fine English name if I wanted to use it. So had my mother. She was Clarice Beryl Sumana, a Tamil woman, and she hadn't any surname, for her mother had been a dancing-girl at a temple in the south—first married to a tree in the funny little way they have and then took to drink and a Frenchman. So you see my grandfather was French. And my mother was pretty. I remember that all right, and she took up with a planter here. He was English. She did the best she could by giving me a grand English name. It was all she had to give. I'm Iris Violet Lilavati. No surname of course. Didn't I tell you I was a mongrel!"

She stopped and drank thirstily again and went on, not in the least conscious of me as anything more than a listener for something locked up which had to pour out of her at last. The strangest situation. Something awful in it too. The quiet night and her hard voice and the European blood in her crying out for its shame and rights against the other darker blood, like something protesting in a barred prison never to be escaped.

"I say," I said; "don't tell me if you don't want to. What does it matter?"

She flashed an angry look at me.

"I do want to. No false pretenses for me if we've got to live together. I was a stray dog when my father went home and she died, and I was packed off to an orphan school. An English teacher there took me off to her house for a kind of slavey when I was twelve, but I'll do her the justice to say she gave me lessons now and again. But I couldn't drudge forever and I got into a Colombo shop when I was fourteen and big for my age, and Tyliol came along with his wife one day to choose her a new hat, and when she went home he asked me out here and I came. That's all. Forever and ever. Amen."

The ugly matter-of-fact way she told the thing made it more hideous, and I was too ignorant of the country to see that she couldn't have done better and might have done much worse. I thought I saw perversity in the hard bright bow of her lips and metallic luster of her eyes and, after all, what could a girl be but a beast who would take up with Tyliol? Beauty or no beauty she gave me a physical shudder at the moment like the scream of a pencil on a slate. Something in me winced, for her story seemed to impinge on my own life like a raw stain. How could I stick out living with her and Tyliol in this pit of a place? She made the thing impossible.

She read my thought like a witch and shifted into a kind of ironical humility that I liked even less.

"My old aunt down at Kilmalcolm lines was a pretty girl once. She's a hag now picking tea. I go down once in a blue moon and see her—duty you know, family feeling—and I just think, 'Will it be ten or twenty years before I look like that?' There's a deep line like a snake's mouth from each nostril to her chin, and her throat hangs like a brown leather bag. Sometimes I see those very lines in my own face when Tyliol cuts up rough. Oh no, we're really not nice people to know! I'd get out if I was you—good and quick too! It isn't pretty here for a nice English boy with brown eyes and a taste for good behavior."

She pointed to Tyliol slouched in his chair. His looks didn't commend his way of life.

I certainly thought of retreat. Beauty isn't always enough to hold one with everything pulling the other way. She propped her lovely dimpled chin on her two hands, elbows on the table, and stared at me, her eyes green as a cat's in lamplight and laughed unpleasantly.

"Well, go! I can tell you you'll not like it when he biffs me because Ramsamy has spilt the sugar in the

soup. Pack up your troubles in the old kit bag and
be off tomorrow!"

Her tone was rasping. I would have gone straight
back to my room and begun the packing if I had known
where to go, but I was so strange to the island yet that
I hadn't a notion what to do and precious little money
to do it on. You can't live for nothing in Ceylon. I
knew that already. But still I stood up and was beginning some commonplace that matched her repelling
voice and face, when suddenly she broke down and
began to cry and in the strangest way.

Not a muscle of her face changed or altered, but the
tears brimmed and overflowed like water running down
a window-pane. It was a horrid moment. It took my
heart in a most painful grip, awaking all sorts of
strange tendernesses for misery—the feeling you have
when you see a starving dog, a bleeding horse. Her
tears were like blood from a grievous wound. I made
a step forward.

"Don't, don't!" I cried. "I didn't know you minded
it and that made it awful." I was very young. "It's
easier now. You can't stop here. Get away tomorrow.
I shan't stop long myself. It's a devil of a place."

She looked up with wet eyes, the lashes clung together in little points; there was a sob in her voice like
a child's.

"That does me good. Don't bother about me. I
wanted someone to pity me, for no one ever did. All
the same, I can't go. There isn't a door in the island
open to me. I'm a"—she used a frightfully plain word
—"and a mongrel not worth the bread that's wasted on
me. If I went—well, you know the only thing I could
do, and if it wasn't Colombo it would be Cairo, and
that's a hell for girls like me. The whole world is, if
you come to that. For you see—"

I found myself saying, "Tell me!" almost breathless. Her face had taken on such a quivering loveliness that it was as if a satiric mask had slipped and left the real woman behind visible for the first time. My eyes clung to her, but she was not listening. She went on:

"I've had offers down in Colombo but there's something in me that sickens at it—vomits! It's a hard life up here, but I keep him straighter than he'd be without me. That's how I pay my way. Other things too— if I told you—"

She hesitated on a long sigh. I came a little nearer but did not venture to touch her hand though I was drawn to do it. She got up as if to end the audience and stood facing me as I said again: "Tell me!"

"Not yet. Never, most likely. But there's things here —wonderful. You watch, and if I see you have eyes in your head—" Again she hesitated then added wistfully: "May be you'd better up-anchor tomorrow all the same! You're but young—all said and done!"

"I'm older than I look. Much older than you. You're a slip of a girl."

"Nineteen, but the dark blood in me is older than that. Well, good night, and thanks for favors received."

She reached up and turned the wick down lower, and the stench of kerosene filled the room like a wave.

"And you won't let me tumble him into bed?"

"Not I. He'd have our lives tomorrow. He's not to know you saw him."

"But the leeches and—"

"Leeches your granny! D'ye s'pose I leave him alone here? They'd suck the blood out of him until he was a dead waxwork in the morning. No—when my lord sleeps out I sleep out too."

"Do you mean you sit up all night with that hog?"

She shook her head smiling and pointed to the door that led into the house to bid me take myself off. The veranda was filled with shadows, her face white in a lost gleam of moonlight like a woman's drowning in a sea of blackness of the vast night outside.

Tyliol moved uneasily, and the jackals were crying now, that queer thin cry that slips between flesh and bone like the blade of a knife. We seemed out in the middle of it in the veranda with the dying light still marking us out to all the world and the black veil of night covering all the world. So I went in and left her, full of feelings rather than thoughts that I can't describe even now.

I knew next day, and after, that I had penetrated into some rare mood which I must not expect as my right. Tyliol had the head to be expected, and his temper was simply obscene. Least said soonest mended on that point. Lilavati had seen to the grub. It was plain but good enough, and the podian and cook ran like riggers when she called or gave an order. The bungalow was not particularly clean, but that was a thing quite outside Tyliol's sphere of interest and therefore hers. Watching, I saw she met him at all points he demanded, but not a step beyond. You would have expected for instance with all the gorgeous blooms outside that there would be jars of flowers in the veranda and dining-room—the words sound so stately that I could laugh as I write them! Not a bit of it.—Not a flower, a leaf, anywhere to soften the harsh ugliness. Tyliol never noticed a flower. That was enough. They never intruded.

As a matter of fact he never noticed anything as far as I could see. He would go over the Estate but very seldom came near me, and I never knew a man of fewer words. He lived shut up in a kind of sulky silence. Still, for all his shortcomings I must own he knew his business. The place was run well, as far as I could see, in spite of his brutalities to the coolies, though when and how he looked after it I couldn't for the life of me say. This made it easy for me to learn my business and I did learn it and that's about all I could say for Tyliol.

In the same way she fed the coolies' miserable dogs, bandaged their wounds, healed their mangy coats with stuff the Vet sent her, brought humanity and sympathy and some sort of order into the tumbling, yapping dog-world of the Gaunt-Willock Estate, but never a dog came near the bungalow though you could see she loved them. They would follow her like shadows to the edge of the garden, hungry-eyed, submissive, as the outcaste dogs of Ceylon—the Untouchables of animal life—are always. Then she would stand a minute there and look at them in a way they understood, wave a forbidding hand, and the lean pack would turn and go slowly down the hill again like things deprived.

I came on her one day about a month after my coming as they trooped off disconsolately and she stood watching them—beautiful as Circe with her swine—not that I would compare even those poor souls with swine. They had the good dog-soul in them in spite of their rags and tatters and their being the wreckage of their kind and anything but fit companions for a girl. The sun was powerful, but she never felt the heat like a European and stood under a hibiscus bush with the scarlet pendent flowers and glossy leaves hanging behind her like a rich illumination in a Middle-Age psalm-book. They were crimson jewels and she burned in the midst of them with splendid color like a veiled lamp. She had nothing to shield her head, and her hair was blood-amber in the glow. Indeed she dazzled me with her beauty and a kind of sumptuousness, like the swooning perfume of the ivory-white temple-flowers that grew all over the garden on their gnarled and silver trees. She had a cotton dress of the tawny red that the coolie women love to wear with their heavy earrings and metal collars, and that stung a kind of anger in me. Why should she cheapen herself to their gaudy savage taste? But I left that for the moment.

"You shouldn't mix yourself up with those beasts. There's a lot of rabies going about everywhere, Thambiraja tells me; and everyone of them should be shot. I'm willing to do it myself."

She looked at me coolly.

"You can shoot me first if you take to gunning. If rabies comes it comes, and if any of my dogs get it I'll attend to it myself, thank you all the same."

She was a good shot. She had a way of practicing with a light gun of Tyliol's on marks she put up for herself—I supposed for want of anything more lively to do, for there were no books in the bungalow. I had won so little of her confidence since that first night on the veranda that I suppose there was a touch of jealousy upon me. I had looked for much, but she held off steadily and went her way and was mostly busy in ways I never saw or understood.

"I believe on my soul you really like those brutes," I said unbelievingly.

Her eyes drove defiance at me. "I love them! They're mine and I'm theirs. They shouldn't exist. They're a pest to others and nothing to be decent about to themselves. So am I. Well—we like each other, we pests and miseries! We don't ask you to join the party. Let us alone, good gentleman!—that's all we ask!"

She put on the gipsy's whining tone to a nicety and held out her hand as if for money. I was furious. I

had meant nothing but sympathy, but she always flung
it back in my face. If I had thought the mystery was
open to me since that first night I was much mistaken.
All I knew was that she kept Tyliol in whatever sort
of order was possible to him and kept herself to herself. Beyond that, what she did or felt day or night
I never knew. Ignorance curbed my anger and made
me cautious now. I said as kindly as I could:

"You should have a decent dog for your own. It
would be a kind of companion for you in the house.
Say the word and I'll get you a good fox terrier.
Thambiraja knows of one—"

"No, thank you. What? And have Tyliol make it
a target for running kicks when he gets the jim-jams?
Not me! Besides, before very long I'm going away."

"Away?" I said blankly. The sunshine slipped like
water from every glittering leaf and was gone. Had
a cloud come over it? The world turned gray. She had
seemed as fixed a part of everything as the group of
palms about the bungalow, as the coolies, Tyliol—
everything that made the Gaunt-Willock Estate.

I stared at her confounded:

"You can't. Tyliol'll go to the devil."

"I should have thought he'd arrived by now," she
answered drily. "However, cheer up! I can quite understand you wouldn't want him on top of the other
comforts of the Gaunt-Willock. Who are Gaunt and
Willock, I wonder, when they're at home! But I'm only
going for a month, and I'm not going for six weeks
yet. Just a little holiday. One doesn't want to give in
to the luxury of living here always."

I passed over the irony. "Lilavati, we can't do without you. You'll surely come back?"

It had come on me with a rush how necessary she
was, how everything turned on her, every rag and

crumb of decency in the house was what she contrived
and planned and fought for. I couldn't face the life
without her—no, not for a day. Alone with Tyliol?
Never!

"Oh, I'm bound to come back fast enough! Where
else am I to go? Cairo?"

The bitter jeer of her tone! How could I get at her
behind the smoke screen she made for herself? The
smoke got into my throat and made my eyes smart
and of Lilavati I knew nothing. I spoke with what
dignity I could, and was priggish, not dignified:

"You hurt me very much. I hoped for something
like confidence and friendship between us, and one
could do with a little of both in this hell of a place.
Yet it's beautiful too, beautiful!—if it weren't for
Tyliol.

"Poor Tyliol!" she said with a half-smile which I
couldn't interpret. "Yes, he's not exactly an attraction.
But you know, Temple, the life here isn't so bad all
through, is it? The coolies are decent fellows often,
and the women—I couldn't help liking them if I tried.
And the babies— But, no, it's no good yet. The dogs
are gentlemen every one of them, though they do wear
shabby coats. I like it better than—Cairo!"

I could see that something about Cairo, some word,
some shame, had left an ineffaceable stain on her mind.
She had seen in a dream of horror the beautiful jeweled, painted butterflies dancing with men of every
nationality on God's earth—the property of each and
every one of them at a price. Cairo was her notion of
hell, a blaze of gold and drink, and jewels and lust
and bitterest self-contempt. The brutalities of Tyliol
were clean compared with that. I knew Port Said and
was inclined to agree with her.

Suddenly it struck me like a revelation that "fallen

woman" as she was—though indeed she could not have
had far to fall from—Lilavati was living a fine sort
of life here. The house revolved round her and she
ran it somehow. She ran Tyliol too, as the finely
tempered machine of a car obeys a drunken driver's
hand and forges ahead in spite of him. Me—she ran
me. I knew who went through my things and saw to
keeping them in order. Who guided the fractious cook
and podian? The dogs? The coolies? It wasn't until
she said she was going that I thought the stars would
fall on the Gaunt-Willock Estate and do it in if Lilavati went. I looked at the cotton frock that had vexed
me. Made by herself—I had heard the sewing machine whirring late into the night—it ran into precious
few rupees—poor little gaudy gown!

And she might have been driving down Bond Street
now in her Rolls-Royce with diamonds like swinging
lamps at her ears, and men to obey her whims as if
they mattered very much more than any divine de-
crees—Tyliol's drudge, my housekeeper, mender and
maker. That was a moment of revelation.

"Lilavati," I said, and something choked in my
throat, " do you know what I think of you?"

"Quite well, thank you."

"What?"

"A worthless good-for-nothing slut of a Eurasian.
A blot on the decency of the Gaunt-Willock. A—"

"That's nonsense. You've been reading cheap lower
middle-class novels. Wash! Why don't you read stuff
worth while for the lamps in your eyes? No—that's
not what I think. You're beautiful—you know that
yourself, don't you?"

She had no fear I was love-making and answered
quietly, "I don't know," but a little surprised for all
that.

"Well, I think you're the whitest girl I ever knew. Sheer white, right through to the bone. I think the way you stick by this stinking leaking ship is white through and through. I don't know how you do it, but it's done."

I have never seen a more amazed look than the one she turned upon me.

"Have you by any chance gone mental?" she said. "For there's an asylum for idiots somewhere in Ceylon, though I can't say where exactly. You know jolly well I stick to the ship because if I go overboard it's deep water—and sharks. I stick to it because there's nothing else."

"I know that all right. You've rubbed it in. But you could stay and let things rip. You don't do that. You keep things going. D'you think I don't know what you do with the coolies and their women? D'you think I don't know the Gaunt-Willock wouldn't hold together a week if you didn't pray and preach and canoodle them into doing what you want? They'd have knifed Tyliol long ago, but for that. And I don't blame them."

There was a long silence and the palm fronds creaked overboard. I shall never hear that dry sound on a breeze without thinking of Lilavati. She was pondering deeply—her mind fixed on something beyond me. At last she raised her head. I noticed then for the hundredth time the beautiful direct look in her eyes. They were so lovely that they had held me away from what was behind them, but now I saw a something lovelier still.

"I believe I'll make a clean breast of it," she said and paused, striking her shoe lightly with a little stick she carried, then went on gravely. A mood I had never seen before.

"D'you remember the night you came? I knew then you were decent but I thought you might be a fool—they often are! Well, I said then I'd tell you things some day if I saw you had eyes. Now I'm going to make a bit of the business clear. There's lots more when I know you can see more."

A changed Lilavati. The sunlight spattering through the leaves made her radiant in a shower like rain. I might have been beauty-blinded but for the feeling of being up against something more—much more—important and gripping. I can't explain it—let it go at that!

"Well, it's true. I do hold the show together. It's *my* show. It's been gradually slipping into my hands the last three years. Tyliol's going a bit mental with drink and I've got to do it. We used to go through the accounts and business together until I got the hang of it and now most times he doesn't even know he hasn't done it himself. I make him think he has. I write letters in his name to Gaunt and Willock—I've forged it times out of mind and he doesn't know and they don't know, and they say all's going fine and the profits were never so good. Of course I know the rise in rubber has helped me, and all the world's drinking tea now. . . . Persia never used to take a pound and now she's drinking tea—Persia's half killing herself with it. We can't grow it quick enough, and if we had twice the land we'd do four times as well. I'm rubbing that in on Gaunt and Willock. You know it. Naturally all this isn't a picnic, for Tyliol has lucid intervals and he goes clean off the deep end when he knows he wants to grip and can't, and can't even remember what happens. And he's awful to the coolies—you know that. But you see I have their blood in me and they know it. I can talk their lingo for it's mine. Besides. Tyliol doesn't know, but I've raised their screw to what Barwood and Stolz are paying on the Mirandola Estate and that's the show place in the island; and the poor fellows and their women are as proud as proud that they're worth it. And they are! Gaunt and Willock approved and they're getting more than their money's worth in the return in work!"

To say I was confounded is to say nothing. The sunshine and glittering palms and the girl swam about me in dazzling confusion. For I had known Tyliol was a brute—a damned cruel foul-mouthed brute, but I had said to myself that he had a grip on things for all that. If he used the coolies like beasts he paid them like men, and there were allotments of money for their poor wedding beanos and for women in child-birth, and the kiddies had their whack once a day of good heartening food that didn't swell their stomachs like the green stuff they ate, but put blood into them. And the houses were whitewashed and decent as far as could be. Mind you, this wasn't cossetting. It was what the decent estates do, but decency and Tyliol had so little in common that you never would have suspected that point of view in him. Still, I gave him credit for being a beast but a just beast and wondered he never went down to the lines to see how well his notions worked. They were a long step away, to be sure, but still I wondered. And now—

"Do they know?" I gasped when I could speak.

"Not they!" she said scornfully. "I declare I thought you'd more sense. No—they stand what they do from him because they think he's a heart of gold, or whatever you call it, under a rough skin. He'd have been knifed unless."

"But Gaunt and Willock send authorizations and approvals?"

"The letters go through *me!*" she said grimly. "Or rather they don't. And I type Tyliol's answers, and he signs them when he's drunk or else I sign them for him. All I wonder is what'll happen if either of them come along this way!"

My mind was sweeping through all the aspects of the case, moral and otherwise.

"But they're paying the brute for work he doesn't do. If—"

"They're paying him less than the managers of the Mirandola get—a jolly sight less—and if they weren't satisfied— Look here!"

She pulled a paper out of the little red bag she carried and read out a sentence.

"We know and fully realize from all your information, corroborated by knowledge of other estates, that we have every reason for the fullest recognition and gratitude for the smooth working and fine results you give us— etc., etc. Any steps you may take for giving the coolies due comfort has our approval, etc., etc."

"I've lots of that stuff," she said, snapping the bag on the papers. "You know as well as I do that's true. We're doing right well here. And when you've learned your business and come into the accounts you'll understand it better. Now, which of the Ten Commandments am I breaking?"

In a maze I tried to consider, for when you come to forgery and lying you've got to think a bit to get the landmarks clear. But not one occurred to me at the moment except about keeping the Sabbath Day holy and that didn't click. I stared at her.

"D'you mean to say you run the whole show? give the orders for stuff and everything?"

She answered carelessly: "As you see. Tyliol rides about and blethers and Fernando and Perera bring the

indents all written out to him for confirmation and I—
confirm them. Or don't. But they only think he's
thought it over when it's different."

"But he's drinking more heavily. How long will it
last?"

"God knows. I don't. But what I think is—you must
be learning to boss the show. Suppose I wasn't here.
Well, you must be able to step in when he drops."

I saw that. I saw the whole scheme—splendid! Then
some decency in me raised its head.

"It's you should have it, Lilavati. Not a soul else
deserves it."

The scorn in her eyes!

"I? A girl? A Eurasian? A woman that's been forg-
ing and cheating? It's you or a raw manager out from
England—if I drop. And I've done things here—well,
I'd like them to go on. Even the dogs get their grub
every day."

I knew that. I had seen a big pot boiling down at
the lines with scraps that came from the house in
buckets and scraps the coolies threw in when human
ingenuity could get no more out of them and the bones.
And there was poonac in the brew, and the dogs fed
once a day and they were more decent than the gaunt
skeletons elsewhere. I had liked our coolies for it. But
it was Lilavati. I declare I forgot she was beautiful.
Other things put it in the shade. I said simply:

"What can I do, general? I'm under orders!"

"Learn to take hold. Don't slack a minute. Tyliol
may last two years. Then take on; you can!"

"And you?"

"I haven't thought that out yet. Don't the Christians
say 'sufficient unto the day'?"

That struck a new note.

"Aren't you a Christian, Lilavati? What are you?"

You see I wanted to get at the dynamo that worked her.

"Guess!" she said. Then laughing, "Little boys mustn't be curious. I've got my own ways. Now, you know the ropes. I couldn't have kept this up when you knew more and you'll help to hold things straight."

She waved her hand and went up the steep way to the house and I stood there lost in amazement. The courage—the dash of the thing! The clean certitude with which she had gone at it and conquered. I had a lot to chew on.

Business took me down to the lines that day, and I noted as I had never noted before that the children were well-fed—beautiful dark, straight little slips. The women had food to eat to hearten them for their work in the tea and rubber plantations. I looked into the shaded *crêche* with its open-spaced roof and walls, where babies were swinging in hammock cloths from a bar of wood. Their contented voices filled the air like the little noises pigeons make when they preen their feathers in sunshine. A woman of the Vellala caste tended them, for that was the highest caste on the Gaunt-Willock and even the coolie mothers objected to a woman of lower caste handling their babies. I noted another thing I had thought sensible in Tyliol. Water was piped to two taps in the lines, and the women coming back tired with work had only a step to fill their vessels. I knew at Kilmallock and other estates they had a long walk before they could fill them and come back heavily loaded.

Up to this I had envied the creepers on the Kilmallock and Mirandola shows. They had decent fellows at the head and a certain amount of society and amusement and so on. There had been times when I was thirsting to chuck the Gaunt-Willock and get back to the decencies. But now—I thanked my stars it had been impossible. It's a good moment in a man's life when he sees a clear way before him and knows what has to be done and that he can do it. And who could fail with that girl ahead? Not I. Not any man with anything more than the spirit of a rabbit! People threw mud at Tyliol but they all owned up that he knew how to run a tea and rubber estate. So he did! I had my cue and took it. He was the figurehead, but she and I were captain and crew.

That day a man came over from Mirandola. He was riding and leaned over from a fine chestnut gelding to speak to me. I had envied that mount. I didn't envy the bloomingest millionaire that ever lived now.

"I say, Temple," he said, in his smooth well-bred English tones that sounded like home, "I haven't time to go round hunting up your boss and you'll do as well. You know he has written about a lorry instead of using all those confounded bulls and carts—"

I didn't know, but smiled intelligently.

"Well—his notion to have a joint motor lorry with you and us and Kilmallock, to collect all our stuff and take it straight down, has caught on. He said very truly that the wastage in these bulls on these damn roads is awful and it's not only a brutal business but it would pay us to be clear of the contractors. Tell him we're on, and Sigerson has all the lorry specifications."

"I'll tell him. He'll be awful pleased. He was calculating we'd save a lot if we pooled on that."

The lie slipped off my tongue like butter and was well received. Keston laughed:

"Your man would be an ace if he didn't lift his little finger so often. As it is his show is very decently worked. I wish our lines were as good as yours. Can't get the boss to see it. We get crimps about the place that you never see, I bet."

"No—the crimps give us a wide berth!" I said, and it was true. "Our coolies know when they're well off."

He rode off whistling—awfully well turned-out, and not a thought of envy did I send after him. Something in me was shouting aloud for glee. I walked like a king under the palms to find her and didn't know—not then—that among her other little industries she was making a man of me and out of poor enough stuff all said and done.

She clapped her hands when I told her.

"That ends *one* little hell here," she said. "I'd an inkling they'd jump at it. You'll see some fun at tiffin."

I did. The talk was indifferent and chiefly between her and me, Tyliol throwing in a few heavy interjections and drinking a jolly sight more than he ate. He was about half seas over. Presently she said:

"Mirandola and Kilmallock are getting a move on. I heard it awhile ago. What d'you think's up?"

"Some blasted foolery, you bet. New-fangled stuff that cuts no ice with me."

"Not when there's money in it?"

He pricked up his ears. "What's that?"

"Oh, nothing to write home about. Only the contractors have been doing them in with the bulls, and they're going to have a lorry between them. Send the stuff straight down and have no more bother with the contractors."

"Well, I'm not going to do it here! I bet it's blooming humane rot about the bulls. Let 'em work—what are they there for?"

"That's true!" she said laughing. "Who cares for a bull? But there's money in it. Fernando heard they'd worked it out at a save of ten per cent and more on haulage charges. And what with lame bulls and sore necks and drunken carters it's enough to drive you mad the way it is. I'd like to see the contractors' faces when they know Mirandola and Kilmallock are through with them!"

That was the right note. He chuckled:

"By George, yes! If I get a bit of my own back from those damn contractors I'll think the thing over. S'pose Mirandola and Kilmallock would pool?"

"Well, as to that—Temple could find out," she said cautiously. "Don't let's show we want them. Let them want us."

Then he blazed out at her for interfering. Who was she to thrust herself in, etc., etc. He'd do it and he'd write the letter and he wouldn't wait a day, and he'd smash her face in if she interfered.

"Do I ever interfere?" she asked humbly, her eyes cast down.

"No, but you jolly well would if I was fool enough to let you. Come into the office after tiffin, Temple, and we'll put it through and damn the bulls and the carters."

She went off after tiffin, and Tyliol dictated a fool of a letter, and I brought it to her and we sent a sensible one. Was it compounding a felony? God knows; I don't. At all events the bulls and the money were saved. The lorry specifications came. I passed them and in a few weeks the purgatory of the hill was ended and the lorry came and went with precision. Tyliol boasted to the men who rolled up that he had initiated the whole business.

"Nobody thought of it until I wrote. Fellows here can't see before their noses," and so forth. That claim was admitted. Certainly his letter had set the ball rolling. His fame as a manager mounted.

The more I watched Lilavati the more I marveled. One day I came in and found her shuddering on the sofa with a black bruise on her temple. He had knocked her down and in falling her head had struck the table and— Well, I saw red. He was out about the place, swearing at large, and I got up without a word, to follow when she caught me by the wrist and held on like grim death.

"You shan't go. Promise me. What does it matter? It isn't the first time and—"

"It shall be the last!" I said with what breath fury left me. "Let me go. Don't turn me into a skunk that can stand by and see a woman misused. I never see him speak to you but I want to ram his teeth down his throat. I'll do it now."

But still she clung to my wrist and gradually the fury died out of me before the power in her eyes. Believe it or not, day by day I learned that Lilavati had wells of power besides which my angers were child's play. Her look caught me now with an intensity that I felt to be as much above me as a man's strength exceeds a child's.

"Sit down and don't be a fool. What's a knock on the head? There's a lot of trash about this kind of business, and a woman worth her salt can take a kick as part of the day's work. You can't quarrel with Tyliol. He'll hoof you out if you do and I want you."

I saw that, but—my God, her beautiful bruised face, pale as death, her suffering heroic stedfastness! I pulled myself together.

"Lilavati, why in God's name do you stick it out? Let's go. I'll work for you like a brother. I'll ask nothing but to look after you. Let's shake clear of this foul business and Tyliol."

"Oh, yes!" she said with her smile, "and have all

Ceylon say you took up with a Eurasian mistress of
Tyliol's and chucked your business. Much employment you'd get, you innocent! Look here, Temple. I'm
not going to have my work undone, and if you and I
leave Tyliol the whole show isn't worth a sneeze. I'll
stay and you'll stay, and if he does knock me down,
let him! I'll get up again. If you really want to help
me, swear to me that if I die you'll stick to the Gaunt-
Willock."

I knew already that the estate and the coolies and
all were more to her than anything earthly. Deliberately I say it. That was the one thing to be proud of
in a life that had no other pride.

Briefly, I promised. Then indeed the great eyes shone
in her face. She glowed beauty on one. All the music,
art, poetry, in the world was in the lovely glance she
gave me as she released my hand. It taught me how the
moon pulls the tides, how women have driven men out
to the ends of the earth to gain the hidden heaven they
hold. I could stick Tyliol or the devil if she ordered
me.

"And now I'll tell you something!" she said in a
voice of melting sweetness. "D'you remember I said
there were wonders here? Well, if you knew what I
have to hold on to, you'd laugh at Tyliol. Poor Tyliol!
Poor everybody that doesn't know! Oh, Temple, if ever
you know *that!*"

She laughed to herself as one who sees the inexpressible—the secret of all beauty, all wisdom—was shining
in the oceans of her eyes. I said, as I often said with
her, "Tell me." I suppose I had always had the romantic in me and she caught it. That's the way any sensible
man would sum up the situation, but I knew that formula left out some ingredient that vitalized the whole.
She knew it, but I didn't. Again she laughed.

"I have something that makes all this swearing and blowing and raging mere—poppycock! Did you ever see a child stamping and roaring! That's Tyliol. But —would you believe me if I told you? No. You must see for yourself. Now I'm going to lie down. My head's wishy-washy."

I went off, sore with rage and ignorance, out to where the coolies were tea-picking. It isn't hard work in a way, but it is exceedingly tedious; and in a hot sun standing, picking, picking, there are a good few things I'd rather do if you ask me. And I went past them and on.

Let me be honest. In revolving many things the thought had struck me more than once: could she be giving Tyliol drink that she might rule the brute in him, and if so, could I blame her? Could I blame him if he turned and rent her? I was in deep water between the two of them, and strange fancies were coming and going in my head.

There was a place, very beautiful, on the slope of the hill where the palms grew golden and shining. They were the king coco palms, particularly aristocratic in the palm-world, and the water of the nuts a delicious drink. They made a kind of avenue and I walked along it with the golden green rhythmic swaying overhead, thinking of Lilavati and how in the world I could extricate her and myself from Tyliol's mess without breaking up her work. I noticed nothing until I saw what I took to be a little grave under a palm. It was so small that I doubted, but its rounded shape certainly suggested the notion. At its head grew a white, deliciously scented flower that we call the jungle rose though it has nothing of the rose about it, and on it lay two flowers of the blood-red hibiscus. But the whole thing was only three feet long—if that.

I thought then that it might be a dog's grave—one of the poor beasts that grew like weeds down at the lines, and I stopped and looked at it with that notion. But it didn't appeal to me. If it were that, Lilavati must have done it for no one else would, and she hadn't a bit of that kind of sentiment. She would share her own dinner with the living dog, but the life once out of it I couldn't see her willowing over a grave. Not she! And the two withering flowers were newly put there that day. The sun hadn't yet quite burnt them up.

I walked on and still the thing puzzled me, and after I had done my work and the sun was rushing like a rolling wheel into the Indian ocean I went in and up to the veranda where Tyliol was having cocktails and she a lime-soda. They were talking in the usual way and no notice was taken by either of the fact that the mark on her temple was black against the golden velvet of her skin. I don't know now how I kept my hands off the brute as he sat sipping and talking in his low rasp about the great things he'd done that day and the fool she had been, with a side-shot at me now and again to vary the music. I stuck it out as long as I could and went in and threw myself on my bed.

That night a great moon was dawning over the shoulder of the hill, and silence came with her as she rode the heavens, like the awe that goes before a queen. A wonderful night. You could scarcely see a star, the radiance so drowned them and flooded the world with light and with shadows black as ebony. It was only in the shadows that you could see the twinkling points of fireflies. Otherwise they swam invisible in glory.

How could I stay in the veranda with the kerosene lamp where Tyliol was snoring? Lilavati was not there. She had vanished in her white dress down the path that led to a stream rippling from a spring in the rocks to the river below—where the coolies washed their clothes in the ruddy brown water. She went about the jungle at night as fearless as a leopard. I longed for a talk with her—her strength of purpose to buck up my weak-kneed depression, for it was up-hill work often at the Gaunt-Willock in spite of the glow in her eyes. I went out round the allamanda bush and down the slope.

Now—believe me or not as you will.

At right angles branched off the way to the grove of king coco palms. I declare on my soul that in that awful moonlight—queer word, but I know what I mean!—they shone like silver beaten and burnished, and the shadows under them like black velvet, so wonderful that I had to stop and look whether I would or no. It was something you wanted to get near to, to understand, to make it yours, a language you knew the alphabet of and craved to read the book and couldn't. I stopped and fell into the breathless silence and the shadows, like part of it.

First a snake went across the track on some business of its own in the night—a cobra. You could see every trick of the pattern and its deadly grace of motion; swift as an arrow it writhed across and was gone. I saw them often and nothing to fear, for they never go for you, but that night it meant more and was part of the secret alphabet I saw but couldn't read. Then at the far end I saw Lilavati in her white dress coming like the meaning of it all, seeming rather to float in moonlight than to walk, for her little feet were in shadows like black water. If I could only watch. If I breathed I did not know it. Like the snake she was on her own unknown business.

She stopped and made a soft call like a bird; a naked

child ran out of the shadows and into the lake of light
with two hibiscus blossoms almost black in the moon
hanging from her head. What of that? She was good
to the coolie children. They ran round her like the
dogs. But this child was white as mother-of-pearl. The
moonlight shimmered over her like the lights in pearls
when they turn the white of a woman's bosom to
tawny. Flawless, milk-white, rose-white, and her head
was a mass of gold curls. Her face I could not see, but
she fled straight to the girl, and Lilavati dropped on
her knees and they were clasped together in an embrace
that had all the motherhood of the world in it.

How can a man move when he sees a thing like
that? I stood in the dark and saw them in the flooding
light, and questions beat in my brain and got no answer.

A white child on the Gaunt-Willock and lost in the
palms at night? Not lost, Lilavati had come to meet
her. I could see her look as she knelt and clasped the
child, and the child clung to her and they stayed mute
so long in that passion that they might have been a
marble group arrested in love eternal. Each hid the
other, I couldn't see their faces, and how long I stood
or she knelt I shall never know. I could no more have
moved!—I was in the same vibration. It held me too.
Saying this I use a word which would never have
occurred to me then. I have learned it since. I knew
then only that I was sensitive to what they felt. That
was all.

After a long time Lilavati stood up leaning over the
little head. With clasped hands they came towards me,
the child treading through the shadows with bare feet
as if she moved through water and the moon full in
her face. It was too far still for me to catch the features, but she looked up at Lilavati and I think she

did not speak. Perhaps the understanding lay too deep
for that, as mothers say it does often with a baby.
When they came nearer Lilavati knelt again and
wrapped her arms about the little naked body, and now
I saw her face.

I had never seen her smile before—at least never
like this. It was love's passion bathing in its own
delight. She did not speak—but her lips were pressed
to the upturned face, to the bare shoulders. She lifted
the child and they clung together. I dared not look. It
was too intimate and lovely. When I dared again as
she moved, she stood alone. The child was gone.

Had she run into the palms with bare feet where I
had seen the cobra pass? I had heard no sound. It was
impossible to guess which way she had escaped. But
that Lilavati should let her go alone, should only stand
looking after her with an expression I can put into
no words known to me, was terrifying—a white child
in the tropic night and its dangers!

It broke the spell. I moved—I came out of the shadows and she turned and saw me. Instantly the mask
fell over her face again—like a cloud over the moon.

"And what are you doing here!" she said in her
hardest voice, and Lilavati could be hard. "I thought
you were up in the veranda with Tyliol. This is *my*
place at night when I want to get out of it all for a
bit."

Her look was dismissal but I stood my ground.

"I don't want to butt in and you know it. I hadn't
a notion you were here. But all the same this slope
reeks with snakes and Fernando saw a leopard here two
days ago. You shouldn't—"

Her eyes fixed and held me. "Snakes? Leopards?
What's that to me? D'you suppose I've never seen them
before?"

"Yes, but—I saw—"

"What did you see?"

I swear I couldn't tell. I didn't know. For suddenly it was all mirage. Had I seen? Was I dreaming? I lost faith shudderingly in my own senses. It was the night, the moonlight, such things don't happen. Even a man who drinks only water may go a little off his dot with a glaring moon like that. It blurred, blurred in my head. It all disintegrated, and for a moment my mind with it, and I forgot, forgot utterly, except that something had knocked me silly. It was the clammy fear night leaves behind it. No less—no more.

"I don't know what I saw," I said stumblingly. "It was the shadows. All the same, let's come along. It's the snakiest place on the hill—"

My voice trailed off and my heart-beat was all wrong for a minute and I hadn't the faintest notion why. A horrid thing to feel. It made a rank coward of me. But I could hardly drag one foot before the other, for my own imagination terrified me like the ground slipping away in an earthquake. That I could think I had seen an impossible thing and then forgotten what it was? That's the gate of madness, and remember the sun strikes on your head like a sword of fire in Ceylon. I thought I was going mental.

"Hold hard a minute. I'm a fool, I believe I've had a touch of the sun. It was hell with the lid off today."

I was gradually reassembling my mind now—the parts were clicking again. But her eyes were steady, quietly possessing me.

"A fool? It looks like it. But what did you think you saw. I want to know. I will know."

"Oh, chuck it, let's go up to the house. I saw nothing. Come on!"

She fell into step beside me, putting her arm through

mine, and we went slowly under the palms. Reaching
the last of them where the path climbed the hill, she
halted and looked back and I with her.

The moon had floated higher above the trees and
swept the alley with a besom of light. No shadows.
The glare of tropic moonlight and emptiness. Nameless
fear took me again—it was waiting. All was waiting,
listening. Vibrations I had never moved in—shapes
and forms utterly strange to human experience—were
at work under the black shadows where the snakes
crept invisible. Anything might happen and freeze us
with fear.

Us? Lilavati made a sound—a motion; she dropped
my arm and turned, her hands stretched out as if to
something behind us. I turned instinctively and saw
nothing but her face fixed on some sight invisible to
me.

A sighing like a breeze ran through the palm fronds,
something retreating—receding into formless space. I
could not stand it. I couldn't endure an instant longer
with her beside me and the whole universe of perception open to her and shut to me. I had no place in it—
none—and whether I ran or walked I don't know even
now, but presently I was at the top of the path near
the veranda and, thank God, the lamp was lit and
shattering the awful moonlight and Tyliol was gone.
I put my arm round one of the posts, the sweat running off me like water and my heart pounded like a
man's I had once seen collapsed after a Marathon. I
mean I could see the frantic beats under my loose shirt
like a thing trying to leap out of my body and escape.

And for what? Because imagination had taken
charge instead of reason, and in the disappearing dream
I was as helpless as a child or an idiot to deal with my
own mind. If that's what lunatics feel when they see

the keepers on them and no one to believe them—no, not even themselves—God pity them! But what had Lilavati seen?

It was minutes before my heart steadied and I relaxed as a man does after the strangling of a nightmare. And then I heard her walking up the path and she rounded the allamanda bush and came up the steps and straight to me.

"For God's sake, Temple, what made you bolt? Tell me what you saw."

The entreaty in her face roused the sick beating of my heart again. She stood with a hand on the table, leaning on it for support. I had never seen anyone so deadly white. My voice was thick in my throat.

"I saw something, but I don't know what. The awful thing is that I can't grip it. It's all melting away in my brain like a cloud changing shape. But what did *you* see?"

"Nothing. What should I see? But you—you!"

She shook at my arm as if to shake the truth out of me, but I stood dumb. I had seen Fear. Nothing more, but enough.

Suddenly Lilavati dropped to her knees, hiding her face in her arms on the table.

"I'll tell you. I'll tell you, Temple. You're good. You're the only man that ever was decent to me. Don't think me mad! Don't! But you'll not understand. How could you? How shall I make you?"

I could say nothing. I stood there—that was all, and her shuddering voice went on choked with dry breathless sobs.

"Temple, you asked once if I'd any religion. I don't know. My grandmother had awful gods, and my mother saw things—and her dreams! She'd know when a man was booked for his coffin. I've seen her

look at many a one and say he'd got his reservations
in a week or a fortnight, and it was true. And once—"

She lifted her face to emphasize the truth and stared
at me with distended eyes like lamps of darkness.
Something choked in her throat. She got up and stood
tall under the lamp.

"She told me I had the sight too. She said 'People
walk in the dark and all sorts of things go on round
them that they don't see, lovey. But *you'll* see. *You'll*
know.' "

She halted a minute then went on with a rush.

"There's real things you never see, Temple. Lots of
them. But *I* see them. You don't believe it. How could
you?"

There was silence and only the undertone of the
jungle like the breathing of some monstrous life beside us, never ceasing night or day. Then, with hands
locked together as if to concentrate strength, she spoke
again.

"One day when first I came here I was sitting on the
veranda and there was a glass jug of water on the
table. The sunlight was on it and I stared and my eyes
dazzled and in a second I didn't see things round me
but far off, like my mother. Tyliol was down the hill
in the south plantation, but I saw him and into him and
he wasn't a puzzle to me any more. I'd got the whip-
hand in some ways. Not all, mind you!—but some."

"That's how you make him do things?" I asked with
a creeping fear along my tingling nerves.

"That's how. I look into him and he gets drowsy
and he's got to do it. But mind you, Temple, I don't
use it for myself. I wouldn't. If I did that to him he
couldn't beat me nor swear at me, but I won't do that.
I won't save myself. Only the work and the coolies and
the dogs. I haven't got the strength yet to make him

decent. I don't love him any more like I did, but I love
him like a sick child, and if I could I would. You bet!"

"You loved Tyliol? You love that brute!" The
loathing I had for him made even the wistfulness of
her voice and eyes revolting to me in and for a moment. I shall never forget her astonishment.

"For God's sake, Temple, why else d'you think I
came here? What other reason brought me?"

"To get away from the foul set-out you told me of.
No decent woman could love Tyliol. You make me
sick when you say a beastly thing like that."

I remember she looked at me in exactly the same
way as a mother looks at a foolish child. There was
even a faint smile on her beautiful mouth.

"Tyliol wasn't always such a soaker. He seemed a
long sight above a mongrel like me. 'A gentleman'
you know. Oh yes, he was a cut above any man that
had made eyes at me! Anyhow I loved him. But when
I got the sight I saw he was only a silly fool that can't
be trusted with himself or anyone else for two secs.
A most awful fool! And I saw I must take on for him
and I did and I love him still, only—not like I did.
No, not that!"

Suddenly, with comprehension I realized the broken
dream, the strong resolve. She was forcing understanding on me. I listened spellbound to the story of a
suddenly enlightened soul. It falls to the lot of few to
hear that tale.

"I wasn't quite sixteen then. You know we half-
breeds are older than your women, and I'd just found
out I was going to have a baby. I was most awful glad
—I've got that streak in me. Even a puppy or kitten
I'd die for and I thought—well, no matter! I slipped
on the steps of the veranda and it came to nothing.
Nothing at all—not even a grave to show for it! But

one night when Tyliol was awful drunk I went down
to where you saw me tonight, and the moon shone like
day on the palms, my eyes dazzled and I saw again and
there was a baby in my arms. Temple, I'm telling you
the truth before God. I felt it like a living child, warm
and soft—a small little thing, the size it would have
been if it had been born, and I walked up and down
clean mad for happiness. And when the moon got
above the palms it was gone, but I knew it had been
there and I'd get it again."

"And you did?"

"Every night when the moon is nearing the full I
go and she comes and— Oh, my God, Temple, is it
only a dream? It can't be only that if you saw it too.
You did, didn't you? And wait till I tell you—when I
went along by the palms next day, for I couldn't keep
away from them, I saw a little grave as if a child was
buried there. And I want you to know I'd been thinking all the time that if I only had a little grave I could
cry over I'd be half happy again. You can feel you
had it if there's a grave to go to, but if there's nothing—"

Her hands stretched out for understanding; her face
yearned for it in a very passion of motherhood. But
how could a man feel that or know the meaning of the
agony of love that had possessed her? I shook my head
mutely. She misread it.

"Ah, Temple, you think I'm a fool—but I see it. It's
there under the palms, but it's not a prison like graves
are—it's just a little place where she sleeps sometimes when she's not with me, not always, you bet!
Now she's grown older she has all sorts of fun round
the place that she tells me. For she grows like other
children—so she isn't only a dream—she couldn't be.
D'you remember the day when all the dogs down to

the lines barked like mad for joy, and we saw them running past the veranda like the hounds up to Newara Eliya? That was Savitri—they were playing with her —I see it often."

Her eager eyes softened into a kind of hopelessness. "I'm talking like a half-baked idiot. It's true, but you can't believe it. You're saying, 'She went off her dot when the child didn't come to anything.' But I must tell you, Temple— Look here! I was a fool of a girl before, always cutting up rough with Tyliol and the place going to the dogs, and the coolies and their women and children the most God-forsaken miserable lot God ever took it into his head to forget. But from the first time I had that baby in my arms I knew I could do any mortal thing. And I've done it! All but making Tyliol decent, and that'll come too one day."

She had done it. Men might say Tyliol soaked, but they never failed to add there wasn't a better run estate in the whole island than the Gaunt-Willock— that no man had a better sense of managing his coolies.

But there's more to say. As she spoke memory broke on me like a flooding wave. I remembered—I knew what I'd seen and that it was true sight and not her power on me as on Tyliol. My brain and something deeper came to heel like a dog. She hadn't done it—I had seen for myself. The true sight. But the things she told me came like revelation. No wonder she had done what she had. The strength of the universe was behind her. Her love had conquered more than death. It had created—as they say God himself creates—a child and all the wonder of it from nothingness.

"Don't you see," she broke in, "that I'm the happiest girl in all the world? If the child had been born —Tyliol didn't want a brat he said—well, he'd have misused her if I'd died. He might have chucked her

overboard like I was chucked. She'd have been sick
and sorry like other children and when she grew up
it might have been—Cairo or Colombo. Life isn't a
picnic for anyone—not even the luckiest. You take it
from me, Temple, there's something in having a kid
you need never be afraid for, living or dead. She's got
the Key of the fields, that one! And she's passed it on
to me. Ah, we pick up things night and day—*we* do!"

She waved her hand above the moon-drenched
world, and awe swept up about us as if she had summoned it. The night meant more than ever night before. The shadows were the cool of water. I felt the
jungle rejoicing far off in its mighty heart, and the
wild things moved through it in a truce of God. Oh,
to see with her—to know all! I got only the dim reflection of what she knew for certain, but what it meant
has lasted me for my life so far and taught me— But
I shall come to that presently. The lamp had flickered
out for want of oil and the moonlight flooded in like
an ocean of pure glory.

"Temple," she said, "I wasn't a fool to tell you, like
I thought when I began. I've got the sight and I tell
you you've got the eyes that'll see too, some day. I
know now why I told you. That's why!"

I leaned forward across the table and took her hand;
it was cold as ice with intensity of feeling, and her
face blanched like death. The blood had all rushed to
her heart to feed the burning love in it. Love? She had
enough for the child, for Tyliol, for me, for every
coolie, every dog—every plant that lived on the place.
She had enough for the world if all the seas had gone
dry. Her channels were open to the fires that warm the
sun. We looked in each other's eyes and she understood
before I spoke.

"No dream, Lilavati, no dream. I saw her in your
arms. I saw it clear as you did. Look!"

We turned to the allamanda bush and together we saw her laughing and waving to her mother and the allamanda flowers bleached white as pearls in the moonlight about her.

Lilavati leaned across the table and still holding my hand kissed it. Kissed it. While I live that hand shall never do a cruel or dirty thing. She smiled at me and went down the steps and they were hidden by the bush, Savitri laughing and leaping beside her.

There is little enough to tell now. Oceans really. Everything in a world that I'm learning to understand better daily, but one can hardly expect people to take these things for granted if they haven't seen for themselves, and those who have don't want telling. They know and smile.

In a week Lilavati left without saying why or wherefore and I had little chance of a word with her, for no girl was ever busier. There wasn't a thing or person she left unvisited or uncared for. I heard her give strict directions for the pi-dogs and their feeding and I can see her now with a mongrel pup, one of a poor unwanted litter but beautiful in its way, held to her breast while she gave her orders. Little Savitri stood leaning against her, looking up with laughing eyes. I always saw the child with her outside the house now, but never once inside it, not even in the veranda. All that was Tyliol's domain and something stronger than walls kept her out. But she would wait under the allamanda bush, and then—then!

I went down the long path with Lilavati to reach the little bull-drawn hackery that was to take her on the first lap to civilization.

"Temple," she said as she went, "supposing anything was to happen to me—" Her tone made me uncomfortable. I loathed her going.

"What could happen? Unless the bull takes to sprinting—which doesn't seem likely."

She laughed in her own quaint way. "Oh, there's lots of ways to snuff out. Well, suppose and suppose! Would you stay with Tyliol?"

"If you told me to I suppose I might. But not for love of Tyliol."

She considered that a moment then said: "No, of course. Love of the job. It's a clean bit of work after all. Eh?"

"It's yours, that's enough for me."

How her bright eyes shone. "Honest Injun? You're a good sort, Temple. I love you." She said it so soberly and earnestly that I don't suppose the vainest blighter in the world could have misunderstood her. I didn't, at all events.

"You don't need telling the answer to that. Yes, I'll stay. But, speaking on general principles, don't snuff out. There's room for you here."

"Yes. And there!" she said. "I've never been sorry for what I told you. I know by your eyes when you see her, and—I like you to."

As a matter of fact Savitri was running down the path before us like a white butterfly and as light. Exactly as if she had wings.

"What has she in her hand?" Lilavati asked suddenly.

"White flowers like water-lilies. Beautiful—But I don't know where they grow."

"I do," she said, and no more.

We were now at the bottom of the hill. I helped her into the hackery and felt the pressure of her hand. She wore her terai hat and it was gray and she had a gray dress. Perhaps it was because she was going that I thought I had never seen her so lovely, with her eyes

shining under the broad brim and her queer half-wist-
ful smile. She leaned out.

"We've been good pals, Temple. Take care of yourself till I come back."

I waved my hand. The handsome little bull broke
into a kind of shambling trot. I stood and watched
until the palms took her, than turned and went slowly
up the hill.

No use to describe the place without Lilavati.
Tyliol was awful. He never mentioned her and though
a letter came here and there I didn't even know if it
was hers. I spent the days in missing her at every
turn, and wondering fretfully why she had gone. I
wouldn't touch the pile of mended socks she had left
on my table, for I wanted them to stay just as her
hand had put them.

Every night when there was enough moonlight I
went down to the palms and did sentry-go thinking
of her. Every day when I had a minute I went there
and passed the place where I had imagined the little
grave. I say "imagined" for I could see it no more.
I believe Lilavati and I had both outgrown it, as I
shall outgrow a lot more silly stuff that holds me now.

Never a sign of her or of the child. It seemed the
place had forgotten them and the touch that made it
worth while was gone.

On dark nights I sat in the veranda, and Tyliol
drank and snored. I would have been sick of the whole
show but for keeping things going for her, and I did
that and he didn't butt in.

The moon came again slowly rounding to perfection
and I went down one night as usual to the palms after
dinner. We dined early and in Ceylon there's very little
light after six anyhow, but the young moonlight was
exquisite—not much power, more like a shy girl look-

ing through leaves, half-frightened to see how you take it. Lilavati had been gone a month. I had my pipe and strolled to and fro on my beat thinking of her and wondering when she would be coming back. I knew she would be glad to come—I knew her heart. If Tyliol had had the best of her I hadn't missed my best in her either. I heard her voice saying: "I love you. You know that."

What I tell now may not be believed, but it's God's truth for all that. As I turned I saw the child. She leaned against the stem of a young palm and was looking steadily not at me but past me as if at something that came swiftly up behind me; it might be the beginning of a breeze in the airy palm fronds, but it came with a rush, and Lilavati passed me running, and the child sprang to her and they clung together.

They never saw me. It was not for me this time. I stood and something crept through me—like strength and all the good of the earth when it flows up the trees like warm blood and gives them life. Then after a bit I turned and went up the path to the veranda. I don't even know if I saw them there or not any more. I had got a sight deeper than my own eyes.

As I reached the steps of the veranda there was Tyliol sitting by the table with his elbows on it and his chin on his hands. He hadn't shaved for a day or two, and his face was grim and gaunt in the lamp-light as he stared down into the jungle. A boy ran up past me and put a telegram before him. I was in the veranda as he opened it and I saw him read it. He pushed it to me and got up and went in. I read:

"She died after the operation this afternoon at four o'clock."

I can't tell what I felt. How should I know? From his room close by came an awful sound—the sound of

Tyliol sobbing like a man fighting for his breath in great seas.

The end of what I have to tell is the strangest part.

I stayed with him. I would have stayed in hell for Lilavati. From that day he touched no drink. Never again. I can swear to that. But he got stranger and more shut off every day. He had a small bungalow run up for me at the foot of the hill, saying he knew he wasn't particularly good company and it was natural I should like to be to myself and have things my own way. I certainly preferred it. He grew more silent than ever; even over the work he never used an unnecessary word where a gesture would do; and then he would go off up the hill and if I had to pass he would be in the veranda, never reading but staring out into the jungle. The coolies were horribly frightened of him though he never misused them now. On the contrary, working along her lines, he saw they had all they ought to have—perhaps even a bit more; not one of them but was glad to stay and others to come for the sake of the decent treatment they got. I remember when Willock came out (a good sort himself) he told Tyliol before me that he and Gaunt had such confidence in his management past and present that he could do exactly as he liked about them and no questions asked. That confidence was justified and I know what I'm talking of.

I never liked Tyliol, but I grew to feel there were things I couldn't understand in him and they were probably better than I guessed. Lilavati has not finished her work.

No—not she! That kind of work has no end. I have passed that veranda at night and seen her standing by the allamanda bush, holding the child by the hand and looking at Tyliol as he sat staring out over the jungle.

They would stand there motionless. No sound from any of the three, but as I got more knowledge I could feel the vibrations passing between them, could even see them. If it hadn't been for the things I picked up daily I'd have been lonelier in my bungalow with young Scriven (a good fellow) than Tyliol in the silent house on the hill.

But her work was not through with me either. I saw her every day—and the child. They went laughing about the place. The dogs knew it—I can answer for that—and there was an old man (whom Tyliol formerly would have kicked off the place, but who now had a cushy job to keep him doddering about) that used to point along the sun-flecked paths. He knew I saw, and his toothless wrinkled old smile and pointing hand included me in their happiness.

But there was more for me. In all sorts of strange ways Lilavati is at work. I have her sight now. I see things that it isn't possible to tell to any who have not known the same things and they are more worth while than anything else I know. I am fully content with the Gaunt-Willock—and no man needs more. I shall never move on.

Sometimes on moonless nights when young Scriven is off and away to some dance or lark at other estates (we have a decent road to the place now) I sit in my own little veranda and try to think out *what* Lilavati knew. But reasoning cannot hit the mark—its wings shrivel in the sunshine. Yet I know that somehow she had got through to the spring that fills all the cisterns. Her cup was never empty and all the thirsty could drink there. She had power—she knew. She could shoulder any burden and carry it singing. She has no burdens now. She laughs.

Last night I walked under the palms and she sat

there with the moon in her eyes—more beautiful than in the old days. She smiled but did not speak though her lips shaped my name; and I realized the strangest thing—even that the life of Lilavati herself was dream, symbol, parable, with the eternal and changeless sunshine behind it. And so it is with us all. The cry of the blind man for light is the world's desire. To see—to know. To break the prison and be free. And for me and herself she had won it. And perhaps—for Tyliol in a far-off peace.

The Horoscope

For it is a true saying that a man never believes anything sincerely until he can afford to laugh at it.

DAY BY DAY IN A STREET IN LONDON WHERE THE great doctors and surgeons dispense their wisdom, for sale at fees calculated in that obsolete coin the guinea, patients roll up in motors of the best or taxis of the worst for sentence of death or respite. There never is acquittal; but a respite of twenty, thirty, forty years is good enough for the average man and he goes away rejoicing. A queer enough position for the judge who pronounces sentence and sits in the intervals wondering what culprit will next be arraigned before him! I, as one of the doctor judges, have as my culprits the victims of obscure nervous and mental troubles. This was not the original line I took in the profession. It was forced upon me by circumstances and a training very unusual in the western world, and though I refuse to commend it as cheerful, a more interesting one does not exist and it will become more so as wisdom grows. I use the word "wisdom" deliberately, for it asks more than the knowledge which every clever man can acquire. To be honest, I should call my branch a vocation rather than a profession, and it is in the nature of things that the vocation chooses the man rather than the man the vocation. It had brought me some uncommonly queer cases already, and in the story I tell now it brought me the cheeriest and queerest of the lot.

I sat in my consulting room one day wondering whether anything could overtop the extraordinary case that had just made its exit, when my man ushered in the unlikeliest-looking patient I ever beheld. Sir Francis Bethune. I had had his name on my list for a week.

Figure for yourself a man of forty, alert, broad-shouldered, with bright eyes of an excellent hazel and a jolly smile to match their kindliness. A gentleman in the best sense of the word, every inch of him, and as there were a good few inches that speaks for itself. He made the rather drab room as cheery as a May morning when he came in. But what does perfect health of mind and body do in a mental specialist's consulting room? The look of it cannot be mistaken by the experienced eye. It needs no cataloging. I prepared myself immediately for the unusual. It came.

He had hardly patience for the preliminaries, leaning forward, straining like a dog who scents rats, and the moment I laid down my pen snapped out his question:

"I want you to tell me, doctor, if I'm going mad?"

It was impossible to help laughing, the thing was so patently absurd. He looked distinctly aggrieved.

"Considering I've come all the way from Devonshire to ask you that question—Yes, I know I look all right. I *am* all right if you come to that. But still—"

"Tell me your story," I said encouragingly. "I needn't tell you you seem in the pink in every way. But still—as you say— Go on."

A rich man with a fine place in Devonshire, rich in friends also, fond of moderate luxury, a good glass of wine and a good table, given to hospitality, with a strain of the adventurous which had made him a bit of a traveler—unmarried, but engaged. There were the background of the picture and as to what the picture would be I could not even hazard a suspicion.

"No man enjoys life more than I do," he protested. "It grips me at every point. Now, take sports. I'm master of the Harriers and a member of the Watercombe Hunt. The stag-hunting on Exmoor and foxhunting are the delight of my life. I'm known for a decent shot. Golfing, everything. I hadn't a blessed crumple in my blessed rose-leaf. The girl I'm engaged to is Miss Fleurette Leslie. That speaks for itself."

Dimly it did. My life does not lie along those lines, but I had faint remembrance of beauty, gonged by the newspapers and resonant all over the fashionable continental resorts as well as in London. It was associated with the name Fleurette. So much I knew.

"I ask you—could any fellow have more to keep him chirpy?"

"It's a long list."

"I should say! Well—listen." He pulled a paper of notes from his pocket and looked it over. "My log, so to speak. I'll tell you how it began. Where am I— oh, here."

His tone now changed and became impressive.

"Hartstaple Meet. Yes. Well—it was a splendid field. Never saw better. The whole countryside, and we drew at Kilway and started as fine a fox— But I needn't go into that. A glorious run. We killed at Blackman's Copse, and little Euphan Murray was blooded. Her first kill and she rode like a Trojan!"

"Blooded?"

"Bless me! You know! The huntsman smears the blood on her face and hands her the brush. A fine old ceremony. Well, I was looking on, relishing the child's pleasure, when—will you believe me?—quite suddenly I turned as sick as a dog. I had to turn back inside Blackman's Copse and vomit."

"Riding on too full a stomach? A hunt breakfast?"

"Lord love you, no! *No.* The sight of the blood all

over the girl's face, the bloody rags of the fox and
the hounds over them—suddenly it knocked me over
like a shot bunny. *Me.* Me that loves everything manly
and open-air! But wait—that isn't the worst! When I
got out of the copse, white as a table-cloth to my very
guts, I found myself saying to Dornish—Lord Dornish, the master of the Foxhounds!—'I call that a
beastly bloody brutal sight, don't you?' I shall never
forget his face. Naturally he thought at first I was
joking. He said something jolly and I sidled the mare
up to him—it was Black Bonny—and said furiously:
'I'm damned if I don't write to the papers and show
up a fashionable crowd of men and women like this
laughing to see an innocent child brutalized like themselves before their eyes.' When I say *I* said it, the
impression I had was that it was the devil speaking
through me but I couldn't stop."

His eyes were fixed upon me haggard with consternation.

"Astonishing! What happened?"

"He backed and looked—I was going to say, looked
round for help. I pushed after him. 'And let me tell
you, my lord,— "My lord!" To Dornish!—that a man
of your years who encourages a thing like this should
be sent to penal servitude for ten years.' I could hear
myself shouting over the field. People stopped talking
and grouped and listened, and Trumpleton, the beastly
old farmer that hates the hunt, cheered somewhere on
the edge of the field. I give you my word if I could
have dropped dead straight off the mare I'd have
thought Providence showed its good sense. In the face
of the whole county! I couldn't stop myself. I damned
them all for a set of bloody cowards and I rode off
that field, a broken man, and that damned old Trumpleton cheered me from over his gate."

I have seen many cases but never one in more urgent need of sympathy. I suggested:

"They might think you were a sheet in the wind, as the sailors say. Had it been a wet night?"

He shook his head with a bitter smile.

"One small whisky and soda before bed. Drunk— not they! They know too much. But that isn't the worst. I stretched out in a big chair when I got in, simply because I'd had the shock of my life. For God's sake understand it wasn't *me*—*I* was all right then, thinking just what I always thought. It was— What *was* it in the devil's name?"

"Let me hear the whole story before I form my judgment."

"Dalgleish was coming to stay a couple of days— my lawyer—to have the first talk about the marriage settlements. A topping good fellow though he *is* a lawyer. Well, he turned up later—just before dinner. And now, for God's sake listen, doctor. I went up to dress. My fellow had put out everything, and as I stood and looked at them for a minute I—I couldn't put 'em on. Give you my word. Couldn't stand anything black and stiff, and the trousers I particularly abhorred. I plunged at a wardrobe and hauled out a magnificent crimson silk dressing-gown, shot with gold and trimmed with gold frogs and braid and cord and tassels, that my aunt sent me from India and I'd never had on my back since it came. And I put it on and sent the other slops flying on the floor and so I went down to dinner blazing like fireworks and not so much as a collar."

I was going to speak but he interrupted:

"It was as if there were two me's inside. One that knew the right thing; the other and much the stronger that would do what he jolly well wanted. No use arguing; he'd *got* me. It was only because it wasn't there that I didn't tie a whole rainbow round my head and go down with that. I was craving for color as a man does for booze. You should have seen Dalgleish's face when I sailed in. He tried to be polite though." Sir Francis wiped a damp forehead and said hurriedly: "Would it be out of order to ask for a drink? It's almost as bad to tell the damned thing as to live it."

"Certainly!" I said, touching the bell. "What shall it be? A whisky and soda?"

He looked at me indignantly: "Spirits? Never. Do you happen to have any sherbet? Lemon with ice, for choice."

I am seldom at a loss, but I own this floored me. Startled me also. I shook my head.

" 'Fraid not. How about a lemon squash?"

He said grudgingly: "Very well. Lots of sugar, tell them. Stiff with it."

It was brought and the tale proceeded.

"Dalgleish nearly fainted when I appeared but said he supposed it had been a hard run and I was done in. I didn't dare contradict. We went to dinner. I suppose nothing earthly could make my butler turn a hair, but when I walked in— You know how you feel when the air's all full of thunder. I saw him and the footman look at each other and no wonder. Well, the *hors-d'œuvres* were all right—just a kind of *sambal* like they have in Ceylon. I was as hungry as a hunter and ate that and the soup—cream of celery. And then came the fish. Trout, doctor, killed that morning, with sauce —oh, my heavens!—and when it was at my elbow on came the awful feeling I'd had in Blackman's Copse and I found myself saying: 'Take the beastly dead stuff away. Quick! Bring me a poached egg.' "

"It was clear from the first your stomach was up-set," I said gravely.

"Stomach? Lord pity the daft! I wish all your patients had a stomach like mine! Just you wait. There was a sweetbread next and Dalgleish ate it while I sat with my poached egg and loathed the brute. A sweetbread! Even now—well, never mind! Then came a little turkey pullet from the Home Farm stuffed with chestnuts, and if there's a thing I love—but it was no good. I knew my fate when I smelled it. I almost screamed to have the corpse taken away and two more eggs brought. The butler said, 'With 'am, sir? You've ate nothing!' and I nearly brained him. He won't try that trick again! The savory I could do with. It was stuffed olives with something clean, and the ices I wolfed. *Wolfed!* Dalgleish had an eye on me and after dinner he said: 'I'm sure you're not up to business tonight. Let's take it easy.' But I wouldn't. We spread out the papers and began work."

He looked at me as who should say, "Prepare for a shock!"

"We'd reached the point of discussing my wife's income when I died either with or without children, and Dalgleish said in a professional way: 'Needn't consider the position for many children. Let's take two as our limit in calculation and—' Suddenly I found myself standing up and gesticulating. 'Dalgleish!' I roared. 'Kindly keep your unpleasant opinions to yourself. A large family I intend to have. Isn't it one's plain duty to one's country after a war that bled the country white? And furthermore—let me tell you that in such a case I'm all for polygamy and I intend to introduce a bill in parliament to enable every man with sufficient means to have two wives or more.'

"He sat up, petrified by my manner, seeing I was in earnest, though God knows I couldn't have been, and then dropped back into his chair so heavily that I

thought he'd go through the seat. I can see his fishy
eyes now, glowering at me.

" 'By George!' he said, 'I know you're not drunk.
But otherwise—'

" 'Otherwise I'm saying what many able and excellent men from Abraham down have said and done
before me. I ask you, sir, what's to be done with the
superfluous woman? Is she never to know the blessings of a husband and a family? Is a man not at liberty to have a change when he pleases? I mean to set
an example that all shall respect. Instead of sneaking
about private love-affairs as they do over here, I shall
settle my wives openly and honorably and expect the
countryside to call upon them or to have done with
me.' Dalgleish giggled; he said: 'Have you said that
to Lord Dornish? Anyway I hope you'll dot them over
different parts of the property, for if Miss Leslie—'
Then I blazed up and told him I didn't pretend to
have been better than other men, but if he couldn't
respect honesty and patriotism—and out came a thundering long tirade about worthy people who'd had a
string of wives, and there I was in that fool of a
dressing-gown lecturing Dalgleish about people I had
never heard of before myself and, if I had, would
have loathed. First he listened a bit while I walked up
and down shaking my fist, and then he laughed until
he was as helpless as a baby. Next day he went up to
town and I felt sure he'd never keep the thing to himself, and yet if I opened my mouth to say I'd been
a fool out popped some new argument for polygamy.
He wasn't laughing when we said good-by. Nor was I.
So I felt it was time to come to you."

I own my opinions were in a jumble. The man was
irresistibly comic and yet frightened out of his senses
and the whole ridiculous business was a martyrdom

that only those who know the fine old crusted type
of Englishman can understand. It appeared that he
read the lessons every Sunday in the old Norman
church on the property, and I could see the terror in
his eye lest he should come out with some appalling
harangue instead of the appointed prophet. I knew he
believed that a man who had committed blasphemy
against the sacred fox had laid himself open to all the
obscenities of the Pit. My conviction was that he took
the visitation as a heaven-directed judgment for that
crime.

"But what I want to ask you, doctor, is to come
down and stay with me at Brakespeare for a few days
and watch me. You can't tell in this interview. I feel
my better nature asserting itself under your eye. I
realize I was a madman. Down at Brakespeare it
seemed the only sensible way to behave. That's the
awful part of it. Come down, I entreat you."

Naturally I refused. My work—

He broke in: "Money's no object. Name your fee.
You see before you a ruined man. Not a soul has come
near the house since that outbreak in the hunting field,
and when Dornish had to write to me the other day
about the chairmanship of the county council he wrote
exactly as he does to Petty-Foggins, the attorney at
Scrumpton. And I haven't been near the hunt since.
Couldn't."

I cannot detail our argument. It took about half an
hour to beat me to my knees and then I consented to
make arrangements for a week. He hailed me, almost
with tears of gratitude, as his life-belt and went off
to lunch on what he described as a lettuce and a few
beans, leaving me completely at sea. I own it. This was
a variety of mental trouble which had never as yet
come my way. Such reversals of thought and experi-

ence are certainly often a form of insanity, but so they also are of what is favorably known as "conversion" in spiritual circles, and many humanitarians would be disposed to take the latter view.

He undoubtedly left me with plenty to consider.

A week later I got down at four o'clock to Scrumpton station and there was Sir Francis Bethune on the lookout on the platform and a fine Rolls-Royce outside. My first question he answered with a desponding shake of the head:

"Worse, if anything! I can only say that if I met such a Jane Amelia as myself anywhere my warmest wish would be to kick him into a ditch and sit on his head. I've sent an order that all poultry killing is to be stopped at the farm. No beasts are to be sold to the butcher, and I've resigned my mastership of the Harriers and written the most awful letter you ever cast an eye on—"

"Not to the papers?"

"To the papers—local and London. And worst of all Miss Leslie and her mother come down tomorrow and the devil to pay. Here's the wire."

I read aloud: "Hear you're a fermented old loony nowadays. Hold up till we get down. Fleurette."

"Evidently she takes it as a joke," I said.

"Takes everything as a joke more or less. Her mother doesn't. Thank God, you're here!"

We were bowling along a lovely Devonshire lane—the blue Exmoor heights rising softly above the richly wooded country. A little river flowed softly through lush meadows where the red Devon cattle lay or browsed. A lovely land—a fair heritage.

"All mine round here!" said the owner gloomily. "That river's crammed with trout. Crammed. And if there's a thing I love better than a grilled trout it's catching him— *Now* I could as soon stick a hook in your gills as a fish's. Lord, help us! What have I done to deserve this!"

I was silent. That last remark had started a wholly new train of speculation in my mind as to the case. What had he done to deserve it? The law of cause and effect applies in the ridiculous quite as much as in the august, and while it was all I could do to control my laughter, perhaps I began to see a filtering ray of light in the gloom. I said cautiously:

"That's the very point. What have you done to deserve this dislocation of experience?"

He turned on me furiously:

"I can answer that. Nothing. Nothing whatever. I've been a humane man, always a regular subscriber to any society that helps lame dogs over stiles—children or animals. I've been a steady sportsman, and a good sportsman always loves animals. Why shouldn't he? And yet"—his voice wavered and became uncertain—"I don't know. Half my time it seems to me I'm a converted brute and half that I'm an Englishman degraded into a crank—a faddist of the most despicable type. Which am I?"

"We must get to the cause before we discuss the effect," I answered.

We were running smoothly through the ups and downs of the great Brakespeare Park—a most beautiful place, magnificently wooded, with the river Mote winding through it in pools and cascades fresh and clear as its springs on Exmoor—a heavenly sight under the beeches on that warm March day with its vibration of spring. It soothed the eyes with coolness and peace. There was a sound of lowing cattle in the distance and he pointed down that way.

"The Home Farm."

Here and there cattle were grazing on the rich grass, or deer glimpsed between the trees.

"The best venison in Devon," Sir Francis said sighing, and sank into sorrowful reflection. We swept through the gardens nobly planned—the herb garden, the Dutch garden, the Italian garden, and by one, sweetest of all, the cottage garden with a toy dairy where the happy lady of the manor might superintend her dairymaids, at work with cooled hands and white dimity tucked-up dresses on the cream and butter and cheeses for the great house.

It seemed to me that a man might hold all the loveliness and joy of this paradise and yet consent to part with a bloody background, but this I dared not utter. A doctor must retain his patient's respect if they are to work together, and his would have tumbled like a card-palace at such a folly. The house had a mellowed beauty not often to be seen; a great Jacobean stateliness in warm red brick faced with white, and a piazza at one side, above a rose-garden where lords and ladies (now otherwise engaged) walked in silks and satins three hundred years ago and felt their wealthy world could never crack and dissolve in dust. Above the door was the coat-of-arms with its supporters, and a whirlwind of setters and terriers rushed out to meet their returning master, wild with joy.

"*They* like me right enough," he said, stooping to caress the little grizzled heads of Pepper and Sauce— the Dandie Dinmonts who led the flight. "They always did. And I've got a notion you can laugh at if you like that they've been even nicer to their poor old governor since he's fallen from his high estate. Eh, what's this?"

Two letters decorously presented on a silver waiter as he set foot inside the door.

"Oh, I say—tell Mrs. Malpas to have rooms got ready for Lady Leslie and Miss Leslie tomorrow. Here —hold hard, doctor. Look!"

The first was a formal acceptance of his resignation of the mastership without a word of regret. The second, a stiff statement that he would probably himself recognize that his strictures on fox-hunting and his late letter to the local papers and the Times on the subject would for the future preclude any friendly relations between himself and members of the hunt. A most ill-judged letter in any case and one to wound him to the core. It was signed "Dornish."

He turned into the library, pushed me a chair and threw himself into another, and there was a moisture in his eyes that won me to even better liking for the great baby (as I had called him to myself) than I had already.

"Every man and woman in the countryside was my friend—close friend, and now there isn't one that would give me the time of day. They call me a Bolshevist!" he said with his hands over his eyes. "A man feels it!"

"I shouldn't be apt to call such turncoats friends myself. Are the women as bad as the men?"

"Oh, well—follow my leader, you know. Certainly the letter I wrote was a stinger. I've deserved it all. I shouldn't grumble."

He pushed a paper to me.

The letter was excellent, from my point of view, temperately worded and dealing with the cruelties involved in stag- and fox-hunting exactly as I liked to see it done. I say, *my* point of view, for the training and discipline of my life, into which I will not enter here, convinced me as a young man that blood sports are inexcusable from more points of view than one, that it is only in case of need man may kill, and if he does it with a certain regret and pity then, so much the better. As a medical man I was naturally alive also to the merit of the simplest food on which health can be preserved. Therefore the letter interested me amazingly. I hadn't thought the man had it in him to put his points in such a clear-cut forcible way. No wonder the Hunt didn't like it, and the more so because the Devon Times and Gazette devoted a leader to it plumb on his side; and it appeared it had been followed by a shower of sympathetic letters culminating in a gorgeous outburst from Trumpleton heading all the farmers who hated the hunt going over their land. Very good letters too, some of them, but none to equal Bethune's. His remarks on digging-out were masterly.

"You see!" he said woefully. "The whole countryside's up and it's war to the knife. I'm an outsider. I'd best cut the show and sell the house and live—God knows where! Unless you can cure me, and even then I suppose I could never live down such a catalogue of horrors."

"We're alone," I said, "and the door's shut. Now, tell me, Sir Francis, don't you think that's a rattling good letter of yours?"

"In a way—yes," he admitted grudgingly. "I'd be hard put to it to answer that second paragraph. But even if I thought it I'd have been damned before I wrote it."

"Don't you think it?"

He was desperately confused. "Sometimes I do. Sometimes I think it's piffle—just because it contradicts experience. But watch me—watch me and smell out what got me into this fix. It'll mean a regular class war in this jolly old shire or I'm a Dutchman."

An excellent dinner was served. The cook had risen

to the situation and nothing better can be imagined from start to finish. I noticed he enjoyed it thoroughly and that his look of outdoor health hadn't undergone any diminution as yet. He had the air of a mighty hunter suffering from a long frost when scent won't lie—waiting angrily and impatiently for a break in the weather.

We spent the evening talking on books and politics, and in both he came out much stronger than I should have expected. He had dreams of writing an account some day of his own travels up the Brahmaputra and the extraordinary experiences he had in his journey up and beyond the source in Tibet. I led him on to talk of them, for it took his mind off his present ones and the ever-deepening shadow of Lady Leslie's arrival next day. He was frightened of the daughter, and the mother awakened all the terrors of the future son-in-law. But we kept off the lady as far as I could steer, and I can honestly say that the more we talked the further I found myself from any conclusion.

He gave a really spirited description of the long reaches of the great river and the amazing jungle clothing the banks, with retreats in which strange dwellers, men and animals, still lurk and deal out death to the unwary.

"Up in the foot-hills by a reach called Tonda in British India we found the wildest stories of gods and men, and now I come to think of it I may as well shut up Brakespeare and go off exploring there again. I left a lot of questions unanswered and it's a fine life if one has no better."

"Miss Leslie?" I suggested.

He shook his head and turned the subject.

"They had the usual yarn up there of a kingdom that was great once upon a time in the mountain val-

leys. Jewels and women and wars—you know the kind
of thing. I didn't pay much attention except when they
brought me this. They made me pay a biggish bit but
I liked the look of it, though no one can make head
or tail of the things on it."

He pushed the electric lamp over to my side of the
table, and getting up brought me a most beautiful old
copper vessel, a large and somewhat egg-shaped bowl
with a wide flat rim. I am ignorant of such things,
but I believe a large proportion of silver must have
been smelted with the copper, for the sheen was extremely beautiful with an appearance of silver playing
over gold. It had been necessary to clean it when they
tried to decipher the signs engraved on it, and I looked
at them with a magnifying glass.

"They look astrological."

"They are—and nothing else. But the worst of it is
none of the astrologers can read them. There are some
signs they know, but used in different connections, so
there it rests. But the Tondas, as we called them, had
a story that the rulers of this kingdom, which was
not far from Sikkim, came up to the hill country from
Central India ages ago and were great Indian princes;
not a man, woman, or child of them would intermarry
with the Mongolian peoples about them, though they
were on friendly terms. They kept rigidly to their own
ways, and measured distances off so that no Tibetan
might come nearer to them than ten, twenty, or forty
feet, as the case might be."

"That certainly sounds like India!" I said.

"Yes, and the kings got all their women up from
India. There was a regular trade route. They worshiped Indian gods. But to tell you the truth, doctor,
I can't fix my mind on the Tondas with Lady Leslie
in the offing. Let's return to my troubles, if you don't

mind. There's a lot to be said for a harem and no official mother-in-law."

We relapsed into gloom and I was forced to realize that the upset had really been a very great disaster in his life. It would set him as alone in Brakespeare as ever he had been in the wilds of Tibet unless, indeed, there was redemption in Miss Leslie. A tactful woman might master the situation even with the fox and stag and their English worshipers pulling against her. That is, if—

Too large an "if" I knew, directly my eyes lit on the beauty. I stayed upstairs discreetly until I was summoned down and then went unwillingly. There was a cackle of ladies' maids on my floor; a lumbering of trunks large enough for an ocean voyage. The shrill squeaking of an unpleasant Italian grayhound. The atmosphere of quiet was gone, and a trail of perfume reached me from an open door as I passed. A thing I hate! It haunted the library also and strengthened as Lady Leslie, bland and brazen, creaked in a stiff corset as I was presented and bent her head with an enameled smile. She was a malignant prophecy of what her daughter would be in twenty-five years—a very large lady tightly braced under a fashionably easy dress, which generously disclosed massive arms, shoulders, and a wealth of bosom. The scanty field left to the imagination could secrete little illusion of the slimness aimed at.

But the daughter was beautiful, and her manners and dress were the last word in modern distinction. She was slight, tall, and erect as any handsome boy of twenty, with a toss of short black silky curls which would have done him no discredit. A lovely little Jewish nose and arrogant upper lip stained a blackberry-juice crimson would have been arresting even without

the dark sleepy eyes hidden in heavy lashes. Her face
was pale as ivory, whether by art or nature I cannot
say, but the whole effect was that of a frontispiece to
a book of decadent verse decorated by some artist
whose name would sooner or later get into the papers
with an unpleasant caption. How a healthy-minded
fellow like Sir Francis could have found her congenial
was one of the unanswerable mysteries which pervade
the mating of men.

She smiled with careless languor as I made my bow,
but for a flash her eyes were inquisitive, and as the
long lashes subsided I knew that both ladies promised
themselves I should be thoroughly sifted later.

"We think all the mischief began on that unhappy
hunting day, Dr. Livingstone," began my lady. "We
think dear Sir Francis had been overdoing himself,
don't we, Fleurette?"

"Looks like it!" said the beauty languidly. The tones
were slow and golden, but as she spoke all loveliness
slipped away from her as far as I was concerned and
left only heightened amazement at the man's infatua-
tion. Under them I could detect the shrewd soul, bal-
ancing chances, with cunning in its bad little eye. Each
word was a drop of icy rain on passion. I knew that
even damns were too dim to illuminate the blackness
of her fury at this sudden let-down in her lover's consequence. The woman inside her was curling away into
repulsion from the man sitting a few feet from her
and painfully trying to make the best of things by
pretending that all was as it used to be.

What had happened before I appeared? The air of
the room was electric—I saw that he was fighting
down shock as well as she. It is my trade to read the
cipher of expression, and when I saw his eyes rake
the shining slimness of her beautiful silken legs, dis-

played by a skirt so short that sitting dragged it above
the knees and gave glimpses of her thighs, it was with
the very repulsion that had seized him at other accustomed displays of life far less appealing to the pri-
meval instincts. I cleared decks for action. We were
in for it! Coming, coming!

"We'll all count on Dr. Livingstone to pull you
right, old thing," said Fleurette, slowly glancing a
seductive little smile in my direction, "because it's a
sheer blithering nuisance. I did so want to ride over
and see Lettice Dornish's bull-pups when I was down
here again, and now I suppose they'll cold-shoulder
me too."

"Even the bull-pups! Well, I shouldn't wonder,"
said a voice I should never have known for his. "Suppose you try!"

She pouted languidly.

"What, and get kicked out? It would be simply
sterile to shut my eyes to the fact that we're particularly putrid outsiders just now. No thank'ye, Frankie.
I'll go for a run with the Harriers tomorrow morning.
That'll be rather valid, I think."

The Harriers—of which he had resigned the mastership! Here was a bolt from the blue! He turned a deep
mahogany red from chin to brow through his tan.

"Suppose you do!" he said, and pulled himself up
sharply.

Mamma perceived the danger. "Fleurette! Fleurette," she said with a hint of steel under a purr,
"you silly child! You tease! But Francis knows you
so well you can't tease *him* any more!"

Fleurette yawned. "Why shouldn't you flounder
about after me, Frank? I declare that's rather a valid
notion. Lettice Dornish used to go simply soupy about
me, and if we turn up together like in the good old

days I believe the hatchet'll be buried on the spot. Do, Frankie?"

He sprang up suddenly, looking eight feet high as he stood, opened his lips to say something, shut them and walked violently out of the room, banging the door behind him. I got up to follow but she curved forward and put her hand on my coat sleeve. Her face was real and sagacious in a moment; her eyes greedy for information.

"What in the name of mercy—what *is* it, doctor? Is he mad? Will he get better?"

The mother had risen too. They hemmed me in. I said briefly that I could offer no opinion until I had examined the case further. She relaxed into a tinkling little laugh.

"Well, all I can say is—if he's going to give up life and behave like a fermented old centenarian, I'm not on!" And Fleurette turned sharply away to the window.

We all have our own tastes, and heaven forbid I should disparage other people's; but I thought her the most unattractive woman I had ever seen in my life. Beauty itself can edge the dart with repulsion sometimes and it did here. I got out of the room and knowing he had run to earth went up to his room and knocked. He opened the door and asked me in—white with inward struggle.

"Sit down!" he said thickly. "That ends that. Did you know I had the horrors come over me when I looked at her thighs exactly as when I saw the fox cut up the other day. She sat there—perfectly heartless, shamelessly immodest, the finished— No, I won't call any woman that—of the modern world. She's gone with the rest of my old life."

"But is it reasonable? You chose her, knowing all

that. You found no fault with her dress. It's what all the women wear but a little more so. Mightn't what she said be more manner than anything else? Her talk isn't real. It's the fashionable cant of the minute studied from the magazines. I knew where every word came from. She may be a good sort underneath."

"And I thought it piquant!" he said, grinding his teeth. "I was enchanted when she told me she was getting 'perfectly oozy' about me. There was another—but she laughed me out of that. Said 'that kind of virginal dither would blue-mold me in a week.' It was 'quite too fragrant and Victorian.' The fool I've been. Get them out of the house, doctor, or you'll have an asylum show on your hands. One doesn't marry women like that. One keeps a handful of them and gives them the go-by when one's had enough. I've had enough."

I made it clear that I could not possibly speed the parting guest in that way, and, as he glared at me, added:

"But I've no objection to saying you're very unwell and can't turn up at dinner. That by my advice you're taking a bromide. Kept up tomorrow morning that might do the trick."

"Then do it!" he said, looking at me like a man distracted. "God bless this bust-up, or whatever it is, for saving me from *that*. I begin to think it's 'a soul's awakening' or whatever it is they call that oleograph you see in all the cheap picture shops. Perhaps after all I shall like myself better when I get used to myself. I don't now."

I confess I went down with some trepidation. Lady Leslie received me with enthusiasm, the beautiful Fleurette languidly but with a sharp ear pricked for fog signals. I provided them. I said Sir Francis was in such a state of excitement that I had judged it better to keep him extremely quiet and alone. After which we went into dinner, as ill-matched a trio as you could find in the length and breadth of England. I liked her less with every word. A cheap mind tricked out with the rags and spangles of fashion. Suppose the man's aberrations condemned him to an asylum, wouldn't even that be better than life with a woman to whom all things that men should value were contemptible names and no more? Upon my soul, the problems were thickening!

Her mother ate and drank a little more than was desirable and went frankly to sleep directly after dinner. The girl wandered listlessly about the room, bored to tears, resourceless, sick of her own company, a butterfly winged for a short flight in the glare of the electric lights from artificial flower to flower, and then —the long cruel winter of age, disease, death. As a life-companion—oh, Lord!

I went upstairs and told Sir Francis I had heard her say to her mother that she felt like a blanc mange, that Brakespeare was a musty old hutch and she thought it would be a strategic idea to get a move on after lunch.

"Excellent!" he said. "I'll write when they get back. Not but what Fleurette could be amusing if one took her in pillules and with a few other sorts to put pepper in the soup. I'm done with rot, doctor. I'll live my life in my own way. There's room for it here and I'll take women as men do in the East—as an amusement and not an end. After all, we give them all they've got. If we collapsed, no more for my lady!"

He talked like this for an hour, and I shall not report his talk, though a lot of it was inexpressibly comic in a queer guileless way that he couldn't savor himself at the moment. Nothing noxious. A harmless let-off of sexual gas. But amazingly un-English in tone. I couldn't place it. I couldn't place him. I was utterly at sea.

Then with difficulty I tore myself away and went off to my room feeling about as perplexed as any psychologist could fairly ask to be at these sudden cyclones and revulsions. It was not madness, I knew, and yet any outside observer would certainly have said he was as mad as a hatter. I stood by the window a moment staring up at the constellations—the armies of immeasurable Law looking down upon our apparently lawless earth swarming beneath. Ants in their dark galleries if we knew no better! And at that exact moment two thoughts flashed through me. One, that this outbreak, whatever it might be, had a singularly oriental complexion. The other that an oriental friend of mine—Pundit Devaraja (I will not give his real name, for reasons) happened to be in London at the moment, and that oriental psychology has explored certain byways which western psychology has hitherto cold-shouldered with relentless dignity. A wise and learned man is a very present help in trouble and Devaraja had all the instructed Indian's zest for the unusual. His diagnosis might clarify a suspicion which had struck me in the same flash as I stared at the wheeling of the Great Bear down the sky. Yes—I knew that I badly wanted a quack with Devaraja!

Next day I sent a telegram and told Sir Francis (closely barricaded in his bedroom) what I had done and to a certain extent why. He agreed in unmitigated astonishment, and he never would have agreed if he had not reached the point where hope survives resistance. Miss Leslie had made a gallant attempt to storm the citadel, knocked and in a whisper of music suggested they should have a ten minutes' talk in his dressing-room.

"And I'll be so good, Frank. I'm so unhappy that I think my heart will break. Do, *do!*"

Silence from within. Commissioned, I issued by the dressing-room and declared my patient invisible. He had, in fact, a blazing headache and I had ordered him to bed. She opened her sleepy eyes with a vengeance, then glared at me like a tigress before she turned and went downstairs. They left after lunch, and in the evening Devaraja arrived.

It may be imagined that I had some difficulty in explaining the situation to him. His knowledge of English was perfect but not so his knowledge of English mentality, and that a man could be suspected of insanity or Bolshevism because he preferred not to eat flesh and had developed a sudden dislike to blood sports was a kind of insanity itself to his mind. Naturally the humor of the situation escaped him entirely while to me it triumphed over all else, though I was obliged to keep that point of view to myself. Where I could scarcely hang on to my professional gravity Devaraja saddened, and made the preposterous situation inexpressibly comic by his grave and pensive laments.

"These English—these English! Because the man has come to his senses they scorn him! What a nation of sausages!" he ejaculated. Then he sat drowned in meditation and finally emerged with a truly Indian suggestion:

"Has the man ever had his horoscope worked out?"

"Never. I could swear it."

The very notion appeared a blasphemy against the landed gentry of Devon.

"He should. It may reveal the reason of this awakening."

Astrology! Well, I never censure anything I know nothing of, but I must own even Devaraja's arguments and eulogies had never hitherto exactly captured me. It might have something psychic about it—that had been my utmost concession, coupled with the argument that as the sun doesn't actually pass through the signs of the Zodiac at all it appeared that the so-called science crumbled before it started. I repeated this now and he, a former reply:

"In this world the ignorant of us naturally conform to the phenomena about us. The wise do so also though they know them to be only the symbols of eternal truth. Judge by results."

I immediately asked him to draw a horoscope, for as to the date and time required I was certain Mrs. Malpas, the housekeeper, a family heirloom of price, would not be wanting to herself and us on such a point. I dared not confront Sir Francis either with an Indian or a horoscope unless matters should take a very unexpected turn.

I was right. She gave not only the date of birth, but a paper with fullest particulars including hour and minute, headed with the pious ascription: "Praise God from whom all blessings flow!—My lady safely delivered of a beautiful boy." And in the full rush of information she happily forgot to ask why a doctor should need such early information.

Devaraja sat down with an almanac, forgot the world, and before we went to bed laid down his pen and called me:

"Many horoscopes have I worked out, my friend, but this is the strangest I ever beheld. I thank you for giving me such an opportunity. You know little of astrology and our methods differ from the English, but I will use your phraseology and—"

I interrupted to beg that I might be spared details as far as possible, in view of my ignorance. He smiled.

"Therefore I will merely mention that Aquarius is

the rising sign. The sun was in Pisces and the moon in Capricorn. With Aquarius rising Saturn rules the House of Life."

I am no astrologer and cannot therefore report Devaraja literally,—I can only give the points as they struck me. I gathered that the Sun was in the second house and the moon in the twelfth, Mars in Sagittarius supported by planets in Aries. The sun and moon in the ascendant. And what they were all doing there escaped me entirely, especially when he added that there were peculiarities which exhausted the major influences of the horoscope.

Here I entreated explanation, and he replied:

"Have patience. I will spare you the rest. The salient points are these. The native was born of elderly parents, the mother about forty-four, the father fifty. He had a fall at the age of four which injured the skull and accounted for rather an irritable, nervous childhood. That influence was overcome at the age of twelve. He traveled, saw the world, developed a fine harmonious nature and—"

Here I interrupt to say he gave me much information as to the patient's life and temperament which I regard as private. He then resumed:

"The moon in Capricorn gives an extraordinary attraction to India, Aquarius rising gives a deeper nature than could be suspected from the exterior. It may be taken to insure the resurrection of past desires. The position of the moon also indicates the recovery of memory. All this has been startling in the extreme, so much so that I desire in addition to work out one or two horoscopes of his former lives and am confident that we shall reach a perfectly clear explanation of his present conversion. Conversion, as they call it in the West, is often a return to a previous life experience."

Conversion! I trembled at the prospect of breaking this view to Sir Francis. Fortunately he had decided to go up to London by the 7:30 train next morning to discuss the broken engagement with Mr. Dalgleish, so there was no need for a meeting between him and Devaraja and I had time to consider the situation.

"But can you get at his past lives by astrology? Can you get the horoscope of the past? That seems a big jump."

"Certainly. I have made a study of the Tibetan 'Astrology for the Dead.' It takes the moment of death as a basis for the calculations and amongst other things gives the land and condition in which the dead man will be reborn on earth. I shall get the aspects from his present life and horoscope."

"And how on earth will you get the moment of the last?"

"Difficult, but with our Indian methods we can work back though it takes a long time. Then we shall not speculate—we shall know."

"And what do you think has happened now?"

"A rare case, but not unique. I believe a former life has suddenly broken out in this. The moon's influence has not been strong enough to insure memory but it will come, and then all will fall into harmony. Very extraordinary cases of conversion or change are often brought about by this."

"You think then that an oriental past in a former birth—"

"I am certain. I will work out the calculations when I go back. Treat the native meanwhile as an Oriental. Encourage him not to repress his feelings but to respect them. The Englishman is gone, and—to use your homely proverb—it is now between two chairs he stumbles. You must hoist him on to the oriental one.

The English lunatics will never forgive a sane man. But I must have the Tibetan calculations to work from."

"Judging by appearances this is a hit in the bull's-eye. But the causes?"

"I will work it out. I will not see him. Better wait until we can meet fraternally. He will improve as his true nature expands."

As he rose his eye fell on a silvery shimmer on the fine Jacobean table at his elbow. The bowl picked up by Sir Francis on the upper levels of the Himalaya.

"This is ancient Tibetan work. I should say about the year 800 A.D.," he said with interest, and took it in his hands, drawing near the light. He turned it over and over while I stood patiently. Presently:

"This is most interesting. Astrological—and of the time and method I just spoke of. Could I put in a long-distance telephone call and ask my pupil to bring down the book tomorrow? Might I stay another night? This is a great treasure. It might even help me in your friend's calculation."

It was arranged, and the pupil, a wheat-colored young Indian with a very intellectual face, arrived next day at lunch-time and departed swiftly without a word to me or breaking bread in the house. Devaraja sat the whole afternoon and evening over the jar making hieroglyphic notes and repelling all interruption. It was not until ten o'clock at night that he rose, shut his book and said, "Done!"—with the fire of enthusiasm blazing in his black eyes. He rose and addressed me like a public meeting:

"This is one of the finest examples I have ever seen of a death horoscope. It is by a highly skilled Tibetan astrologer and was to be buried with the dead man—a king, many centuries ago, of a people on the great plateau which ascends to the mountains. He was an Indian—apparently from Behar. It was to await his rebirth."

I had had such marvels from Devaraja that nothing could astonish me, but when it is remembered that I had never mentioned the history of the bowl to him I think it may astonish others. I rose instinctively to listen and leaned on the back of my chair.

"The horoscope gives the color, the key and the governing *mantram* [charm] of the native's life. These correspond with the horoscope I drew for you yesterday. He was to be reborn in a high position in the West, to live an alien life for the first half of his life and finally to break through and remember the past, enabling an ignorant Western people to realize the existence of a system of thought quite unknown to them. He will die at the age of ninety, having lived to see his children take the same path and with the utmost distinction. I think your case is clear. I need only add that he will regain his kingdom."

He looked at me in mild triumph. I relaxed into the chair almost petrified by this turn of the wheel, for he gave me full information and I received it with the respect due to his knowledge and my own appreciation of the solution of a most difficult psychological problem. It had come to me clothed in comedy, but a very different aspect was turning upon us now, and it is hard to express the interest with which I would await developments.

Devaraja said:

"To recover his memory is the point. Let us both concentrate upon that in our meditations tonight and at dawn. The planets are in a peculiarly favorable aspect for the native. We will not lose the opportunity. You note of course how his karma led him straight

to the Tonda country. You can't cheat karma! That
also brought you and me here and placed the bowl in
my hands."

We separated and I went up to my room and, sitting in moonlight with the starry heavens wheeling
above me, I concentrated upon my patient. Memory.
Memory. That was the strong current I sent to him.
And I received the impression that the aerials were
in receiving order.

"It was a good night," Devaraja said briefly on bid-
ding me good-by in the early morning. "Tell me what
comes to my brother in the waking of memory."

My brother! And the owner of Brakespeare—English *in excelsis!* But I held up and promised, profoundly certain that Devaraja had set me on the right
trail.

Sir Francis came back after Devaraja had gone and
immediately invited me into the library eager to hear
what had happened with regard to "the Indian pundit."
There was that in my face which forbade any less
respectful term. He then volunteered that he had written in London to Miss Leslie saying he was sure her
distaste for his changed view of life would render it
impossible for her to consider him any further as a
possible husband and that he agreed in what he knew
would be her decision.

"That's the gist of it!" he said. "But a blind man
could see it was final. It reminds me somehow of the
parody:

> "I've learnt life's lesson to my cost,
>   When all is said and done.
> 'Tis better to have loved and lost
>   Than to have loved and won."

He was humming this absent-mindedly but cheerfully
when we went into the library.

"To think," he said, "that Lady Leslie will never sit here again! I wonder if it's because of that I feel so light-hearted this morning, doctor? so reconciled to the loss of other things I set such store on? Well— on with the dance! What did he say?"

I led off with a question. Had there been anything unusual? Had there been anything specially remarkable about his dreams of late?

He hesitated.

"Now you mention it—yes. Nothing to write home about, but I've been dreaming a lot about that place I told you up the Brahmaputra. Queer confused dreams. But I can account for it because I had been reading over my diaries. What then?"

"Can you remember any snatches of the dreams?"

"Very little. But I did dream I went back there and they gave me a rousing welcome and offered me six wives of noble blood. Pretty girls, too."

"Do you remember if in the dream they were the people you saw when you were there, or long-ago people?"

"That's queer! I suppose, long ago, for they were all in full fig and in some sort of a hall with pillars with elephants and horses springing from them. A wild kind of panorama. Very like the movies."

I questioned further, got one or two more interesting facts and began:

"I don't expect you to believe what I'm going to say. In fact you won't, and the best word I expect is charlatanism. Still, it's true. What has happened to you is the recrudescence of a former life with all its instincts and prepossessions. You have inherited the mentality of an Indian prince, ruler of a small kingdom under the greatest of the Himalayas—a kingdom the very name of which is now not on the map. You are thinking, feeling, desiring, as you did in that life but with the wider knowledge imposed on you by this."

I stopped expecting a rush, a roar, and coruscating fireworks of bad language—culminating in a furious request to leave the house. Silence. Then—I looked up to see a smile dawning upon his face.

"Thank the Lord! *Now* I can speak. My good sir, I was afraid to be frank even to you, for I believed you'd give me up for a loony. The truth is that I knew in my heart I was on the right track when I started all this, though it was damned inconvenient and I wouldn't own it even to myself. I was really afraid I was going balmy. But last night I went to sleep with a head like a bomb, simply bursting with bothers, and in the night I came awake as clear as a bell and I knew what had happened just as you tell me. I remembered the whole show. I could take you and show you where I lived—everything. You see I've always believed in rebirth since I was in India, for it's the only logical way out of the problem when all's said and done. But naturally I wouldn't breathe it, for it would have put the rector off his dot and thrown me out of touch with all the charities. As bad as the hunt! But now—"

He paused, looking down and smiling gently as if at an agreeable thought. I was speechless for the moment. He resumed:

"I can't be worse damned than I am, and now I'm going to let myself go in good earnest and say and do precisely what I think. I shall come into the open."

"But you said you hated the—the transformation. That the real you didn't think these things."

"I was ashamed to say anything else. But not now. *No*. I love animals and they me and I'll be their open friend henceforward. They want one, God knows! I'll have a Birds' Sanctuary and a Home of Rest for Aged

Animals and I'll go in for pushing their claims right
and left. And I'll not only remain a vegetarian but
I'll have Bernard Shaw down to lecture on corpse-
food at the village hall, and make the local magnates
lap it up. And I'll prosecute the hunt when it goes
over my land, and I'll establish a harim or remain a
bachelor whichever suits me best. Why shouldn't I
follow my natural bent?"

I slowly recovered speech. Remember all this was
before he knew the astonishing confirmation of the
copper bowl! I told him that next and almost floored
him.

"By George!" he said, and sat down. Need I add
more on that head?

I returned to London that evening loaded with bene-
dictions and two superlative checks for Devaraja and
myself. I noted that his manners already were princely,
and there was a tendency to treat us both as faithful
adherents to the crown. He was looking over a book of
famous Orders of Chivalry when I said good-by and
I suspected him of an intention of founding an order—
of, say, the Indian Elephant, with a Knight Com-
mandership apiece for Devaraja and myself. At the
moment he was with some effort controlling his tendency to the splendors of oriental raiment. That was
bound to come sooner or later.

I laughed in the train until I was obliged to smother
my head in the Devon Gazette from the suspicious
glances of my fellow travelers. You cannot laugh pub-
licly in England as a soloist without incurring the
direst suspicions. It affronts the national gloom.

What happened was this. The papers announced
soon after that owing to discoveries among the
archives of the India Office, his Majesty had been
pleased to create Sir Francis Bethune, Maharaja of

Tonda, and that the Maharaja had embraced Hinduism. They left the particular brand uncertain, floored by their ignorance of such niceties. He came to see me and told me the county had accepted the situation and all was forgiven and forgotten.

"Not that they like it," he added with his usual candor. "Naturally they couldn't. But now I'm a maharaja the feeling is—What can you expect from a pig but a grunt? So English! A stupid race!"

I noted the tone of the distinguished foreigner already fully matured, and his happiness radiated joy like a Christmas fire.

"But I mean to live up to it at Brakespeare!" he added. "A certain amount of state and ceremony is due to that kind of thing, and my own memories, with Devaraja to coach me, have given me the right tip."

It was natural that a little later he should go to India. He married the daughter of the Maharaja of Covindapur, the most enchanting young woman, lovely as a lily and with eyes like blue lotuses. She had a voice sweet and low as a fugue played on bluebells. Of course no one could resist the Maharani and they became the rage in London and among the splendors of Brakespeare, especially when the true story got into the papers, as it was bound to do. She could scarcely drive in the park for the crowds that thronged the streets, and her appearance (veiled) at a Durbar at Delhi drove the whole world nearly wild with excitement. I heard on a side-wind that Miss Leslie was frantic with jealousy at seeing another in the limelight which might have been hers. The affair has certainly brought India into the limelight also and with a thrill of romance never as yet awakened in the British soul. As to the birth of the heir—words fail me!

Here I must leave the story to the future—where

many developments await it. Later Sir Francis was given a peerage (in reality for services to the Conservative Party) and is already known in the House of Lords as "the member for India." A delightful elephant has been acclimatized at Brakespeare, on which the Maharaja and the Kumaraja take their airings in the park. I am confidently expecting its appearance in London.

The horoscope Devaraja has drawn for the heir predicts events which will certainly make England sit up and take notice of India when they fall due. Meanwhile his father's reminiscences of ancient glories are among the most interesting things I know, and it is conceded that the maharani must have been the chief consort at her husband's court in Tonda, though for want of knowledge of the hour of her birth even Devaraja cannot be logically certain. The zenana is as yet undetermined. Perhaps one wife is as much as English degeneration has qualified the maharaja to handle.

The Thug

I HAVE PRESENTED MYSELF SO MANY TIMES AS JAMES
Livingstone, a specialist in psychological troubles and
disturbances, that I have given myself if not my
readers reason to marvel at the strange and abysmal depths of human personality which come before
me almost daily in events that would often be incredible even to a man of my profession but for the guar-
antee of terror and deadly doubt which certifies their
reality to the sufferers. Sometimes one gets a cheerful
and humorous blink into the supernormal, and I have
had many cases which convince me that the humor and
irony of the unseen world out-top that of the seen as
much as do its beauty and terror. But more often it is
the other way in that uncharted country—the psyche
shuddering on the brink of some experience with
which it cannot cope and so falling prostrate and conquered. And, by the way, the man who is once face to
face with the Unseen must learn the first rule of the
Game and beat it in upon his being. It is this: "He
who turns his back is lost." The motto on the standard
is always "Push onward." With the Emperor Akbar I
may say, "I never saw any man lost in a straight
road."

My strangest stories I dare not tell. They are meat
for strong men—for those who have had their own
experiences. But this is one that may well rouse fear
and something better than curiosity. Worth telling, in
my opinion.

I was sitting in my consulting room in Harlington Street, London, when a patient whose name I give as Hampton was shown in—a tall sinewy, extremely dark man of thirty-six, strong in the jaw and with dry, close-shut lips which gave the impression of limitless strength and courage. I summed him up instinctively as the born adventurer, probably with a strong dash of alien blood—Indian, for choice. I saw him galloping, hell for leather, leading a forlorn hope on the perilous frontier where the hills open a more perilous way into India, or quiet with folded arms on the deck as the ship sways to her last plunge. He walked firmly into the room even with a touch of swagger (my patients do not always show off so well!) and sat down four-square in the chair. Then the clock struck, and at the sudden little silver noise, the mask dropped. He started like a man stopped by a bullet. Ripples of nerves ran over his face and throat. I saw him grip his shaking hands in one another, and go as white under his dark sunburn as a ghost-seer in midnight by a churchyard wall. I could see the heart-beat hammering under his thin coat, and I knew I had one of my worst cases on hand and settled down to it. I had to give him a tot of brandy before he could command the working of his lips enough to tell his story, and it came out in terrors—shall I call it?—moans, ejaculations of shame and fear, which oblige me to give it in my own way and not in his. But I keep to the stern truth. God knows it wants no garnishing.

I skip the medical details and come to the kernel of his terror. That was lest the need of earning his living (he had to support a mother and sister) should drive him back to India. He had been combing England since his return for any job that would give him five or six hundred a year, for on that they and he

could scrape along together, but the war and the inrush
of women to business had blocked all ways and, so far
as he could see, it was India or nothing. Then, could
I cure him, and could I tear the root of his fear out
of his heart so that he could face it somehow, anyhow? That was why he had come to me.

So much for the prologue. Here is the terrible story.
No one loves and knows India better than I, but there
are the paths that skirt precipices deeper than Everest's,
there are the jungles where lurk worse than the tiger
and the cobra.

"Save me. Cure me!" was his cry. "Shake the
instinct out of me if instinct it is, and I'll bless you
the longest day I live."

Hampton was in the employment of one of the
largest business firms in India. They dealt in many
commodities, and his own branch of work led him
half over India and put him in touch with Indian
bankers and money-lenders, Mohammedan and Hindu,
and many other strange personages that the Indian
Civil Service man may never come in touch with all
his life. He made the best use of his chances, for
knowledge pays, and had besides an unusual knack of
picking up languages. He was first-rate at Hindi and
Persian, and had three or four other tongues or dia-
lects at his fingers' ends. This made him valuable. His
pay was good, his commissions excellent, and but that
he was an honest man he could have made money hand
over hand in *bakshish,* which is always in the background of racial transactions out East if a man will
lower himself so far. But Hampton never did, and his
abstention gave him a clean-handed reputation among
the dark men, and he stood high with East and West.

There never was a man better pleased with his life
and himself, and even the climate suited him as if he

were native-born though, dark as he was there was not a single drop of dark blood in his veins. Not a crumple of any sort in the rose-leaf.

Now it happened one day nearly four years before I saw him that he was obliged to go south on business in one of the great States of Southern India. He was immensely bucked, for everything Indian took his fancy, and he was working up quite a serviceable knowledge of architecture. And about Dhondapur lie the magnificent ruins of the dead grandeurs of the Gond princes, broken palaces built of a kind of black stone richly carved by the finest craftsmen of the south into sinister beauty. Some stand outside the little town in the famous palm groves near the new dak-bungalow (rest house)—one by a beautiful little tank in the public gardens. He promised himself a rare treat when his business was over with Faiz Ullah, banker and head of a great house manufacturing rich stuffs.

He reached the little station in the afternoon and decided to send his valise to the dak-bungalow and walk to the house. Easily found in that small place and a fine one at that, with the usual shut-up and secret look which the rich Indian (and especially the Mohammedan) prefers. The wealthy Faiz Ullah stood just inside the open door as if waiting for him, and paid him the compliment of ushering him in himself to the fine old-style room surrounded with gorgeously cushioned divans, where the business was to take place. No servant appeared.

"I knew when the sahib's train was due and his face is bright in my eyes; so much respect have I for the Kumpani he represents. Be seated, sahib, be seated, and do honor to my house."

The most picturesque old fellow. He might have been the Emperor Akbar's court banker if such a per-

son existed. He wore a very full-skirted coat of rose
satin girt about the middle with a gold-embroidered
Persian scarf. Tight-fitting white trousers wrinkled
down to his ankles and on his head was a closely tied
turban in the Moghul fashion with a handsome gold
clasp at the side.

Hampton noticed that he started at the sight of him,
but he explained and apologized at once.

"For indeed, blessings of Allah! the likeness of the
sahib is great to a nobleman who used to honor my
house in days past. May the lights of Allah enlighten
his tomb! I shall not easily look upon his like and the
mere resemblance made glad my memory."

They got their business partly done and made an
appointment to continue it next morning, and then in
honor of the guest-right Faiz Ullah disappeared for a
moment to order refreshments.

"Allah forbid, sahib, that you should cross my
threshold without sharing my bread and salt."

He was an important person to please in his way
and Hampton had no motive for refusing, especially
as refusal would be a slight. His host returned with
some handsome carved figures in ivory for his enter-
tainment and with them a whole set of wooden ones,
beautifully shaped and painted, each about three inches
in height.

"And of these last I beg the sahib's gracious acceptance. Allah forbid that I should offer what is unworthy
of a great man, but these, though of wood, were
wrought by a mighty maker and are so fine a rarity
that in India is none like them. Those of his Highness
the Ruler of Jaipur are dirt in comparison."

Hampton oscillated between thanks and rejection.
It was of course his rule never to accept a present of
any cost, but these things though interesting certainly

looked to him as if fifty rupees would be their outside value. And they were interesting. He felt he had seen something of the kind before but couldn't remember where.

"But what are they?" he asked.

"Blessings of Allah, does not the sahib know? These figures represent the Thugs, the famous murderers who once haunted all India until the mercy of the beneficent English government put a stop to their wickedness."

Hampton stooped over the tray on which they stood, intensely curious. Everyone has heard of the Thugs, but few know the truth of what is the most extraordinary and murderous religious system known to history. He knew little more than the name and he asked his new friend to explain the meaning of the drama which the figures were acting.

Squatting on the divan beside him and holding him with piercing dark eyes, the banker took up figure by figure in slender amber fingers and in his low monologue began the snaky subtle windings of the murder story known in India as Thuggi.

"And I need not tell the sahib learned in our tongues that the word 'Thug' means a deceiver. Deceiver, indeed! Their net of murder and loot spread all over India until the great East India Kumpani showed its mercy by discovering and punishing these evil-doers."

"But do you mean to say that a great system of wholesale murder and looting could go on under the eyes of the company's officials and never be suspected?" asked Hampton, fingering a group of two where one with a knotted yellow handkerchief had flung it about the neck of the other and with a twist strangled him. The corpse was dropping sideways heavily.

"Sahib, how could it be known? There were then no ter-ains, and travelers went and came alone or in twos and threes like birds, carrying their merchandise with them on mules or ponies. They encamped for a night in the palm groves outside a town, or they rested at the caravanserai for a night and then they journeyed on into the jungles and the tracks again, and who but the tigers or the Thugs could say how they ended? It was no one's business. I can tell you this, sahib, that my grandfather stood by Sleeman Sahib, the great colonel, when the informer Feringhea revealed to him that the very grove outside the town where the colonel sahib governed was a *bhil*—a murder place—of the Thugs and angrily he refused belief. He said:

" 'May the face of the liar be blackened! This thing cannot be.' And Feringhea answered:

" 'Command them to dig, sahib, now—here, where you stand!' and at the colonel sahib's foot they dug, and there lay, head to feet, fourteen bodies of men and women, and the sahib turned aside and vomited."

It was at least profoundly interesting. Hampton looked at the figures with curiosity, and then at the old man. His eyes glittered in the shadows with eagerness to tell his story.

"My grandfather was a writer in the office of the colonel sahib, and, sahib, these are the very words he wrote for his master." He repeated them in Hindi with the perfect memory of the Oriental:

" 'If any man had told me that a gang of assassins by profession resided in the village not four hundred yards from my court, and that the extensive groves of the village of Mundesur only one stage from me on the road were one of the greatest *bhils,* or places of murder in India—that large gangs used to rendezvous in these groves, remain in them for days together and carry on their dreadful trade all along the lines of road with the knowledge and connivance of the two landholders by whose ancestors these groves had been planted, I should have thought him a fool or a madman; and yet nothing could have been more true. The bodies of a hundred travelers lie buried in and about the groves of Mundesur.'"

The old man chuckled to himself as he ended:

"So said the colonel sahib! If he had known that at Kingoli the leader of all the Thugs of that district was the rich merchant Hari Singh whom all the sahib people honored, what would he have said? But then how could the colonel sahib tell? Hari Singh would go away on his journeys—what more needful for his barter and commerce? And how could any sahib know that this good man who worshiped in his temple with offerings to the gods, had with his own hands strangled seven hundred and sixty-eight men and women? Surely the khan sahib"—now why did the banker give Hampton an oriental title of respect?—"will laugh when he hears how this Hari Singh befooled the sahibs! Once he asked the sahib in charge of the district for a pass for bringing up rich cloths from Bombay, and he and his men went out and met the owners and made friends with them and murdered them every man and brought in the cloths with the pass and sold them openly in the bazar and mocked at the sahib's beard! He murdered these persons only five hundred yards from the bazar and buried them. Who knows but that the sahib himself bought a few of the cloths? One must laugh at such skill, khan sahib; is it not true?"

To his consternation, Hampton found himself laughing aloud in the strange silk-hung room, with its great divans where a man could couch in peace and forget the changes of time outside. Here in the heavy-smelling quiet might surely reign the morals of a day when murder was a jest and loot an honorable business.

How still it was! Some of that queer incense charged with musk which they use in India was burning in a brass pot finely carved and pierced. Its thin blue spirals circled in the air and loaded it with over-sweet perfume. The old man's piercing eyes held his like rivets. He fancied languidly that he could see the deadly story shaping in them like words. Was he thinking the thing to him or speaking? Hampton could not tell. Half drugged, half drowsy, he listened, and still the refreshments made no appearance and still the hateful story glided on with the fluent deadly grace of a snake. Was he himself an Oriental listening to a racial saga with which he could sympathize—the shackles of his western standards falling from him like withered garlands? Again he could not tell.

"Thuggi was well planned, khan sahib—well planned. The band was divided—each man had his own duties. There was the captain whom all must obey. See!—this is his figure, with the gay scarf knotted about the waist. These two are the *sothas*—the inveiglers, whose duty it was to win the trust of travelers by promising them protection on the dangerous journeys or seeking protection from them. The arts of the *sotha* were endless, and he was chosen for his pleasant looks, his frankness, courtesy, and art in making his company desirable. He went into the bazar to meet with the unwary and engage him in talk, terrify him with the dangers of the way, especially from wandering bands of Thugs, and finally induce him to join

forces so that they might go together through the
dangers, and reach their destination safely. Their destination! It was the *bhil*—the murder-place! But that
was only their own affair—and the Thugs!"

He chuckled at the humor of the notion like the
thick gurgle of water from an underground spring and
Hampton echoed the chuckle. It was humorous to think
of grown men walking into such a trap as easily as
hungry birds! They deserved what they got. A queer
business. And unknown to all the watchful officials!
"Did it pay?" he asked.

"Pay?" The old man shook his head like the malignant dwarf of a fairy tale. "You may wager on that,
khan sahib! See these pearls and emeralds. They were
dragged from women's strangled throats and from the
little boxes hidden cunningly under silks and cottons
in the bales on the ponies' backs. Oh, the Thugs knew!
They knew."

He rose, shimmering in his rich coat and edged
towards a cabinet of fine Amritsar work. He pulled out
a drawer and emptied a tangle of necklaces and strings
of jewels on the orange silk and gold cushions of the
divan by Hampton—grass-green emeralds, the pink
rubies worn by the poorer folk, deepening into the true
pigeon-blood from Burma. Cut gold beads, round,
cylindrical, enameled, jeweled—occult, beautiful things,
many worthy of honorable places in museums, nearly
all splendid. Seals and sigils, cut with the emblems of
strange sorceries—a wonderful heap for a man to see
outpoured like wayside seeds before him. Hampton
fingered them, let them run smooth and cold through
his hand, touched the round bright jewels to his lips to
feel their cool.

"A fat trade!" he said at last. "But had they no
pity? Had they no fear—these Thugs? How was it?"

The old man answered eagerly as if he hoped for a recruit.

"Fear? What fear, khan sahib? You knew better than that in the good old days! The skill of these men! They were masters of the smoothest deceit in all the world. How could the ignorant call them murderers? After all, a man must die, and how better? There was no fear—no pain. There was no defiance, no violence about the Thug. All his methods were kindly, courteous, and trust-inspiring. No doubt most of the victims never realized by whose hands they fell. That is the beauty of Thuggi—it was the friend to whom you trusted for help and protection who was the secret Death. They loathed a brutal slayer."

"True—a quick way through the Gates of Fear," Hampton's dreaming voice said. Was it all a dream—the jewels, the old man, the room heavy with poisonously sweet odors? The gliding voice continued:

"And what had they to fear—these gallant Thugs? When a band was formed the first thing they did was to win the ear of the district authorities. Many of the hereditary landholders of India and head men of villages had had for many centuries private understanding with them and helped them handsomely, receiving in return a fixed percentage or laying a special tax upon their houses. You will see, khan sahib, this suited the Thugs perfectly. It was a reasonable kindly arrangement. Then, too, many of the mendicants of the villages were also in the league and their retreats in groves and shady places were exceedingly useful in many ways, the holy men enticing travelers to camp under their protection. Of the smaller rajahs and princes many also added to their incomes by the patronage of Thuggi. No, they had nothing to fear and the great goddess knew how to protect her own. Their password of *'Ali Khan bhai salaam*—Hail to Ali Khan my brother!' carried them safely all over India."

"But, good God!" said Hampton—and even in his drugged ears the invocation rang strangely—"you can't mean it was a religious business too! Murder—"

"Murder is no murder when it is pleasing to the gods!" said the soft voice—or the glittering watchful eyes—which he could not tell. "True, it was for gain —but for more, much more. Remember, khan sahib —search your memory! There is a goddess great and worshiped— See, I whisper her names—Kali, Bhowani, Durga. She, she it was who taught the first Thug to strangle. She who showed him the quick twist of the *rumal* that kills a man before he can cry out. She herself instituted Thuggi and promised her special favor. She set forth also that the reward of her votaries was the plunder of their victims, and they need never fear detection, for she herself would dispose of the bodies of the slain. Aho, she kept her holy word! This lasted for happy ages, when at length two unworthy Thugs, wild with curiosity to see how the goddess fulfilled her promise, kept wicked watch on her proceedings and found that the way her Divinity disposed of the bodies was by devouring them. Furious at the detection, she blazed forth in her majesty and announced that though she would not withdraw her protection, her servants must in future shift for themselves by burying the bodies of the slain, and that only the closest attention of her omens would save them from ruin."

"May her name be honored!" said the voice of Hampton—or was it the thought in his bewildered brain? Dim memories stirred in his mind like a nest of newborn snakes.

"Honored, indeed. And by Moslem and Hindu

alike," said the old man running his hands through the heaped jewels and holding them up to flame in the lamplight (How had a lamp come? Was it dusk?) "What other deity is honored by Moslem and Hindu? How else do they meet as brothers? Each band of Thugs carried her sacred pickax, which represents her teeth, and on this they swore their oaths. The knife stood for a rib of the holy goddess, the strangling cloth the hem of her garment, and this cloth or hand-kerchief was always white or yellow to please her eye. See these figures—they carry it so, khan sahib! When the band moved it was by the guidance of her omens. To hear the cry of a hare was ruin—you must fling down your plans and return, for so she ordained. To hear the bray of a donkey on the left especially if answered by one of the right was her omen of brilliant success and promised many victims and glorious plun-der. So with many other sounds of the jungle or the roadside, and the Thug who did not obey them as her servant sworn would sooner or later certainly pay dear for his wickedness. Oh, they neglected nothing—those just and faithful men! They knew her love and wrath too well!

"After a success a sacrifice was always made, the *Toupani*—a solemn rite which if neglected could only bring the furious vengeance of the goddess. At the *Toupani* coarse *gur* (sugar) was laid by the sacred pickax with a piece of silver as an offering, and after due prayer the *gur* was shared by all who had qualified by strangling. The untried could only look on and envy. The Thugs knew that those who had eaten this *gur* became utterly changed in nature, and that whether they would or would not they then had a Thug's heart for life and death and could never break away from the profession. So powerful was this spell that this happened even to those who might taste the *gur* accidentally. But the Thug was a good and worthy man. Here is his rule—you knew it once, khan sahib:

" 'Be as kind as you will to those about you, affectionate to your kin, give alms to the needy, follow the ordinances of your faith, Hindu or Moslem as it may be, but remember always that you are a Thug and are vowed to relentless destruction of all whom the goddess throws in your way.' And never did they spare! Why should they? They would strangle their own mother or father to please the goddess."

His voice ceased. Refreshments had appeared mysteriously, for Hampton could not remember having seen any servant enter, and stood on a magnificent tray of Jaipur work at his elbow. The drink was sickly sweet sherbet. There were sweet cakes and what looked like brown *jagri*—the sugar of the palm tree. The old man offered him a morsel in a long thin gold spoon embossed with garnets and turquoises.

"And that," he said, "is one of a set that a merchant named Ahmad Khan was bringing from Benares for the marriage of one of the Gond princes. But the Thugs got him and his bones lie in the palm grove by this town, and their captain sold the spoons to the prince for a fat bag of money. Taste this sugar, khan sahib, that is the famous *gur* of the Thugs. Something to boast of—having tasted it! Blessings of Allah, it made brave men—heroes! There are few like them now. Few. But some."

Dreaming awake, as it seemed to him, Hampton took the little gorgeous spoon and tasted the thick brown stuff, but his drowsy hand refused to hold the spoon. It sank beside him. His head fell back on the cushions and he knew no more. Whether it was sleep or a faint he could not say.

When he roused himself his first conscious thought was a mad longing to be away and out of the room. It was dusk—a lamp burned dimly in a sea of shadows, the air was loaded poisonously with the fumes of incense. His host was cringing before him with glittering snake-like eyes uplifted, holding the tray in his hands with the odious figures ranged on it. There were the *sothas,* leaning forward smoothly and courteously to talk with the wretched traveler, who listened so eagerly. There were the stranglers—one with raised rumal, ready to fling it about the victim's throat. There were the grave-diggers and—

Loathing seized Hampton. He kicked the tray brutally aside as the old man muttered, "Accept the gift, khan sahib," and the figures fell clattering to the ground. He rushed through the outer room like a man possessed. No one waited there—none of the accustomed crowd of servants about a rich man's door. It flashed on him with a kind of horror that he had not seen a single living soul in the place but the smooth and snaky old man who had told him—what? He could not remember, but a fog of horror hung about him like foul rags. He found himself in the ill-lit street with people coming and going silently on padding bare feet, and the outer air was like a cool hand laid on his beating temples. Had his wits left him? He asked the way to the rest house, and a dark hand pointed, and he set off, walking at the top of his speed, confused in mind, only certain that a miasma of horror clouded the place. Frightful things had happened but what—he could not tell.

Did the frog-faced keeper of the bungalow know— who met him with such servile courtesy on the veranda as he came stumbling up through the moonlight shade of the grove of palms?

Hampton had a raging headache, his hands were as hot, his body as shivery, as if he had picked up malaria in the town, and yet that could not be. Was it the little poisonously sweet cake he had eaten? It was never the morsel of sugar. Business or no business he would never go near that cursed house again.

I stop here to say that while he repeated his story to me I watched him keenly, and the feeling gripped me that even in telling it he was re-hypnotizing himself. To my mind the whole atmosphere was hypnotic and the notion pleased me. The illusion, whatever it might be, would be more easily dealt with. Naturally the idea of drink had crossed my mind but there was no sign of that in the man—I could trust my experience there. I was yet to learn that there are things in human nature which leave all experience behind.

His brain must have been pretty well confused when he reached the dak-bungalow, for he fancied, while he waited for the usual dinner of tough curried fowl, that he saw quick dark figures and dim lights slipping about through the palm grove. He spoke of that to the squint-eyed khansamah, who salaamed and rejected the notion.

"By the protection of the Inaccessible One the place is very quiet at night, huzoor, and no trash from the bazar come and go here. The Presence may leave his possessions lying about, and this unworthy person can swear that none will touch them."

Unable to eat and sick with headache he resolved to get to bed as soon as possible and took possession of the dak-bungalow bedroom which all travelers in India know and hate; the hard bed, mosquito-netted, the bare roof, the general discomfort and air of passage as if people halted there longing to be up and off again with the dawn.

He could not sleep. The rats and rat-snakes in the roof were too active. Regiments of rats had made the hinterland of the ceiling their castle and the snakes were up and doing. The rush and rattle, the fleeing squeal, and thin whine of mosquitoes in the air kept him awake and tossing with a throbbing head.

Suddenly bed became unbearable. He could not tell why, but he sat bolt upright and forgot the hunting party above. It was urgent that he should go to the window and look out, taking the chance of a snake writhing along the bare floor. He stood there with a cold shuddering premonition tempering the sweating heat of the room. The few lights of Dhondapur twinkled like distant fireflies.

Hush—what was that? Two men were standing in a shaft of moonlight between the palms. They were in turban and loin-cloth and whispering eagerly as they looked toward the bungalow, eyes a-glitter with quick animal interest as they watched him. One turned to the other and whispered. A donkey brayed on the left— another answered on the right. Far off rang the thin squeal of a jackal rising crescendo into a thin howl.

What then? Any man who travels in India is used to these things. He must get to bed. But a word to the keeper of the bungalow next day would not be amiss in case these fellows were *budmashes* (scoundrels) from the bazar with an eye on his valise.

The two stole forward on noiseless feet, and—beckoned to him. Beckoned to the English sahib standing above them by the height of the veranda. Familiarly, and with a kind of fierce glee. Unheard of! Natives to summon an Englishman—and as if with understanding between them! Never!

Here Hampton became vague. He said he knew— he was sure he called to the keeper and told him there were suspicious-looking characters about, but he could not remember whether the man answered. When he looked again the two had disappeared.

But there was a small flickering fire among the palms, and men sitting about it. Travelers? Arrived too late for the caravanserai in the town. No—not that. But what were they so busy about?

By the fire—on a bit of coarse matting lay a pickax. It was raised so that he saw the two anchor-like teeth shining in a jet of flame. There was a plate with something indistinct lying on it—it might be money. And the men sat round these objects silently and as if they were sacred, and waited—but for what? Hampton could not tell.

It was then that a fierce curiosity ran along his veins like a rage. The dangerous secret rites of these dark peoples should not concern an Englishman, but they did—passionately. The fire flickered, the silent naked figures sat about it—one apart as if ostracized from the central sanctity—and it grew on Hampton that this thing concerned him intimately and that there was no more sleep for him while the moonlight ran down the palm fronds like water and the silent figures waited. Waited. Yes—he could see them turning to the rest-house, pointing, beckoning.

An irresistible urge was on him. He pushed open the door that gave on the veranda and went out in his thin silk pajamas and bare feet. Bare feet, where the white man would have shrunk from the evil grace of the cobra's gliding or the nip of the black scorpion. But his feet looked dark in the shadows as he went.

I must halt to stress the agony—yes, the servile agony of terror which possessed Hampton here. His own degradation sickened him. It half sickened me, half inspired me with contemptuous pity to see a white man fallen so low. He was mad with fear lest I should reject his plea for help—the deadly need that streamed out of him like life from an incurable wound. I felt what was coming but I mastered myself and told him to go on.

"They were in a ring when I got out," he said, "and they stood up and salaamed and made room for me, and one and all they said together:

"*'Ali Khan bhai salaam!'* in their different voices, some high, some low. It made a queer and terrifying medley of sound."

"Welcome to Ali Khan, my brother." To a white man. Hampton said:

"Oh, something in me knew what it meant all right, though I couldn't yet shape it into anything understandable. I was quite at home with the good fellows, though I was white and they were dark. But was I? The moon shone very queerly on my hands and feet, for it made them as dark as the others.

"'Welcome, khan sahib,' said the handsome old man with a grizzled beard and green turban, and, 'Welcome,' said they all. I slipped down beside them by the fat packages of merchandise half cut open. In the small one by my feet were strings of pearls, and of emeralds uncut but good—some cut also, such as I had seen at the old devil's in the town.

"'Aha, these travelers were good *bunij* [merchandise],' said the old fellow with his hawk's beak of a nose. 'Our *sothas,* Govind and Pir Shah, went into the bazar at Dhondapur and there was the merchant trying to bargain with the keeper of the caravanserai for a quiet corner. Our men knew well that by the favor of the goddess he had goods worth hiding—he was so touchy about the quiet. So they went to him and said:

"' "Why, Amir, are you trying to bargain with this

dirty thief for a flea-bitten corner in the caravanserai when there's a fine grove outside and good space for your tents, and good company? Where are you going?"

" ' "Why, to Salimshah,' he said doubtfully.

" ' "And so are we; and our leader, one of the rich merchants there, Azam Khan, was saying just now we should be the better for a few good comrades to strengthen our hands for the country between this and Salimshah has a bad name for wandering Thugs, and it's as well to be on the lookout."

" ' "Thugs!' said the merchant, and they saw him whiten in the sunlight and knew they had a coward to handle. "Yes—and am I to leave the caravanserai and trust myself in the groves with strangers? No, thank you, my friends. I prefer bugs to Thugs." ' "

The old man with the green turban blinked at Hampton and laughed. He said:

"Too long to tell you, khan sahib, how they coaxed and wheedled him. There never were two fellows with such smooth tongues as Govind and Pir Shah, and they very soon made him see there was no sense in paying good money for a dirty corner there when he could have the fresh air and the moonlight and safety for nothing. They told him the bazar thieves were like sea-sands and that's true—may Allah blacken their faces! Dirty rogues! So now, khan sahib, he and his young wife and girl and their servants join us in the hour, so we must finish our sacrifice and hide the plunder. The grave is made ready already yonder."

He pointed to a grove on the left where the lantana bushes grew up thick and strong a little beyond the last rank of the palms, and Hampton looking towards it saw that he was seeing right through where the dak-bungalow had stood. He had just come from there but on this glaring moonlight night it did not seem strange that it had lifted like a morning mist and floated away into the unseen. His head was still bewildered.

"Come, *jemadar* [captain]," said one of the band. "The sacrifice to the great goddess, or what luck can we expect with this new *bunij?*"

While Hampton told me this, I noticed a change coming over his face very terrible to see—especially to a man like myself whose business it is to decipher the inner from the outer. I have described him as he was. Now his lips tightened over the teeth and showed them white and gleaming. There was a dull spark in each dark pupil and the whole face had the profoundly guarding watchfulness of a beast of prey. In my own mind I said:

"A homicidal lunatic—and not of English blood." I had not yet probed the depth of the horror.

He propped his lean chin on his two fists and centered his roving eyes on me. He found it easy enough to speak now. The shame and pleading had disappeared and given place to a kind of sullen pride.

"So we sat in a ring about the fire, all of us, and eight were the *bhuttotes*—the stranglers, and there were the *shumsheas* who hold the hands tidily of the *bunij* when the handkerchief goes round their throats, and the *sothas*—the enticers—ready to help where they were wanted, and the *lughais,* the grave-diggers. A fine band of handy fellows. Hindus and Moslems—and brothers all!"

He had drifted into the story and was half acting it, playing his part dramatically. It possessed him. He forgot me.

"And now we each sat solemn and silent, remembering the dreadful goddess that Hindu and Moslem

Thugs worship. No tricks with Kali! Her drink is blood. Her food, human flesh. She wears a necklace of skulls about her neck, and her earrings are dead bodies —she does not lack for jewels! And there our captain made a small hole before the pickax and hid the piece of silver and poured a little of the coarse sugar into it and he raised his voice and cried aloud, with clasped hands uplifted in prayer :

" 'Great and all-powerful goddess—you who have for ages given your protection to your beloved Thugs, help us from on high, from below, from all round, and fulfill all our hopes.'

"We all echoed the prayer and the *jemadar* taking water shook it over the pickax and into the hole. Then the Sacrament of the Gur—the holy sugar—was divided among us and as it was handed to me I drew back and said:

" 'How can I share it—I who have never yet strangled man, woman, or child!' And they laughed aloud a stifled laughter. 'You, khan sahib! You who have six hundred victims already to your count—the best hand with a rumal in Southern India! Do not mock the goddess with jests, but eat.'

"And I ate."

He looked into my eyes until the darting glance seemed to pierce me.

"And if you yourself ate that sugar by chance or by choice you too would be a Thug for life; from the king's palace, from the office, from the study you would break forth to take the life owed to the goddess by her servants." He paused and resumed his story.

"So I ate and was glad and only one sat apart looking longingly at the rest of us, for he had not yet killed his man, but that night he would qualify, for the merchant's girl was allotted to him, being young and tender and not likely to fight for her life. And to me they allotted her mother and with old remembrances on me I said:

" 'Is it well to strangle the women? It is known the goddess is angry if her own sex is attacked. I knew a man, Ayub Amir was his name, and none in this world had such luck. Under his house was buried the wealth of princes. Unluckily, but it was his kismet, a dancing-girl of Aurangabad won his heart and with the cunning of women she smelt out his secret, and when he told it to the band (as he was oath-bound) he was commanded to kill her himself and no other. So he took her out into the jungle for a day of love, and there with his own hand he flung the rumal about her throat, and watched the eyes start in her head, and bundled her into the grave by the running river. But he never had a day's luck after. A hare crossed his way as he went back to the town, and the sweat ran down him like trickling oil, for he knew the token of the deity's desertion. And the English got him and he hung and swung on the gallows. I will never kill a woman.'

"The *jemadar* laughed. They all laughed.

" 'We have killed hundreds of women and no harm. Ayub Amir loved the slut and his heart died in him when she died. That was not the goddess's doing. No, khan sahib, do what you must, and praise the goddess for your strong hand and wrist of iron.'

"So I agreed."

The devil's change in his face so distorted it that for the first time I questioned whether I should be alone with him, knowing India and knowing the history of Thuggi. I interrupted him here. I said:

"I begin to see light on your story; I must devote full time to it. Allow me to arrange the next visit with my man. It won't take a moment."

He agreed without a grain of suspicion.

At the door, I whispered to Jenkins, a powerful man and not without experience of odd happenings in my consulting room, to be near the door. Also I put a little steel friend upon whom I knew I could rely in my pocket. I could see the blood lust in the man glowing from spark to flame. He went on as if there had been no interruption—absorbed, forgetting all else.

"The carts came lumbering up in the moonlight. The noise and talking of the six men with it startled me. Would the people at the dak-bungalow hear? The *jemadar* gave me a knowing leer:

" 'Not they! They are in with us. They get their division.'

"He stepped forward to the merchant who was dismounting from the cart. In the first, his women were sheltered from sight.

" 'Welcome, Amir, to safety, and a band of good companions journeying like yourself to Salimshah. Safety in numbers! As we came along we heard of a band of six merchants murdered and plundered by the accursed Thugs. So I had my own fears and it is well we came together. What is the government doing to let such snakes defile the earth? Shall my men help yours to set up a tent for your household? They will have more comfort than in the cart.'

"All was smiles and good-fellowship. A tent was pitched, and behind a shelter the veiled women entered it with their ayah. And then we men went to supper and to enjoy ourselves. One of the merchant's servants sang divinely to the lute, and he gave us songs of the beauty of women and the wines of Persia to stir the blood. But I tell you this, doctor, not a lustful thought stirred in any man there. The true Thug is a good man—a religious man. He insults the honor of no

woman—no, not if she were lovely as a houri. But
the songs warmed us and it was rare sport to see the
old man drinking his wine and praising us for good
fellows and to know that his breath was in his nostrils,
and so with them all. They sat there, doomed."

The Englishman had dropped away as though he
had never been. The unashamed Thug sat before me
with burning eyes lit by the devil of murder. I listened
with perfect quiet and professional attention. It held
him in check, though he had long forgotten that he
needed healing and pity. He was a man glorying in the
most exciting blood-sport in the world.

"So we sang and laughed and knew that from the
tent bright eyes were peeping, quick ears listening. I
heard a woman laugh softly. Little she knew that behind each of her father's men sat a stout Thug, singing and laughing but with his hand on his rumal, waiting for the signal.

"Oh, it was a gay death-party. May all end as
jovially! And suddenly:

" 'Bring tobacco!' called the *jemadar* loud and clear,
and in a flash the rumal was about every throat of our
guests and the death-twist given. A gurgle—a smothered cry and all lay dead at our feet.

"Some cry, some sound must have reached the
women, for the tent curtain lifted—they rushed out
screaming. We two were ready for them—the new
Thug was as quick with the rumal as if he had had my
years' practice behind him, and the girl was dead at his
feet before she had time for another cry. I have no
need to praise myself. My skill was known from
Peshawar to Madras, and the mother fell beside her as
the girl dropped.

"The burial took not twenty minutes. We laid them
in the grave head to feet, made the incision in the

abdomen that is needful, and smoothing all over trampled it smooth, and who could have told what lay
underneath? The ponies and plunder were ours—a
splendid booty. The old miser was as rich as Kubera,
the god of wealth."

Hampton sank into a reverie, staring at the wall,
and so sat a moment. I wondered what would be
uppermost in him next minute, and held myself ready.
It was unexpected when it came.

I saw the Asiatic die out. His dark lean face was
working slowly into the western impulse. Fear, doubt,
hesitation were in the pitiable look he turned upon me
presently. I relaxed my guard and watched him with
intense interest. This was a problem worth unraveling
if the thing could be done.

"How did you get back to the bungalow?" I
prompted, judging my moment.

"God knows. I don't!" he said bewilderedly. "I only
know I woke in the beast of a bed, and the snakes
were quiet overhead and the grove was empty. They
had gone on. I went out to the lantana bushes, and
though I knew where it was I could see no sign of the
bhil. The Thugs do their work well. But that morning
I felt alone in the world."

"Did you speak to the khansamah?"

"The keeper?" His eyes were as helpless as a lost
child's. "But I tell you, doctor, it wasn't the same man.
It was a fine upstanding fellow with excellent chits
which he showed me, from all sorts of big bugs who
had used the place. How could that be? And he handed
me a letter from the banker I had to see on business,
asking why hadn't I come yesterday, and was Hampton
Sahib sick, and should he attend him this morning?

"My God, I thought I was a dafty then in good
earnest. I questioned the khansamah about the man I

had sat with the day before. The name was right, yes, but that was not the house I should have gone to. I described the old banker. They had never heard of him. The man who owned that name was young, and known and liked everywhere.

"What was I to think? Where had I been? What devils had I fallen among? What poisons were running in my veins? The banker came and he was what the khansamah had told me. I had never seen him before, and I dared ask no question—none." He stared at my face like a lost man as he ended his horrible story.

"Cheer up!" I said. "It was a bad dream—a nightmare. You had awaked and can sweep it out of your mind for good."

"Can I? Where was I that afternoon? And"—here his voice sank into a broken whisper—"on my hand was a ring I had never seen before, and in my pocket a string of pearls."

He held out a ring to me—a table-emerald cut with a swastika—of great value. I own that as I took it a shudder ran through me. And yet the story was incredible—utterly incredible. Take it that the man was mad—the most natural supposition—then there were a hundred ways in which he might have come by the thing, and his brain twisted its existence to its own mad uses. I gave it back and still harped on the dream, but could raise no hope in him. He went on, heavily.

"What do you say to this? I went back to our headquarters at Calbay. I had a comfortable flat there and an excellent khansamah. I had all the world could give me. My firm valued me more every day. They made me a junior partner. I was beginning to forget the accursed thing when—one night, suddenly, the possession came on me. Do you still call it a dream? I

slunk out and down to the lowest street in the town.
I left it an Indian. I gave the password 'Ali Khan bhai
salaam' to a man I had marked down there and joined
a band. That night we waylaid four travelers on their
way to Durgaghat, and the next night, eight; and from
that on, the gate was opened to hell, and every week
I was an Englishman high in honor, and every week-
end a murdering Thug doing what I lusted to do.

"That first Monday morning I had a wedge of gold,
two heavy gold jingles such as the women wear on
their ankles, and a string of pearls. And my gains
mounted up. What could I do with them? I started a
strong box at my bank and put the things in it and
there they lie. I dared not sell them. How often did
this happen? I can't tell you. It would come on me
with a rage like a wolf's for blood, and I could no
more resist it than stop breathing. All I know is I have
a second strong box there crammed with jewels and I
dare neither sell them nor look at them. God help me!"

The story seemed perfectly incredible. It was easier
to believe him mad.

"But did the papers take no note of the disappear-
ances? You don't mean to say men and women could
drop out like that and nothing said? It's incredible."

"Why not? There are always the snakes and tigers
and dacoits, and who takes stock of chance travelers
in out of the way places? Of course it isn't like the
good old days. Money isn't carried about as it was,
and you have to go much seldomer and more carefully.
Still, there are good pickings if you know how—especially with traveling nautch-girls and the like. And
God in heaven wouldn't have suspected me. No man
has a higher character, and our *jemadar* was one of
the most respected Moslems alive—a really religious
fellow with his prayers five times a day. Stricter than

strict in the Ramadan fast, and a family man with a wife and four children and as sure of heaven as of his faith. The thing could never be known. But look here, doctor, the devil of it was that in between I would be the white man and I felt I was going mad between the two lives. And I got malaria and that meant leave, and as the ship pulled out from Calbay I felt the dark man die in me. Horror and terror of myself drove me half mad, and my abject fear is that if I go back to India the thing may come on me again. It will—I know it will, and the devils will have got me again, and I shall go down—down to hell."

An awful entreaty glared at me from his eyes. I had the feeling of a man slipping down the slope of a precipice, clutching at every tuft of grass—and in vain. The abyss yawning beneath him.

What could I do? I could not find the poor devil employment in England? I could not counsel him to sell the jewels that murder had brought him and that might give him to death. I could not honestly certify him as a homicidal lunatic unless on the presumption that every murderer is mad, which I don't believe. And above and beyond it all the supernormal, that I felt more than understood, glittered fatefully like firelight upon black waters. Doomed he was, but if not by his own doing, what was his responsibility? A difficult question indeed.

I said:

"The case is such a difficult one that I must take time to consider it and with an Indian friend of great psychological experience."

He shook from head to foot with his thin hand on my wrist. "You won't give me away?"

"Not I. Doctors can't. But I may help you if I get his wits to back mine. Tell me—did you ever go back

into the street where you met the old devil who gave
you the *gur?*"

"Yes—I saw the house. A fine old house, but empty.
I asked and the people said no one would live there—
a bad man had had it once and the place was full of
devils. I believe it with all my soul."

Assuring myself that he had felt no temptation to
Thuggi since leaving India I got rid of him with some
difficulty and, directly I got a minute, rang up my
friend Devaraja, the great Indian scholar and psychologist. He came the same evening and I put the case
before him, with my own comments. The belief I had
formed was that in a former birth Hampton had been
a Thug and that the old self had broken through into
the present. But solution I could see none. As a man
sows he must reap and there is no more hope of evading the penalty than of running away from your
shadow in a noonday sun. That belief governs all my
thoughts and every day I live in the world confirms it.

Devaraja sat revolving the matter. His fine pure-cut
face in the turban, which he never discarded though
he wore coat and trousers in London, carried such
wisdom in its meditation that I relied on him beyond
all powers of description in these abysmal problems of
the soul when they came before me and concerned
Asiatic happenings.

"Of course you are right as to the cause," he said.
"He had been a Thug in a former life and he came
under the evil influences of Dhondapur where Thuggi
was at its worst, and that set all the combustible stuff
aflame. He surrounded himself with the worst thought-
forms and they led him straight back to Thuggi; it is
difficult to separate what is dream from what is true in
his story—but undoubtedly he has been at work. There
are the jewels."

I said: "My own opinion is that the only solution is suicide. I shall tell him frankly that I think the case incurable and leave him to draw his own conclusion. He has good stuff in him and he'll take it."

Devaraja looked at me with brooding eyes.

"No case is incurable; what right have you to preach any gospel of despair in a world where there is no room for it? Suicide is the flight of the coward—and to what? To you and me who believe in rebirth there is no solution there. How can he evade his doom? Suicide offers no more solution than as if he emigrated to America. Without expiation and penitence he will only have to face it all over again on a worse stage. No— no. There is a harder road and steeper climb for the man if he has the stuff in him that you guess."

"And what is it?" I was baffled.

"Tell him to turn informer and hand the band over to the law and himself with them," said Devaraja raising a solemn hand.

"Good God—such a thought never crossed my mind. An Englishman! He couldn't for the whole race's sake. An informer is a lower beast even than a Thug—and to be both—never!"

He looked at me as one who pities a fool, every line of his face hardening.

"Then let him do it as the Indian he is when he murders as the khan sahib. And as to the others—do you want his friends left untouched, left loose to slaughter men, women, and children? But as for him— look at the expiation! He will be scorned by innocent and guilty alike. The informer is the world's hatred. There is not a living soul but will spit upon him—the coward, the traitor! If there is good left in the man show him that way and he will take it."

"He will die sooner!" I said confidently.

"Possibly. And if so, he chooses his fate. But give him the chance of fulfilling his duty to society and to himself. You owe him that. Then, wash your hands of him if you like."

"But how—how is he to do it?"

"Tell him to 'go Indian' for good when he gets back and get all the information he can. He evidently can easily be a Hindu when he chooses. Let him go out and be lost in the teeming millions. Let him stage a disappearance of Hampton Sahib and have his jewels sold for his mother. Then let him turn informer."

"My heavens, Devaraja, you are ruthless! Death would be a million times easier."

"And therefore it is not for him!" he said gravely. "Let us get his feet on something solid for the next start. Penitence and expiation. The government won't hang him. His services will have been too valuable. They will do worse. He will work out his sin in agony. They will send him to the Andaman Islands for life. That is a hell which will probably save him a worse in his next rebirth."

A hell indeed. Those lonely islands in the Bay of Bengal inhabited by the worst criminals and those who guard them. And an Englishman! I own my heart sank. I pleaded his powerlessness to resist this outrush of hidden lava from a burning core. Devaraja sternly reminded me that that last life had been his doing and had itself sprung from some immitigable evil in unremembered days.

"Shall I speak to him, or will you?" was all he would say. I pleaded in vain but in my heart knew he was right.

Eventually we tackled the poor wretch together. Was it the former birth in Asia that made him so quickly amenable to Devaraja's view of his responsibility? He accepted it, made a frantic plea for suicide, and when that was set before him in its hopelessness of escape, took the alternative with what I could have sworn was a look of relief in his dark tortured face. I shall not easily forgot how, when he stood up and we rose too, he thanked me for my good will and the light it had thrown on his problem and then turned to Devaraja.

"I ask you to clear up the last doubt. What about the jewels? Can I honestly leave them to my mother and sister?"

"I think so," said Devaraja with knitted brows. "You—none of you knew who your victims were. They have never been claimed or sought, have they?"

"Never."

"Then have them sent to England for sale—or South America. Yes, that will be best. And now we part. I wish you the upward step, the healing agony, the far distant attainment."

He moved no nearer to the cowering man, half blasted by his doom, but he made the beautiful Indian salutation of the joined hands raised and the slightly bowed head and Hampton responded. He turned on me with a look I never wish to see repeated in this world; it haunts me still at times; and went slowly out of the room, his shoulders bowed as if under an intolerable burden. Afterwards I was ashamed that I had not given him some sort of Godspeed. I might have shaken hands. But I could not—the sight of that slender-fingered gripping dark hand of his, lithe and strong as the coil of a snake, sent shudders down my spine. I could not. May I be forgiven!

Devaraja had reached a wisdom where as yet I could not climb. He did his bit. I failed.

He and I watched. The papers duly announced that Mr. Hampton was returning to Calbay. He sailed by the Andrinenburg. So far so good, but even in the routine of my work I could not forget that ship plowing her way true East and carrying a man to worse than death. *He* would not mix in the deck-games. No. He would be silent and very preoccupied, and women would avoid him and men say he was devilish bad company. I made that voyage with him in a very real sense though as yet I could not believe he would have the strength to carry the thing through. I said this often to Devaraja but he thought otherwise.

"He will do it. He has seen the thing in its naked truth," he would answer. "I would stake my life on him."

And still we watched the papers.

The Andrinenburg reached Calbay and for a fortnight nothing happened. Then:

> Grave anxiety is entertained in Calbay as to the safety of Mr. Enright Hampton, junior partner in the well-known firm of Messrs. Hartright, Calson and Cronenburg. He is known to have arrived by the Andrinenburg on 8th October and should have presented himself two days later at the office. In spite of energetic search by the police nothing has been traced.

There was half a column of theory following this, ending with the highest praise of Hampton's unblemished character and the grief felt by his friends. There was the usual theory that he had been murdered and flung into the sea, with the usual hope that early information might be received.

"It never will!" said Devaraja. "What way have you and I, my friend, of knowing what hell tastes like? Doubtless we knew it once, but we have outgrown the memory. That man burns in a living flame."

I was silent. And still I could not believe he would conquer.

A month later he was forgotten and the Indian papers were ablaze. An informer, a miserable scoundrel, had given away the secret of a band of Thugs roaming unsuspected through the jungle ways in far-away places and disposing of unwary travelers quite in the good old style. Horrible details were given. The informer was known as the "Khan Sahib," and though himself the worst of criminals his death sentence would certainly be commuted to life-long imprisonment in the Andaman Islands in view of the public utility of his treachery.

The papers rang with descriptions of the despicable wretch's demeanor in the witness-box. He was suffering badly with malaria, they said, and presented a dreadful spectacle of cowardice, shame, and terror. Even the prisoners looked more human than he. Terror was to be expected, for deadly hate glared at him from the crowd in the dock. But so far as his evidence went he did not flinch, scoundrel as he was. He admitted his own guilt with theirs—a frightful calendar of crime—and endured the universal loathing with what some described as apathy. At all events he asked and expected no pity.

"I think," said Devaraja in his serene way, "that man may be a hero in his next birth. He has seen the light and marches straight for it."

The murderers, sixty in number, were one and all condemned to death. Such a thing had not been known for half a century and more. But there was no single extenuation, and seeing no hope they confessed the justice of the sentence, only praying with one voice that the informer might suffer also, but apart. Even they scorned to die with the traitor. That was not

granted. His life was to be the reward of his treachery
—the government was immovable. The reptile must be
protected. And still Devaraja and I watched. He said:
"I question whether they will get him to the Andamans alive. There is no man held in such hate or contempt in India. But for his sake I shall regret it if he
escapes by death."

I was silent still but for a very different reason
indeed from my first. I thought Devaraja pitiless. I
hoped for the mercy of steel or shot. I felt that expiation had been made.

Once again the papers rang with the loathed name of
the Khan Sahib.

As they were leading him to the boat, strongly
guarded and handcuffed between two Sikh policemen,
a man darted forward from no one knew where. He
flung a bottle of vitriol into the prisoner's eyes as he
walked bowed and shuddering among his guard. He
fell to the earth, not mercifully dead but blinded for
life. The other was seized and taken amid the wild
cheers and applause of the crowd, who had somehow
got wind of what had happened. There was no pity on
earth for the murderer who had added treachery to his
crime. It was all for his assailant.

There was no pity even in the heart of Devaraja,
and I also perhaps had by that time learned the solemn
unfolding of the Law, merciless in its working that so
it may save. It was awe rather than pity that moved me
as I read of Hampton's immeasurable agony. For he
had conquered. I owned myself mistaken.

Our last paragraph, much later, announced the de-
portation of the Khan Sahib to the Andamans. Of him
I know no more, but I think much. Devaraja read the
news with a kind of sober exultation.

"The Divine is good to him," he said, "for the gate

of the senses is closed that his sight may open on the light that survives when sun and moon and lamp and fire are extinguished; the light of the immortal Self within. We have dismissed him from our compassion, my friend, and now may rejoice. The guiding hands have caught his and he marches to the unstruck music."

I cannot call this one of my cures, nor yet Devaraja's. We knew it was out of our hands. The Celestial Surgeon had the man on the operating table, and I dare swear he comes out of his ordeal whole and clean.

Hell

THE STORY I AM ABOUT TO TELL IS SO STRANGE THAT
if it were not a part of my own experience I would not
vouch for it, knowing as I do through what misty
zones of self-expression revelation often reaches one
through others. Setting aside the charlatan, the fraud,
and the self-deceiver, the most truthful people often
struggle vainly and most misleadingly to relate experience, for the simple reason that we really have no
language as yet to express anything but the forms of
consciousness presented to us by our senses. St. Paul
states the difficulty in his well-known phrase "and there
saw things not possible to be uttered." They are not
possible, but yet to certain persons the attempt conveys
notes like the harmonic which echoes a struck string,
and this impinges on their own consciousness, reviving
old forms of consciousness or presenting new. St. Paul
and other mystics knew that this attempt must be made
if there is any hope of seeing the bud of dawning
knowledge flower into the thousand-petaled lotus of
day.

Therefore I say what I know, though it must be
understood it was much more real than I can say.

It begins with a dream to be very briefly told. Some
dreams are an open gateway to truth and this was one
of them.

My body was in Canada. My consciousness was
walking in Kensington Gardens. For those who do not
know the place I will say it is exceedingly beautiful,

with ancient trees overshadowing great stretches of grass and wide and narrow paths where one may love to linger in the shade. There are quiet little ways where one may be alone with birds and squirrels even in the busy time of the day, and at evening time it is lovely with long shadows, a glimmer of water from the Serpentine, and the peace of the old red brick palace dreaming among its stiff Dutch gardens and stately lawns.

In my own dream I was walking slowly down a little green byway to the long stretch of water, meditating on things very foreign to the old English setting, when I saw a woman coming quickly up from the water to meet me, silently as people come in that mysterious land of sleep. Her feet made no sound. She was like a picture suddenly thrown on clear air. She was middle-aged, fretful-looking, with anxious eyes and a hurried apologetic way with her hands, which were clothed in shabby gloves. Her dress was shabby too. I believe she had once been pretty in a limp, ineffectual way. I had an impression that her voice would be shrill and a little peevish. I thought she was going to ask me the way.

No. She stood in front of me in an attitude which suggested nervous trouble in every line of face and body and said the oddest thing I have ever heard in such an encounter.

"I do wish you'd speak to me. You're the fourth silent person I've spoken to today. We live near here, but although we go out nobody ever comes in. *Nobody.* You can't think how it gets on one's nerves—always being together and nobody saying a word. Will you come?"

One does odd things in dreams. I said with some astonishment; "Yes, if I can be of any use. But when?"

She said vaguely: "Oh—well—soon. I must be go-

ing now. We have to be in before dark. Good night.
It's the most hideous existence."

I said, "Good night." Trees, woman, gardens drifted
away on a dream-breeze. But the impression was left
for a moment clear-cut. Helpless pain and distress. A
promise. But how? Where?

Not long afterwards in circumstances I had not fore
seen I was in Kensington, staying within easy reach of
the gardens and beautiful old palace. I often walked
there, but I did not remember the dream. The impression was dormant. She had got into my world for a
moment from some strange world of her own and had
walked out again. Besides, my mind was fully occupied
at the moment with a book I was writing and arrangements for returning to Asia.

One evening I had dined alone and early and the
evening beauty of the gardens drew me. The broader
walks were full of people. A few lovers sauntered along
the narrow ones, so lost in their own dream that as
far as the outer world was concerned they were phantasmal. They neither knew nor cared who passed. I
turned down a little path I knew which leads to the
upper reach of the Serpentine, quiet, lonely. As I
caught the first glimpse of tranquil water I saw a woman coming towards me.

It seemed as ordinary a happening as the coming of
any of the other people who had passed me on my way.
I scarcely looked at her as she came slowly on. Then
I saw she meant to speak to me and I half stopped.
She was shabbily dressed in faded-looking black. Her
clasped hands were clothed in shabby gloves. She had
an anxious, slightly bewildered expression, and my first
idea was that she was a stranger who had lost her way
and was going to ask for directions. She walked
straight up to me, nervously as if half expecting a
rebuff, and said the oddest thing.

"I do wish you'd speak to me. You're the fourth person I've tried today. We live quite near here but though we go out nobody ever comes in. *Nobody.* You can't think how it gets on one's nerves—always being together and nobody ever saying anything. A dreadful life. Will you let me talk to you?"

Honestly, I thought her a little insane, or at least mentally deficient. In either case pitiable. Nothing worse. I could not have been afraid of her if I had tried. I said soothingly:

"If you wish. If I can be of any use."

She said vaguely: "Certainly it would be of use. May I walk with you a little? It's really horribly lonely."

She spoke in as many italics as Queen Victoria in her letters; every second word was underlined. It would be wearisome to give it and it was wearisome to hear. And still I did not in the least remember my dream. It all seemed one of the odd things which may happen at any moment in London. One accommodates oneself to them if they are possible. If not, one invokes a policeman. I said at once:

"Certainly. Shall we go towards the palace?"

She answered: "Oh—well—yes. But you see I want to tell you all about it. I'm *sure* I've seen you somewhere before. Shall you mind listening?"

I said, "Not in the least," convinced she must be a little daft, to put it mildly, but taking it as a gentle and milky daftness unlikely to attract attention. I tried to think how one should talk to people like that and said something about the gardens. Did she often come there?

"Fairly often! When I'm not in Kensington High Street looking at the shops. I think Barker's windows are lovely, don't you? I spend hours there watching! those adorable manikins—and now and then they have

a dress parade! Have you heard? The loveliest girls—
as slim! I can't think how they do it!"

I asked cautiously (with a nurse-attendant in my
mind); "Do you go alone?"

"Oh, always! I can't get anyone to go with me. In
the old days in my flat two or three people used to
come in and have tea. Now they never come near me.
I *can't* understand why."

She looked at me as if asking me to explain the
situation. It might have been comic to find oneself discussing dress parades with a perfect stranger if it had
not been—what? Tragic. That was the word. There
was a sense of awe like thunder clouds banking up in
the air. And then—

Suddenly as a lightning flash I remembered my
dream. This was the woman, and instantly I saw there
was something in this strange business—something to
be faced and understood. The commonplace dropped.
We shed it like a garment and were face to face with
truth of which I could understand nothing. There was
certainly nothing in the woman herself to arrest one.
Her helpless fretfulness suggested feeble personality at
best. But she meant something, for all that. Wary and
wakeful, I asked:

"But have you no friends? Is there no one where
you live? Are you alone?"

"Certainly not," she answered with a little backbone-
less pride. "I live at a boarding house near Holland
Park. You know, you go up Church Street and turn
to the left before the top. It's before you come to the
rich part. A 'horrid little garden with Michaelmas
daisies and Virginia creeper over the house."

"And several people live there?" I asked, humoring
her but feeling the enigmatic something which filled the
air more strongly every minute.

"Oh, yes. There's Mr. Colfax. He lost his money

speculating on the stock exchange. He quite hoped to be a millionaire. Now he does nothing but advise some nephew who's trying to get on in the druggist business. And Mrs. Simmons; she was a dressmaker, quite fashionable, but now she's a little—well—mental, you know—and makes things for bazars. And Mr. Methven —he drinks, but not violently. We shouldn't tolerate it if he did. I believe he does something for a destitute aunt. And Miss Ellcot goes out once a week to look after somebody's children that can't afford a nurse. That's all."

"But," I said, pitying the dreadful stereotyped life, "you are quite a little society among yourselves."

She answered hurriedly:

"Oh no, no! We never speak to each other. And Mrs. Spinks our landlady, though perfectly respectable and the food quite good, never speaks a word to any of us even when she carves at dinner. I'm—I'm—a little afraid of her. Then we sit all the evening and stare at each other or at the wall. Very bad manners I call it. My great-grandfather was a bishop and I ought to know. . . . Would you mind coming down this way? We're so very public here."

She led the way to a quiet nook behind the trees.

Here I pause to say that one does not follow strangers in London—least of all in the parks and in twilight. But those who know the plane on which we were at the moment may on that plane go safely in perilous places. Fear is a denizen of the world's atmosphere. It dies in clear air, and where there is no fear is no danger.

We found a great elm sweeping its branches about it like the robe of a goddess. The dusk hung in it like veils of softness. In its twilights she waited for me to speak.

"Do you never try to start a little talk?" I asked.
She shook her head vaguely.

"Well—no. There's a something—let's call it constraint. They're what I call secretive—so ill-mannered. I get a little frightened sometimes. And every day I come to the gardens and speak to all sorts of nice-looking people and ask them if they won't look in on us once in a way and give us a start. Just the way I've spoken to you, you know. Perfectly friendly. And a very odd thing—" She hesitated and looked at me cunningly from sideways eyes as if to see how I would take what was coming.

"What is the odd thing?" I prompted.

"Well, you'll hardly believe it. No one ever takes the slightest notice of me. I might not exist. It's as if they neither saw nor heard me. Shocking bad manners. And I the great-granddaughter of a bishop! You can imagine how I feel it. You're the first person who ever took the trouble to answer me, I expect you're well-connected too. I feel as if I'd seen you somewhere. Perhaps you've been presented at court and I've seen your picture in the Daily Mirror."

"I feel too as if we had met before," I said. "But how very strange that no one answers you!"

"Amazing if it weren't for present-day manners. Only yesterday such a nice old lady was sitting just over there." She pointed to a seat under a tree. "Some children were flying kites and I sat down by her and made some perfectly well-bred remark about them. She never even looked at me. Can you imagine? She took out a letter and began to read."

Now as she spoke, a feeling of strangeness crept over me which I cannot describe. This is where the inadequacy of language comes in. It was utterly disconcerting. Not fear—not in the least—but the knowledge of a something deeply secret—the nearing of the supernormal. You stagger for a moment before your footing is secure. I have known it before and since, and it never deceives. And yet—a middle-aged woman, shabbily dressed, with a strong sense of gentility: Surely nothing more commonplace in the world? But yet *again* I knew the normal was rending apart and giving way to the impossible—the true.

I am going to use an extraordinary simile. I was in the state of mind drummers produce when they beat a swift tattoo like the mutter of distant thunder and it rises louder—*louder*—LOUDER—until the tension is all but unbearable and the nerves strain at the leash. Nothing was insignificant from that moment. I began to assemble my mind and subconscious and to examine her in every flicker.

Outside the trees it was still light—underneath twilight. She stood looking anxiously at me from dusk which spiritualized her until her face was like white foam flowing away on black water. I hung on her words as profoundly as if they were a thing to be earnestly considered. I said with the eagerness I felt:

"Do tell me how you came to live at the boarding house. Did you hear of it by chance?"

Her look clouded; she picked aimlessly at the beads on her sleeve.

"Odd you should ask that, for it's just what I can't answer. I often worry myself about it. It's really a horrid place. Cheap lace curtains and an aspidistra in a red pot in the window—you know the sort. And what do you think I have to do? Why, to look after the little servant-girl next door—a vulgar little slattern! She has a lover and she's going to have a baby. Revolting, I call it. What *would* my great-grandfather have said!"

I was stalking her now with such care that I almost trembled lest a wrong word should startle the whole thing into empty air.

"But why have you to do it. Who told you to?"

"No one. I just have to. I don't know why. She's wild with fear and she comes to the partition between the gardens and I go out and listen. She likes it."

"That's kind of you!" I said. "You have the gift of sympathy."

She shook her head helplessly.

"I haven't a notion why I do it. However, you asked how I got there and I can't explain. Do you think it could be loss of memory?"

"If you would tell me the story as closely as you can we might piece it together."

"Yes—I will. You can't imagine the comfort of having someone to talk to. We sit round the whole evening and never say a word. Mr. Methven drinks. Mr. Colfax smokes. Mrs. Simmons stares at the window, and Miss Ellcot at the fireplace. I've never heard their voices. Awful, isn't it? Then they go to bed."

"And you?"

"Oh, I read novels—I like the passionate ones with beautiful rich women and sensual strong men—I always did. Then after nine I go out to the partition between the two gardens and Julia comes and cries for half an hour. I've planned for her to come as my maid if I can find a flat. I *can't* go on as I am. They're all so frightfully secretive. You never know what they're thinking. Sometimes I wonder—suppose if it were something dreadful? I could scream out loud when that comes into my head."

She whispered that and her eyes were roaming swiftly like a hunted hare's. There was unworded terror hiding in them.

"They never come out here. That's why I like it," she added with an assumption of courage.

"Then you don't know how any of them got there?"

"Not a bit. The landlady is very respectable. The eggs and butter are quite decent, and the tea is made at the table, which I always think so nice. I have a little gas stove and kettle in my bedroom and make a cup for myself when I want it."

"Do you mind telling me your story?" I ventured. "It really is like something in a book."

"Ah, you don't know yet how romantic!" she said slyly—with a kind of furtive pleasure. "If you talk of romance!—And to think of the awful place where I have to live! . . ."

An interruption here.

A young man came down the path above us, going quickly as if to an appointment. He half halted and spoke to me, slightly raising his hat.

"In case you're a stranger, madam, the gates close in an hour, and it isn't wise for a lady to be here alone so late. Pardon me!"

He went swinging on. "Alone?" she looked at me and I at her and knowledge crept through me like cold water in my veins. Now I knew why I had felt the supernormal looming up like the roll of distant thunder-drums, now I knew why no one had answered her but me, why her eyes were full of secrecy and fear. Did it frighten me? Not in the least. I have had my training in a school which understands these things and their kinship with us. But I was tense as a bow-string now with expectation. I drew as near as I dared, knowing I must not touch her.

She said fretfully: "*Now*, you see! It was you he noticed, not me. I ask you— isn't it the worst possible manners? One feels so ignored—so bewildered. It's

like the awful house where I live. They never speak to
me. Never. Do you know I sometimes have a feeling
they don't know I'm there."

She looked at me in bewilderment. Dully. I said:

"You must allow for their ignorance. Do tell me
about yourself."

That collected her as far as she could be collected.
She was eager to talk about herself, as if the act of
realizing and being realized would give her the kind of
life she believed she still possessed. She was only holding on to shape with my realization of her, and the
appearance fed on that vitality. Were we sitting between the roots of the great tree or standing looking
fixedly at each other? I cannot tell.

"I had a little flat behind High Street—more down
the Earl's Court way, quite superior, the bedroom
opening into the sitting-room, and the use of the bath-
room. My own furniture. The cabinet had belonged to
my great-grandfather the bishop. People used to say,
'Ah, that speaks for itself!' My means were very small,
you understand, but that doesn't touch the question of
gentility, does it?"

"Not in the least. What did you do all day?"

"Oh—well—I read novels. I'm a great reader. Don't
you like those passionate sex novels? And then—I had
to trim my hats and mend my stockings and so on.
But what I really liked best was to go up to High
Street and look in at the windows and price things.
They change them so often. Delightful!"

"The theater? Concerts?"

"Well—no. Seats are so frightfully expensive now.
But I never found the day long. I lived in a kind of
thought-world of my own. Lovely dreams of the sort
of things I'd do if I could afford it. I don't know anything pleasanter than to sit by the fire with the tea-

table beside you and just dream like that idly. The things you want to happen."

"No friends?"

She drew herself up with primmed mouth.

"You see, if one is well-connected it spoils one for second-rate society. No. Except Miss Maynard and the rector's wife and Mrs. Godsal— But I was perfectly happy. And now those awful people! Sitting round me like tombstones. If only I knew how I got there. Then I could get away!"

I made a mistake, I said: "May I know your name?"

She shuddered back as if a rough hand had touched her.

"No—no. It wouldn't be suitable. I'm surprised you asked!"

I should have remembered. These manifestations do not willingly tell their names. It hurts them in some way we cannot understand. I apologized hurriedly, terrified lest I should lose her and added: "Then your life was quite self-centered. No outside interest?"

"Oh yes—the shops, you know, and I had my Daily Mirror every day and the Evening News, and Mrs. Godsal who owns the flat and lives in the ground floor came in sometimes. I was as comfortable as a cat by the fire."

"Had you a cat?"

"No, I dislike animals. I could have gone on forever in perfect content and then a horrid thing happened."

She hesitated and I knew exactly why. This kind of manifestation can never bear to allude to its last earthly moments and yet cannot keep off the subject. It is like having a hidden hurt or disgrace which must be always skirted—never directly approached. I question if most of them understand at all what has happened, though the vibration hurts them.

We were interrupted again. One of the park care-takers went by and called out:

"Gates closing in half an hour, lady. Take the first turning down to Kensington Gore."

She saw him—heard him.

"Very impertinent to interrupt! Well—one snowy day just before Christmas, High Street was simply lovely. They had the manikins in ball-dresses—exquisite! I couldn't keep away, so I just went up and took it all in and then I allowed myself tea and fruit salad in the tea-room. I never enjoyed anything more. All the people coming and going—delicious! I bought some cakes and a pair of gloves—these gloves, and came home. And that very night—oh, just a trifle, but I had a sore chest and I couldn't breathe very well. People are so silly. I should have been all right if they had let me alone. And then the expense! They would have a doctor and nurse. I won't dwell on it—I hate sick-room stuff. However they kept me on milk, and I simply got starved out, and one fine day—I fainted. Nothing more. Just fainted."

She stopped a second, her eyes glinting strangely at me in the twilight. I took it composedly as one should. They often do not know they are dead. I think she doubted and needed reassurance.

"A very common thing to happen. And then?"

She was immensely relieved and resumed her confidential tone: "You know one has the oddest dreams while one is coming to. Do you care to hear?"

"Immensely!" I said.

She simpered and went on: "I was in a meadow covered with blue flowers as thick as daffodils in spring. Millions—and the sky and sea met in the most extraordinary blue sparkling light you ever saw—like when you look out into the horizon. Blue—blue, everywhere—bathing in it. Exactly like the sea. I do so admire it off Brighton Pier. You know?"

I did know with a vengeance. This is the Clear Light after death described in a great system of thought never known in life to the little flitting fatuous being before me. I listened in awe indescribable.

"Blue—blue, piercing, flooding everything like all the arc-lights that ever were. It made my eyes dazzle. All the flowers gave out light. It flamed—flamed blue. Sparkling, rising, tremendous! I tried to hide. It was enough to blind one if one hadn't shaded glasses. All the scent of the flowers went by me like wind."

I listened breathlessly, for reasons to be told later. I knew, I knew! Again I heard the approaching roll of thunder-drums which precedes revelation. She must have been vaguely conscious of it too, but she went on peevishly:

"There was the most awful roaring noise like thunder. I had never heard the trains so loud before. I was simply blinded with light and deafened with noise, and there were the doctor and nurse chattering in the window and taking no notice of me. Me, the patient, if you please! I screamed out: 'Do put the blind down, and for goodness' sake shut the window. The arc-light at the station is shining bang into my eyes and the trains are roaring like thunder.' But it went on—perfectly awful! Someone, I think it must have been the doctor, said loudly, exactly like the booming of a great gong—so inconsiderate in a sick-room: 'When Reality is on you, cling to the Light. It is yours. It is you. Know that whatever visions you see are only your own imaginings. They are hell. Cling to the Light, the Light! It will save you.' Do you think it could have been the doctor? Or the Salvation Army in the street? They are frightfully noisy!"

"But you could not do it!" I said pityingly. "It was too bright. You could not understand!"

"Understand! It was perfectly ridiculous. I got up and pulled down the blind myself with the queerest feeling that I was lying on my bed all the time. That shows how weak I was—but I wouldn't give way to it, and presently I felt stronger. Then I said out loud so that they could hear. 'I shall report you, nurse, for neglect of duty. As to the doctor, he must be mad!' And I walked into my dear little sitting-room and sat down. Oh, the comfort of it—after that awful Light! You seem to be an understanding kind of person so you'll realize it. It was simply new life to me!"

Oh, terrible fetters and cages our own thoughts make for us! She had seen the Symbol of Divinity, and she shut herself into the base little prison from which Death had tried to free her! I looked at her with pity inexpressible. She could not read a ray of it.

"I just sat down. Heavenly! The noise had stopped and the fire was burning brightly. You know—the nice lights and shadows all flickering about. My tea-table was pulled up to it—tea and hot buttered toast, and a letter on the table. I don't often get letters. Never now! I tore it open. My uncle had died and left me Five Hundred Pounds a year." She said it in capitals. "Now I could go to Brighton and have a good room in the best boarding house on the Steyne. I could buy the five-pound dresses at Barker's. I had often and often dreamed of all that, for the poor man had an aneurism. So horrid to die so suddenly! I used always to be thinking what I would do if I had money. Wasn't it perfectly heavenly! Money! I loved it and never had it. And another letter—"

Here she minced a little. Her manner grew coy and her eyes narrowed.

"I wonder why I tell you everything. Well—long ago—he fell in love with me. You can see I was pretty. He had a wife—a perfectly horrid woman. No sympathy between them. And—well—I had a baby. Naturally I couldn't keep it. I got it adopted. He left me because of that, afraid his wife would get to know. But I was always wishing he would come back. Well, this letter was to say he couldn't do without me, and would I meet him at Tencott—our old meeting place by the Thames—on Saturday."

She paused a moment and looked at me bewildered:

"To tell you the truth I'm not perfectly certain how much I dreamed all that about him and how much was true! I used to think of nothing else—picturing things, dreaming awake and asleep, lying in my bed, crying and longing and pressing my hands on my eyes till I used to see him come into the room. My whole body wanted him. And then I used to think—Oh, but how awful if I had a baby. I got that on the brain. But we had such heavenly times. No one ever knew. Such a gentleman! He was manager of the bank where I had to go once a quarter to sign my annuity paper. It must have been there he noticed me. Don't you think so? Wasn't it a romance? Oh—his kisses, his kisses!"

Now I listened with perfect understanding. This had been her dominating complex, as modern science chooses to call it, though I know a much wiser and more ancient wisdom which not only classifies but explains causes. The complex of her miserable life was manifesting before me now in the only form in which the so-called dead can manifest in the world of appearances. The spirit—never. That is beyond all reach of human invocation. The thought-complex which sums up the experience of a lifetime, bad or good, futile or noble—that is what people pick up at the séances—the only thing which is responsive to the thoughts and prejudices in themselves. The Spirit! They might as well summon the Almighty to manifest in response to table rappings or the little out-reach of thoughts bounded by the brain. But the finite thought-complex can after death be brought in touch with other thought-complexes above· or below it in the scale of evolution, as it can by telepathy or such familiar manifestations in life. Is the process desirable? This is not the place in which to discuss that point. Proof of immortality it gives none, for the atoms whirled together in a human complex take time to disintegrate and re-form. Proof of immortality there is—infinite as immortality itself, but it is not to be found along that finite road of changing moods and consciousness.

She babbled on until I caught her up again.

"And the Light was gone?" I asked, pitying this poor consciousness, shaped of illusions, manifesting in the fear and bewilderment of her abortive life. Such pity one accords to the blind beseeching faces seen behind the guarded doors of an asylum. "And you dreamed him again?"

"Dreamed? Why, there was his letter on the tray! Don't I tell you? I was as happy as a queen. The only thing that fretted me was that the cabinet belonging to my great-grandfather the bishop was gone and they had arranged the furniture differently. So inconsiderate when I was ill! I rang to ask for Mrs. Godsal who owns the flats, but I suppose the bell was broken, and she always gave herself airs. Nobody came anyway. But I *did* enjoy my tea and I wrote to him and said I would come and went out and posted it. Do you think it was wrong? His wife simply meant nothing to him and he adored me. I love those passionate men who just take possession, don't you?"

I said: "Did the Light mean *nothing* to you? Nothing at all?"

She answered: "Oh, the light on the Thames that day! It was sunset and all the river glowed like fire. We were in the copse where we always met. We sat in the ferns—exquisite! I can smell their crushed smell now. He was beautifully dressed in flannels and a blue tie. Such a gentleman always! People used to look at him when we walked together. I had a dark blue foulard—beautifully made with the new dipping sides to the skirt. And *passionate*—oh, such a man! Love simply burning me. His wife nothing—I everything! I was even glad he was married—the secret between us was so delicious. How we cheated the dull people who couldn't guess our happiness! I thought how I'd go to the bank next week, and he would just look sidelong at me and we would know. Once he touched my foot under the table when the clerk was there. Ours was a true marriage. What's a mere ceremony compared with things like that?"

"Did you ever think of your dream-child?" I asked.

She looked puzzled. Not sorrowful. Puzzled.

"I don't think so. That was one of the things that would frighten me. But that wretched Julia talks of her baby. Of course that's quite in a low class of society. I believe the young man is a grocer's assistant. Sometimes it reminds me. But of course, if such an awful thing happened, a lady could never acknowledge it. Julia's what I call shameless. She means to pay someone to look after it until they can marry—and then she'll take it. Don't you call that very animal? But for my darling lover's sake I shall help her a little with the payments, now I have five hundred pounds a year. I had a kind of notion I might let her have the child in the flat if she turns out useful to me. She wouldn't be so likely to leave me then."

If I could only tell the thoughts that poured through me! Was she any madder than the millionaire prisoned by his counting-house, chained to his gold, the king dreaming of dominion, the shifty politician with his greased palm itching for more, the enchanting beauty whose body will be slime in a few years, the famous actress, the man or woman who pushes to any goal of success anyhow, everywhere? I declare that to me she stood an epitome of the world bartering its birthright of bliss, beauty, power, and the whole universe for a mess of pottage. I looked at her with mingled horror and sympathy. Dreams—the dreams of the lunatic asylum, the lies of the senses tossing us hither and thither, and behind them the divine spirit eternally one with the Divine. She did not even know that she could no longer react upon the world she loved. Or that she was a mere thought-form weakly manifested, soon to be disintegrated and re-formed. Until then ineffectual as a dead frost-bitten leaf. Could anyone believe her to be a spirit returning to give news of things unseen? Had she been a little more highly evolved she would have chattered of a Christian, Indian, Buddhist, or Mohammedan heaven—whatever had been the husk of symbol molding her thought-forms in life. A more modern education would have permitted her to babble of whiskys and sodas and cigarettes.

One does not marvel at these manifestations but at the ignorance which accords them any dignity or authority. With the highest thought-forms few indeed of us can hope to come in touch for very obvious reasons. With the evil or ignorant thought-forms it can never be difficult.

When I caught up with her again she was saying fretfully:

"And then I think I must have lost my memory

just a tiny wee bit! Only the effect of the illness, you know. The effect of that horrid Light and the noise in the street when they ought to have kept me quiet. Because a most extraordinary thing happened. I was just as happy as could be in my dear little flat, if they hadn't moved the furniture—and I can't *think* what's become of the bishop's lovely cabinet—but I sat there all day and nobody came, and I began to think the housemaid must be on holiday. And then it occurred to me that it would be pleasant just to run up and have a look at the fashions in Barker's windows. I do love that. Well, I went up—the street crowded, all the women simply *glued* to the windows and the things perfectly lovely. There was a dress of peach georgette with silver—five pounds. I thought, 'Well, that's the very thing if we go to the theater together. I must go back for my check-book,' and suddenly I knew I had forgotten where I lived! Did you ever forget anything like that?"

Her weak little eyes were urgent upon me, frightened—exactly like a rabbit's if you take it in your hand without the love and understanding that all animals respond to. I said:

"I forget little things sometimes, but they come back."

She answered, shuddering: "But this didn't come back. I couldn't remember the street, the number. I couldn't even be sure whether it was Bloomsbury or Notting Hill Gate and I had got mixed up with something in Brighton. Horrible! It was simply awful. I stood as if I were looking in at the windows and women chattering all round me about hats and stockings to match the dresses. Then they mostly went home to dinner, and I couldn't stand there all night and I hadn't so much as a roof to shelter me. I couldn't think. I was half mad with fear. I felt in my pocket and even my purse was gone. Only a few loose pence."

I understood what had happened. The first thought-form after death had broken. Unconscious self-judgment (the relentless, the unbribable) was appointing her a new hell—or rather let us call it a new school for the molding of possible thought-forms a shade higher in the scale of evolution. Then she would be turned out upon the world again in rebirth, to do the best she would for herself. I listened enthralled. Heavens, what a task before this puny creature—to hew out the divinely lovely Galatea sleeping hidden in the marble rock of her selfish futility. What ages would it take?

"So I went up to the policeman who stands at the bottom of Church Street and said"—I could see her saying it with her little mincing ineffectuality—" 'I'm so worried. I've lost the address of my lodgings and I don't know the way back. Can you help me?' You can think how unpleasant it was! He looked me up and down and said, 'Haven't you any card, mum? Have you tried your pockets? Try again.' So I just felt in my pocket—very old-fashioned, but I always have one in my slip'—and there I found an address. He read it and said, 'The green motor-bus takes you up within five minutes of it,' and I got in, thinking how lucky I was, and asked my way when I got out."

Her eyes filled with tears. She dried them with a raggy little handkerchief.

"I walked along, planning to have a muffin for tea and to speak very seriously to Mrs. Godsal about the cabinet when I got in; and lo and behold! there was no flat. There was a shabby garden with bushes of Michaelmas daisies—just that pale insipid color I hate —and I went up to the house and the door was open and—oh, the very queerest thing!—I knew it was where I had to go and I just walked upstairs into my bedroom. The landlady looked out of her den and said, 'Oh, that's you,' and there I've been ever since. Now could *you* help me to remember where my dear little flat was? I would give anything to be there again."

I shook my head. "How can I? But there are other things I might help you to remember if you would let me. As a matter of fact I think Julia—who seems to be a sensible girl—will be your best help at the moment."

I had of course seen that this unwilling help to Julia was the best she was capable of as yet. It was a hopeful symptom that her mind had invented Julia and was playing with the thought of doing something for her—the only hopeful thing—a narrow chink of light in the darkness of her prison. I noticed too that everyone in the miserable household apparently had their feeble filament of care reaching out to others—all except the landlady. I felt something sinister there that I could not decipher, though no doubt she was in the scheme of the eternally right and necessary.

"Julia indeed!" she said scornfully. "A little slattern! She knows it's very kind of me to notice her at all, especially as she's lost her character."

"Do you still go for your annuity to the bank?"

Again that bewildered look.

"Not now. Some arrangement seems to have been made with the landlady and I don't have to pay her. Could it be by the municipal authorities, do you think? But I have really lovely clothes when he wants me again—a violet and gray georgette and beautiful furs and so on. My wardrobe is crammed. Five hundred a year goes a long way with a single woman's wants. Still, the place is simply awful. I wouldn't tell you at first, but I get *deadly* frightened. They never speak to me or to each other. We just sit round in the evening and stare and no one notices what I have on or thinks what an interesting life mine is. They are *extremely* second-rate."

I asked: "Do you ever think of their lives?"

"Theirs? Why, there's nothing to think of. You never saw such grim old fogies. They might all be mummies. But—I don't know who you are, but I *have* seen you before, and I see I've interested you— Couldn't you come in tomorrow evening and just talk to them a bit? The fourth house to the left after you get into Roslyn-Ware Street. You'll know the shabby lace curtains and those horrid Michaelmas daisies. Come about eight o'clock. We're always in then."

"Where do they go in the day?" I asked. Again the bewildered look.

"I don't know. You see, we don't talk to each other. I can't remember now how I heard what they do. The landlady said what I've told you when first I came. Since then she never speaks. Will you come?"

For reasons of my own I said, "Yes"—and as the words left my lips there came the usual shouting of the caretakers to clear the gardens.

"All out! All out!" It had grown suddenly dark under the trees, and they were menacing like mysterious shapes in ambush down the long paths with neither moon nor stars hanging upon the boughs. A chill breeze stirred the leaves. Before my eyes I saw her figure melting, receding, disintegrating. Her foolish shrill voice said faintly:

"Dear me, how very inconvenient! The *idea* of hustling us out like this! I was just going to say—"

All was gone but darkness. I ran as quickly as I could to the gate leading into Kensington Gore and

scraped through as it clanged. I stood outside panting, but not with fear. The pitiable helpless creature!
To what rebirth is she destined? Will the little lusts for
little pleasures be on a plane a trifle higher? I think
so. Hell is a process of education slow but sure. She
will have outgrown the illicit loves of the dream bank
manager and have developed into (say) platonic
adoration of some gentleman who leads an influential
thought-circle with Asiatic affinities. She may write
soulful unrhymed verse, a meager allowance of six
lines to the poem. Something after this fashion:

> A wave thundering in
>   Breaking in aimless foam,
> The ocean passions of my soul
>   Break on the rocks of fate
> And withdraw shuddering
>   Into the profundities of the abyss.

Her dress will be expressive of the depths in sexual
passion and psychic implication. She will choose a
modern poet for her confidences in Kensington Gardens and will show him the first chapters of an autobiography of infantile, adolescent, and adult complexes
chiefly centering on the indecent. I cannot fit the hell
to this particular exposition of individuality, but since
she manufactures it herself with unsparing diligence it
will be ready in due course.

Meanwhile I wended my way to Roslyn-Ware Street
next day guided by the omniscient policeman. A narrow street, sordid and mean, vocal with the crying of
babies and scolding of overtaxed women, from open
windows closely draped with cheap lace curtains the
worse for soot. I found the house, the fourth on the
left. Pale Michaelmas daisies bordered an untidy path

with an ill-cut weed-grown flower bed on either side. A shabby Virgina creeper nourished in sooty air hung wearily about the house. The windows cried aloud for cleaning and in the center of one, exactly between the loop of the curtains, stood an aspidistra in a red pot.

I turned the tap on the door which represented an electric bell, and after a scurry inside, a faded woman in a black apron appeared and opened it grudgingly. I said I had heard rooms were let there and she drew herself up instantly.

"Oh, dear, no! No such thing, Mr. Horner (I am Mrs. Horner) lives here and we occupy the whole house. Good afternoon."

I got a word in edgeways as she shut the door.

"Do you happen to know if there is a young woman named Julia in service in either of these houses?" pointing to the right and left.

"Certainly not. No servants are kept."

She banged the door.

I walked down the narrow path wondering many things. Did the Horners guess what terrible company they kept—what things sat in their rooms and were about them night and day? Was it a miasma of misery and shame condemning themselves to the dulness of listless despair? If I had gone into that terrible parlor, would my clearer eyes have seen Mr. Colfax, Mrs. Simmons, Mr. Methven, and Miss Ellcot sitting there in deadly silence staring at each other? Was the sinister landlady ever on the watch over her inmates, hidden in some den they could not guess? Unknown, untellable—a mystery brushing me with silent wings as it fled.

I regretted Julia. The invention of Julia with her tears and hopes and weeping courage was the only promise for the future.

To sum up. A woman to whom I told this story asked: "Why should the wretched woman have come to you?" I answered that I believed my knowledge of the subject and reaction to her wants might have helped her. But how can I tell?

Years ago, Sir William Barrett, whose work in the study of psychic events cannot be forgotten, gave me his little book on thought as a creative force and with it a powerful impetus along the line of that study. If he had known what we know now of the same study in Asia, with what tripled emphasis he would have asserted the power his own insight presaged. Remembering that book, on returning from Roslyn-Ware Street I took down another one on the art of dying (old when Tibet was young, for from that strange country it comes), that art in which so few are versed though one and all must meet the Inexorable face to face. Surely it would be well to give a little thought to a matter so inevitable and upon which personal experience enlightens only a very few. I took the book into the sunny gardens and sitting under a great elm in dappled shadow read as follows:

"At the moment of death the consciousness of objects is lost. There is what is called 'a swoon' in which is beheld the Clear Light of the Void, in other words the high consciousness which sleeps in us all under the every-day consciousness which our senses present to us. This Clear Light is seen as the glory of spring—but that is only a symbol representing an infinitely indescribable joyful experience. If the dead man has the power to recognize that Light as his own higher consciousness he is freed from all earth bonds and passes on to perfect union with bliss. If he cannot, if the Great

Light dazzles him and he shrinks from it, then his consciousness passes into lower and lower thought-forms, appearances as fashioned by his thoughts on earth. Thus entrapped by his earthly consciousness he still inhabits and exists in them. *In these his consciousness can touch other earth-consciousnesses.* By those he is gradually drawn downwards from the Light into the earthly atmosphere where he is eventually reborn to tread the sad round of earthly experience. It is said that those who have rightly practiced yoga, or the great science of concentration, recognize the Clear Light and rejoice in their union with it. For them births and deaths are ended."

Sitting under the tree with the little happy squirrels flitting beside me, I recalled how closely her earthly experiences had imprisoned the consciousness which represented my sad visitor, and how, if untrained, I, too, might have received her as a spirit and visible proof of immortality. I repeated to myself the great verse which sums up that true knowledge.

"Never the Spirit was born, the Spirit shall cease
    to be never.
Never was time it was not. End and beginning
    are dreams.
Deathless and birthless and changeless, abideth
    the Spirit for ever.
Death cannot touch it at all, dead though the
    house of it seems."

Yes, and the feeble fluttering pulse of life in her will strengthen steadily until it beats in time with the mighty heart-beat of the universe, and then—gradually, marvelously, her growth will shatter her bound crippled consciousness as an acorn shatters the vase in which it was planted and spreads into a mighty oak rooted in earth but soaring to the heavens.

> "Though I was born on earth, the child of earth,
>   Yet was I fathered by the starry sky."

I shall meet her again elsewhere when the chrysalis wings tremble in their folding.

I close with the strange and beautiful prayer of these Tibetan people who have studied death as eagerly as life. The prayer of those who just are born, being dead:

> "Alas, when the uncertain experience of Reality is dawning upon me, setting aside every thought of fear or terror, may I recognize whatever visions appear as the reflections only of my own consciousness! May I know them to be only apparitions. May I rejoice in the Clear Light of my own highest consciousness!"

And the answer:

> "When the Clear Light is seen, sparkling, bright, dazzling, glorious, be not daunted. That is the radiance of your own true nature. Recognize it.
>
> "From the midst of that radiance the sound of Reality reverberating like a thousand thunders will come. That is the sound of your own true self. Be undaunted, fearless, unawed.
>
> "If you cannot recognize your own thought-forms for nothingness, the Light will daunt you.

the sounds awe you, the rays will terrify you. And ignorant, helpless, you will be imprisoned in your own thought-forms and must wander the earth again as its prisoner."

A strange thing to read in Kensington Gardens under the ancient trees. For all such prisoners of the self-consciousness let us pray the prayer of Enlightenment.

The Man Who Saw

IT IS THE TRUTH THAT IF YOU WOULD KNOW A COUNtry you must know something of her religion and of her literature; for the first is her soul and the second her mind, and if you know something of these two and know them sympathetically you will not be far from that inner spirit which is a compound of both and makes the nation a living entity. Knowledge is the other name for sympathy. I have never been in any country of which I did not know something—however little—of both. It has been well worth while.

Camping up the Himalayas some years ago, when I knew less than I do now of psychic study, I had reason to realize this, and the chief delight of a glorious time was that to my tents hidden in the mighty pine forests came everyone who had a story to tell or some bit of ancient wisdom to divulge. Sitting outside the tents or in the little matting hut which the men ran up as easily as a bird building its nest, they came to have a cut doctored or an ailment cured by the potent medicines of the sahib-people, and because they knew it would be valued the payment would be something unforgetable—some flash of beauty, wisdom or wonder that has irradiated life, or, if it were not that, the momentary union with their own strange natures, so alien in ways that matter little, so human and near in those that matter eternally.

But through a man of my own people I was to receive what at that time might truly be called the Greater Illumination, and when I think of the snowy peaks storming heaven, and the vast loveliness of the world outspread beneath them, I think of my friend of a week and rejoice.

His small camp of two tents caused me some regret when it sprang up as unexpectedly as mushrooms,

"Where the whispering pine-trees murmur the
secret they sigh to tell."

—for the solitudes of those vast mountains and valleys set one free to mighty contemplations and enfranchisements and one does not welcome unsympathetic intrusion. Little did I know that it was to be a landmark in my life—the passage of a soul so stored with instinctive knowledge and strange experiences that I mark the day I met him with a white stone of remembrance and gratitude.

Camps are almost always friendly and he came across at once to ask if I had anything helpful for a bad cut on his right arm. It was clear that he could not attend to it properly, and as that little service often falls in one's way in the wilds I had everything ready, and it led to unusual sympathy and friendliness for the week that we were side by side—with experiences of vision impossible to forget, for the man was a true seer though a hardy cheerful Highlander whom, except for the hidden power of his Celtic blood, no one on earth would have connected with psychic powers. I was to understand the why and wherefore of those later. I shall call him Armytage. I wish I had any power of conveying the extraordinary things he said and knew and the matter-of-fact, careless way in which he said them.

"I've always been a ghost-seer," he told me when, we had reached the stage of interchanging thoughts. "Of course I know they're not really spirits, but it's very strange when you realize what a creative power thought is. I once knew a man who was forming a devilish (and quite unfounded) belief about his wife. I saw it take shape objectively and stand before him in the room. It always went after him while I knew him. He murdered her in the end."

"What was it like?" I asked.

"It gave you the feeling of a very small deformed human thing that had points of likeness to the bear form, but had none of the honesty and wisdom of a bear. A horrid thing with a nosing snout. Not really animal at all. A misbegotten thing of vile thoughts. The manifestation of animal thought is always innocent and beautiful though sometimes as cruel as the flash of lightning. Have you noticed how interesting it is to see a group of poor mange-eaten, starved pariah dogs and the tremulous, timid beautiful thought-forms that go with them, something like a flock of white birds but more human? Fear and undying hope and belief that someone will intervene in their hopeless misery."

I saw at once that fate had brought a true seer to my door and rejoiced.

He took it for granted that recognition will soon come of the necessity for cultivating the power of seeing the true thought-forms of things, instead of the distorted forms perceived by the senses, and that the way to this power is through the Indian form of concentration known as yoga. I had heard little of that then, though enough to rouse the keenest interest and resolution. He was himself skilled in that science. He said laughing:

"And when that time comes people will have to be as careful to keep their thoughts in order as to keep their bodies clean. Sickening revelations are made often enough now to those who can see."

We were sitting outside the tents then in a kind of opening of the trees that fell away disclosing the sky and the radiant silence of the mountains. It came into my head to ask if he could see the reality of an eagle sailing before us, floating grand as a frigate with motionless flattened wings on some high mountain current of air—and if so, whether he could make me see it too.

"If you're that sort," he said carelessly. "Not otherwise. If you've had the right sort of drill in past lives and in this. May I take your hand?"

I gave it and, as it lay in his, suddenly I saw that with the eagle went an image clear as crystal, glittering in the sun. It appeared to be all eyes—shining eyes turned everywhere, radiant, unspeakably watchful and keen and swift—a most beautiful shape, but so unlike anything I had ever seen that I stumble in trying to describe it, for even as I thought I had got it the light fluctuated and changed, and sometimes it was a ruffle of wings like shafts of glory. Flight and vision in perfected essence. Either and both.

"I know," said Armytage, "I see that too. It's like the Beasts in Revelations 'full of eyes within.' By the way those Beasts represent the essential thought of all the animal creation as the Divine thinks it. But of course that can't be described. It's only a shot at it. My God, if I could tell all I see! Of course I live in the world of sight, for I see these things always."

I looked at him in amazement. He was not in the least the mild-eyed melancholy type of lotus-eater who lives within the verges of reverie and ecstasy. I felt the <u>practical force</u> of the man from the beginning as clearly as I feel my own—a blue-eyed, strong-jawed person, with an important profession demanding much use of the reasoning and authoritative faculties. Whatever power he had, he had earned it.

"But," I asked, "don't you find it fearfully confusing to live in the world of the senses and the real one together? You seem to use both sights at the same moment as one does binoculars, whereas most people who have them turn one or the other vision off under certain conditions. How do you manage that sort of double vision? It sounds rather dizzy."

"Not a bit of it. You look here! You see that pine-tree casting a strong shadow eastward. Does it puzzle you for a moment to distinguish what you call the real pine-tree from the shadow? Not it! Well, I'm like that exactly, <u>only I see the *really* real thing</u>, and what you see as real is its shadow to me. But a very curious thing that I haven't got to the bottom of yet is that I don't see what *you* call the shadow of things at all. I'm trying to work that out."

"Do you mean that looking at that pine-tree you don't see the absence of light its solidity makes on the ground?" I was utterly astonished.

"Not a sign of it. Mayn't it be that we only fancy things are solid? I don't know yet. But I see what *you* call the real tree as the <u>shadow of the truly real tree</u>—so I get <u>two things</u> from it as you do; and that's enough for me."

"You don't mean that what I see is nothing?"

"Good Lord, no! It's only that we people see the real thing and not the distortion the world calls real. Now that eagle—I saw the feathered thing as a clumsy sort of attempt <u>following the real vivid radiant living</u> thing that was all perception. The <u>feathered thing was</u> its shadow."

His face gave out a kind of light while he spoke.
I said:

"That was the way with me too, while you made me
see it."

"Oh, you'll see all right soon! Probably in your next
life," he said carelessly. "You could see a little now if
you chose. But one must be uncommonly careful what
one says to the blindies. They want all the world to be
as purblind as themselves, and the best word you get
is lunacy."

"But tell me how you gained these powers," I
pleaded.

It seemed every moment was a golden treasure
which once lost might never be recovered. He answered
with the same careless certitude.

"You see, I'm one of those people who remember
their last birth and more. You can row up against the
stream of the life-force if you know how and get back
to the last port. I was a yogin at Badrinath, and a
jolly good life too. But I gave everything the go-by
except cultivating the powers for the sake of power,
and that won't do, you know. I was as proud as Punch
of the queer things I could do. So now I have to have
my nose to the grindstone and work at the practical
side of things. That's truth too of course, and you've
got to master it. Never have your head in the clouds.
The true mystic is the most practical Johnny on earth
and very bad to come up against in business. There's a
tip for you—as true as taxes. That's all bosh about the
practical side of things being illusion. It's only distortion and seeing the wrong values."

I fully agreed and asked: "Have you lost your yogic
powers?"

"No—no! I couldn't see what I do if I had. Besides
a gain is never lost in the universe. Once a yogin
always a yogin. Sex, for instance, doesn't interest me

personally a bit and life is much more interesting without that fetter. It seems the funniest obsession to me now. I see men and women—" He halted, laughing and wholesomely. "And the potty little stories and fuss about it all. There are far more interesting things!" he added. "Everyone gets through with that after a certain stage of development."

"Does it make women more or less friendly with you?"

"Depends on the woman. But mostly it helps to bring out the innate friendliness in women that sex smothers. I like women amazingly. And when they reach the point where sex doesn't count they can be great yoginis. I've known two. Tell me, would you like to see the reality of that little river leaping over the precipice?"

"Would I!"

He pointed to a great dove-gray cliff above us with a dwarfed pine-tree clinging to it here and there to drink scanty life from its stony breast. Over it poured a small rushing river from some high unseen glacier, shattering in silver on the rocks below and gliding away through flowers, grasses, and banks of maidenhair fern shivering with delight at the beauty above and below. It was so lovely in itself that to think of it as the shadow of some more perfect loveliness was impossible.

He took my hand in his firm cool clasp.

Instantly, above the water, curving with it, following its crystal folds, I saw—how can I describe it—something that was swiftness, light, and passionate joy concentrated into a being that struck me dumb. I saw it first an arrow of sunshine, as it led the wild race of water like a thing loosed from the hand of a god. Distance could not daunt it. It was eternal. It was what the plunge and luminous transparency of all water mean. In a moment more it was hovering music made visible. I had never seen music before, but I have known since that it is a symphony of light and color and that all the arts are one and indivisible when seen by unblinded eyes. What it must be to see music, sculpture—the beauty of words as pictures—all, all, as a radiant unity! It would be worth the sorrows of millions of rebirths to attain to that. This time I knew I had never seen water before. I cannot see it otherwise now. But this sight is not through the eyes.

In this and other things he showed me I learned another thing. To the true perception these essential forms of nature are not as the poets describe them. They are not personal and sexed. The soul of the river does not take the shape of a nymph. No—no! Either the Greeks had not seen, or, seeing, invented the woodland, river, and sea-nymph forms of perfect human beauty as symbols of what they could not hope to describe in any words. Possibly other people see differently, but it was Armytage's experience, and—since I have had more experience—has been mine, that it is as I have said. Why should all life be humanized? One cannot say that the forms of divine spirits are human in appearance. They fluctuate. Armytage, passing a temple dedicated to Maheshwara and entering the outer court, had beheld the image not as an image at all but as a moon rising above mountains unspeakably serene and remote. Some day these symbols, for symbols they are at best, will be translated for the world's wider use.

What Armytage was struggling to express (and I carry on the struggle) is that the natural world as we see it exists and subsists from the real—the spiritual world, as the effect from a cause. But happy, indeed, are those who can penetrate the cause, for celestial

continuous good

order reigns over the disorders of earth. I pass on to a strange story which he told me of the Shalimar, that famous garden in Kashmir which the Mogul Emperor Jehangir made for the woman to whom he had given not only his heart and soul but his empire—Nourmahal, known as the Mistress of the World. And I must declare that this story was the stranger, because I knew of an Englishman who had a vision of the same sort in that enchanted place. I have touched upon it in a story I named "V. Lydiat." But Armytage's experience was so much clearer and stronger as to convince me that these (so-called) dead thought-forms could be reproduced at any time by those who have attained percipiency.

But this was the story of Armytage.

Year after year he had come from Southern India to the North, to the snowy mountains which hold this jewel in their citadel, drawn by an influence he could not parry. He thought of the place, wrote of it; it would have come between him and his work if he had permitted it, and his dream was to make his home in Kashmir when his work was done. He told me he owed it much illumination.

Ten years ago one late summer's afternoon after a long day's dreaming on the Dal Lake, he pulled his little shikara up the narrow stretch of waterway which leads to the Shalimar Garden, made long centuries since for the lovely ladies of the Great Mogul, as they called him in the western world.

The pavilions of the emperors, their fountains, the secret paths bowered in roses, all are still there, but the little jewel-feet no longer pace them and the jewel-laden hands that wove the roses into garlands have pushed open and closed the door of Eternity and are seen no more.

Their hidden pavilions are thrown wide to the careless gaze of men who never heard their names or stories, and whose life-blood would formerly have washed out the crime of beholding the hidden beauties of the emperor's gardens. And this man was himself on this errand and it was when he had secured his shikara at the upper end of the way that leads to the Gardens of Dead Dreams that his story began.

He saw an Indian woman alone before him, walking very slowly and wearing the all-concealing *burka* with only slits for the eyes. That was strange. Often as he had been there before he had never seen a woman alone. They come by twos and threes or with children and friends. Her garment made no rustle, her feet no sound as she went, but that is common enough. Naturally he passed her easily and did not see her face. Night was now dawning in twilight, and it was only by the interest his many visits and gifts had made with the men in charge that he was permitted to come at such a time.

"For already the place had got hold of me," he said. "I couldn't keep away from it. I've made the history of the Mogul Emperors and their women my own, and every place of theirs is more real to me than any other on earth. But I'd never been at the Shalimar so late before and what I had in my mind was to spend the night in the great pavilion. Think of the beauty of it— in the night and moonlight! It dragged me to it."

I could think very well. There are few places on earth combining such beauty with such memories. A man might well dream as Armytage dreamed. I can answer for that. The pavilion is noble, surrounded by water and its cool. The pillars of the pavilion are of splendid black marble from Pampoor.

At the gate he was delayed by the absence of the

custodian, and here the veiled woman overtook him and seeing why he waited signed to a gardener within and bade him go in search of the man, speaking Hindi, which Armytage of course understood perfectly. That also was a strange circumstance. These women never put themselves forward. It should have been the other way over. He should have spoken.

Her voice was clear as a thrush's song after rain, syllabled with sweet precision giving the impression of a language acquired and no birthright.

He thanked her in the same tongue and she made some slight salutation but no reply, then drawing apart stood there in motionless silence until the man came hurrying up and unlocked the gate which opens into Wonderland. Then she passed in before him, the man following humbly. The fountains were silent, each sleeping in its crystal prison, for they play only at stated times or for special visitors, and now dusk was falling over the gardens. Suddenly she turned to the man with a gesture of calm authority and ordered him to set them playing. She was obeyed at once and immediately the diamond jets were sparkling all along the four terraces rising in gradation to the noble pillared hall at the upper end—surrounded by water and fountains filling the air with the wild music of the hills. She waved the man back imperiously and went on alone, disappearing up the steps on the left side of the terrace.

Dusk came with sovereign quiet in the lonely gardens, and Armytage moved almost as quietly—so strong was the influence of the place. He climbed the steps at the right, and forgetting all but the beauty wandered onward and up until he came to the undefined boundary where the garden passes into the wild loveliness of the first ascent to the mountain Mahadeva.

There he turned and came slowly down through the roses to the pillared pavilion among the fountains. How long he took he did not know. The moon was plashing and dipping in the broken water the fountains made before the pavilion, and the white woman sat on the steps above it looking stedfastly down into the change unchanging of its dancing gold. He ventured in passing, as it were, to say a word. It had crossed his mind that a woman so alone, so confident, could only be one of the two well-known beauties of the royal city, who were accessible even to foreign speech and admiration.

He thanked her for the sight of the fountains and added a little clumsily: "I believe a charge is made for their playing. Allow me to settle it with the man."

She replied without the least embarrassment: "There is no charge when I command. I have full liberty here, by his Majesty's order."

She used the word *"Hazrat,"* and Armytage's impression was that she referred to the reigning Maharaja of Kashmir.

"I come here very often. I have done that for a long time," she added. "There are certain nights I always spend here."

In very great amazement he asked: "Alone?"

She shook her head and said slowly: "But you also love the place. You may stay." The permission was so royally given that it became a command.

"I will stay," he said.

It was at this point that he tried to describe to me this lady of the hidden face, but it was exceedingly difficult, and he wrestled with words which would not impart his meaning—so that I could only seize it here and there like glimpses in reflecting water shadowy and vague.

She never detached herself from the background of beauty formed by the starry night and the shadowy vastness of the mountains, and was no more companionable than they, so he said. He had the strangest sensation—it seemed that he was looking at a picture formed and projected from some other consciousness than his own—not for his benefit, far from that, but as something into connection with which he had strayed unknowing. Was it alarming—did it inspire a sense of danger? I asked. No, but of suspense—of unutterable expectation. So might a man bidden to see a king's show wait alone and in a corner the rising of the curtain. Yet she walked beside him.

"Do you live here?" he asked at last, feeling the silence an unbearable strain.

"I live in a house by Lahore," she answered. "But I come here. There are nights when the Shalimar calls me, and I cannot stay away. It calls you also. Look!" And suddenly turning, she swept her arm upward, drawing his eyes to the pavilion and behind them.

To his amazement it was bathed in soft radiance from myriads of lights gleaming between the black pillars, wreathing the base and roof, glittering like beautiful constellations in the tossing fountains. Dim figures moved against the radiance, scarcely discernible but living, moving.

"The place has come alive!" he said under his breath. She turned her eyes on him through the slits in her veil, which made them terrifying as a masked face may sometimes be.

"Did you think beauty ever dies?" asked she, and turning from him went swiftly up the steps, waving him back, as though to say, "No further."

But he could not think, could not obey. Slowly, irresistibly, something drew his feet onward and upward toward the tossing water, the steps, and the lights. Half-way he climbed, and then a mysterious something stopped him like a wall of ice, transparent and chill as death, closing the way. Thus far and no farther indeed, and so he halted, longing yet unable to move. But he knew very well after that what it all meant. He was looking on at a masque of thought in which there was no part for him.

After that point as he tried to tell me what had happened his speech was burdened with the unutterable. It tottered beneath it. He had seen her unveiled and glorious, standing a head taller than her women, jeweled like the night itself with moon and stars.

"But they were not people from Srinagar—you must have known this," I said. He shook his head. He knew other and very different things. Did they sing? Did they speak? I asked.

No, neither. They were there. There was music—a lost kind of music—but they did not make it.

And as he spoke, halting, stumbling, I remembered the other man who had seen the same sight in the same place. And he too had been compelled to all but silence. Could he find any words to tell me of the loveliness that dominated Asia in her day? He struggled with words—doing his best.

"Impossible to describe as music. Nothing ever like it; her color pale gold and rose mingled wonderfully, lengths of silken hair midnight black, robing her in curl and wave like water, nearly to the sandaled feet. Brows of beauty, and the lightnings of deep eyes behind cloudy lashes—imperial height. Having seen this which centered all beauty—what could remain for admiration and wonder any more?" So he said.

"The other women?" I asked. No—they were there like stars about the moon, but he had not seen them.

All the long night he had remained fixed gazing—
gazing as the earth stares at the stars in a cold ecstasy.
He never closed his eyes, never felt his heart beat nor
was conscious of a breath. Nor, he thought, did they
move—but that he could not tell. It might be that they
were absorbed in the same deep dream or reality, but—
No! It was beyond him.

He saw and loved and remembered.

That was the story. The vision, if vision it were,
faded as the gray dawn stood silent on the mountain
tops, leaving his eyes empty, and then he stumbled
down the long ways to the gates and waited there, rapt
in memory and the sense of loss, until the man came
and unlocked them terrified to see an intruder.

"But you let me in last evening when the lady bid
you?"

"Huzoor, what lady? Lady sahibs do not come with
the night to the Shalimar Bagh."

"The lady who bid you set the fountains playing."

"Sahib, they did not play. It is an order that they
do not play at that time nor at night."

Armytage turned and looked up the gardens. Not a
sound—not a ripple, yet the moment before they had
made music in his soul.

"They played all night from the moment you let
me in."

"Sahib, I did not let the Presence in. How have you
entered? There would be great anger if it were known,
and this poor man would be dismissed in shame. Nor
have the fountains played, for at night I looked in
and all was still."

Armytage argued, entreated, could make no more of
it than that. But of course he understood very well.

"I shall go there again, some day," he said, "because
I've learned a lot since then and I should see it quite

differently now. All that was only the empty shell, like echoes in a dead house. But of course I couldn't get in touch with the real Nourmahal. She's working out the facts of life somewhere and I wonder where. It's very difficult to get them in a jeweled zenana, I fancy. But did you notice that point about her house at Lahore? Her tomb is there and she thought she was tied to it. Isn't that grim? Beastly things, tombs. They often imprison the thoughts of the dead. Everyone should be burned in radiant flame with the right mantram [sacred verse] and the ashes thrown to the winds. I have to attend European funerals sometimes and by the power of my yoga I see things well—unpleasant."

I agreed heart and soul. Our funerals are frightful contrivances for us and for the dead. I asked whether he thought it desirable to cultivate the power of coming in touch with their thought-forms at séances and through the other media used in modern times.

"Lord, no! It should be all as natural as breathing if it comes, and never through a third person. Always direct. Besides it should really not possesss anyone who hasn't control of the beginning of the powers. All sorts of things may happen. I once knew a man who fell in love with a dead woman. They have some ghastly stories of that in Japan and the case I knew was pretty bad. No—it's fools who take risks like that."

I could only assent, for I knew he knew what he was talking about, but later knowledge has assured me he was right. We know too few of the rules of the game to play tricks with danger. I asked him then if he thought it possible that one could influence lower forms of consciousness—had he had any experience of that? I read to him from my notes the very remarkable story which the Emperor Jehangir, the lover of

Nourmahal, tells in his interesting autobiography. It runs as follows and is worth giving in his own words, for all the emperors of that most royal house had the gift of the pen. So writes the emperor:

A king came to a garden in the heat of the day. He saw an old gardener at the gate, and asked if there were any pomegranates in the garden. He said: "There are." He told him to bring a cup of pomegranate juice.

The gardener had a daughter adorned with grace of person and beauty of disposition. He made a sign to her to bring the pomegranate juice, and the girl went and at once brought a cup full of pomegranate juice, and placed some leaves over it. The king took it from her hand and drank it, asking the girl what was her reason for placing leaves over the juice. She with an eloquent tongue in a sweet voice represented that it was not wise to drink off quickly a quantity of liquid when bathed in perspiration and in such a warm air. Therefore she had placed the leaves by the way of precaution that he might drink it slowly. The king was charmed with the maiden and her sweet ways and the thought crossed his mind to take her into his zenana. Meanwhile he asked the gardener: "How much profit do you derive from this garden every year?" He answered: "Three hundred dinars." The king asked: "And what do you pay the Diwan?" He answered: "The king takes nothing from the trees, but takes a tenth of the cultivated crops."

It came into the king's mind that there were in his dominions many gardens and countless trees. If then he were to get a tenth of the garden produce as well, it would mount to a large sum. Hereafter he would order a tax to be levied on garden produce.

He then said: "Bring me a little more pomegranate juice."

The girl went and after a long time brought a small quantity.

The king said: "The first time you came quickly and brought more. This time slowly and brought less."

She answered: "The first time I filled the cup with the juice of one pomegranate. This time I pressed out five or six and did not get as much juice."

The astonishment of the king increased. The gardener humbly represented: "The blessing of produce depends upon the king's good will. It occurs to me that you must be a king. At the time when you inquired of me the income from the garden your disposition must have changed, and consequently the blessing passed from the fruit."

The sultan was impressed and drove the idea from his heart. He then said: "Bring me once more a cup of pomegranate juice."

She went again, and quickly bringing a brimming cup gave it into the sultan's hand.

He praised the intelligence of the gardener and explained the actual state of affairs and begged the girl of him in marriage.

"And," adds the emperor, "this true tale of that truth-preserving sultan has remained as a memento on the page of time. I trust that Allah (to whom be glory!) will always incline this suppliant towards what is good!"

So for the Pepys of the East, and as I laid down the note-book I asked Armytage whether he believed it, adding that I did, for I had known a man who was always conscious by the vibrations of pain when a plant thirsting for water was in the room, and recently the scientific wisdom of Sir Jaganis Bose, going as far as instruments can take him, has justified my then conclusion and has given us to believe that beyond his discoveries of physical consciousness in plants stretches (as in man, but otherwise) the territory which instruments and reason cannot explore—that of the psychic consciousness of the plant world. We little know yet how the baser thoughts of the world constrain and control the beauty about us.

Armytage laughed:

"Of course it's true. Plants have an amazing consciousness. I never pick a flower. Jehangir knew all that and more from his Indian teacher, the yogin Jadrup Gosein. There are not only open references to his teaching in Jehangir's book but all sorts of signs of the yogin's influence. If Jehangir could have chucked drinking he'd have been a big man, but even Nourmahal couldn't fight that, so it was his fate. But about you— Now, look here! You try alone. Look steadily at that pine standing out from the rest. Steadily. No, I won't touch you. Try and concentrate with all the little you understand. Concentrate on the tree. But you must be alone. I'm off to my tent."

I sat, concentrated on the tree, and in a moment forgot him. My mind focused into a ray playing on it steadily, though at that time I had had little experience. I cannot tell how long it was before I felt response. Along the ray traveled what I will call vibrations, stirrings of consciousness unlike yet allied to my own. It was a terrible effort to hold on at first, but presently the force I had invoked was holding me in touch. It became effortless. Threads of light and color wove and unwove like a reflection broken in water. Now they were reforming suddenly. I no longer saw the great tree except as a shadow—as its own shadow cast flat on the earth by sunshine, but in its place stood—what?

Something of pure light, a mild yet vivid flame that projected what I had thought the real tree as its shadow, green as the transparence of aquamarine with moving light that circulated through it, breaking into pale fire at certain points—where I think (but this I cannot know) the greater branches would spring. The upper part broke into feathers of flame—but I knew that flame could never burn. It was cool as water. It was growth, life, the ardency of sunshine, the sweeping of heavenly rains drunk in delight by the psychic roots. It swayed softly as on a wind of the spirit with all its glory of leafage. It was a divine thought of beauty such as no eye can see nor ear hear until both are opened, and yet it was allied to the poor shadow it cast upon earth which must wither and perish in its due season, while the essential stood immortal. All light is one, the cosmic life-blood, but it takes different shapes for its manifestations. The united life of all trees stood revealed to me. The conception—the primal idea of them.

I am ashamed to say—but truth is best—that the poignant beauty which I desired to draw into my own life-blood and could not (though that too may be learned) broke me down, and the tears streamed from my eyes, and in those pitiful human tears—which were joy and grief intermixed—the vision vanished. The pine-tree stood before me again, silvered with hanging lichens, beautiful indeed, but concealing its mystery as the rough shell hides the pearl. They show their innermost no more than we do.

Armytage came back after I had armed myself against the cruel feeling that Beauty had shut her door against me forever. He laughed at the notion. In his hand he held a paper—he put it in mine. With a few pencil strokes he had roughly indicated his own vision of the tree—and it was mine also.

"You see?" he said in his quick way. "But don't you attempt to do it often until you've got much further in concentration. There must be no effort. Mind you, I don't pretend I've got very far and *I* was born with this sight owing to my knowledge of concentration in my last life and the one before. That's the beauty of the law of cause and effect. It never lets you down and it never lets you off. You can trust it. I could tell you what station you got out at in life last time if it would help you."

I said I would rather find it for myself. I knew it would be simply that of a hard worker and one who was not afraid to hunt the truth in dark places and—

"Oh, that of course!" he cut in. "People can see nothing if they haven't made some kind of effort. You can't exactly fatten in sloth along this road. For one thing, it's much too interesting. No—you weren't anybody in particular but you knew and were dumb—selfish, keeping things to yourself. Now you can talk, but you pay for it in other ways. By the way, a runner has just brought me a message: one of my men is ill in Bombay, and I'll have to chuck the rest of my holiday and get back."

I condoled but his happy eyes cut off condolence. He was perfectly cheerful.

"My life is a hard grind at the practical all the time, but it's quite good going at Bombay if you live the way I do. My diggings are not far from the Parsee

funeral place—the Towers of Silence, where they
leave their dead to the vultures. It sounds horrid—
and give me burning every time! Just a clean pyre,
and so an end of the body. But I was going to say—if
you ever come that way I'll try and show you some of
the lovely things I see in connection with that. I'll tell
you one: not long ago a Parsee child's funeral went
up and they led a dog in front—dogs drive evil spirits
away, they say; that's why they do it. Well, I stood in
my garden, and I saw the dog ahead simply struggling
to get free. Leaping, making the deuce of a racket.
Why? In front of him ran the child—laughing, hands
thrown up, face sparkling with joy, blown like a bubble
in a wind—and a man walking after couldn't even hide
his tears though it drove him nearly mad to show
them. And the vultures were wheeling above. Oh, the
fools we are! The almighty idiots!"

I said: "But Death wears his mask close-fitted and
it's a terrible one. It takes eyes to see the joy within."

"True—too true. But you know better and you'll
know better still. If you work at yoga you can take all
you want. You know that's a rule of the game. But it
isn't easy. You don't get something for nothing along
that road. And now—as I strike camp early tomorrow
—would you care to come outside tonight and I'll show
you something you won't forget in a hurry? It'll be a
kind of good-by, though I'm certain we shall meet
again. I think you'd better come, but promise me to
tell it when you think the psychological moment has
come. People really should know."

I promised; presently he spoke again:

"What I want to make you see now," he said, "is
what's going on all round us. You see empty sky and
space and all sorts of trees and mountains and inani-
mate things, and human beings strutting in the fore-
front of the stage, monarchs of all they survey. Well,

what I want to show you is that there's a mighty drama going on about us all the time and actors we never even guess. We're rather small beer until we know our rights. I think you'll be astonished."

I said: "Not so much as you think; I know it."

"That's one thing. To see it's another," he answered tersely. "You'll not forget this."

It was night with a glorious moon floating in the wine-dark abysses of sky when I heard his quick step outside my tent.

"Come now. It isn't far. And will you walk very quietly and promise not to be startled? There's no reason on earth why you should be."

I promised, and we went, walking softly from the small clearing into the edge of the pine forest and to a crag where I had often sat, overlooking a small mountain valley with the royal roar of a river thundering through it. Only an occasional tree stood here and there, and vision had deserted me, for I saw them as lovely but ordinary pines. The valley was empty save for a few jutting rocks.

"You can't see anything?" he asked anxiously. "Well, that's rather a nuisance. I thought—after the pine— However, no matter. Let me take your hand. This sight does not come through the eyes."

He took it and for some mysterious reason I was still blind. I had slipped out of the vibration.

"Oh, I say!—this won't do. You've *got* to see. Would you mind if I hypnotized you?"

I shrank a little.

"Just as you like, but you know we Orientals don't do it like the westerners. I wouldn't hypnotize a dog like that. All we do is to inhibit the every-day mind and set the higher consciousness free. I say, 'I loose you. Go.' Wait. I see you don't like it. I'll set myself loose first. Watch! But when you want to rouse me breathe on my hands."

He folded them like an image of the Buddha. It was the yogin speaking now—the adept in the psychic powers. Silently I watched him draw his thoughts inward "as the tortoise draws its members into its shell"—so says an Indian book. I watched him with profoundest interest. His open eyes reflected the moon as he sat like a graven image, motionless, breathless. I ventured to lay a finger light as a breath on his hand. It was as cold as ice, as if the very blood of life had retreated to some inward citadel. I was for the first time in my life witnessing the psychic trance, and it affected me with the deepest awe and wonder. If that could be—if the heavenly heights could be stormed in that way, then the world indeed is heaven and the narrow prison of the breast is the courtyard of the sublimity of the universe.

How long I waited I do not know, but finally I stooped and breathed upon his hands. At first no sign or motion but gradually as the breath, which is the symbol of human contact, warmed his hands he moved, his eyes closed. It was as though he slept, and presently waked as naturally and simply as a child in the dawn. I said:

"Touch my hand. I believe I shall see now."

He touched it—did not even hold it. And I saw. But not with my eyes.

A rain of what seemed to be drops of light was falling between me and the valley below. Just as a heavy fall of rain may blind one to what is beyond, so did this. It was dazzling, tinctured with rainbow colors as though some glory invisible shone on it. Presently it cleared as a shower ceases and a few drops fell fitfully.

I saw a thing so amazing that I think I put my hand before my eyes as if *they* were seeing. Light— light traveling everywhere on its errand of life, growth, sustentation, and destruction. And this light— every ray of it—was myriads of living beings thick as vibrations in light itself, but they were also terrific energy, pursuing ends I could only decipher here and there. I saw a beam touch what I should now call the shadow of a mighty cliff—what the world would call its reality. It slid over it gently as a moonbeam, but as it did so great masses of rock and snow broke in avalanches of horror from the cliff and were lost in thunder in some unseen abyss. I know—and how I cannot tell—that a village was crushed beneath them, human agony and blood and tears that were as nothing in the path of immutable law. Lightly again as a moonbeam the ray shifted—I saw the innumerable divine life vibrating in it as it sped to its goal. It swept the desert slopes of a mountain and it was summer, and blossom and fruit burst into a glory of life. The sky, the earth were covered with these crossing, shifting webs of life and light. They moved on a law beyond me, but law. I heard the awful roar of an earthquake opening its jaws to seize its prey, and the lightbeam traveled across it leaving ruin and dwelt on a sleeping city with the radiance of peace.

> "It slayeth and it saveth, nowise moved
> 　　Except unto the working out of doom.
> 　Its threads are life and love, and death
> 　　　and hate
> 　　The shuttles of its loom."

Now indeed I saw it as a divine pattern, weaving itself into starry beauty thrown upon what I had thought were the wastes of space. The planets and stars, suns and systems, were the geometry of its vast design. Sometimes I saw a Hand, a Face supernal, of great Beings who guided and directed, themselves the slaves of law; but what stood above and beyond it eye hath not seen nor ear heard, nor if they had could any tongue tell.

Sight was failing me—declining into the human, I caught one last fragment—a bear passing through the pine forest alight with Presences. He saw—he stopped; the light swept him and he fell dead. But I saw a seed of light detach itself from the useless shell of fur and broken forces, and rounding into a little orb sweep upward and join one of the wild webs of light swaying across the sky in their terrible illumination. Lost—nothing is lost, my heart cried as it shouted with the sons of God at their work, I too—I too—but the human broke under it. It staggered and fell in the onrush of vision. I saw no more.

Presently in the quiet of the moon-drenched forest I woke as if from sleep, refreshed as though I had been washed in the very sources of life. At first I could not speak. I could only say:

"I have seen the Truth."

"And will never lose it," he answered, "though the earth mists will cloud it often. You have seen that death and life are one."

We sat in silence for a few moments, seeing the earth floating fair in the ocean of moonlight. Is it believable?

That was not many years ago as time goes, but who would have then believed that the air is full of unheard music to be trapped in wires and caged in each man's house for his service? None. And, though this vision of Cosmic Force is far otherwise—when man lays aside his reason and uses his consciousness, he will see the high Intelligences at work about him and rejoice. But that vision must be developed within a man and not by the external aids of microscope and telescope. We should find another word for it than "sight."

As he went back he said:

"Remember always that the waking state is the furthest from truth, and most people know only that. Therefore go very cautiously. Wait your time to tell what you know. It is not yet."

True, but I think it begins to be "now" and I think this from the search of the world for light, as known to me personally and generally. If only a few hear and seek, it is the beginning of the true order of supermen. The dawn of mystic philosophy—age-old as it is —is only now broadening into the day.

"Well, good night and not good-by. We shan't lose touch. Tell me if you write anything about Nourmahal. Having seen her I feel I like to have all the news. In my next life I mean to have a training school in the good old Indian fashion for training people in psychics. It's badly wanted, but in this innings I have to learn my own lesson, to keep my feet on earth and make things gee in this poor little old world."

He clasped my hand very kindly. His vibrated with force and health.

He struck camp very early next day, but ı was awake, and it seemed typical that this Spartan whose drink was water only should depart singing gaily and stepping out to its rhythm a song of Hilaire Belloc's. It sounds forth the praises of beer.

> "They sell good Beer at Haslemere,
>   And under Guildford Hill.

At Little Cowfold, as I've been told,
  A beggar may drink his fill:
There is good brew in Amberley too,
  And by the bridge also;
But the swipes they take in at Washington Inn,
  Is the very best Beer I know."

It died off in the pines, and the rhythmic steps had the zest of one heading straight for the Washington Inn. One of the most interesting people I have met in a life of many interests. I look forward stedfastly to meeting him again.

He wrote four times at intervals far apart, long and fascinating letters which I have his leave to publish when I will, and I think there are perhaps enough people now to be interested in experiences so valid and wholesome. They should not be for the instruction of myself and a few friends only. I answered at long intervals and then I heard no more, but I am certain he is not dead. I believe he has learned his lesson among his figures and ledgers and has gone up into the mountains, and that when I return to them I shall meet him again with that extraordinary look of eternal youth in his face which the great solitudes give to their worshipers. I shall go up and over the Zoji Pass, and he will be sitting on a rock over the upper Indus watching the flying spray in rapt delight, with all the unspoken instinct of the beautiful animal subconsciousness added to the diviner one of man's utmost happiest attainment. He will be as much a part of nature as the mountains and river, but I shall not fear to break into his dream, for I too have made a few steps since we met. And he will look up and say with his old good-nature:

"Hallo! So you got in, did you? Didn't I tell you? And you don't want to get out again. Good stuff, isn't it? But don't talk for a minute. Look! You don't need my hand now."

And he will point and I shall see and we shall both be silent.